PURPLE
REASON

by
Doug Mennen

2016

Purple Reason by Doug Mennen

Copyright © 2016 by Doug Mennen
Cover Design by Natalie Powell
Editing and Interior Design by Charity Singleton Craig

ISBN 978-0-578-18559-0
Printed by CreateSpace, An Amazon.com Company.

Table of Contents

Acknowledgments

I want to thank my wife, Kym, and sons, Leighton and Jerrick, for tolerating my on-going obsession with actually finishing a novel. Nothing in this life is better than family.

I also want to thank two good friends, Darbi Evans and Denise Newton, for taking the time to read and critique the first draft. Your willingness to do so was central for me in rewriting areas that were, well, bad.

And a special thank you to my preliminary editor Kathy Mayer of Lafayette, Indiana. The simple truth is that without your help this book would never have gotten to a place where it moves forward.

Everything we do in life we do for the first time once. Take a risk, ask questions, and learn from those who have been there.

Cast of Characters

ELECTED OFFICIALS
Jackson Niles............................President of the United States
Miller Redding..................Vice-President of the United States
T. Wilson Reed.. Speaker of the House

WHITE HOUSE STAFF
Anthony Sinclair .... Chief of Staff
Susan Mercury .... President's Secretary

ADVISORS TO THE PRESIDENT
Clayton Sims .... Senior Advisor to the President
Hamilton Cochran .... Republican Party Chairman
Jack Langley.. FBI Director

MEMBERS OF THE PRESS
Peter Mercury.................................. Washington Post Reporter
Kyanne Fitzgerald............................. Washington Post Editor
William Conner .... CNN Reporter

Sam McBride ....Montana Rancher
Victoria Niles.....................................Supreme Court Nominee

CHAPTER ONE

Dreams Come True
Thursday, June 4, 2037

W hen I was a young girl I used to stare in the mirror thinking I could see my soul," the woman said without looking up.

The older woman next to her on the park bench sat silently, her deeply lined face showing no emotion. As dusk descended, the air was unseasonably cool, and the usual crowd had thinned out.

"I think I felt more alive back then than I do now," the young woman went on. Her expression, too, was blank.

The old woman rubbed her hands together and fidgeted with her purse as she glanced back and forth between the other woman and the ground.

The younger woman sniffled as she laughed at herself. The light breeze blew her strawberry blond hair across her blushing cheeks. She made no effort to pull it away. A few tears had managed to make their way onto a strand of hair and now hung there in desperation.

"Are you okay, dear?" the old woman finally asked. She had noticed the dangling tears yet couldn't help but allow her tired blue eyes to follow a passing jogger.

"Yeah, I'm okay," she answered as she stood, wiped her eyes and pulled her jacket closed. "Dreams come true, you know," she said softly as she looked around, then turned and walked away.

The old woman watched as the stranger slowly disappeared into the night.

THAT SAME DAY in Washington, the new President sat alone in the Oval Office as a conference call began.

"You are going to have to make them mad," one of the voices on the call insisted.

"I know. We all knew this would likely happen," the President answered.

"They aren't going to do anything until they have to," another chimed in.

"We don't know how ugly this will get, but we should be prepared for the worst," the President said. "We don't know for sure how deep the resistance is going to be. But we do know we can be a lot better than we are. And we also know that we ran against these two parties, and we won. All of you need to be ready for whatever happens next."

President Jackson Niles ended the call, left the White House and immediately boarded the Marine One chopper. After a rigorous and exhausting election and several months of frustrating and fruitless policy battles, he was on his way to a few days of relaxing with his old friends.

CLAYTON SIMS SAT alone on the front porch at his family's lodge on the edge of Flathead National Forest in the wilds of Montana. He sipped Scotch and read while his staff prepared for the arrival of his old friends. The massive lodge was constructed of hand-hewn beams and filled with the mounted heads of dead animals and pictures of family members dating back to the earliest days of the American Republic. Inside, the lodge smelled like the den of an old English manor. The aroma of natural wood mixed uncomfortably with the stench of cigars and Scotch. There were few feminine touches. Even the items arranged to accent the rooms had a cloak of masculinity that dominated the aggressive and heavy feeling of the space.

A stocky, robust man, Sims grew the family fortune through shrewd investing, or what some would call insider trading, back in the 2020s. He battled his tendencies toward arrogance when he deemed it necessary. He detested meaningless chatter, and he refused to participate in activities in which he had no interest. His world was black and white. Luck didn't make his father a successful investment banker, and luck didn't put Sims where he was now. He allowed little time for lounging at the lodge, but today was special; he was recently appointed Senior Advisor to the President. It was necessary to relax for a few days.

THE SMALL GROUP of rich, highly influential and powerful men who gathered had met when they traveled through prep school and a variety of East Coast colleges together. The group had stayed intact since then, and now, twenty-some years later, one of their own had reached the pinnacle—the presidency.

Jackson Niles, a 46-year-old Independent from New York, a lawyer, war hero, and father of two, recently was sworn in as the 48th president of the United States. He was a man impossible not to like. A leader by attitude, he possessed a sincere can-do spirit. A gifted speaker, he drew emotion out of every situation. Even his harshest critics finally gave up trying to pin any of the many supposed scandals on the candidate. Nothing ever stuck, and all charges were rebuffed by moral outrage and indignation, leaving the accuser looking the fool.

The room held anything but lightweights. One of Sims' old buddies, Hamilton F. Cochran, was chairman of the Republican Party after serving three terms in the Senate. Another, T. Wilson Reed, a Democrat, was the new Speaker of the House. Both had been in Washington since graduating from Yale. Although from different parties, they remained good friends. In fact, their political affiliations were more about family histories than deeply held personal views.

During his campaign, Niles said both parties would be represented in his Cabinet. As an Independent, he had little choice. So as longtime friends and confidants of Niles, Cochran and Reed expected to be included in the administration.

The President paid little attention to the parties and had been openly critical of them during the campaign. He had promised that a new chapter was about to begin in the American story. "Political parties," he had said, "would matter much less."

In addition to Niles, Sims, Cochran, and Reed, two other friends from the old gang were there. Jack Langley, a West Point graduate and retired military officer, had taken the post of FBI director. A driven, focused, dedicated former Army colonel, Langley took no crap and trusted no one. If not for the invitation from Niles, he would surely be at his desk instead of in a Montana lodge sipping Scotch.

Rounding out the group, Anthony Sinclair had served in several administrations and knew Washington inside and out. He received his doctorate in history and political science from Georgetown; his depth and knowledge of the world surpassed the others, including the President. He was a practical man, with a slow and steady approach to life. Named the new White House Chief of Staff, he considered the post something he had trained for all his life. Like the President, he stood tall, an athletic man. He did not enjoy politics. He enjoyed accomplishment. Deep down, he loathed the process politics required all people and ideas to pass through. People like Langley, hawkish and intense, worried Sinclair. There were few absolutes in Sinclair's world, an attitude Niles always found comfort in.

There had been others in the group besides these six men, but the others never excelled or took less visible career paths.

Take Sam McBride. A Montana rancher and state militia leader, he was the President's best friend back at Yale. McBride, however, never took to law school. He knew he would never take to the lifestyle of a high-powered lawyer, either. While he loved studying the law, he felt it was rarely applied accurately. So much of society seemed wasteful to him. To McBride, the ranch answered all the questions. Life was simple out there. No politicians, no politics or egos, only simple survival. In Sam's world, friend helped friend, and business was still done on a handshake. He was a militia leader, that was true, but he was no radical. He loved America, but he hated bureaucrats. That's why he was not in the room today.

Sims, Cochran, and Reed hated him. These men loathed the independent, radical individualism that McBride stood for.

The six friends who gathered would stay a few days, fishing, drinking and telling old stories. If they needed something, it would be flown in. All was well. This was celebration time. This was the old gang. The President was in his element. He could kick his shoes off, put his feet up and relax. Still, the Secret Service detail standing outside the front door reminded his friends of reality—Niles is "the man."

"MR. PRESIDENT, WHAT role do you have planned for your VP?" Sims asked, as the group settled in after a day on a nearby trout stream. He seemed to enjoy saying "Mr. President" as much as Niles enjoyed hearing it. Sims spun the ice in his Scotch glass as he looked across at the President. He made no attempt to hide the smirk on his face.

"Still fishing, Clayton?" the President replied with a touch of defensiveness about Miller Redding. "Maybe you'll do better indoors."

A chuckle made its way through the room as Niles smiled at Sims. Sims was not good in the outdoors, and the fact he had not caught a single fish while the others succeeded brought smirks to everyone's face.

"The guy is a mystery, sir," Sims said, feeling more empowered than normal due to his native surroundings.

"Come on, Mr. President," said Langley, "Everyone knows he's only involved because he's a Californian. How many electoral votes was that?"

Langley glanced at the others as he spoke to ensure they knew he was joining the inquisition.

"Now hold on, guys," Niles said, not liking the path or the tone. "Let's get something straight right now. Miller Redding is my VP, and whether any of you like it or not does not matter. He is bigger than this room. There are other people involved, campaign people, money people, big thinkers, you know? You may not like him, but he helped get me elected, period. And, by the way, for the next few days call me Jackson, or Niles, but don't call me 'Mr. President.'"

He hoped he had set the tone for the next few days with this exchange. Niles knew the "old gang" was just trying to determine their boundaries. But there were a lot of agendas in that room, and not everyone considered the "old gang" as important as the new President.

Niles glanced around at his old friends with a friendly but sarcastic look. The President had mixed emotions about the loyalty of the crowd, but as an Independent, he was somewhat stuck with the involvement of the two parties and their power elites.

By Saturday, the conversations had become more about women they knew back in college than public policy. After six or seven hours of cocktails, tongues loosened, and "think before you speak" lost its virtue. After the President and his Chief of Staff, Sinclair, retired to their individual rooms, though, the other four threw a few more logs on the center fireplace and began to discuss the next four years.

"It's amazing how every campaign says the same stuff year after year. Don't you think so, Jack?" said Speaker Reed in his usual reserved, almost sheepish style.

"Campaigns are only words, Wilson. It's the actions that matter. You know that," said Langley as he waived his hands in the air. "It's all bullshit. You know that as well as anyone."

"True, buts let's face it, not much changes from year to year," Reed countered, searching for support and thrusting his cane in Langley's direction. Reed occasionally used the cane to offset an arthritic hip, but most of the time he used it as a pointer. He enjoyed the feeling of "being armed" and the comfort it gave him. He was a bright man, but his small physical stature had created a deep streak of insecurity. A personality trait magnified by the obvious—some would say hideous—enormous comb-over atop his head.

Cochran picked up his Scotch glass. "Still, I've been in DC a long time now, and I've seen little that amounts to real change. You know what I mean, Jack, real stuff, meaningful things. They don't change." Cochran laughed as he finished the sentence in the tone of a man accustomed to having the last word.

Langley shifted in his seat as Cochran stared him down.

"You know I'm right," Cochran said.

Langley shifted again as he cleared his throat.

"For God's sake, Jack, why don't you take the gun off your hip and get comfortable?" Cochran shouted.

"I always carry a gun," Langley answered nonchalantly.

"Yeah, we all know that," Reed chimed in as he adjusted his bow tie.

"I've been shot at by lunatics too many times," Langley said.

"Well, I think you're safe here," Cochran mumbled, with a chuckle that shook his large belly.

Langley spent the majority of his life in the military, and while he had grown comfortable not being in uniform, he was not comfortable without a sidearm. He was not a particularly handsome man, but he was always well dressed and neat. His pistol was always concealed in an interior holster, so only his friends knew it was there. His constant fidgeting and rearranging while seated would have tipped off anyone familiar with the type of holster he preferred.

"I bet he has another one in his boot," Reed said, pointing his cane at Langley while adjusting his comb over with his other hand.

"You want to try and look?" Langley asked, his eyes meeting Reed's. Reed did not continue the confrontation.

Sims returned from the kitchen with a bowl of chips. "Are you guys back to talking politics again? I wanted to hear more about that redhead you dated our sophomore year."

Everyone laughed and turned to look at Cochran, who sat with an amused smile on his face.

"I think we covered that earlier, Clayton. Besides, I think that Suzie Q you ran around with our senior year is a better story," Cochran said.

Laughter erupted as they remembered the girl. She had pursued Sims with a determination that even he came to admire.

"We all underestimated that girl's perseverance, didn't we?" Langley said as he snickered over his Scotch glass.

They all laughed and acknowledged that she was one determined young lady.

"I think you all underestimate our old friend, the President, as well," Langley added as he glanced at the others.

"Wow, talk about killing a moment," Reed muttered as he reached for the chip bowl. "But I disagree, Jack. I think we all know Jackson as well as a guy can be known."

"True enough, Wilson, but I think you will find that as President he intends to shake things up a bit," Langley said. "Those weren't campaign slogans to this guy. Hey, I've been in foxholes with him, and I've heard this stuff for twenty years now. You guys better get ready for some action. He may not be right, but he's going to go for the brass ring."

Langley sat his drink down and sat back to light a cigar. He usually appeared stern, and even when forced to relax, the expression never left his face. He wore his thick black hair short with no strand out of place. It highlighted and defined the lines in his face and the ruggedness of his complexion.

Cochran struggled a bit to get up from his oversized chair and took a cigar from the humidor.

"Jack, you know the people are basically happy in this country, right?" Cochran asked. "Why would anyone want to shake things up a bit?"

"Are they?" Langley asked.

"Are they what?" Cochran countered.

"Happy?" Langley shouted.

"Of course they're happy," Reed said as he jumped into the conversation. "People bitch and moan about the same crap year after year, but if you tried to change things, they would bitch about the change. Hell, people want to bitch about something." Reed, too, grabbed a cigar.

"Hell, Jack, you've already pissed off Jackson. We all can see it," Reed said as he changed subjects.

"Oh I've pissed him off many times before," Langley said. "We disagree on a few things, but it's not anything the President didn't see coming. I've always disagreed with him on something. We used to argue while being shot at." Langley laughed and puffed on his cigar.

Still standing, Cochran looked down at Langley.

"What's the matter, Hamilton?" Langley asked. "You think the President is going to sick that redhead on your ass?"

Once again, they all had a good laugh.

"Hell, I hope not. I would hate to go through that again. Although I wouldn't mind seeing that tail walking down the hallway," Cochran said, laughing as he headed back across the room to the big leather chair he had occupied earlier. "I don't know, fellas," Cochran said as he landed in the chair. "Change can be a good thing, but on the other hand, it can be dangerous, too. You never know where it stops."

Sims had been taking all this in as he nervously downed another Scotch. "I like things the way they are, Jack. But, hey, it doesn't really matter anyway. The court would block or hold up anything big. Those old bastards have been there so long they've probably taken root on those chairs. I think they like the privilege that comes with their status quo."

Sims, Cochran, and Reed sat quietly for a moment, unsure what Langley might be thinking.

Langley stared at the fireplace, a glass of Scotch on the table next to him. A billow of smoke had formed over his head from the cigar he had been puffing. Langley hated the idea of "privilege," even if he was in that class. He was a populist and believed in change for the betterment of all. He had seen the impact of a privileged class suppressing a population through wars, and it made him restless and nervous—nearly all the time.

Cochran finally stood and walked over to the others slumped in their seats. For a moment he stood looking at Reed, Sims, and Langley, and then began to laugh. Cochran was a big, fat man, with a big, round head. His laugh filled a room. He was not a man you would want to have as an enemy. He was ruthless. At prep school he had been teased without mercy about his weight by two upperclassmen. It went on for an entire semester. During his second semester, his two tormentors were arrested in New York City for public indecency. The police found them running naked through Central Park. They had been spray painted from head to foot with fluorescent yellow paint and had apparently spent the evening trying to hide from a group that found them rather appealing. Cochran had never admitted any involvement, but his best friends, especially Reed, Sims, and Langley, always thought he had been involved. Cochran had made regular trips to the city where he grew up. His family owned a chain of moving businesses throughout New England. If anyone could transport two naked, painted, and probably screaming teenagers into the heart of New York, it would have been Cochran. Either way, the two never bothered him again. In fact, no one ever bothered him again.

"Change," Cochran said. "Every president gets elected declaring he is going to change things. And what changes? Nothing, not a goddamned thing. And nothing is going to change this time, either. Oh, we'll have debate after debate, but in the end, a few little tweaks will take place, and that will be it. Then the guy in the chair will declare his victory, and that will be the end of it."

Cochran stood puffing his cigar. "The people don't really want things to be any different than the way they are. People think they do, so they vote for change. But in the end, it's a bunch of bullshit." He downed his Scotch and chuckled as he walked to the bar. "We all waste too much time talking about change," he mumbled.

"I think the Republican Chairman makes a good point," Speaker Reed declared as he raised his glass.

SUNDAY MORNING BROUGHT helicopters, family members, other guests and formality back to the lodge. Niles was once again "Mr. President." That night, they were all back in Washington and none too soon. One of the Supreme Court justices had announced retirement on the Sunday morning talk shows. The President must have been living right, for the first one to quit turned out to be the justice he had hoped would leave. The President already knew who would be nominated—a woman from his hometown who was also a Yale grad—his sister, Victoria Niles.

She had the credentials. She was an accomplished judge and before that a successful New York attorney. They had discussed it. They knew there would be a howl of protest from both sides of the political spectrum, but it was worth it. She was a constitutionally minded judge. As a candidate, the President had promised he would replace any retiring justices with people of superior credentials, as long as they were committed to the intent of the constitution. He felt strongly about this.

Victoria would be confirmed, he was sure, because no one could argue against her credentials. In the opinion of many, she would be on the short list of potential nominees regardless of who occupied the White House.

As expected, news of the President's nomination brought both the Democrats and Republicans out in force immediately. Outraged that this new President would nominate his own sister, they were interviewed on every talk show in town.

The American people, however, seemed unconcerned. National polls showed that only a small number were following the event. And why should they? Partisan sniping had become the rule, and most people couldn't care less. The economy was good enough, let her be a justice, what difference could it make? The usual social ills were still rampant, but so what, the problems were always the same.

The President was not shaken by the hoopla in Washington. It would be thirty days before the confirmation hearings. They would be ready.

THE FOLLOWING TUESDAY, President Niles sat in the Oval Office with Sims, Reed, Cochran, and Sinclair. Langley was unaccounted for, a recent trait of his that was beginning to annoy the President. They were waiting for Victoria Niles, a striking woman at 42. Most of the men in the room were inferior to her intellectually, and they knew it. Victoria, however, possessed the same disarming charm of her older brother and never intentionally made anyone feel inferior. She had never married, and with the exception of the President's old friend, Sam McBride, she had never wanted to.

Victoria and Sam had met when she arrived as a freshman law student at Yale. Jackson and Sam often assisted her with first year studies, and soon, Sam found himself tutoring Victoria one-on-one. Neither of them took life lightly. When the relationship turned sexual, it was difficult for Sam to accept. His high school sweetheart, who was at home in Montana, awaited his return.

The entire affair lasted two years. Their love was real, passionate, and deep—the first time for her, a surprising second for him. Victoria had caught him by surprise. Her mind staggered Sam. He had never encountered a person with such a powerful sense of commitment, curiosity, and passion. In the end, though, it was their mutual commitments to differing ideals that drove them apart. That, and Montana.

Victoria loved Sam to this day, but she loved the big city and her career more. She would never live "out there," away from "the action," not even for love. Besides, she had known her career goal even as a college freshman—she would be a lawyer, then a judge, and then a Supreme Court justice.

At precisely 10 o'clock in the morning, Victoria entered the Oval Office. "Good morning, Jackson," she whispered as she hugged her brother.

"Good morning, Sis. Are you ready for this?"

"Yes, I am. I have been waiting a long time for this day." She already knew everyone in the room and greeted each of them with a professional handshake. She was dressed in a black skirt with an off-white blouse. A black blazer adorned with an American flag pin added to her crisp, clean look. At 5'8" she seldom wore heels because they often made her taller than most others. Today, though, a pair of sophisticated and elegant black pumps completed her attire. Victoria walked to a table containing coffee as the others paused and watched.

"May I get anyone a cup of coffee?" she asked.

The entire group, a bit surprised by the offer, quickly declined. Victoria turned back to the table knowing full well the unlikeliness of her offer. She smiled to herself in a moment of satisfaction.

"I know you said 'no,' Hamilton, but I know how much you love your sweetened coffee."

"We all do know each other so well," he said, smiling as he accepted the cup she offered. The moment broke the tension in the room as the others moved toward the coffee and rolls. The President watched the scene knowing full well what his little sister had done. The two exchanged a quick smile, Victoria feeling the approval in his eyes.

The tension in the room soon deflated as everyone moved about fixing their coffee and placing rolls on small plates.

"Okay, why don't we all find a seat, and let's get started," said the President. "I expect Langley any minute. Clayton, ask my secretary if she has heard from Jack or the Vice President."

Sims set down his coffee cup and plate and left the room. The President's secretary, Susan Mercury, had known the President for years.

"Susan, have you seen Langley or Redding?" Sims asked.

"You mean the Vice President, don't you?"

"Yeah, whatever, you know what I mean, Susan."

"No, Mr. Sims. I haven't seen either of them yet this morning."

"Well do something to find them. We have a room full of people in there."

"Susan's tracking them down," he reported as he reentered the Oval Office.

"All right," said Niles. "Let's start without them."

Meanwhile, Susan began buzzing offices, searching for the missing participants. A loyal, assistant to Niles, she was a lot like the President's sister, with one exception. She valued her family over a career. She only came to Washington with Jackson because she was sure that her husband would be ready to retire from his newspaper-reporting career in eight years when he turned sixty. They would each do a stint in the capital, sock away as much money as possible, and retire to their farm in southern Indiana.

Susan had gone to high school with Victoria but had chosen a small Midwestern college over the Ivy League. There she met Peter Mercury, a journalism grad student who would become her husband. He was about as average as one can be in virtually every way—except one. He distrusted government to the extreme. His family had a history of activism, and he had grown up on a diet of civil disobedience. His only great fear in life was the power of centralized government. He distrusted "power hungry" politicians but found his own professional stimulation in reporting their every move.

As Susan continued her search, Langley came jogging down the hall.

"Have they started yet?"

"Twenty minutes ago," Susan replied. "Mr. Langley, have you seen the Vice President?"

"No," said Langley as he entered the Oval Office.

"Jack, if you think the entire government is going to wait on you, you are badly mistaken," said the President. "Who the hell do you two think you are, and where the hell is Miller?"

Niles had known Langley for forty years. He was well aware of his rigid, clock-watching, and paranoid demeanor. If Langley was twenty minutes late for a meeting with the entire inner circle, there was a reason. The President was determined to find the answer. In the meantime, he would dress him down before the others to remind them all who was in charge.

"Okay, Jack, after we're done here I want to see you alone. In the meantime, here's the plan. Next Sunday we are all going to hit the airwaves for this nomination. I mean everyone. Cochran and Reed will be working Congress with our yet-to-be-found Vice President. Meanwhile, Sims, Sinclair, and Victoria will be on the morning talk shows. It's important that we show Victoria's feminine side. I don't want those media jerks dumping on her because she's single. The American women will support her if we make her known to the public. We have about four weeks before confirmation begins. We need to use it wisely. Any questions?"

The President scanned the room, looking for signs of dissension. "I'll have Susan draft your talking points on the nomination. Be sure to get these items across. This is an important part of my plan. Let's not screw it up. Unless anyone has any other issues? Okay, everyone out but Jack. Victoria, will you wait for me outside and join me for lunch?"

"Of course," she said. "I'll be with Susan."

"Great."

The President buzzed Susan. "Have you heard from Miller?"

"No sir."

"Have you tried his home or cell?"

"Yes, sir. There's no response anywhere."

"Have you notified the Secret Service that we have a missing VP?"

"Yes, Mr. President. They replied that he is somewhere in the White House."

"This is ridiculous. He's somewhere in the White House, and he can't make a 10 o'clock strategy meeting."

"I'm sorry, Mr. President."

"It's not your fault, Susan. Let me know when you locate him."

"Yes sir."

By now it was nearing 11, and the President was not at all pleased with the pace of the day. He looked across at Langley for a moment

"Jack."

"Yes."

"Why were you late?"

"I'm sorry, sir, but I was delayed on my way over by a traffic accident."

The President could see the seriousness flash across the director's eyes. He had seen that look before when they served together in the military.

"Was it serious, Jack?" the President said, trying to tone down the harshness of his own speech.

"I'm not sure, sir; we didn't get that close. It must have been rather bad, though, by the number of ambulances and police cars. Even from a distance I could see the blood on the side of the car."

Langley sounded genuinely worried. Having been in the worst of the fighting in Syria during the Suppression War, he had seen awful things. The President had been in that war, too. It was horrible, but it was there he had made his name. He had saved perhaps millions of lives by attacking and neutralizing a nuclear weapons lab operating in a bombed-out village. The village was full of nuclear bomb "parts" smuggled from across the continent. Enough parts that forty-eight hours later, small nuclear missiles would have been distributed across the area, they later learned. Niles' actions made it a bad time to be a terrorist.

"Jack, I need you to stay focused on this confirmation," the President said. "It's extremely important that we be ready for some sleazy charge against Victoria."

"You're talking about McBride, Mr. President?"

"Yes, Jack, I am. It was a long time ago, but . . . "

Langley interrupted, "But now he's a terrorist, and ..."

"God damn it, Jack. That's what I mean. He's no more a terrorist than you are. Knock that shit off. Your job is to protect her from that kind of thinking."

The President's face grew red. "Jack, I want you to be ready with the facts."

Langley leaned forward and stared into the President's eyes. "Mr. President, he's a leader of a private state militia."

"Damn it, Jack." Niles was incensed. "I will not sit here and debate this with you. I don't care what happened twenty-five years ago. The people don't care what happened then either. Drop it and be ready, or, quite frankly, I'll have your ass. She's my sister; she will be confirmed. Period."

Langley was in shock. In the 40 years they'd known each other, he had never seen this side of Jackson Niles. It scared him. Victoria scared him. Most of all, Sam McBride scared him. The inner circle knew about their relationship at Yale. They were a rat pack. Victoria and Sam had lived together for a year. Whoever would have thought that two law students living together could be discussed in conjunction with a Supreme Court nomination 20 plus years later? Langley didn't believe Victoria would be confirmed. He didn't want her confirmed. In his opinion, any woman who could love McBride could become a liability once on the court. Why did the President insist on nominating his sister first? It was undoubtedly a slap in the face to the two parties. But why a family member? There were other choices available, better ones as far as Langley was concerned, and among the inner circle, Langley was not alone.

"I'll take care of it, sir. Is there anything else?" Langley almost mumbled the words, unsure of what might set off the man he suddenly felt he no longer knew.

"No, Jack, you may go."

Langley walked to the door expecting his old friend to defuse the moment with some funny comment. It never came. He opened the door and walked out. Down the hall, he could see Victoria sitting with Susan. "What a pair," he thought to himself.

As he passed them, he smiled politely but made no comment. He was far too shell-shocked to engage in conversation. All he wanted was to return to his office.

Susan was walking toward the Oval Office as the President stepped out. "Mr. President, I received a message. The Vice President has been in an automobile accident. Sir, it sounds serious."

THE SCENE AT THE hospital was sheer chaos. Reporters swarmed the lobby looking for news. From what the police were releasing, the VP had been driving his all-electric, green roadster to the meeting. He had convinced the Secret Service to allow him this liberty from time to time because it reminded him of his home and freedom back in California. Unfortunately, on this occasion, his wife was in the passenger seat of the car. The car had struck the pillar of an overpass head-on as he traveled the turnpike. He was traveling in the far left lane, undoubtedly at an excessive speed. An eyewitness said she thought a large truck trying to change lanes had bumped the car's rear bumper, sending the car careening down the embankment into the pillar.

In the emergency room the ER doctor was discussing the Reddings' condition with a group of medical specialists and a few government officials. Most visitors to the hospital ER would never see a doctor the caliber of this ER physician. He looked old and tired, but in reality, Francis Keys was a world-renowned neurologist. His long gray hair and round glasses left him looking out of place. Those judging on appearances might mistake him for an old man with no other options but the grungy task of emergency room medicine. "The Vice President is in surgery right now. His injuries are severe and his condition precarious at best."

"What about Mrs. Redding?" a young redheaded woman from her staff asked.

"She's in that room over there," the doctor explained as he pointed to a room within the emergency wing. "She has severe head trauma, but her vitals are stable. We have her sedated as any movement could cause a serious setback."

"May I go in there?" the redhead asked.

"No," the doctor snapped.

"What's the prognosis on our Vice President?" a large secret service member asked abruptly. The man had a deep, loud voice, and his large stature made his presence almost ominous.

"Well, like I said his condition is precarious."

"I don't know what that means."

The doctor looked at those gathered as he struggled to give them the simple answer they wanted. "He's in very bad shape."

"We need a specialist in here right now," the large secret service member said into a small microphone attached to his suit cuff.

"I can assure you the Reddings are being treated by the best there is."

"With all due respect ..." the large man started to say.

"I need to get back to work," the old doctor interrupted. His eyes flashed with obvious annoyance as he surveyed the group. "There's a medical coordinator standing right over there. She can take additional questions and also fill you in on the quality of the team we have assembled." With that Dr. Keys walked through the group and entered the room of Mrs. Redding.

IN AN OPERATING ROOM upstairs, a group of surgeons worked frantically on Miller Redding. It was an ironic fate for this reluctant politician. He had served as California's governor twelve years earlier—for one term. He did not seek reelection. Each year brought new expectations about an announcement to run for the White House. It never came. He sat out the primaries again and again. He was once considered the most likely candidate for president. Instead, he slowly slipped into anonymity, baffling the pundits. Then, suddenly, the blond-haired, blue-eyed Californian appeared at the Independent Convention and announced he would accept the vice presidency if it were offered. The press was in shock, the Democrats and Republicans terrified, and the nation fell into frenzy. His participation almost guaranteed victory. A New Yorker and a Californian on the same ticket, and each the most popular man in their respective states.

But Redding was an enigma. During the campaign, he touted Niles' lines, echoed Niles' words, and generally made sure to deflect the light onto the prospective president. It worked. They carried most states and all of them west of the Mississippi. Redding was the kind of politician the media loved. He talked a moderate line. As a governor he fought for environmental issues, reforms in immigration, strengthening states' rights regarding education, welfare reform, and other measures. He was not typically associated with "hard core" politicians. He stayed away from moral and religious issues; he found no place for them in politics. At the same time, he believed strongly in individual responsibility and rights. However, he was a frustrated governor. Most of the propositions he fought for and won were challenged by the courts and never implemented. After four years, he had had enough. "Why?" many wondered, "would he get back in the arena now?"

Back at the White House, the President sat in the Oval Office with his sister. Sims, Sinclair, Reed, Cochran, Susan, and even Langley had joined them to await news on Redding. The room felt like a hospital waiting room. The President and Victoria discussed the administration's legislative plans. As the group gathered, the conversation expanded to include all those in the room.

Again, as in the lodge a few days earlier, the conversation shifted to the fact that not everyone thought the nation was ready for major change. In addition, some thought a few Supreme Court justices would likely hold up the President's most coveted prize—term limits on the House of Representatives. The President and Vice President had carried nearly all the states, yet they were hostage to continuing gridlock. It was no secret either that Victoria Niles would be grilled on this issue by both parties, which could delay, or even derail, her confirmation. In fact, her stance on many issues offended both parties and nearly everyone in the House and Senate, and the representatives were sure to take out a lot of the frustration they felt toward the President on his little sister.

WHEN THE CALL CAME from the hospital, everyone in the room gasped. The injuries were fatal. The Vice President was dead.

Langley was the first to ask to be excused. Had the Vice President really been driving his own car? Was this an assassination attempt? Langley saw conspiracy in everything. After expressing his regrets about the Vice President, Langley left to be brought up to speed by the Secret Service team in charge and the head of the Washington Police Department.

Susan hugged the President, excused herself, and went back to her desk. Reed and Cochran also left as Sims, declaring he had work to attend to, walked to the door.

Sinclair, Victoria, and the President sat quietly for a moment. The gravity of what had happened was becoming clear. Redding was the main focus of the President's "West Coast" supporters. His loss would be politically catastrophic. Finally, the President spoke. "Perhaps we should prepare a statement."

"I agree," said Sinclair.

"I'll leave you two alone," Victoria said as she approached the door.

THE NEXT MORNING began with a White House news conference. By now, everyone knew that the Vice President had been killed, but no one had declared it an assassination. How his absence would affect the administration—that was now the issue.

In the fourth row of the pressroom sat Peter Mercury. He was one of the new faces in the crowd, now employed by the Washington Post. The paper was thrilled to have one of its best reporters sleeping with the President's secretary. Not that Susan would ever violate the President's trust, but Peter's connection couldn't hurt. Besides, the paper had tried for 15 years to get Peter to Washington. He was highly respected among his peers. In the reporter "fraternity," he was considered the best "no name" reporter in the country. Peter liked it that way. He hated personal attention; he never wanted to end up on the other side of the microphone.

When Press Secretary Claire Simmons entered the room, she was flanked by Langley and Sinclair.

"Good morning, ladies and gentlemen," she began. "As you know, we experienced a tragedy yesterday afternoon. Our prayers go out to Shelly Redding. I would ask as a personal favor that you say a special prayer for Shelly. Her injuries are severe. It will take some time, but she will likely make a full recovery. The Vice President and his wife were on their way to the White House yesterday morning at 10:00 a.m. Their car was struck by a truck as it was changing lanes. The driver of the truck did not stop. This morning the FBI is searching for a black truck, approximately 20 feet in length, and the same general style as a small construction-type van. The FBI does not consider this an assassination at this time. However, because the driver of the truck did not stop, we are keeping that possibility open."

Simmons stepped back from the microphone and paused. She let out a bit of sigh and placed both hands on the podium.

"Please turn off the cell phones and stop talking," she said as the weight of the last few hours and the noise in the room bore down on her. Slowly, the reporters stopped and gave the press secretary their full attention. The room looked unusually messy because many reporters had camped out waiting for news. Empty coffees cups and food wrappers had been pushed under chairs. The room had also taken on an uncomfortable odor since many present had not showered or changed clothes for nearly 24 hours.

"We have general descriptions of the driver and one passenger, but neither of the eyewitnesses was close enough to get much detail," Simmons continued. "The FBI will release a composite drawing as soon as it is available. At this point we do not believe that the driver of the truck knew that he hit the Vice President."

Again Simmons paused and stared down at the podium. Those gathered glanced about as Simmons gathered herself.

"She knows more than she's sharing," a woman from APN whispered to her colleague.

"No doubt," the man in front of them said over his shoulder.

"Mrs. Redding will be returning to California for extended care as soon as her condition stabilizes. The doctors have informed the White House that her injuries will require at least six months to completely heal. I am sorry we do not have more information, but because of the ongoing investigation, the flow of information will be restricted. We will take a few questions."

"Bill Smithers with the New York Times. Mr. Langley, why was the Vice President driving himself?"

Langley had been prepped to expect a long day. He was ready for this question. "The Vice President has often chosen to drive himself to work. As some of you have reported in the past, he is a dedicated environmentalist and often drives his electric car rather than ride in the limousine. It is a personal choice. The Secret Service, while not endorsing this habit, could not force him to give up that choice."

Langley held off from showing any emotion as he gave the explanation. The idea was ridiculous to him, but it was the script, so he played along.

The Press Secretary stepped back to the podium and recognized Peter. She nodded in his direction.

"Peter Mercury, Washington Post. Mr. Langley, where was the Vice President coming from in such a hurry?"

"He was en route to the White House. We assume that he was coming from his home or office."

Langley stepped back to allow the next question.

"Bill Conner, CNN News. Director Langley, to follow up on the last question, wasn't the Secret Service at least tailing the Vice President, and why isn't the Secret Service Director at this press conference?"

"No, and I don't know."

"Oh, come on," Smithers groaned to himself at the reply.

"This is bullshit," Smithers' boss said softly as she leaned over toward him. "Somebody had to have eyes on the VP—they know more."

"Mack Scharer, Fox. Mr. Sinclair, is it normal for the Vice President to be out of Secret Service protection?"

Sinclair was not a regular at press conferences or reporters' interviews. He brought a calming influence in the middle of a storm, though. The President had said early on he intended to save Sinclair for such occasions. His credentials were familiar enough that the press did not immediately attack him. His slow, methodical answers would take the excitement out of a frenzied reporter. The press respected him. After the election he had become known as the "smartest man in Washington."

Sinclair stepped up to the microphone. "Ladies and gentlemen, the Vice President was killed in a tragic accident. We simply don't have all the answers yet. The Vice President's arrangement with the Secret Service must be reviewed in the wake of this accident. However, I'm sure the President would agree that the important issue at this point is that Shelly receives the best care available."

Sinclair stepped back, and the Press Secretary came back to the microphone.

"We are going to have to cut this short as the Chief of Staff and the FBI Director have to attend a previously arranged meeting with the President. Thank you all."

Quickly they were out of the room and down the hall. Langley turned to Sinclair, "I don't need you covering for me."

"Apparently, Jack, you do. It is not appropriate to answer a reporter's question with a 'no' in such circumstances. It is not as if he was accusing you of anything. You should try not to appear defensive."

Langley turned and headed to a side door. He was not included in the upcoming meeting.

Sinclair proceeded to the Oval Office.

"Good morning, Susan."

"Hello, Mr. Sinclair, did you get any sleep last night?"

"Of course, but I don't think Jack is doing well." Sinclair was concerned, not only for Langley personally, but for the effect on the President that Jack's defensiveness could have.

"Why do you say that?" she asked.

"He's on edge, Susan. I know you see it. Sometimes the guy acts as if he thinks everyone is against him. He needs to stop and take a deep breath every now and then."

"He can't, sir. He's a driven man, and lately he seems distracted. Something is really eating at him. He worries me, too."

"But driven to what, Susan? For God's sake, he's the Director of the FBI, what does he want?"

"I think the President sees him differently than we do because of the war. You know they both saw some terrible things there. I think it get's to the Director."

Sinclair hung his head. He'd heard them talk about the experience. Tears would run down Langley's face when he and the President discussed the war. They didn't talk of it often, usually after a few drinks and only when close friends were in the room.

"I suppose I'll never understand what they feel inside about that war," he said. "I'm glad I didn't see it for myself. Still, I hope Jack can lighten up. If he doesn't, he won't make it long in this pressure cooker."

Sinclair walked slowly toward a picture hanging near Susan's desk. The scene was an old painting of Washington D.C. near the time of the Civil War.

"Times like this make me think of Lincoln," Sinclair said softly, as if he were alone.

"To make matters worse, the President said Jack saw the accident on his way here. It's why he was late for the meeting," Susan said.

Sinclair continued staring up at the painting as Susan talked.

"Jack makes me a little uncomfortable sometimes," she confided, taking advantage of the rare opportunity to have a more personal conversation with Anthony Sinclair.

"Why is that?" Sinclair asked as he gave Susan his full attention.

"I don't know, really. He's so intense all the time. I've never seen him relax or have a normal conversation." Susan paused as she slid her chair closer to her desk. "My goodness, I'm sorry. I shouldn't say such things."

Susan fidgeted with her keyboard. Her discomfort was nearly paralyzing. "Please forget I said that," Susan added nervously as she kept her eyes on her screen.

"Susan, it's okay. He makes me a little uncomfortable, too. He always has, but I know he's a good man."

"You better go inside," Susan said. "You don't want to be late—not these days."

Sinclair entered the Oval Office. Niles was on a conference call with Reed and Cochran. He motioned for Sinclair to sit down and put the call on video speaker. Now Reed and Cochran joined the President in the Oval Office via holographic imaging.

"I will never get used to this crap," Cochran grumbled as his image appeared in the Oval Office while Sinclair and Niles appeared in his. "I can't even roll my eyes or scratch my balls anymore with this damned technology."

"Where were we? Oh yes, I agree with you, but right now I want to concentrate on the legislative package," Niles said, now looking Reed and Cochran in the face. The President was again trying to rally his legislative team.

"Mr. President, with all due respect, the legislative package is not ready," Cochran said, his voice filled with determination as he paced his office around the image of Sinclair and Niles.

"Besides, Mr. President, we can pursue both," Reed said as he fidgeted with his comb over. "In fact, I think we can get more accomplished if we push back the legislative agenda we all agreed to. The bills are not quite ready, sir."

Reed's suggestion stemmed from a group of bills the President and his staff had already prepared that his advisors felt would accomplish what they had promised during the campaign.

"And, sir, if we wait, we could swamp our opponents with so much activity they won't know where to turn," Cochran added.

"You two aren't suggesting we use Victoria's nomination as a sacrifice, are you?" the President asked, his voice heightened. "I do not want to hear such a suggestion."

"Absolutely not, Mr. President, but her nomination will bog down the Senate," Reed said. "We are suggesting we wear our opponents down, sir. They can only take so much."

Reed was persistent but different than Cochran. He was thin, fit, and quiet. As freshmen Congressmen, the two had been referred to as Laurel and Hardy. Nobody called them that anymore. Most of their enemies were gone. The few that remained were old and tired.

"Okay, gentlemen, you win," the President replied, knowing that his old friends were not going to relent. "We will do as you suggest. Don't let me down."

"Thank you, sir," they both replied, and then, as he ended the call, Cochran added, "We'll get you everything."

"They'll get you everything?" Sinclair said. "Sounds a little scary, don't you think?" Sinclair was uncomfortable with such pronouncements.

"We must remember, Anthony, they have been in this business for many, many years. They have waited a long time to be in this position."

"I suppose you're right, but what form will these bills be in when they arrive out of committee? They don't really believe they are going to get these bills passed intact, do they?"

"I think they do," replied the President

"I'm sorry, sir, but that's ridiculous. Nothing passes through that place intact—especially good laws."

Sinclair got up and walked to the window, looking out at the Capitol. "That must be the most frustrating place in the world to work."

"Why do you think compromise is a bad thing?" the President asked.

"It's not the compromise, sir," Sinclair answered. "It's the 'politics,' the undoing of a good policy for reasons not in the public interest. We both know that someone will object to our proposals, not because they necessarily disagree, but because they want something for themselves."

"Come on, Anthony, you know that's the way it will always be."

Sinclair turned to the President. "After 260 years of democracy, you would think we could agree as a people on what is appropriate."

"Times change, ideas take on new meaning, what was right fifty years ago won't work today. Look at our program. Who would have agreed with it 25 years ago? You know all this; you've said the same words to me at some of my low points. What's bothering you?"

Sinclair stared out the window again. "I dreamed for 30 years about being in this room, at this moment. I hope we don't spend the next four years arguing about changes that never get passed. I know we will end up compromising—everyone always does. Are you prepared to do that?"

"It depends on the subject," the President answered.

"Trying to get the House to pass term limits is like asking them to fire themselves," Sinclair said as he walked over to a chair and took a seat. "I think that issue holds up everything we send over there," he added. "We should try for some of the other items first and then circle back to those kinds of changes. I don't agree with trying to do all this at once."

"It's obvious how the people feel about this issue," the President countered.

"The public always wants every member of Congress thrown out—except for the one from their district," Sinclair offered with a slight smirk. "Congress is never popular."

"True, but I was clear during the campaign. I will not go back on that promise," the President declared as he looked across at his old friend. "I would rather submit that part first, by itself, and fight it out."

The phone buzzed, and Susan's voice came through the intercom.

"Mr. President."

"Yes, Susan."

"Clayton Sims is on his way in."

"Thank you, Susan."

Sims entered the room and immediately began outlining a timeline of action.

"We have to get these bills into a more manageable format before they go to the floor. Now is not the time."

"We know, Clayton," Sinclair responded. "We just hung up with Reed and Cochran."

Sims stared at Sinclair for a moment. "Do I have a role here? Why am I not told about these things?"

"It was impromptu, Clayton," Sinclair said.

"Very well," responded Sims. "Let's review some of the problems with this wording."

"I have it here on my desk," Niles said. He picked up a pile of papers labeled "Federal Reform Act."

It contained many reforms to many programs, but its core message was aimed at term limits for the House of Representatives and new restrictions on campaign finance. After passage, House seats would be up for grabs every two years, and anyone meeting well-defined requirements would be eligible for federal campaign funding. Outside money would no longer be allowed in the races. The well-connected rich people with their big campaign donors would be out. The schoolteachers, factory workers, small businesspeople, moms, dads, and everyday Joes would have their House back. The super-PACs, Citizens United, and the crazy laws that allowed such things would be repealed.

In the President's opinion, that was the founders' intent, and it was time to make it law. Professional politicians would no longer spend a career in the House. Opinion polls ran as high as 75 percent in agreement with the President's plan. However, there was open opposition in many areas of Washington. Within the Senate and the House, several Democrats and Republicans had vowed a fight to the death to stop the undoing of their power.

The President's plan called for the act to be submitted all at once in both the Senate and the House. It would be an onslaught of talking heads pushing one basic ideal—everyday Americans own the House. America was going to be remodeled by the common people.

The plan called for the "Federal Reform Act" to be submitted about the same time the Senate would begin hearing Victoria's nomination to the Supreme Court. All of these events would take place with the administration missing its Vice President.

THAT AFTERNOON, Susan and Peter were to travel to south Florida to celebrate the birth of their first grandchild. Their son and daughter-in-law both worked as photojournalists, specializing in environmental issues. They had made their home in Key West to document the effects of the ozone hole on America's favorite vacation spots. Perhaps, if someone got a bad burn on vacation they might begin to listen to the warnings of scientists worldwide, they thought.

During the flight to Miami, Susan and Peter discussed the events of the last few days. The press knew as much about the Vice President's accident as Susan did.

"It's such a tragedy for Miller. He seemed to be such a pleasant and thoughtful man," Susan commented.

"Yes," replied Peter. "Perhaps this will slow down the administration's plans."

"I don't think so, Peter, though no one has commented to me," Susan said, being sure to demonstrate that she knew no more than her reporter husband. "I can tell you that the event has affected both Sinclair and Langley. They were both tense and somber, although they both think they're okay."

Peter listened intently. He was interested more as a husband than a reporter. He worried about Susan. This job was a lot more intense than being a private legal secretary.

"And poor Langley, he was in the traffic jam behind the accident. He actually saw the blood on Shelly's side of the car. It really shook him up."

"Susan," he said, again thinking like a reporter, "Langley never said he was at the accident scene during the press conference."

"He's rattled; I'm not surprised he would leave something out." Susan did not want to be the unnamed source for a "hot lead."

"I doubt any administration has had as many of its key members racing around town in their own cars as this one. It seems odd to me," Peter said. "Where was Langley going?"

"To the White House for a strategy meeting, and that's enough, Mr. Mercury. Press conference over." Susan fluffed up the pillow between her head and the plane window and slumped in her seat.

Peter knew there would be no more discussion. Sleep seemed like a good idea anyway. They would be on the red-eye back to Washington in the morning. It wasn't long enough, but all things considered, it wasn't bad.

THAT NIGHT, VICTORIA Niles sat in her suburban condo outside Washington. Her nomination to the Supreme Court was the culmination of a lifetime of hard work. It was an appropriate time for her to reflect on the last 20 years. She thought for a second about calling Sam but quickly realized how ridiculous that would be. They hadn't spoken since Sam broke off the relationship when he left Yale. She knew little of his life in Montana. She never asked Jackson about Sam. She was too proud. Besides, it was Sam who had left her.

Instead, she dragged out old photos of their short time together. The last semester they spent together was magical. They lived in a small bungalow on the edge of campus. It was a modest place, but to her, it was as close to heaven as she ever came. They had spent the summer before the fall term fixing it up. The two painted the walls, planted flowers along the sidewalks and porch, and planted a garden in the back yard. They even put up a privacy fence out back with a baby pool in the middle of the yard.

Looking at the pictures, she recalled the seemingly endless days and nights of that summer in their back yard. They made love at night under the stars on a patch of grass near the flowers and in the baby pool when the sun was high in the sky. They cooked meals on Sam's little homemade grill and took naps together in their hammock under a big shade tree after dinner. How many times, she wondered, had they awakened in the morning tangled up together in that hammock?

It was the happiest time of her life. It was the only time she had shared a house with a lover. But her memories of that time always concluded with the same anger as she confronted how the relationship ended.

AFTER THEIR SHORT TRIP, Peter and Susan landed in D.C. then went their separate ways from Dulles Airport. Susan went to the White House and Peter to his office, where he grabbed a cup of coffee and a bagel and headed for his desk. The senior editor, Kyanne Fitzgerald, a brilliant reporter and writer from South Carolina, quickly ambushed him. She had been in Washington 20 years. There was nothing about this town she didn't know.

"How was your trip, Peter?" she asked.

"Too short."

"That's the price you pay for this profession," Kyanne said with a wink. "How are the kids and grandbaby?"

"They're fine. I wish we could have stayed longer," Peter said as he yawned. "I'm still tired," he said as he stretched his arms over his head. "Kyanne."

"Yes, Peter."

His change back to investigative reporter was obvious.

"Did you know that Jack Langley drove past the scene of the Vice President's accident?"

"No. Where was he going, do you know?"

"According to Susan, he was on his way to the White House."

"Should you be repeating this, Peter, if it came from Susan?"

"She told me this as if it was no big deal. She said he was all shook up because he saw the blood on the side of the car. It was the reason he was late to a strategy meeting."

"Perhaps, Peter, it *is* no big deal," Kyanne said.

"But here's the thing," he replied, his blood rushing. "I've been thinking about this all night. He lives by Northpointe."

"And the FBI headquarters is on the opposite side of town from the accident," Kyanne said as she began to see the mystery for herself. "Why was he driving around on that side of town at 10:00 a.m.?"

"And another thing: he was in his own car, which, I admit, is not so strange in this administration. Still though, where was he coming from? The police report did not indicate that traffic was held up long. I think he was running late anyway. He was obviously somewhere other than home or the office. Where was he and more importantly, why?"

"Follow him, Peter."

"What?"

"Follow him tomorrow morning and see what he does," Kyanne said, giving these instructions rather nonchalantly. As if following the FBI Director around town would be no big deal.

"He'll get up and go somewhere. Let's find out where."

CHAPTER TWO
So Do Nightmares

When Susan arrived at her desk that same morning, Victoria Niles was already waiting.

"Good morning, Susan."

"Hi, V."

"Are you okay, Susan?" Victoria asked. She could tell Susan was bothered.

"I'm okay, just tired. We caught the redeye back from Miami this morning. It has been a long eighteen hours."

"How are your kids and the new grandbaby?"

"They're fine, and she's beautiful. They're naming her after me. I was so thrilled. Holly is going to be such a wonderful mother. She's so happy."

"That's wonderful. I'm so happy for you both. I know how much your family means to you."

Victoria loved to hear about Susan's kids. It filled a need in her own life. Victoria had always been close to them all.

"Is Jackson in yet?" Victoria asked as she sat down and looked at Susan's baby pictures.

"No, didn't he tell you?"

"Tell me what?"

"They all went up to Camp David for the day. They're preparing to launch the legislative package. I'm sorry. I thought you knew."

"I guess I shouldn't be told everything," Victoria quipped. "It would probably be considered crossing the line. I just had a quick question. I'm heading to New York for the day. My old law partners are being literally chased down the streets for info on me. They've asked me to spend a day outlining the 'official' answers."

She laughed and got up from her chair. "Please let Jackson know where I am, and I'll call him in the morning. Oh, and by the way, do you need anything shopping-wise? I am going to spend the evening in the shops. If I get confirmed, I may find clothes shopping rather difficult. I'm going to take advantage of these last few days of anonymity."

"No, I don't need a thing. Please be careful, Victoria. There are a lot of nuts out there." Susan couldn't imagine being a public figure. She could barely stand being recognized as the President's secretary.

Victoria left through the side door and headed for the airport. She loved New York and had a full day planned with some of the many good friends she had there.

As she drove to the airport her head was filled with thoughts of Susan's new grandbaby.

"That is something I will never experience," she thought. At times these thoughts would make her sad, but she had made her choice in life. Since her time with Sam in law school, she had never met anyone she would have been happy with. Still, her mind often drifted to the life that would have been had that relationship not ended. She would try to picture the kids they would have had, the house they would have lived in, all the tiny details that would have comprised their life together.

Victoria pulled into the massive airport parking garage and drove for fifteen minutes before she found an open spot. When it was built, the planners said it would be twenty years before it would fill up in a day. It took five years. She carried only a shoulder bag as she headed for the elevator. She was at the far end of the garage on the lower level—about as far from the elevator as she could have parked. She thought how fortunate it was that these garages were well lit and supplied with security personnel on each floor. Otherwise, they would be rather scary. As she passed the middle of the garage, she saw the door open to the "safety shack," as they were called. She walked over to pre-pay her garage ticket, but there was no one there. As she turned around, she heard a voice.

"May I help you, miss?"

The man speaking looked like one of the security guards. Still, Victoria felt her heart race a bit. It surprised her. A cold, empty parking garage can frighten even a Supreme Court justice. Suddenly, she felt a hand on her shoulder. She tried to move. She felt an object against her side. She heard a car coming down the ramp at the end where she had parked.

"Thank God," she thought. "Someone is coming."

The car pulled up to them. "Get in the car."

The door of a long gray limo opened. She couldn't see anyone inside.

"Get in the car," the voice repeated, as she felt a knife against her ribs. The hand on her shoulder tightened, and the knife was moved to her throat.

"Get in the car or I'll cut your throat right now."

She was terrified. She had lived in New York nearly her entire adult life. She had been mugged twice and fought off a rapist once. In fact she hurt that attacker so badly that the police found him in the nearest emergency room. But this was different. This wasn't a robbery or a rape. Her mind raced trying to figure out how, if at all, this might be related to her nomination. *Who in the world would want to try to scare her or influence her this way?* she wondered.

A black cloth bag was pulled over her head and a zip tie placed on her wrists. She was shoved into the car. Immediately the doors were locked, and the car sped off.

Once on the highway, she heard a voice over an intercom in the car inviting her to relax and enjoy the ride. She was told nothing else.

She recognized the sounds of traffic, the noise the tires made when the road changed from concrete to asphalt and back again. She counted the river crossings as each made a hollow sound under the car. After about an hour, the car suddenly stopped. The door opened, someone got in, the door closed, and the car moved again. The person rummaged around for a few minutes, opened a drink of some kind, and sat there. Victoria said nothing. After about twenty minutes, he reached over and pulled the hood off her face.

"Sit up straight, Tory,"

"My name is not Tory," she replied.

"Does anyone call you Tory?"

"No," she replied defiantly.

"Between you and me, it will be your name. I want you to know who you're talking to when I call or visit you. Do you understand that I'll be calling you 'Tory'?" the man asked as he leered at her.

"We'll see," Victoria answered with a cold stare.

"Really? We may not get along as wonderfully as I had hoped. You see, we actually do believe in most of the same things. But there are areas, assuming you believe what your brother believes, where we disagree sharply."

The man's voice was deep and rough. He had the kind of blond hair you get from spending too much time in a chlorinated pool. He was about her age. Lean and fit.

"We will not tolerate our government being dismantled by you and your damned brother," the man said forcefully. "The people I represent are getting worried, and they're ugly people, Tory. They're the kind of people who kill presidents and their families. Do you understand me?"

He touched her hair.

"Who are you?" she asked. She was afraid, but not for her life. It was obvious this guy was part of a group that wished to influence her.

"My name is irrelevant. What is relevant is that you fear me."

"Why should I fear you?" she asked, feeling a bit more secure that her physical safety was not in question.

The man stared out the window for a moment. He then reached into his pocket and took out a handkerchief in a small zip lock bag. He opened the bag and slid across the seat toward Victoria, placing the handkerchief over her mouth and nose. She tried to hold her breath. She was inches from his eyes. Up close, he looked much more foreboding than at a few feet away. He had on leather gloves. She felt the coldness of the leather against the back of her neck. His fingers pinched her skin as he gripped her neck. His eyes were dark and emotionless, almost dead. She stared into those eyes and then passed out.

SHE WOKE UP LYING flat on the wide, rear seat of the limo. The car was filled with the stink of his cigar—she hated that smell. She was naked, and her hands were zip tied over her head to the door handle.

The man had removed every stitch of clothing and every piece of jewelry. She was absolutely naked. She could not cover herself in any way. With her hands tied over her head, she could not roll over. She struggled for a few moments and then finally gave up. Obviously she was going to have to lie there whether she liked it or not.

By now, the man was seated in the bench seat across from her and drinking what appeared to be wine. She could smell the fruity bouquet and for a brief second found herself surprised that this cigar-smoking creep would be sipping a glass of wine. He stared out the window. Victoria could hear the traffic. It was heavy. They were in a city.

"Do you fear me, Tory?" the man asked without turning his head to look at her.

She turned to look at him. Taped to the seat next to him were pictures of her taken while she was passed out. In the pictures, she was wearing strange clothing or nothing at all, surrounded by drugs and other paraphernalia, not the typical look of a Supreme Court justice. She couldn't remember anything.

"My God," she thought. "My eyes are open in these pictures."

The photos captured various expressions on her face. She hadn't felt a thing.

"Are you afraid of me, Tory?"

Victoria began crying uncontrollably. The man's voice became more intense.

He shouted at her, "Are you afraid of me?!"

"Yes, yes, yes, for God's sake. Stop it. Please leave me alone—for God's sake."

Victoria was losing control and crying hysterically.

"Tory," the man reached over and cut the zip tie. "Put your clothes on. You will learn to answer me the first time. The people I represent do not trust you. They do not like you. They are angry with your brother for nominating you. I, however, am confident, now that I've met you, that you will not pursue this nomination. Why not make a bunch of money in private practice? The pictures will be released to the press during your confirmation hearings if you decide to go forward."

The man again stared out the window. He finally turned to her, his teeth clinched and the lines across his forehead defined by rage. "You could never imagine who these people are. They are more powerful than your brother. Presidents come and go, but these people remain in power. If you disappoint them, they will send someone so vicious you will beg me to come back. You will walk away from this nomination. If not, they will kill you, your brother, his wife, their kids, his dog, his 3rd grade teacher, and any other motherfucker they want. Get it?" he screamed.

The man knocked on the glass separating the front of the car from the back. Immediately the car pulled over. Victoria jumped for the door handle. The man reached over and clutched her hand and the handle all in his hand.

"Do the right thing," he said, looking into her eyes, "or we will kill you." He pulled his hand away and she jumped out of the limo. The car sped away. As far as she could tell, it had no plates.

She looked around and quickly realized she was two blocks from her New York law office. These people either knew her plans and didn't want to raise eyebrows back in Washington by straying from her schedule or it was a bizarre coincidence. Either way, she was out of that car. Victoria ran the two blocks and came through the front doors like a whirlwind.

"Victoria, we were getting worried about you," one of her former partners said as he approached to give her a hug.

"Bill, I need a phone and a private office," she said as she dropped her coat and bag.

"What's wrong, Victoria?" Bill asked as he stepped back in surprise.

"Please, Bill, now," Victoria said loudly as she scanned the lobby.

"Okay, okay. I'm sorry, please use mine. Come on," he said, leading her down the hall.

"Bill, is Lucy here?" Victoria asked as she sat down at his desk.

"Yes, she's in the library."

"I need to make a call. Will you get her and send her in, please? Hurry." Victoria scanned through her contacts searching for a number and quickly dialed.

"Jackie, I need some help. I'm desperate. It's life and death."

Jackie Jacks was a Manhattan detective and, without a doubt, one of the best. The two of them had become good friends while prosecuting New York's finest.

"Ask and it's yours." It was the response Victoria expected.

"Jackie, there's a limo on its way back to Washington. It is a newer limo, probably a 2036. It has no plates; the pinstripe is green. It has four antennas on the back with a dish. I need it stopped and held until I get there."

"Do you have a good reason, Victoria?"

Victoria started to cry again. "Please, Jackie, I need help."

"My God, what's happened to you?" Jackie asked, her voice quivering as she realized the situation was serious for her old friend.

"Promise this goes no further unless I say so. Promise, damn it," Victoria demanded.

"Okay, hey, this is me. You know you can count on me." Jackie was scared to hear the story.

"The guy in the back seat took me from the parking garage in Washington, drugged me, took pictures of me, and then dropped me off two blocks from my old office." Victoria was barely holding herself together. "Please, Jackie, find that car, stop it, and hold them until I get there."

"Victoria, I promise I'll find it, but I don't know how long I can hold them if too many other officers show up. But, hey, I'll do want I can. Do you have the same cell number?"

"Yes."

"I'll keep in touch. My phone's on. Have you been to the doctor?"

"That's next," Victoria hung up and headed for the door.

"Bill, where's Lucy?" Lucy was Victoria's law clerk for years, and the two had developed a deep bond, even while remaining professional.

"I told her to wait in the library rather than disturb you."

"Thanks, Bill," Victoria said as she swept past him and headed to the library.

"Lucy, come with me. Bill, I won't be back today."

"Can I help, Victoria?" Bill asked as he followed her.

"Yes, if anyone asks, I was here, and I went shopping. Everything went fine. Oh and take this," Victoria said. She handed him a letter.

"What's this?"

"It's what you're supposed to say about me when those reporters ask. Thanks, Bill."

With that, Lucy and Victoria left through the front doors.

"Lucy, is your mom still a doctor?"

"Yes. What the hell's going on?" she asked. She hurried to keep up.

"The less you know the better. Please get me to her immediately."

The two women jumped in a cab and sped off. Lucy's mom, Monica Blue, worked in the emergency room at City Hospital. Once there, Lucy asked to pass the front desk. Her mom came out when the security guard repeatedly said no. Victoria knew her well.

"Monica, I need your help," Victoria said.

"Of course, Victoria. Anything," Monica said.

"Can we go somewhere private?"

"Of course, honey."

Monica took Victoria's arm and led her into a private room. Victoria quickly took off her clothing and got on the table.

"I've been attacked. I need you to examine me," Victoria said. She lay back, shivering. "I was unconscious, and I need to know what happened to me."

"Oh my God, how? When? Oh my God," Monica mumbled. She walked in a circle.

"Monica," Victoria shouted. "Pull yourself together. Do I need to tell you how important this is?"

"I'm sorry, oh, my God, okay, okay, okay, relax. How long ago did this happen?"

"Within the last 4 hours."

Monica quickly examined Victoria. "You haven't been raped. But you do have some unusual bruises here on your thighs and back." She pointed to the same areas on herself to indicate to Victoria what she had seen.

"Thank you, Monica," Victoria said as she quickly dressed. "Tell no one about this. Do you have a shower in your office I could use?"

"Yes, please follow me."

The women went down the hall into the doctor's private office.

"Victoria, stay as long as you need."

"Thank you, Monica, but I don't have much time. Please ask Lucy not to repeat anything she saw today. Tell her to tell my former law partners that my ex-boyfriend was in an accident and she came with me to the hospital. That's all she knows."

"Okay, okay. I'll do it. What do you want me to do?"

"Say and do nothing. Nothing. Do you understand, Monica? Say nothing. Do you understand? You could put yourself in danger if anyone knows I was here. Unless you see me on TV or hear me on the radio making a charge, do nothing. I'll call if I'm going to press charges or go public. Can you write up a report and keep it secret?" Victoria asked as she turned on the shower and undressed again.

"Yes, Victoria, I will."

"Thank you, Monica. I hope someday I can explain all of this to you."

Monica left the room, and Victoria locked the door and took a quick hot shower. There was no time to cry, although she wanted to. While in the shower, she heard her phone ring. She shut off the water and stepped out to answer it.

"Victoria, where are you?" Jackie Jacks asked.

"I'm at the hospital. Any luck?"

"Yep, I'm in a helicopter. I have the car in sight. We've been following it for about five minutes. They are cruising at 70 mph, and they have no idea we're up here. I had a buddy of mine in an unmarked car cruise by to verify your description. You were right on."

"Jackie, can you get me there?"

"Are you at City?"

"Yes."

"Go up to the roof. A friend of mine runs their Medevac. Start moving. I'll call him. Go!"

Victoria quickly dressed and ran for the elevator. On the roof, she heard a helicopter running. The pilot motioned to her to board.

"Whoever you are, you must be important," the pilot said as Victoria climbed in and buckled up. The helicopter lifted off like a rocket and shot across the sky. From the headset, she heard Jackie giving the pilot directions. Within fifteen minutes she was hovering above Jackie's police chopper.

"Victoria, we're going to stop them. We're going to try to get them to exit, and then we'll pull them over where we can land the choppers. I have an unmarked car and van cruising along nearby; one is already in position right behind them. Are you ready?"

"You have no idea," replied Victoria.

The car behind the limousine turned on its lights and siren. The limo immediately sped up and charged for the far right lane. As expected, they took the first exit and made a run. Jackie's helicopter descended and put a spotlight on the car.

The driver of the limousine was erratic. He pulled over in a warehouse parking lot and jumped out to make a run toward the docks along the riverfront.

Jackie's helicopter landed in front of the car. The Medevac unit landed behind the car. Victoria got out, and the pilot waved and motioned up. He had to return to the hospital. By the time Victoria walked up to the car, her attacker was standing by the hood of the limo with three guns pointed at his head. His driver also had been apprehended and was now sitting in the back seat of the unmarked van.

"Victoria, is this your attacker?" Jackie asked.

Victoria looked into the eyes of the man bent over the car. It was him.

"Yes, it is." Victoria was emotionless.

"Snap a few facial pics, and run him for ID right away. Then put him in the van. Eddy, go back in the chopper with Dave. Venie stays with us. Hey, guys, we were never here. Got it? Push that limo in the river after we search it."

They all nodded.

"Victoria, search the back seat for your stuff."

In the back seat was a briefcase. Victoria opened it. There were the pictures, the drugs, her plane tickets, the camera, a knife, and a copy of today's *New York Times*.

"Thank you, Jackie. You are a godsend." Victoria clutched the items.

"You would do it for me. You want to take these guys to Greystone?"

"You know I do, Jackie. Has anything changed?" Victoria asked with a dead stare.

"No, nothing's changed. Same people, same system."

"God, these bastards, whoever they are, they think they can scare me into submitting to them. They have no idea how wrong they are. Jackie, can I stay with you tonight?"

"Of course. Besides, I need the whole story. Let's take these guys to their new home, and we'll figure this thing out."

In the back of the van sat the man who, a few hours earlier, had terrorized Victoria while she drifted along in a drug-induced fog. Now, he was in for a shock.

"Mister, do you know who I am?" Jackie asked with an experienced edge.

"You're the cop my lawyer is going to destroy."

"Oh, you think you're going to jail?" Jackie asked. "No such luck, pal." She laughed.

The man laughed back, mocking her.

Victoria stared holes in his head.

"You're in more trouble than you could possibly believe. Are you afraid of me? Trust me, I won't have to shoot you full of Demerol and pretend to screw you in order to convince you to fear me."

Venie quickly returned the unmarked van to the interstate and headed to New York with Victoria's attacker, the attacker's driver, Victoria, and Jackie in the back. They were on their way to a place called "Greystone," known only by the members of a secret society of New York law enforcement. Greystone comprised the two lower levels of a three-story basement under an ancient New York bus garage. The bottom floor was like a dungeon. No official record existed of it ever being built. A worker had discovered it 50 years earlier during the rebuilding of the city's water lines. A few police officers, judges, and other members of the city's power elite had decided it would be an appropriate annex to the jail for inmates freed on the "technicalities," like those often resulting from Supreme Court decisions. In total, maybe twenty-five people knew of Greystone. It was a tight club: you could get in, but not out. And of course, there was no reason to get out. Once you were part of the Greystone administration, you were taken care of by the others. Victoria had been invited into the secret society after making a name for herself by prosecuting a string of mobsters who specialized in all kinds of violent criminal activities.

In the opinion of several former judges, police officials, and powerful politicians, the "system" failed the good people of New York when career criminals were freed without paying for their crimes. Greystone solved the problem. No one had stayed alive more than a year in this place. Over the past decade, crime had increased so dramatically that certain segments of society had begun to crumble. Unless something was done, three-time, four-time, twenty-time losers were left to walk the streets. The result was a "network" of such underground places that sprang up throughout the country. The crime problem was brought under control within a few years. The method may have been illegal, but to many people, Greystone was a shrine.

"You're home," Jackie announced as the van entered the bus garage, turned through an entryway and stopped on a large freight elevator. The elevator descended two floors. When the doors opened, Jackie and Victoria got out of the van and walked to a large metal door.

"Bring him in," Jackie commanded.

Venie got out from the driver's side, reached into the back, and pulled the blonde man out of the van.

"Let's see what's in his wallet," Jackie suggested.

Venie dumped the wallet's contents on the floor of the van as the man stared at Jackie.

"A little cash and one charge card," Venie announced.

"What's the name on the card?"

"Hiatt Montgomery."

"Ok take another picture and research the name," Jackie commanded.

"Smile for a picture," Venie said.

Before the man could flinch, Venie had taken another picture.

"We do that so we can figure out what you used to look like when we find you dead," Venie smirked.

He opened the metal door and led the man down a dimly lit hallway. Halfway down the hallway, Venie swung open another solid door with only a small opening covered with a heavy metal plate. He pushed him into the small room and told him to take off his clothes. Montgomery was standing naked when Victoria Niles walked in.

"People like you require the rest of us to keep places like this," she said. "You attacked me to scare me into quitting. I don't quit. I'll be back tomorrow, and you're going to tell me who you are and who you work for. If you don't, this door will be closed for good. Do you understand? Now get in your cell."

Victoria pushed the man backwards.

The room was 8x8, damp and cold. There was a bucket of clean water and another bucket for waste. A small bulb in the ceiling about twelve feet above his head provided the only light in the little room. A pile of cardboard and an old blanket lay in the corner.

"You two are dead," Montgomery hissed as the door shut.

"Put his driver in that room," Jackie commanded Venie, as she pointed to a room at the end of the hall.

THE NEXT MORNING Peter sat in his old green truck waiting for Jack Langley to leave his home. Peter loved driving the thing. It had been his dad's, and the two of them had restored it at the farm Peter and Susan bought in Southern Indiana. But while he loved having the truck around, he worried about how conspicuous it appeared. As he waited, Peter checked his email and made sure his camera was ready for whatever he might see later. At precisely 5:45, he saw the garage door open and out drove Langley in his black sedan. Giving him about 100 yards head start, Peter started following. Langley drove into the capital but went past his office and continued out of town.

Before long, Langley turned onto a secondary road about thirty miles outside of Washington. He was driving through a quiet little residential neighborhood. Langley pulled into a neighborhood park and followed the road leading to the tennis courts. Peter pulled into a driveway of a house with a "For Sale" sign in the yard, about four blocks from the park entrance. The house was obviously vacant. He got out of his truck, looked at the house for a couple of minutes, and then crossed the street into the park. The park was heavily wooded. Peter walked through the woods trying to remain silent and staying off the trails. He was dressed in jeans and a tan t-shirt and would not be mistaken for a jogger. He proceeded over a small knoll and could now see Langley, out of his car, sitting on a bench next to a small pond. Peter crawled into a large cluster of bushes.

Soon, a woman walked up to Langley.

"Oh great," thought Peter. "He's having an affair." While Peter didn't approve, he didn't feel it was his job to report such a thing—a decision most of his colleagues would not have agreed with.

The woman sat down next to Langley. They appeared to be having a normal conversation. After a few minutes, a man approached Peter from behind. Dressed in casual clothing with a black jacket, he walked right past Peter.

"Thank God, He didn't see me," Peter thought.

The man walked up to Langley and the woman, who both stood to greet him. He shook Langley's hand. The man turned to the woman and said something. Peter took lots of photos, but he had no idea what was being said. "Damn it. What are they saying? Who are these people?" Peter mumbled under this breath.

The man in the black jacket got more animated in his conversation with the woman. Langley was trying to settle them both down. Peter saw him motion downward with his arms, trying to quiet them. The woman poked the man in the black jacket in the chest and shouted in his face. Suddenly, the man in the black jacket pulled out a gun and shot the woman in the head. She fell to the ground. Langley turned and ran to his car. The man in the black jacket walked away, right past Peter.

Peter froze. "What in the hell did I stumble into?" He lay in the bushes for about ten minutes. "Should I see if she has any identification?" Finally he crawled out and ran for his truck. He drove to the nearest empty lot, gathered his composure, and made an anonymous call to the police.

He decided he'd start the drive back to Washington and find out who she was the same way everyone else would. Peter's heart raced. He did not want to return to DC, he did not want the big story, he did not like violence, and he did not want to be here.

"I should have slept in," he thought. After driving about fifteen minutes, he pulled over to use the bathroom and get a cup of coffee. He was shaking and hungry. "I don't need this." Peter took a seat at the horseshoe-shaped counter. "Black coffee, and I'll take a donut." As Peter sipped his coffee, he felt eyes staring at him. He did not want to look up but finally did. Across the counter sat Jack Langley, who was staring at Peter. They were maybe twenty feet apart. Peter tried to act like he didn't notice Langley. Right then, a group of about 10 construction workers came into the restaurant and took the remaining seats at the counter. Peter jumped up and ran for the door. The commotion caused by the construction workers prevented Langley from following. Langley sat there. He now knew what he first suspected when he recognized the reporter: Mercury had seen the shooting.

Peter raced to his office and tracked down his boss.

"I need your help," he said, breathing heavily and shaking.

"You followed Langley, didn't you?" Kyanne asked with a smile.

"Yes, and I wish I hadn't," Peter said.

"What happened?" she asked, switching to a tone of concern as she followed him into his office.

"This must stay between us. I mean no one can know, do you understand?" Peter insisted as he rubbed his head and paced behind his desk.

"Yes, I understand, Peter. What happened?" Kyanne looked around for a place to sit, but the only chair was being used as a place to organize files. She grabbed the stack from the chair and took a seat.

"I saw a woman shot in the head this morning."

"What? What are you talking about?" Kyanne jumped back up from the chair and quickly closed the door.

"I followed Langley to some neighborhood called 'Oak Forest' or something like that. He went into a wooded neighborhood park. A woman walked up to him. They talked. Then a man in a black jacket walked up. The man and the woman argued. I couldn't hear what they were saying. Langley was trying to get the man and the woman to settle down. Then the man in the black jacket took out a gun and shot the woman in the head."

Kyanne stood across from Peter's desk watching her star reporter on the verge of unraveling. She rubbed her forehead, gripped her coffee cup, and then set it down, as Peter went back over the morning's events, this time filling in the details. She realized as she listened that her grip on her coffee cup was starting to burn her hand. She sat the cup down as Peter paused.

"I couldn't believe it. I was hiding in the bushes for a few minutes and then ran to my truck. I called the police from my cell after I settled down and pulled over outside the neighborhood. Then I came here. No, wait, first I stopped for coffee. Langley was there and saw me. He knows I saw what happened."

"How does he know that?" she asked with a look of concern and fear. "How would he know that, Peter?" she repeated.

"I could tell as he looked at me from across the counter. I could tell. He stared right at me."

"Did he say anything?"

"No, he stared at me with the look that said, 'I know you know.'"

Peter was still shaking. "What the hell am I going to do?" he asked.

"He didn't follow you out the door?"

"No, the guy sat there, no emotion, no movement, nothing. Like a statue. He had a coffee cup clutched in his hands; he stared over the rim. God, that guy's a freak!" Peter fell back in his chair and clutched his face.

"Okay, first you have to calm down. Then you need to print your photos. Okay? You need to stay calm, Peter. I don't know what you've stumbled into, but when we find out who the man in the black jacket is, then we can begin to put this thing together. We don't know what role Langley has in this, either. I'm going to check with the staff to see if the police have issued any information on the shooting."

Kyanne was as scared as Peter. However, she couldn't show it. Following Langley had been her idea. She never dreamed Peter would witness a murder with the FBI Director standing by. "What in the world is this all about?" she wondered.

"Peter, let's print these photos so we can spread them out and get a feel for the scene." Kyanne insisted as she walked out the door.

THAT SAME MORNING in New York, Victoria and Jackie were finishing breakfast at their favorite coffee bar, busy as always on Friday mornings, and preparing to head back to Greystone.

"Victoria, you feeling okay?" Jackie asked. "I know you never admit to any pain. You're always okay. But are you?"

"No, I'm not. I feel like shit. I want to go away. I want to disappear for a while."

"Wow, I'm not used to that kind of honesty from you about how you're feeling," Jackie said. In all the years they had known each other, she had come to regard Victoria as one of her best friends, but she had never seen much past her exterior. She had never seen Victoria Niles vulnerable.

"I wish I hadn't been nominated. For the first time in my life, I wish I could watch while someone else does the fighting. I think I've had about enough." Victoria hung her head, letting her despondency show. "I want to disappear, I want out."

Jackie would normally give a "cheer-up speech" at a time like this, but not now, not to this person. Victoria's face was covered in tears; she made no effort to wipe them. Victoria sat staring out the window.

"I want to die," she said. "I was almost raped by that asshole, and all I thought about was catching him so he wouldn't use the pictures against me. What the hell am I?"

"I don't know what to say, Victoria. I wish I could do something."

"There's nothing you can do or say. It's my problem," Victoria said as she wiped the tears with her sleeve.

"Will you tell Jackson?" Jackie asked, knowing she wouldn't.

"I can't. If he knew, he would do something ridiculous. He wouldn't mean to, but he would probably make the whole situation worse. Besides, Greystone would disgust him. He has no idea." Victoria took a deep breath and sighed.

"I don't want to be on the Court right now. I don't want to be a lawyer right now. After Jackson won the election, I realized my dreams were actually going to come true. I've wanted to be on the Court since I was a kid. But it's funny; once it started to become real I see it differently. I sat out in the park one day watching a bunch of kids play, and I started feeling empty. I saw those young moms with their kids and husbands laughing, and I wanted to scream. I made this quest all that I am. Everyone I know sees me through this 'thing' I've been chasing. I used to tell myself I didn't need anything else, but now I feel empty."

Jackie felt unsure as she looked at Victoria. She realized how much their friendship had been a professional relationship, that it had never grown much past the job. An elderly couple at the next table tried to act like they hadn't heard Victoria unload, but their discomfort was obvious. Fortunately, a waitress broke up the moment when she dropped a tray, and attention in the room switched to the sound of breaking glass.

"That's how I feel," Victoria mumbled, as she looked at the glass shattered on the tiled floor.

"Look, you've been through a lot," Jackie said. "You'll feel better tomorrow." It was all she could think of to say.

"I gave up everything to get to this point. I came to hate weekends as I listened to everyone in the office talking about their kids' games or birthday parties or whatever," Victoria said. "I must have looked like such a fool leaving every Friday with my stack of files."

The old man at the next table was now hurrying his wife as she gathered her things and he fumbled with his wallet.

"It's not too late for that," Jackie said softly, as she felt the old couple trying to clear out. "You're a beautiful woman. You can still marry and have a family."

Jackie tried to see through Victoria's bangs, which hung down and obscured her eyes.

"I haven't even had a date in probably three years. I don't even go out anymore." She pushed her hair back and slumped back in the chair. "Hell, I haven't run for ten years or so. I feel jealous when I see people jogging. My clothes don't fit anymore. I look like crap. I feel like crap. I don't like myself anymore. I don't like what this 'quest' of mine has done to me."

Jackie looked at Victoria with a feeling of genuine compassion. She, too, was one of those women who had the job she loved but also had the life Victoria was describing. She understood the emptiness that Victoria felt.

"I know a lot of great single guys, Victoria," Jackie offered with a smile. "I can set you up any day."

"I feel like such an idiot right now. A few days ago I sat in the park baring my soul to some old woman I don't even know," Victoria said without looking up. "Let's go to Greystone and get this over with. Do we have any info on those creeps?" she said in disgust as she pushed out her chair.

"The driver is some bush league career criminal, but the Montgomery guy is former military. The guys didn't find much on him. For the last 15 years or so he's been a nobody."

"Well let's go put Hiatt's head in a vice," Victoria sneered as her anger returned.

The two women left and got into Jackie's car. Greystone was a short drive. A few blocks away, they called Venie on his cell phone. There was no answer.

"That's odd," Jackie said as she looked at her phone.

"He's probably still asleep or maybe his phone's off," Victoria said.

They turned into the old building, drove to the back, and entered the freight elevator. On the lower level, there was no sign of Venie.

"Maybe something happened or he was relieved," Jackie said, searching for a reason why no one was there to greet them.

"Something's wrong, Jackie," Victoria said as she started looking around. "Something is very wrong." Victoria was shaking. Jackie drew her gun and commanded Victoria to get back in the car. "Go up. Right now. Do you hear me? Now! Go!" Jackie was animated but spoke in whispered tones.

Victoria was in no frame of mind to follow her friend around unarmed through the halls of Greystone. She walked to the driver's side door, pressed the elevator button, and rode back up.

Leaving the car on the elevator, she walked around. She was too terrified to sit still.

Down below, Jackie walked the halls of the dimly lit Greystone. Everything appeared normal. As she passed each room she slid open the metal covers in each of the heavy steel doors. The inmates were still there, most huddled on their cardboard. At Hiatt Montgomery's cell, she slowly slid open the steel plate and peered through the opening. In the corner of the room sat Venie, tied to a small chair. He had been beaten severely. His hands were tied behind him with wire, so tightly that his wrists were cut open. He had cigarette burns all over his body, most of them on his face. He was dead.

Jackie knew that her life had now changed as much as Victoria's had just a day earlier. "Who opened the door? Who let them down here?" she thought as she jerked around, pointing her gun in all directions. It was impossible to operate the elevator except from below, unless they had a master key. Someone Venie knew had to have come to Greystone. He let them in. He had to have. There was no other way in. Her mind raced. "I have to get out of here."

Jackie ran back to the freight elevator and pressed the button. The elevator car descended the two floors to the basement. Victoria was not inside with the vehicle. Jackie stepped on the platform, pressed the button and went back up to the surface. Victoria was standing by the elevator.

"Victoria, get in. Someone's been here. Venie is dead. Get in the damn car. We've gotta get out of here."

Victoria began shaking; she was in shock. "Who? How? My God, Jackie, the people who attacked me yesterday knew about Greystone? Where do we go?"

"I don't know. Not home, I can tell you that," Jackie said. "We're going to get on the highway and get the hell out of here until we figure this out."

She raced the car out of the garage.

Victoria and Jackie drove south out of the city as if they were being chased. They had no destination in mind except to disappear.

"Victoria, I have to find out who is behind this. I can't hide."

Jackie was closer to the top of Greystone than anyone in New York. It was governed by a committee of ten, all of them powerful and well connected. They voted on who would be picked up and "registered," as they liked to say. Once you were registered, you were dead. There was no getting out. The committee comprised a former police commissioner, a former police captain, two former judges, two acting judges (one of which had taken Victoria's place when she moved to Washington), two city councilmen, and two prominent and extremely wealthy businessmen, who provided the funding.

Jackie Jacks was scared but in control.

"Victoria, someone on the committee was behind your abduction."

"Maybe."

"Maybe, my ass! How else do you explain this?" exclaimed Jackie.

"There are people above the committee, Jackie. People you have never met. National people. Washington people." Victoria was telling her friend things she would never have disclosed if the events of the last twenty-four hours had not happened.

"We can't be sure it's someone local until we find out who the hell Hiatt Montgomery is. We can't assume anything," Victoria said. "I know you are shocked by this, but Greystone is a Washington-sanctioned program. Not official Washington, of course, but the people who run Greystone are protected by high powers in Washington."

Now it was Jackie's turn to be shocked. "What the hell are you telling me?" she shouted. "The same bunch of assholes that cause our crime problems also allow places like Greystone to exist! Why not change the damn laws, then?" She was irate. She screamed at Victoria as they drove. "You people, you're one of them. You fuckin' people make us risk our lives. God damn you all," she screamed as she drove.

"Jackie, settle down. It's not the same people. We're on your side. That's part of what Jackson's campaign was about. We haven't been running the Supreme Court or the government. We've been fighting the same problem nationally as you are, as I did, in New York. As long as laws allow these creeps to walk on technicalities, we have no choice but to operate places like Greystone."

Victoria looked at her old friend with compassion. "We're on the same side."

"So what now?" asked Jackie.

"I don't know. I'm not sure who to go to."

THAT SAME FRIDAY morning in Washington, Peter Mercury and Kyanne Fitzgerald stared at a series of digital pictures they had printed and spread out on Kyanne's office conference table. What they saw only confused the situation. In the photos, Jack Langley's face was twisted. He was obviously pleading with both the man and the woman to stop arguing. In the photo that captured the shooting, Langley looked horrified and obviously surprised. The man in the black jacket, on the other hand, was void of emotion. He was also a complete mystery. Neither Peter nor Kyanne had ever seen him. The woman's back was to the camera in every picture. They had no way of identifying her.

"Peter, you must remain calm."

He sat down. He didn't want to hear any more, but he also knew he was in this thing up to his neck.

"I called a friend of mine who works in the police department out there," Kyanne said. "She said there wasn't anything to report except a couple of prank calls. I told her one of our reporters had picked up the activity on our police scanner."

Peter stared at the photos. He had the pictures, but someone else had the body.

"Kyanne," Peter whispered. "I need some good advice. What the hell do I do? Who do I trust? Should I go to the police? Should I go to Langley?"

"I don't know, Peter. Do you think you should get them to the President via Susan?"

"No, for God's sake. We're not involving Susan in this. We don't know who these people are. Besides, maybe the President knows all about this."

Kyanne had never had a situation like this in all her years in Washington. She paced back and forth across the room.

"Peter, I think you should go to your farm or something for a day or two, and let's see what shakes out. Maybe something will turn up."

"I can't do that, Kyanne. We don't know what Langley's capable of doing."

"Peter, I think you have to tell Susan about this if you fear for your own safety. She should be aware of the potential danger. Perhaps she can go with you?"

Peter held his hands over his face. His pulse quickened, his face reddened, and his hands trembled as he contemplated his next move.

"I have to talk to Langley, Kyanne. I have no choice. I can't run away."

LATER THAT DAY, Victoria Niles arrived back in Washington. She'd left Jackie at her condo in the suburbs. After driving and talking for hours, Victoria had convinced Jackie to stay with her for a few days to see if they could find some answers. Victoria knew, down deep, that her problems with Hiatt Montgomery, whoever he was, were originating in Washington.

Victoria entered the White House virtually unnoticed as people buzzed around dealing with the business of the day. As she approached Susan's desk, she was disappointed her best friend was nowhere to be seen. She looked around the corner to see the door to her brother's office standing open.

"Good afternoon, Victoria," the President said as he spotted her.

"I'm sorry. Susan wasn't out there, so I thought I would peek in," she said as she entered the Oval Office.

"How are you, Sis?" he asked as he gave his baby sister a hug.

"I'm okay, Jackson. I'm really tired."

"Did your trip wear you out?"

"The trip, the nomination, the move. It's all wearing me out." Victoria could be honest with her brother to a point, as long as she kept the events of the past two days to herself.

"Maybe you should take a vacation before this nomination business gets really serious."

The President hugged his sister again as he gave her a smile. "Once it starts, it doesn't stop," he cautioned.

"I know. Jackson, I have a question for you," she began as she took a seat. She dreaded the idea of Secret Service protection as much as she dreaded the conversation with her brother.

"What's that?"

"I think I want Secret Service protection."

Victoria stared at the floor. She knew a million questions would be coming her way, and she was not good at keeping the truth from her brother.

"I think that's a great idea, Victoria. I've been hoping you'd come to your senses about that. Has anything in particular brought you to this decision?"

Victoria got up from the sofa and walked to the window of the Oval Office hoping to hide her eyes. "I've had a few strange phone calls from some crazies. You know, nothing serious."

At that moment, the President received a call from the head of his Secret Service detail.

"What?" the President said as he looked across the room at Victoria. "Are you absolutely sure?"

He stood looking at Victoria without speaking. "Okay, I need you to stand by. This may be a top priority, and I may need you to come here."

He hung up the phone and took a deep breath.

"What is it, Jackson?" Victoria asked as she turned to face him.

"That was the head of my Secret Service team. There has been an explosion ... at your condo. It was completely destroyed."

"Oh, my God. Jackie was there. My God, they've killed her," she said as she stumbled across the room and fell into the sofa with tears falling from her eyes. "I did this to her. This is my fault." Victoria drew her knees up on the sofa as she curled up. "Nothing is worth this," she moaned. "I'm so sorry Jackie," she blurted out as her crying intensified.

The President picked up the phone and called the head of his Secret Service detail.

"Get over here—right now," he said. Then, turning to his sister, "Victoria, are you going to tell me what the hell is going on? Who's killed her?" He stood looking down at his sister.

"Victoria, please," he said as he knelt down in front of her.

"Some crazy guy came up to me yesterday in the parking garage and said they would kill me if I went forward with the nomination."

Victoria kept her face buried in her hands to prevent her brother from seeing her eyes. She could not tell him about the abduction or Greystone. If the truth ever came out, she did not want him compromised.

"Who was he, Victoria?" the President asked.

"I don't know. I'd never seen him before."

Victoria let out a deep exhale as she tried to gain some composure. "I thought he was some nut. I didn't take it or him seriously."

"Victoria, you're going to disappear for a while. As far as the press will know, you died in the explosion. I'm going to nominate someone else. No person outside this room is going to know you're alive. I'm not going to risk the only sister I have."

He walked to the door outside his office and spoke to the Marine standing guard.

"Lieutenant, you're going to take a trip with my Secret Service head. No one else will ever know about this trip," he said.

"Susan, are you out there?" he asked as he buzzed her desk.

"Yes, sir," she replied.

"My Secret Service head is on his way over. Send him in directly. But no one else is to enter this room. Absolutely no one," he commanded.

"Yes, sir," Susan responded without pause.

Jackson looked at Victoria.

"I love you, but you are not going to die for this nomination. Do you understand?"

Victoria looked up at her brother. "Yes."

"Good."

The lead man on the President's Secret Service detail entered the Oval Office.

"Mr. President," he said simply as he entered and stood before Jackson.

"I am giving you a direct order. You will take the Marine Guard outside that door, and the two of you will escort my sister to my home in upstate New York. You will then return directly to this office. You will not tell anyone about this. Do you understand?"

"Yes, Mr. President."

Jackson walked over to Victoria, knelt down and put his hand on her shoulder, and looked into her eyes. "I know more than you think I do, little sister. Go with them, they can be trusted, and you have to trust me."

The three left through the side door of the Oval Office and walked directly to a waiting helicopter.

THE NEXT MORNING, Jack Langley sat in his backyard, his oasis. He was dressed in a sweat suit. It was a beautiful Saturday morning, warm and sunny. In the middle of the yard was a large gazebo made of white lattice. The latticework and railings were covered with honeysuckle, wisteria, and various climbing roses. Langley's mom was an active horticulturalist and at each visit she added another plant to the collection of color. Langley met the morning here as often as possible. He felt protected, almost invisible inside his overgrown garden. Today, though, he was frightened and already worn down. Next to his cup of thick, black coffee was the morning paper. The headline read: "Supreme Court nominee killed in fire."

Events would soon take on a momentum of their own, he suspected. Langley's mind raced. Peter Mercury was not supposed to be in that park. The man in the black jacket had no reason to shoot the woman. At least not that Langley knew. The woman had been incensed over the man's harassment of Victoria. "What harassment was she talking about?" wondered Langley.

The woman was the only contact Langley had. She had contacted him about some grand conspiracy but had given no names. The meeting in the park was to answer those questions. Now Langley could only wait for a phone call or a knock on the door. "Had Mercury told anyone else about the shooting?" Langley wondered.

And now Victoria was dead. Had the man in the black jacket killed her, too? Langley was unsure who the bad guys were. "What conspiracy? To do what? What the hell was going on?" he thought.

"Should I go to Mercury?" Langley wondered as he scanned the morning's paper. On the editorial page of the paper was an op-ed called "Is President's Movement to Blame?" The article by a longtime Washington reporter speculated that Jackson Niles' program went too far. The everyday person could not be trusted with the scope of power Niles was proposing. The writer speculated that crazy fringe groups were chomping at the bit for the program to be passed because they saw it as the gateway to "independence."

It was the first article of its kind since Niles had taken office. Langley read it, wondering himself if the writer wasn't correct. He had seen fringe groups go crazy in the wars he had been involved with. "It's always the same," he thought.

Langley put the paper down and went back into his suburban home. He should get to the office and contact the President. No doubt, today would be a bad day for Jackson Niles.

AT THE MERCURY HOME, Susan was distraught over the loss of Victoria. They had been best friends since childhood and her loss would leave a hole in Susan's life. Inside their home, not one light was on and all window coverings were closed. Susan, wrapped in a blanket, lay curled up on the end of the sofa. Victoria's passing cut deep into Susan as she considered the life that was lost. She loved Victoria and had held out hope that Victoria would find true love while also reaching her goals. "What a waste," she kept whispering as she thought of her friend's talent and quality of character. "You had so much to give," she cried out as she relived the shared moments of their time together.

Peter, on the other hand, sat on the back patio wondering who to tell about the shooting he had witnessed. He couldn't tell Susan. Not now, that was for sure. She had enough to deal with considering her best friend was dead. Peter was deeply saddened by Victoria's death, too, but he saw it differently. Peter smelled trouble, deep trouble. Something bad was going on, and Victoria had gotten caught in the middle. Peter knew he had stumbled into something big. He wouldn't believe for a minute that all these events weren't linked in some way. Unfortunately, he had no idea who, what, how, or why.

CHAPTER THREE

Off Comes the Scab

In upstate New York at the family home, Victoria spent Saturday morning lying in bed watching CNN. The news special for the day was "The Death of a Nominee." It was a strange feeling listening to the account of her death.

She was relieved to find out that Jackie had not been overlooked. She didn't know how her brother handled the details, but it didn't matter. At least Jackie's family would not be wondering what happened to her. Jackie had a special place in Victoria's heart, and she sobbed as the news switched to focus on the detective. The guilt over Jackie's death made the sadness sting even more. Victoria cried over the thought of Jackie's family losing her. She was a devoted mother and wife. Her death fought for space in Victoria's mind as she watched the commentators switch back and forth between Jackie and her own death.

The home in New York was small, cozy, private, and at the end of a long winding road. It was surrounded by dense woods and looked out over a small private lake. The night before, the President's men had drawn all the shades, locked all the doors, and stocked the house with a few items to eat.

By 10 o'clock, the morning talk shows began to repeat themselves, and Victoria started to wander through the various rooms of the home. Before he became President, her brother had traveled here often to get away and spend the weekend fishing. As President, though, he had made the place off-limits, not wanting to ruin its privacy for the years after he left office. Not many people even knew the family owned the house, since a non-descript corporation the family used for real estate purchases held the deed.

Victoria came down the stairs from the bedroom and headed for the kitchen. A hot cup of coffee would clear the caffeine headache she was feeling. Next to the coffee pot was a note, "Two Secret Service guards will arrive by late Sunday PM—lie low until then." Victoria started the coffee pot and wandered through the home. It had been more than 20 years since she'd been here, not since her parents came here on summer vacations.

The walls were covered in family photographs. In the den, Jackson had pictures of his wife, Vivian, and many photos of his children. The fact that his wife and children were still residing in New York finishing up their school years now seemed fortunate for all. Vivian was not enthusiastic about being First Lady, and the campaign and election had revealed strains in their marriage. Her family was old east coast money and the idea of major change was not appealing.

Jackson had also hung many pictures from previous fishing trips, all of which included Sam McBride. Picture after picture showed the two of them, often with Anthony Sinclair. Some were recent.

She didn't know they had stayed that close. "God, he looks good," she thought. Sam was about 6'2," lean, and muscular. His brown hair was thick and wavy, and his green eyes deep and penetrating. The years had been kind to him, his features only more defined than in his youth. He could still stop her heart.

Victoria poured a large mug of black coffee and walked out onto the deck. It had rained all night and most of the morning but had finally cleared up. The rain had greened up the grass, and the lake looked alive with activity. A variety of warblers flew around the backyard, across the lake, and then back to the many sugar maple trees and bird houses that hung from branches throughout the yard.

"What a beautiful place," she thought, as she walked past the deck to the pier where the backyard met the lake. As a child she had come here every season with the family. Her parents had harvested maple syrup from the trees in the winter, and in the fall as the leaves changed, the woods became the most beautiful place on earth. Today she watched as the yellow winged warblers darted about chasing mosquitos. Victoria sat down on the dock next to the gently rocking rowboat and dangled her feet in the water. "When was the last time I did this?" she wondered.

The roughness of the wood pier against the back of her legs reminded her she was wearing only a t-shirt. The sun had warmed the water and removed the coolness from the air left by the rain. Victoria sat the coffee mug on the pier, slipped off the t-shirt and dove into the lake. The last time she had skinny-dipped, if you could call it that, was with Sam in their little pool back at Yale. Victoria swam across the little lake and then turned and swam back, taking her time. On the side of the pier was a small inner tube. Victoria pulled it into the water, reached up and took a final swig of her coffee, and then pushed off to float on the lake. She wouldn't worry about what's next. For now, it was enough to float across the lake naked, under the warming sun.

AT THE SAME TIME in Washington, the mood at the White House was somber. Anthony Sinclair was handling the President's affairs while Niles spent the day in the family quarters. It was important he play the role as if Victoria were really dead. He took no calls or visitors. All were referred to Sinclair.

On Capitol Hill, Sims, Cochran, and Reed were gathered in Reed's office.

"Thank God that bitch is gone," Sims said. "I've never trusted her." He was tired of holding back his feelings.

"Hamilton, let's not let Niles nominate another problem," Sims said as he picked up Reed's cane and pointed it at the Speaker.

Cochran pushed himself up from his chair and walked to the door. "Keep it down, Clayton. For God's sake, we're in the Capitol."

"I don't give a shit," Sims said as he spun around. "We've let this go too far already, if you ask me."

"You better get yourself under control," Reed whispered. "You go popping off, and it causes trouble for us all. Besides, we don't need people asking questions. Settle down and put down my cane."

Speaker Reed reached out for his cane.

"You need to spruce up this office," Sims muttered as he handed the cane to Reed and looked around. "It even smells out of date in here."

BY LATE AFTERNOON Saturday, Victoria was huddled on the sofa in front of the fireplace. The weather had turned cooler, so she built a fire after spending most of the day swimming in the lake and lounging on the pier. She kept the television off, as she did not care to watch any more news or silly sitcoms. The silence of the house and the warmth of the fire felt soothing. Staring into the fire, wrapped only in one of Jackson's old flannel robes, she sat comfortably in the quiet.

She thought about where she would go next or what she would do. "How long will I be dead?" she wondered. In a way, she liked the feeling. Victoria had felt only emptiness as she approached the nomination. Now, she felt differently, not exactly fulfilled but like the hole inside her had been removed. All her life she had been pursuing one thing and that quest had come to define her. Every friend saw her through that lens. Any man she dated knew her first as the woman who would eventually be on the Supreme Court. It was "her," all of her. Everything she thought or discussed or was perceived to be had become wrapped up in the nomination. Now, if she so chose, in a matter of a few hours the nomination would be gone.

In the silence of the lake house, Victoria drifted deeper into herself. She had come as close to a near-death experience as a person could and still be conscious. She reflected back on her life, viewing her decisions and then the life that resulted as if she were someone else. Even so, the regret she felt cut more deeply into her than ever before. In her mind, she saw even the people she had met just briefly and now could only speculate about their lives. She remembered and then analyzed so many past encounters she had never allowed to move beyond the superficial. She hovered in that dream-like state, drifting off now and then only to be awakened by the sound of the fire cracking. A bottle of red wine slowly worked its way down her, as evening became night.

Suddenly, she was thrust from her trance by the sound of a key rattling in the lock of the front door.

"Oh, my God, who's here?" she thought, as she jumped up from the sofa and darted out the back door and to the pier. She huddled behind some bushes and watched as a solitary figure walked through the house. She watched as the person went upstairs turning lights on and off in each of the four bedrooms. The man—or was it a woman, she couldn't tell—repeated the same pattern downstairs. Victoria was huddled in a ball behind a bush. She was barely clothed, and had no identification, no money, no transportation, nothing. Her heart raced as she wondered where she would go. The back door finally slid open and a figure walked out onto the deck.

"Victoria are you out here?"

Victoria didn't move. "Whose voice was that?" she thought.

"Victoria, are you out here? It's Sam, Sam McBride."

Victoria was frozen in fear. She hadn't talked to Sam since Yale. "Was that really his voice?" she thought.

"Pinky, it's me. Jackson sent me."

"Pinky!" She hadn't heard that nickname since Sam had last used it.

Victoria stepped out from behind the bush and walked toward Sam. The twisted feelings she felt for Sam left her in the unusual and uncomfortable situation of being tongue-tied.

"Why are you here?" she finally asked in an indifferent tone as she approached him.

"Jackson asked me to come and get you," Sam answered in surprise.

"I don't need your help," she said, the memory of Yale surging in her soul.

"Jackson wanted to make sure you were safe," Sam replied feeling unwelcome. Victoria stood looking at him with a flood of thoughts and feelings bubbling inside.

"Jackson doesn't think the explosion was some freak accident. He wants you hidden away in case they realize they failed."

"I can go somewhere else. You need to go home," she instructed Sam, as she walked back toward the pier.

"I'm not leaving here without you," Sam said, jogging to catch up to her.

"Look, Sam, I appreciate that you flew out here and all, but this isn't necessary. Go home. The Secret Service guys are coming back, and I'll go somewhere else with them," she said, turning over her shoulder but continuing to walk.

"Do you think your brother would trust your safety to anyone else? He called me as soon as his office was empty. No one knows I'm here except him. The Secret Service guys coming here is part of his plan," Sam explained.

"All they'll find is an empty house, though," he paused, hoping Victoria would finally stop and turn around. "You're coming with me. And, I'm sorry to say, we're going to Montana."

Sam smiled a little as he said the words, having not forgotten what an issue Montana was to Victoria.

"You're going to disappear. The only people who knew you were alive last night are now going to report to the President that you are missing." Victoria stopped.

Sam looked at her with an expression of resolve. "I'll help you get your things together, and then we have to go."

Victoria followed Sam into the house as she accepted that her brother and Sam were not going to take "no" for an answer.

"I don't have anything here. Only the clothes I was wearing when I arrived," replied Victoria.

"I brought some sweats and a t-shirt for you to wear on the plane. Jackson told me your sizes. There's a pair of shoes in there, too." Sam set down a duffle bag on the sofa. "Bring that robe you're wearing, too. I left it here last fall."

Victoria smiled for the first time in two days. She had forgotten she was wearing only the flannel robe. It was too big for her and difficult to keep closed. Victoria picked up the bag and went upstairs. She changed quickly and stuffed her power suit from the day before, along with the robe, into the duffle and came back downstairs. She walked over to Sam and gave him a friendly hug.

"Thank you, Sam. I do appreciate you coming here," she said looking up at him.

"I have a plane waiting. I landed at a small, private airport about a half hour from here. Before we leave, though, we need to toss this place to make it appear there was a struggle."

The two of them closed the fireplace doors, tossed pillows around, knocked over some furniture, and then drove back to the airport in the car Jackson kept there for his weekends away. Within the hour, Victoria was sleeping soundly on Sam's jet, on her way to Montana, feeling truly safe for the first time in a days. As Sam monitored the flight instruments and adjusted the controls, he glanced over at Victoria now and then. So many memories surfaced that he hadn't thought of for years.

Late that night, after landing at the ranch, Sam sent a message to a phone the President rarely used. "Pinky is home." Niles had waited nervously in the family's living quarters, desperate to see that message flash across the screen.

"Thank God," he thought. "Now I can get down to business." With that, he left for the Oval Office.

EARLY SUNDAY MORNING, Peter Mercury sat in his favorite diner enjoying a quiet breakfast. The stories on his tablet were filled with speculation about the bombing of the Supreme Court nominee's home. Peter believed the shooting in the park was connected to Victoria's death, but he didn't know how. His usual inclination was to blame the government, but this was the President's sister. Peter could only speculate who would want her dead, but he was confident someone in the government was so opposed to the nomination, so scared by the prospect of having Victoria on the court, that they took this extreme action. Peter, though paranoid, was still a practical and reasoned reporter. "Who had the most to lose?" he thought. As usual, he started with those closest to the event, since he believed a deceiver was always in the mix when something big happened.

"Who in the President's inner circle is the darkest character? Who would take such extreme action? Who had the most to lose by Victoria joining the Court?" Peter would explore his thoughts with Kyanne later in the day.

IN MONTANA THAT Sunday morning, Victoria ate a bagel as she watched Sam prepare his horses for a trip. Her life had been completely changed by recent events, but she found herself thinking not about the Court or Jackie or politics but about the last time she saw Sam packing: when he was about to leave her. His decision to leave Yale was abrupt and had left Victoria stunned and broken hearted. She had sat on the front porch swing that morning, silently crying as Sam loaded his car. He had said almost nothing to her other than he had to leave, that a law career was no longer of interest to him and he had to go home. Victoria learned a few days later that Sam had pre-paid the rent on the little house for the next two years on his way out of town. Then a few days later, a card arrived that simply said, "I'm sorry. I never thought we would fall in love. I had to go back home."

She never heard another word from Sam, and other than an occasional mention by her brother, she knew nothing about his life. She knew he had married his hometown girlfriend, but other than that, she knew nothing.

Sam finished up with the horses and turned toward the house. Victoria snapped out of her reverie as Sam entered the kitchen.

"Did you get enough to eat?" he asked.

"Yes, I think so. Where are we going?" Victoria asked.

"I have a small cabin about a day's ride from here if we take it nice and slow. It's isolated and unknown to anyone. We're going there for a few days."

"Sounds kinda fun," Victoria said as she made a face of disappointment. "Why there?"

"I promised your brother you would be safe, and that place isn't on any maps. My ranch backs up to Flathead National Forest. Nobody ever makes it to the backside of the park. It's literally in the middle of nowhere," Sam said. "It's only for a few days to make sure nobody's looking for you. I'm not taking any chances."

Sam walked to the counter and picked up a backpack. "I have plenty of food. Think of it as a long picnic."

"Sam, I appreciate all this, but everyone thinks I'm dead. I can't expect you to leave your family for a few days to look after me. I have other places I can go. I do have friends, you know. You don't have to do this." Victoria was sincere, but her tone was also laced with bitterness.

"I don't need you," she added as she looked down.

Sam turned and looked at Victoria for a moment, looking like he wanted to say something. Instead, he turned toward the door. "Come on, let's get going."

By noon it was obvious to Victoria that Sam was not in a talkative mood. He hadn't said a word since they left the ranch, and he rode ahead of her explaining that he wanted her to ride behind him and the packhorse. She wondered what he was thinking and had concluded that he must be annoyed with this task her brother had assigned him, and, in fact, did not want to be away from home.

"This is all ridiculous," she thought as she rode. "He doesn't want this any more than I do."

Ahead of her, Sam rode along methodically, confident he was doing right by Jackson but unsure of his own feelings. "Never did I expect *this*," he muttered to himself as he glanced back at Victoria. Victoria, noticing the glance, tried quickly to smile, but Sam turned before she could change her expression.

"What was *that*?" she wondered.

Sam kept searching for words to say but found nothing, as years of conflicting thoughts turned over in his gut.

By early evening, the air began to cool, and Sam suggested they camp for the night rather than trying to ride the last few miles in the dark.

"It's too dangerous at night. The horses might spook." With that, he dismounted and tied his horse to a tree branch.

"I'll get a fire started. Look in that backpack and see what looks good, and I'll get something cooked up," Sam said as he gathered wood.

There was a small stream about 25 feet from where they had stopped, and Sam suggested Victoria water the horses while he got the camp set up.

"Lead them. They'll stay over there and drink for a while. They won't go anywhere."

Victoria could not help but notice the beauty and serenity of the place. She laughed to herself as she walked around the area, remembering how she had loathed the idea of living "out west," as Sam used to say. After spending her entire life in cities, she was surprised by the calmness and peace she felt. For a moment she felt removed from all that had happened.

Before long, Sam had a fire roaring, a tent set up, and a hot bowl of soup ready for Victoria.

"I brought some fresh bread and cheese, too," he said as he handed her a small tray.

"Thank you, Sam," Victoria said as she looked up at him. Sam offered a slight smile but nothing else in response.

"I also brought some wine," he said as he handed Victoria a plastic cup filled with white wine. "If I remember correctly, you drink Riesling, right?"

"You have a good memory," Victoria answered without looking up.

"Too good," Sam mumbled as he turned. "That came out of a box, so it may not be what you are used to," Sam added as he glanced back.

"It'll be fine. I still mix my wine with Sprite or something. I'm not a wine snob, Sam. And by the way, I drink wine from a box at home, too."

They both laughed as each remembered, without saying so, their introduction to box wine at Yale. They would often float around in the baby pool with a box of wine next to them. Sam coined the nickname "Pinky" after an afternoon in that pool and the resulting sunburn on Victoria's backside. It was the last time she went without sunscreen on areas that seldom saw the sun.

Victoria sat quietly as she ate the meal Sam had made her. She wasn't hungry, but sitting in the middle of nowhere with a campfire burning was relaxing. "This is good, Sam."

Sam kept silent, but finally told Victoria that there was more soup if she wanted seconds.

"No, this is enough, but I think I might get another glass of the wine." Victoria walked over to a tree stump where the wine box was sitting. "You want some more?" she asked.

"Sure."

Victoria walked over and filled Sam's plastic cup to the top.

"You know, this is the first time we've seen each other since Yale." She backed up so she could see Sam's eyes, but he kept looking at the fire.

"Sam, are you going to talk to me? We've been riding all day and not a word. Now we've had dinner and hardly a word. Come on! My condo was blown up, one of my best friends is dead, the world thinks *I'm* dead, I'm in the middle of Montana with a guy I haven't seen in twenty-some years. For God's sake, talk to me."

"Okay, what do you want to know?"

"Tell me about your family, kids, anything. I don't like the circumstances, but here we are after all these years, and I want to hear something. Tell me about Sarah and your kids, please." Victoria sat down, never taking her eyes off him.

"Victoria, I don't know what Jackson has told you over the years."

"Nothing. I mean absolutely nothing. When I got to the lake house and saw all those pictures of the two of you, it was a bit of a shock. I really didn't know you two were together that often. So I know absolutely nothing."

Victoria reached for her cup of wine, took a drink, and looked across the fire at Sam. It was dark, but when the fire lit up his face, she could see he had tears in his eyes.

"Sam, what is it? I'm sorry. I didn't mean to pry. Sam, come on, it's me—Pinky. You can talk to me. What is it?"

Sam kept staring at the fire without moving a muscle. "It's been a long day," he said as he stood up. "The tent is for you. I like to sleep under the stars by the creek." With that, Sam picked up a sleeping bag, stood up and walked down to tie up the horses.

"Good night, Victoria," he said softly as he walked past her.

Victoria sat in silence, sipping her wine and staring at the dying fire. She really had no idea what had just happened. Sam used to lie in bed talking with Victoria all night. In fact, she used to joke around that she wanted to kiss him just to keep his mouth busy.

"What happened?" she wondered. Victoria had spent many nights at home alone in the darkness wondering about Sam McBride. She always told herself that Sam had loved her as much as the girl from home, but the girl from home was at home—in Montana. And at the end of the day, that is where Sam wanted to be.

The next morning, Victoria woke to the sound of Sam packing up the horses and preparing breakfast.

"We'll be at the cabin in an hour or so," he said. "It's an easy ride from here."

Victoria quietly ate the sausage and fried potatoes Sam had made as he packed up the tent and prepared her horse for the ride. A small coffee pot rested on a rock next to the fire, and Victoria was surprised by how good the strong coffee and heavy food tasted.

"Sam, I am not helpless, you know. Once we reach the cabin, I think you should go home for a few days. I don't want to be a burden any more than I am. I can survive in a cabin for a few days. Go home."

Sam finished with the horses and walked over to Victoria. It was the closest he had been to her since he had hugged her at the lake house.

"I made your brother a promise," he said firmly. "I will stay with you as long as it takes for him, and me, to know you are safe. There isn't anything you can say or do that will make me leave your side. Your brother and I are like brothers, and I would do anything for him."

He stepped back and headed for his horse.

"Okay, Sam," Victoria said, realizing how safe she felt with him. "I'm sorry about last night."

Sam stopped for a moment but didn't turn around.

"Sarah was killed three years ago in a car crash. I thought you knew. You caught me off guard. I don't want to talk about it."

He mounted his horse and started through the woods. Victoria was now the one caught off guard. She hadn't been told and had no reason to know otherwise. She stood there looking at Sam, a thousand questions in her mind as he rode off. "My God, Sam, I'm so sorry," she whispered.

IN WASHINGTON THAT same morning, Peter Mercury arrived at work and immediately headed for Kyanne's office. "You realize Victoria was murdered, right? I mean, I'm not the only one thinking this, right?"

He was fired up, having come to the conclusion that something big was afoot.

"Who do you think did this, Peter?"

"I don't know. I have no frickin' clue. But condos don't simply blow up with the President's sister inside. I mean, it's insane to think that some gas leak would randomly happen to *her* condo. Come on, give me a break."

Peter removed a book from a box sitting on a chair in the far corner of the room and randomly turned the pages. He paused for a moment as the sounds of a group passing by filled the hallway. "I should have eaten something this morning," he mumbled, as the smell of fresh toasted bagels penetrated the room.

"I could use something, too," Kyanne said, also noticing the aroma. "I can't think straight on an empty stomach."

Kyanne had worked with Peter over the years on special assignments when he would come in from New York. He had broken open more stories than any reporter she had ever worked with. "It's only a matter of time," she thought as she watched Peter, knowing his mind was flashing from thought to thought.

"Who had the most to lose from her confirmation, Peter?"

"That's it, Kyanne. That's the thing. Who did? Everyone? No one? Why would it matter if she were on the Court? I mean, the President promised big changes, but so do they all. Nothing is going to change. Hell, it never does."

Peter placed the book back in the box as he let out a sigh.

"If your premise is right, that it was a murder, then you are talking about people who are incredibly connected and powerful, not to mention brazen. What's your gut say, Peter?"

He walked back to Kyanne's small conference table and sat down. "I think all these events—the VP's crash, the shooting in the park, and now Victoria—are connected in some way. Some group has it out for this administration. I don't know why yet, but I think these events are linked. An assassination of the VP and the death of a Supreme Court nominee—it can't be a coincidence."

A knock on the door interrupted Kyanne's response as an assistant delivered coffee and bagels.

"Thank God," Peter declared as he grabbed a bagel and started munching.

"You want some cream cheese?" Kyanne asked as she joined him.

"No thanks."

"Who has a reason or who's the center?" Kyanne asked.

"Jack Langley and the FBI."

"Maybe he was in the park investigating the same hunch," Kyanne said. "Remember that Jack Langley fought with the President in the service. Those bonds go deep, Peter. I wouldn't suspect him yet. He may be trying to figure out the same riddle as you."

"Maybe, but if he's on the same trail, then he knows more than I do, and I need to find him and see what he's been up to since Victoria was killed."

Peter started in on another bagel. "I was hungrier than I thought," he said with his mouth full.

"Peter, if this is what you think it is, then you need to be extra careful," Kyanne cautioned. "I need to know where you're going every step of the way."

"Let's ask the FBI for an interview with Langley," Peter said. "This thing is so weird I want to get him alone and ask him about the diner incident. He'll know what I'm thinking when I call. Let's start there."

"I like it. I'll have the request sent and let you know what I hear. But here's the thing," Kyanne said as she stepped close to Peter, "Right now he doesn't know what you know. Once we make this call, he'll believe you know more than what happened in that park. Are you sure you want to get on his radar?"

"I have to."

"We'll either take a big step forward, or we are going to have to put you somewhere safe. And I mean that, Peter."

"Fair enough. Make the call."

Peter was down the hall heading out as soon as the words left his mouth.

OUT WEST THAT MONDAY, Victoria caught sight of the cabin as the midday sun was heating up. There was a stream close by with large boulders and a few shade trees along its banks. The cabin looked surprisingly nice from a distance, with a small porch along the front and a couple of old rocking chairs already moving with the breeze.

"Welcome to your short-term home," Sam called out as he dismounted.

"I came out here for a few months after the accident and built this as a form of therapy. No one ever comes out here. This is about as remote as you can get. There are no roads anywhere nearby. You're safe here, Victoria," Sam assured her.

Victoria dismounted and walked up the short steps into the cabin. The inside was one big room except for a small bath Sam had built in the back corner.

"I have a gravity water system set up and a small solar heater, so if you want to take a hot shower you should be good to go," Sam said as he unloaded supplies on the kitchen counters.

"Wow, Sam, I'm impressed. This is actually much nicer than I expected, and, yes, a shower sounds fantastic. But where's the TV?" Victoria asked, giggling on her way to the bath.

"Don't press your luck. Let's get unpacked and take the horses down to the creek. Those big boulders heat up and there are a couple of flat ones that make a great place to lie back and relax."

"That sounds great. Can I do something to help?" Victoria asked.

"Change into something for a relaxing day by my natural pool," he said as he glanced at Victoria with a smile.

"Sam," Victoria said as she walked toward him.

Sam looked up and made real eye contact for the first time since he had picked her up at the house in New York.

"Thank you for helping me," Victoria said as she hugged him gently.

"I would do anything for you, Pinky," Sam said as he gave Victoria a long, tight hug. "Now let's take this box of wine and some snacks and go enjoy the day by the pool."

Victoria was relieved that Sam was starting to talk to her. She looked around the little cabin for a moment. A large metal wood stove stood in the corner near a log bed, which looked handmade. Victoria wondered if Sam had carved it himself. Two old quilts were folded in half and hanging on the footboard. On the other wall a rocking chair sat next to a small table with an old kerosene lamp. There were no pictures or anything that looked like an attempt to decorate. The kitchen area had an old hand pump that drew water from a rainwater cistern. The little cabin was sparse, but it had warmth to it that surprised Victoria.

A few minutes later, Sam was walking the horses to the creek with his arms full of blankets. Victoria followed close behind with food and wine. As Sam began to relax and talk to her, Victoria remembered how much she had once enjoyed his company. Sam had been funny, thoughtful, and interesting to talk to. She used to love their long discussions about the issues of the day. He was the first and only man she had ever dated whom she felt was her intellectual equal. And if that weren't enough, when the talking ended and the lights went out, Sam made her melt.

"Let me put these blankets down," Sam said, motioning to two large, flat stones that sloped gently down and into the water.

"Wow, these are almost hot," Victoria said as she stepped up onto the rocks.

Sam layered the blankets on the large stone until the pile was thick and provided a nice cushion. "Later we will build a fire on that one," he said, pointing. "I've spent many nights out here."

After a couple of hours relaxing on the thickly padded rocks, Victoria finally took a chance at a more serious tone.

"Tell me about Sarah," she said.

Sam lay looking up at the big blue sky. He stared out as the question washed over him. It was unexpected, and for a moment, Sam experienced the same internal conflict he had confronted years earlier.

"I really don't want to," he finally said softly. "I'm sorry, but I don't."

Victoria felt uneasy as she looked over at him. Sam didn't seem offended or angry. To her, he seemed empty. "Maybe I shouldn't have asked," Victoria said softly.

"It's okay, Pinky," Sam said, almost inaudibly. "It would be the first time I've talked about her in three years. It's been hard. I'm not ashamed to say."

Victoria sat up on the rock and looked at Sam. "I'm so sorry you lost her, Sam. I really am."

Sam looked at Victoria but did not comment. Victoria paused and gazed across the water. "It's incredibly beautiful out here," she said, deciding a less serious tone was better.

"Tell me about your life," Sam said. "You've been a big-time lawyer in New York, right?"

Victoria looked down for a moment, not quite sure how to answer Sam. She hadn't been that happy before her "death," but she hesitated to confess such a thing.

"Do you have kids?" Sam asked, expecting to hear all about them.

Victoria drew a deep breath, realizing that Sam knew nothing about her life. "I never married."

Sam hesitated a moment, realizing how uncomfortable his comment had made Victoria. He thought about how close he had come to asking her to be his wife. "I imagine with the career you've had, there wasn't time." He struggled for words. "You were a judge in New York, too?" Sam quickly added in an effort to get the conversation going.

"Yeah, for about ten years," Victoria answered as she brushed her hair back.

"Did you enjoy that?"

"Yeah, sometimes. But you get to see the dark side of life every single day. It gets old after a while," Victoria responded without much enthusiasm.

There was a moment of uncomfortable silence as each struggled for something to say.

"You accomplished your goals, though, right?" Sam finally managed to ask, trying to find something positive to talk about.

"I did, but I've had moments lately where I have questioned what I did," Victoria answered.

"That surprises me," Sam countered in a tone of compassion.

"Sam, I made choices. I pursued the Supreme Court nomination. That's what I always wanted. Lately, though, I've felt that maybe I put too much into that goal. I've had my regrets, but I guess that's life."

Victoria shrugged a little as she offered a slight half smile at Sam.

"Have you been happy?" Sam asked in a tone of genuine concern.

Victoria took a drink of her wine as she contemplated Sam's question. "I always thought I was," she finally answered. "But after Jackson won and I realized I would be nominated, it was like it all hit me. All of a sudden, I felt empty." Victoria paused as she looked up at the stream. The scenery was beautiful, but she didn't see any of it. Instead she saw herself, and she felt pain at the vision. She should have felt some satisfaction or at least acceptance, but instead she had only regrets. A great egret glided in across the water and snatched a small bull trout from the stream. "That's satisfaction," she thought as she watched the bird soar away.

"It wasn't that I didn't want to be nominated. I just realized I had dedicated my whole life to something that was up to someone else. Would I have been nominated if my brother had lost? All of a sudden, the whole thing felt different. I felt shallow. I saw the women in the park with their kids and husbands, and I felt like I had been tricked. I can't really explain it. But I guess the truth is, no, I have not been that happy."

"I have been dedicated. I have been strong," she said. "I have been successful. I have made money. I have gained influence. But I have not been happy. That's the truth coming from a dead, 41-year-old woman."

Victoria turned away as Sam stared at her in astonishment. He felt a wave of emotion in his gut as he looked across at this woman he had loved so much. It was hard to hear such a confession.

"Pinky, you should be proud of what you accomplished," Sam finally managed to say.

"I should be, but I don't feel it," she said. "I got to a point where I didn't like myself. Not even a little."

"You're a young woman," Sam declared in a tone of encouragement. "Life isn't over, you know?"

"It's funny, in a way. I think I felt relieved when Jackson told me I was going to go away and be 'dead' for a while," she said. "I felt like I was being let off the hook."

Neither of them made eye contact. "Of all the emotions, regret is the worst," she said. "We can't change the past. We have to live with what we chose."

Sam reached over and touched her on the cheek. "You've been through a lot. You aren't thinking straight. Let's make the best of being out here. This time will pass, and you will see things clearly when the dust settles. You are a smart, accomplished woman. You've been through a terrible ordeal. Let's have some fun, and in a couple of weeks you'll go back to your life and everything will be okay."

Sam kept his hand on her face as she continued to stare down.

"I don't need a cheering-up speech," she finally said as she looked up.

"I don't mean it that way," Sam countered softly. "You have accomplished more at the mid-way point of your life than most people do in an entire lifetime."

"I used to think about leaving New York and being an attorney in some small town. There were a couple of guys I said no to that I sometimes think were wrong choices," she confessed with tears in her eyes. "I saw other lawyers in the city who had full lives. They kept things balanced and seemed a lot happier than me."

Victoria looked away as Sam listened without offering a word.

"I thought many times that I was the smart one and they were settling for less. But all of a sudden I started feeling like I had wasted my life chasing something that didn't matter."

"I don't know what it is about you that makes me open up so much," she said as she took a deep breath. "I feel kinda silly."

"You're being too hard on yourself," Sam finally offered.

"Maybe so. Maybe it's the whole thing. The nomination and then the impact of being sent off as a 'dead person.' I've been forced to look back at life as if it really is over. You know what I mean?" she asked. "Not many people get to do this. I mean the world thinks I'm dead. And I can stay dead if I want. I could decide I'm not going back. I could take on a new identity and start over as a teacher in some little town. Or wait tables like I did in college. It really is kinda nuts and kinda cool, if you stop and think about it. I could stay dead and be a completely different person if I decide to. I could start over. I could be anybody I want," Victoria said, realizing that truth for the first time as the words left her mouth.

Sam looked over at Victoria as he realized she wasn't just "going through" something. She was genuinely rethinking her path in life—both past and future.

"It does feel nice to be outside doing nothing," Victoria said, changing the subject. "Maybe I can work off these 20 extra pounds if I stay out here long enough," Victoria added with a self-deprecating laugh.

"I think you look great," Sam reassured her.

"Before the fire, I had a closet full of clothes I couldn't wear anymore. I was stress eating leading up to the nomination, but once it became inevitable, I was so nervous I couldn't keep food down."

Victoria turned and lowered her legs into the water. "This is actually warmer than I expected. Is that pool over there deep enough to swim in?"

"Oh yeah," Sam said as he took a drink of wine. "But the trick is finding the right rocks so you can walk across that little rapid and get to the deep water."

"So that's hard?" Victoria asked.

"If you go the wrong way, you'll fall on your butt," Sam explained.

"Maybe later," Victoria answered as she pulled her legs up, slid back up the rock and picked up her cup of wine. "I think another drink and a nap sound good," she said as she stretched back out.

Sam dozed off, waking up an hour or so later to find Victoria gone. He briefly panicked as he pushed himself up and looked around. Upstream, he saw Victoria attempting to cross the rocks that led to the calm pool. She carefully walked from rock to rock with a drink in each hand, balancing herself on the wet stones as she gingerly moved across the rapids.

Sam laughed as he watched this beautiful woman from his past walk along the river, oblivious to his presence. Finally, she reached the other side, set down her glasses of wine, pulled off her shirt and shorts, and slowly slid into the calm water. Once in the water, she turned and looked to see that Sam had been watching the entire time.

"I made it," she called out as she raised her arms in victory.

Sam laughed, lifting his glass in a toast to Victoria's accomplishment.

"Your turn," Victoria called out with a big smile.

THAT SAME AFTERNOON, Peter Mercury walked quickly through the DC airport. He had learned that Jack Langley was out for a few personal days and was supposedly out west fishing. Peter knew of the friendships that connected the President's inner circle, so he decided to do a little investigation of Sims' lodge to see if Langley was there with the old gang. Peter wasn't sure what he was looking for, but he wanted to know if Langley showed up.

As he walked, Peter's phone rang. "We have an identification on the shooter," Kyanne reported.

"Tell me."

"He's a bad ass, Peter."

"How bad?"

"Former Special Forces—as elite as it gets. His name is Hiatt Montgomery. Don't mess with this guy, Peter."

Peter ended the call and drew a deep breath as he walked down the terminal toward his gate. He had felt fear before during the many stories he had broken, but hearing Kyanne's description gave him a unfamiliar sensation. "I hope I never see that guy again," he thought as he handed over his boarding pass.

Peter landed in Missoula mid-afternoon and drove east toward Flathead National Forest. By early evening, he had parked the car and was walking through the forest trying to get close enough to the lodge to scout out who was coming and going. He carried what he needed to spend a couple days there, if that's what it took.

He found a spot with a clear view of the front porch, but after an hour of sitting and staring through his telephoto lens, he had seen no signs of life. At about 2 o'clock in the afternoon he heard what he thought was a deer moving through the woods behind him. As he turned to look, a rider on a horse came up the hill.

"Who might you be?" the rider asked, as he came up on Peter.

"I was hiking through the National Park and must have wandered off the trail," Peter said.

"I didn't ask you how you got here," the rider responded.

Peter stared at the rider, whose face looked familiar, but the three-day beard and large hat obscured his features so he couldn't quickly figure it out.

"I have to hand it to you, Mercury," the rider stated. "You are a brave, but I'm afraid rather stupid, man."

Peter now realized he was looking at the man in the black jacket from the park. Hiatt Montgomery, the man whose identity Kyanne had revealed earlier in the day.

"What the hell are you doing here, Mr. Reporter?"

Peter stared up at Montgomery, unsure what to say. He was expecting to find Langley at the lodge. This was unexpected, and Peter was not prepared. The last time he saw this guy he had shot the woman in the park.

"Not talking, Peter?" Montgomery asked as he pulled a pistol from inside his jacket and dismounted the horse. He approached Peter, and before Peter knew what was coming, the man grabbed a rope from the saddle and slipped it over Peter's head. The loose ends fell all the way to the ground.

He jerked the rope tightly around Peter's ankles as he pushed Peter to the ground.

"I'm going to have some fun with your sorry ass," Montgomery said, and with that, he mounted his horse and took off, dragging Peter across the ground. "I suspect you will be plenty talkative by the time we reach the lodge. Of course, that's if you're not dead," he yelled as he laughed and picked up speed.

In the 15-minute ride to the big front porch at the Sims lodge, Peter's clothes were shredded and his body bloodied. Montgomery jumped off, tied the horse to the porch railing, and walked back to Peter.

"I don't think I even need to tie you up, do I?" Montgomery asked as he pushed on Peter's face with his boot. "Okay, I'm going inside for a minute, and I'll come back with some water for you. If you try to run away, I will shoot you in the foot—to start with," Montgomery laughed again as he walked up the porch steps into the lodge.

Peter had been in tough spots before, but this was different. He was not capable of taking on a man like Montgomery under the best of circumstances. But after being dragged through the brush, he was barely able to sit up, let alone run or fight. He lay there wondering what was coming next, and for the first time he considered the possibility that he was about to die. No one knew exactly where he was, and he had no way of dealing with this psycho. As he lay there lacerated, bleeding, and feeling pain throughout his body, all he could think of was whether he would ever see Susan again.

Montgomery reappeared and pulled Peter up to the railing of the porch. He put a handcuff on one hand and attached the other end to a thick wood spindle. "I've got some calls to make about you," he muttered as he removed the rope from Peter's feet. "There's some water and food," Montgomery motioned to a bag he had set down. "You sleep out here tonight. When I get back, you tell me why you're here and what you know. It's that simple. If you don't, I shoot you in the head and no one ever finds you. Are we clear, Peter?"

Montgomery didn't wait for an answer. He went up the stairs and disappeared into the lodge.

BY LATE AFTERNOON Victoria was standing in the shallow side of the rapids, a few feet from the large stones. The water felt a bit cooler, but the sunshine quickly warmed her up as she walked back toward Sam and sat down. "It's incredible out here, Sam," she said softly as she stretched out on the blanket.

It was both familiar and strange for Sam to be looking at Victoria lying there next to him.

"I'm going to start a fire and cook something to eat," Sam said.

"Can I do anything to help?"

"Gather some fire wood?"

Victoria looked around. Along the stream were numerous areas where logs and branches had washed out of the banks. She gathered small pieces and built a pile near the large stones. As she worked, she started to laugh at the simple joy she found in such a mundane task. She had spent all her adult years in the hurried life of a law career. She could barely believe her sudden change of fortune but also the peace and serenity she was experiencing. The cool grass felt good on her bare feet. The big blue sky and the warm sun lifted her spirits.

She smiled as she worked, thinking that for her, life was new. She began to see her "predicament" as an opportunity more than a curse. She felt a sense of wonder and expectation she had not felt in years. She was free from her old life if she so chose and was beginning to feel the lightness she had felt in her youth. She smiled and laughed a little as she walked along. The air felt different. The sun was warmer. For the first time in so many years, Victoria felt free from the quest she had given herself.

Sam had a small fire burning, and a foldout grill over the fire was now covered with two large steaks. "After today, it will be fresh fish," he said. "I have some fruit and veggies, but no other meat.

"Fine by me," Victoria answered as she added to the pile of branches. "I need to eat better anyway."

Sam cut up a bag full of vegetables and potatoes and wrapped them in foil as Victoria looked on. "Would you get me some more wine?" he asked as she watched him work. Victoria reached over for the wine box and refilled Sam's cup.

"Have you ever slept outside?" Sam asked. "I mean, not in a tent, but outside under the stars?"

"No," Victoria said.

"We can sleep out here on this big rock tonight," Sam said. "I'll keep the fire burning, and with enough blankets, you'll be warm."

Sam finished wrapping up the vegetables and placed them on the edge of the fire. "They'll cook real fast inside that foil." Victoria looked at the pile of blankets and then looked up and down the stream. "Where will you be?" she asked.

Sam chuckled a little and then looked up from the steaks. "I was thinking next to you. We would both be warm that way."

There was an awkward silence as Victoria fidgeted with her glass. "I think I'll take the bed inside the cabin."

Sam didn't respond as he wondered what to say next. Victoria was suddenly uncomfortable with the thought of sleeping next to Sam.

"I'll light a fire in the cabin stove after we eat. It stays nice and warm in there," Sam promised as he flipped the steaks.

Victoria sat quietly as Sam checked the veggies and added a little bit of wood to the fire. She didn't know if Sam had propositioned her or if his intent was to sleep. Either way, she was caught off guard and was now feeling uneasy. She had loved Sam more than any man she had ever known, but now she felt differently. She still loved him, but she wasn't sure if she could trust that feeling. He had hurt her badly at Yale. And now, after a lifetime had gone by for each of them, she was hesitant to try it again.

"Sam, I haven't even been on a date in the last three years," she finally confessed.

Sam took a deep breath and tried to keep himself composed as he exhaled. "Me either," he said as he stood and headed for the cabin.

Victoria slumped as she realized the time frame was identical to Sarah's death. "I'm such an idiot," she mumbled. A few minutes later, Sam emerged from the cabin. "The stove is lit and the cabin will be nice and warm by the time dinner is finished," he announced as he sat down.

"I'm sorry about that comment," Victoria said softly.

"No big deal."

The awkward silence that took over lasted throughout dinner. Sam wasn't sure himself if his suggestion had been sexual, but he knew it had been rebuffed, either way.

Victoria was equally uncomfortable. She and Sam had a passionate relationship in college, but that was now ancient history. She'd never been that close to another man and, because of Sam, probably never would.

"This food is delicious," Victoria said politely as she took a bite of a Yukon Gold mixed with onions, mushrooms, and broccoli.

"Thanks."

They finished the meal in silence, since neither could find a casual topic to bridge the discomfort.

Victoria was still attracted to Sam but was unable to find the courage to trust again after all those years of hurt.

For Sam, who had been utterly alone since Sarah's death, Victoria was like a ghost. Never in his wildest imagination had he pictured being out here with her. Even now, after all he had been through over the last three years, he felt some guilt for even looking at Victoria. He was attracted to her. She still moved him, and he was struggling with the feelings. She was the same to him, but she was, at the same time, different. The years had scarred them both.

"I think I will head for the cabin," Victoria announced as she finished her plate.

"I'm sorry, Victoria," Sam said as he watched her leave. Victoria froze in her steps as the apology cut through her. "About what?" she asked.

Sam hesitated, thinking he had struck an old nerve. "I meant what I had suggested, but I have a feeling something else is going through your mind."

Victoria stood looking down at Sam. The anger and hurt she had managed to bottle up for so long bubbled inside her. "Have you ever lost complete respect for someone you loved?" she asked in a monotone voice.

Sam drew a long breath, knowing what she meant.

"God, I loved you, I admired you, I looked up to you, and you fucking left. Like some chicken shit little boy, you packed up and ran away. To feel love and hate at the same time. To be absolutely disgusted with someone and still love them. That's hell, Sam. I can tell you firsthand that is fucking hell. I don't know what you have been through these last twenty years, but I really don't care, either. To me, you are a chicken shit. You left."

Victoria reached down, grabbed her glass, and quickly swallowed the wine. "I lost all respect for you that day. I love what we were, but that's it." Victoria stood looking down at Sam who was now looking back at her. A million thoughts shot through his mind, but he was at a loss for words.

"I'm going to bed," Victoria finally declared as she tossed her empty cup down in front of him.

Once inside the cabin, Victoria let out a deep breath. "I'm glad I'm tired," she mumbled as she walked toward the bath. A few minutes later, she pulled the heavy quilt up and settled into the soft bed. "It is nice and warm in here," she thought as she turned on her side and curled up.

Outside, Sam added wood to the fire and refilled his cup. "I guess I can't blame her," he thought as he reminisced about their past and how he handled his leaving. The sky was clear and a million stars spread out above Sam as he lay there. The air was cool, and he thought how much better he would feel if another warm body was next to him. Sam stayed awake for a while as his mind replayed the days from his past.

For the first time in a long time he was thinking about the time he had spent with Victoria at Yale. He smiled and even laughed out loud as he recalled their time together. It was therapeutic for Sam. He had been torn apart by Sarah's death, and to think of another woman, at this point, was liberating. He was surprised by it, yet even in this moment he thought of Sarah. Through the years they had grown closer, and what was once an almost burdensome relationship had grown to be mutual. Motherhood had strengthened Sarah, and as the years passed, her increased strength had brought them closer. Sam had grown to see her differently. It was in the quiet of the night as he stared at the fire that the last twenty years took on a new meaning. Being in the presence of Victoria brought new insight to his feelings. The advantage of being able to look back, to have perspective, made him realize a truth about his marriage that he had never seen. As Sarah had grown stronger, she had become more like Victoria—at least in his heart.

He thought of how Sarah had guided the children when they were young. How she had protected them when they felt threatened. He remembered watching her in the park comforting their son as he dealt with feeling excluded the first time. The strength Sarah gained as a mom had moved Sam. Had Sarah's transformation triggered love that was actually meant for Victoria? Guilt washed over him. But as the night passed and Sam continued to relive moments with Sarah that had touched him deeply, he began to view them through a new lens. He *had* loved Sarah. First, it was the childish love of finding a friend who could offer a comforting shoulder after the loss of his mom. Later, it was a teenage crush on a girl he had become so comfortable with that his first sexual experience had seemed natural. Later, as young adults, passion entered in as their love took on a deeper meaning. Yet even as their love grew, Sam could still see the dependence and weakness in Sarah that he had resented.

When Victoria appeared at Yale, Sam found the passionate love of an equal or even a superior mind and spirit. He was captivated and awestruck. When motherhood transformed Sarah, this girl he had known so long, into a strong and independent woman, Sam found himself quietly watching in awe again. He couldn't tell Sarah he saw her differently, but he came to believe she felt it. They grew closer, and the relationship grew deeper and more passionate as the kids aged. He finally came to a point where the regret was gone. The decision he had made at Yale finally seemed right. Life was complete. Then Sarah died.

Inside the cabin, Victoria watched the glow of the fire in the small stove. Her sense of liberation was growing by the minute as she examined her situation. She was feeling stronger and happier as she considered her "next life." In the calmness of the little cabin, she was growing. She felt the healing inside as her newfound freedom began to sink in. "I'm moving on," she whispered as she curled up in the old quilts.

WHEN THE SUN FILLED the cabin the next morning, Victoria awoke feeling rested and at peace. "I haven't slept that soundly in years," she thought as she stretched. She found a coffeepot and after adding wood to the stove, soon had hot water. Looking out the window, she saw Sam still sleeping by his dying fire.

On the counter, a map was stretched out that showed the park location relative to Sam's ranch. "If I ride west I can reach that little town," she thought. A few minutes later, she was dressed and had one of the horses saddled. She led the horse out quietly, not wanting to wake Sam and deal with the inevitable confrontation. "This is a little ironic," she whispered as she reached what she felt was a safe distance and climbed into the saddle.

When Sam finally woke up, the sun was bright and warm. He added wood to his fire as he pulled on his boots. "I need some coffee, but I shouldn't wake her," he thought, rummaging around in his pack for a granola bar. "I might as well deal with this now," he thought, turning for the cabin. As he walked, he looked over and noticed one of the horses was gone. "I better go find out where that thing has wondered to," he muttered. Once at the cabin, he froze at the site of a saddle also missing.

"What the hell!" he said as he climbed the steps and burst through the door. Sam stood motionless as he stared at the empty bed. He drew a deep breath as he contemplated Victoria riding alone through the wilderness. Her empty coffee mug sat on the counter next to the map.

"Where did you go?" he whispered. Sam quickly exited the cabin and saddled and packed the horses as his fear rose.

It didn't take Sam long to find the trail Victoria's horse had left. But her coffee mug had been stone cold when he moved it off the map, so she had a big head start. Sam rode hard as he watched the trail weave through the grass ahead of him. Finally, after an hour, he caught site of Victoria riding west through a mountain valley. She was on course to enter a small village of stores and a few homes. "What the hell are you thinking?" he thought as he gained on her. He slowed as he came within a distance where he felt she might hear his horse running. As he drew closer, Victoria looked back.

"Hold on," Sam called out as he approached.

"Let it be, Sam," Victoria called back as she increased her speed.

"Damn it. Stop for a minute," he said as he rode up by her side. "Stop!" he yelled, as he grabbed her horse's reins.

"You're not in charge here, Sam," Victoria said in protest.

"Stop it," Sam said angrily as he pulled her horse to a stop. "You go riding in there and get recognized and your brother pays the price," Sam shouted as he spun her horse around.

Victoria stared back angrily as she contemplated Sam's words. "Nobody out here knows me or gives a damn," Victoria countered as she attempted to pull away.

"Your face has been on the front of every paper and plastered on every TV for the last 24 hours. These people don't live in caves," Sam shouted as he stared at Victoria. "Think of somebody other than yourself," he added with a fatherly tone.

"Other than myself?" Victoria repeated with a scream. "You mother fucker! You have no shame, do you? You fucking bastard!"

She pulled the reins from Sam's hand and kicked the horse. She bolted away as Sam quickly pursued.

"Stop it, goddamn it," he yelled as he again grabbed her horse. "Get off, get off the fucking horse," he yelled as he jerked the reins out of her hands.

Victoria stared back with fire in her eyes.

"Get off the horse!" he yelled again.

"Fine, keep your damned horse," she proclaimed as she slid off the saddle and started walking away.

"For God's sake, will you stop it," Sam demanded as he followed. He grabbed her and turned her to face him. "Hate me if you want. I can't blame you for that. But your brother is in trouble, and you can't show up in some small town in Montana."

Victoria drew a deep breath. Helping Jackson was the one thing he could say that would get her attention.

"Stay out here long enough for him to get things figured out," Sam suggested in calmer voice. "Only a few days—okay?"

Victoria took a step back as she gathered her thoughts. "Okay, but we're riding into that town so I can get some things to change my appearance," Victoria demanded.

"Why?" Sam answered puzzled.

"Because I have plans, and I'm not staying out here for long," Victoria answered.

"So if we do that, you'll go back to the cabin for a week?" Sam asked.

"One week."

The two stared at each other for a moment.

"Okay, let's go," Sam finally said as he handed her the reins.

Once the two rode into the village, Sam suggested they head for a small store near the edge of town. "Tell me what you want, and I'll go get it," he suggested as he came to a stop.

"I need hair coloring, a pair of scissors, and a brush."

"What color?"

"Black."

A few minutes later, Sam emerged from the store with a bag and handed it to Victoria. "There's a bathroom on the back side of that restaurant over there," Sam said. "I'll get a table outside and meet you there after you do your thing."

Sam was halfway through a glass of water by the time Victoria emerged from the bath.

"Don't say a word," she demanded as she sat down. Her long strawberry blond hair had been replaced by shorter black hair with bangs.

"I actually kinda like it," Sam said, smiling.

"It'll do the job, I suppose," she said.

There was no one else seated outside, and before long, Sam had relaxed, feeling comfortable that Victoria's change of appearance as well as her being away from the Washington crowd would keep her unrecognized. The restaurant offered a few appetizers that intrigued Victoria, so they sat drinking fresh mountain water and working their way through the small plate menu. They started with a wild mushroom dip advertised as the "House Specialty." A western version of bruschetta followed, served with something known as buffalo chowder.

Sam finally suggested they head back to the park and find a place to camp.

"Back to the wilderness, Pinky. That was the deal. I know a little spot where there's a hot spring. It's better than any hot tub I've ever been in," Sam said. "You're going to absolutely love it."

The sun was low in the sky by the time Sam and Victoria climbed the rock slope that led to the small hot spring. He had undersold the location. The warm pool of water was about eight feet across and deep enough in places to get completely submerged. Next to the small pool was an area where Sam built a fire and spread out the sleeping bags he had quickly loaded onto the horse's pack that morning. Victoria wasted no time in taking off her boots and was already dangling her feet in the water.

"This feels incredible. The water is perfect," Victoria said, her feet and ankles submerged.

"I bought you some lotion at the market. It's my way of giving you a little civilization while you're out here in my beautiful wilderness."

"I do like your wilderness," Victoria said, smiling at Sam and knowing the unlikeliness of her statement.

"Are you ready to get in my mountain hot tub?" Sam asked as he pulled off his boots.

Victoria was already pulling off her jeans and t-shirt as she slid down into the water. "Oh that is perfect," she said as she sat back against the large warm stone on the pool's edge. "Wow," she added as she let out a deep sigh.

The sky was as clear as it could possibly be and filled with stars. They sat in silence. Neither had any desire to bring up a subject that might reignite the earlier scene.

CHAPTER FOUR

A Dirty Morning

W ell, after a full day of discussions, I'm still getting mixed answers about you, Peter," Hiatt Montgomery said. Peter was still handcuffed to the porch of the Sims Lodge.

"Some of my friends think I should shoot you and let the coyotes and wolves have you. Others think you know something. So they've left it up to me," he said as he sauntered across the porch. "Either way, you're going to tell me what you know. I think you're out here following a hunch about something you've seen or heard. That's what I think. But I don't think you want to talk, so I'm afraid I am going to have to convince you. I'm also a bit embarrassed to admit that I don't have my usual means of persuasion with me out here. You see I was actually on vacation after a week of grueling work. So now I am forced to resort to some old-fashioned tactics to get you talking."

Montgomery took a drink from the whiskey bottle he was carrying and then slipped a noose attached to a long pole around Peter's neck. "Stand up. Walk to the horse stables out by the end of the air strip."

Once inside, Montgomery led Peter to a center column that had a thick rope hanging from the rafters above. He sat the whiskey bottle down on the floor and tied the rope around

Peter's hands. He then walked over to a pulley and cranked the rope tight until Peter's feet barely touched the floor.

"Here is how this works Peter," Montgomery announced, as if teaching a class. "I'm going to whip the truth out of you. Have you ever been whipped or tortured, Peter? I guess I should ask because I never know what people have been through in this life."

Peter remained silent. All he could think of was getting through the next hour or so then finding a way to escape.

"No? I didn't think so," Montgomery said. "It doesn't matter."

Hiatt Montgomery stepped back and grabbed a whip hanging by the nearest horse stall. "I'm afraid this is the best I have."

He brought the whip close to Peter's face. "Now, if this were Rome, I'd have a whip with pieces of metal tied into the ends. Those pieces would dig into your skin and tear it away as I pulled the whip back. That would be exciting and effective—don't you think?"

Montgomery walked over and sat down on a wooden stool next to where he had placed the bottle of whiskey. "Peter, why are you out here?"

"I was looking for Jack Langley," Peter answered.

Montgomery spit out his drink of the whiskey. "What the fuck—you're talking before I even touch you? My God, you are a pussy, aren't you?" Montgomery laughed as he took another drink. "Oh, wait a minute, you're playing me, you little shit. You think I'm fucking stupid?"

He took a long drink of the whiskey and cracked the whip next to Peter. "I hate fucking reporters."

Montgomery whipped Peter, who screamed in pain. "There isn't anybody to hear you," Montgomery yelled as he brought the whip back again. He took another long drink from the bottle. "I would have loved to have been a Roman," he screamed as he brought the whip forward.

Peter was now bleeding from open cuts on his back. "I told you the truth. I was looking for Langley," Peter tried to say between groans of pain.

"I don't care, you fucking dumb ass," Montgomery countered. "You'll tell me the truth in the morning when I come back, or I'll whip you all day. This? This is nothing. Tomorrow morning is when the real fun starts. Think of this as an appetizer."

Montgomery kicked the pulley and the rope loosened enough for Peter to drop to the floor. He laid there motionless. His back and sides where cut open from the whipping. Montgomery sat on the stool drinking the whiskey, muttering in an indiscernible tone.

"There's water in the horse trough. It's all you get tonight." With that, Montgomery, now completely drunk, staggered out of the barn and disappeared.

Peter stayed motionless for a while, sure that Montgomery would reappear and resume the torture. After fifteen minutes or so, Peter managed to stand and make his way to the horse trough. He put his hands in first, hoping that wetting the ropes would loosen them against his wrists. He avoided getting water on his back for now. Though he was sure his wounds were deep, at least for the moment, they felt tolerable.

Escape was Peter's only thought. He knew he had to be gone before the whiskey wore off. After a few minutes of soaking his wrists, Peter decided to crawl into the trough to wash his cuts. The cold water felt better than he had feared, and he sat there soaking until finally the ropes on his wrist began to stretch out. He pulled at the knots with his teeth until he was finally able to slip strands of the rope out through the knots. After an hour or so of chewing and wiggling, Peter freed his hands. He quickly put on what was left of his clothing and began moving around in the darkness of the barn to find a way out. He soon realized how drunk Montgomery must have been since the door he had exited remained unlocked.

Although the moon was nearly full, it was still dark enough that Peter was unsure where Montgomery had entered the property or where his car was located. Peter slipped out the door.

On the far side of the airstrip, Peter discovered a small stream. He decided to follow it as far as possible, crossing it from time to time to disguise his trail. Peter was no woodsman, but he was scared and desperate. An hour earlier he was sure he was about to die; running blindly through the woods now felt surprisingly okay.

As Peter traveled, he became more and more aware of the surroundings and what to expect. Although not athletic, he was a jogger, so he could cover a lot of ground without exhausting himself. He made good progress, quickly moving along the edge of the creek. His eyes adjusted to the limited light, and while still in pain, he now moved fluidly.

WHEN THE SUN began to rise, Victoria was awakened by the smell of fresh coffee. Sam sat on the far edge of the rocks watching the valley below.

"Are you awake?" Sam asked as she stirred.

"Yeah," she responded, stretching her arms over her head.

"Come over here and watch this valley light up as the sun crests over the mountain."

Victoria poured herself a cup of coffee and walked over to join Sam.

The valley was more beautiful than any picture the great artists could paint. A stream running through the middle came to life as birds swooped in and animals began moving about. First she noticed a few elk off in the distance as they approached the edge of the stream. Then, as her eyes focused, she saw a pair of coyotes carefully moving through the tall grass toward a morning drink. As Victoria took in the entire scene she saw the bugs flying over the water as the birds chased them. The surface of the water appeared constantly broken by the jumping fish looking for flies. The scene played out like an orchestra warming up in morning air.

"Watch how each area changes as the sun hits the water," Sam suggested as he motioned toward the valley.

Suddenly, in the distance, they heard a shot.

"What was that?" Victoria asked as she jerked back from the shock.

"Poachers. I hate those bastards," Sam said as he stood and quickly retrieved a pair of binoculars from his pack. "Probably hunting bear, if I had to guess."

He looked through his binoculars as Victoria stood up and peered in the same direction. "There's the bastard," Sam exclaimed, as he focused in on a distant figure. "What a dumb ass; he's out here in street clothes. What the hell is he shooting at?"

Sam panned his binoculars downstream. "Shit!" he exclaimed as he focused on another object.

"What is it?" Victoria asked.

"Some guy is running through the woods, and I think the other guy is shooting at him."

"What?" Victoria exclaimed as she tried to see what Sam was looking at.

"Look toward that clearing over there," Sam instructed as he handed Victoria the binoculars.

She looked but couldn't see anything.

"Over there by that rock pile at the bend of the creek. There's a man squatting down by the largest stone."

Victoria focused the binoculars on the rocks.

"Sam I know that man. That's Peter Mercury. He's a reporter. His wife has been one of my best friends since we were kids. What the hell is he doing out here?"

"A better question is, who's shooting at him and why?" Sam responded.

"Look back to the right by that large cluster of trees," Sam pointed as he described the spot to Victoria. "There's a guy on horseback. He was stopped by the largest tree at the far right end of that cluster."

Victoria focused the binoculars to the far right and then dropped to her knees and began shaking.

"What is it, Victoria?" Sam asked as he knelt down next to her.

"That's him. That's the man who kidnapped me."

"What?" Sam exclaimed.

"Look, I can explain all of that later. We have to help Peter. That man on the horse is crazy. He's dangerous! What are they doing out here? They must be after me. My God, Sam, they're after me. How could they know?" Victoria was crying but also pissed off that her old life had found her in the middle of Montana.

"We have to save Peter, Sam. We have to. That lunatic will kill him."

Sam went back to his pack and returned with a rifle. "I can pen that guy down from up here. You go saddle up the horses. When I fire, you head down to your friend. If I have to, I'll shoot the guy's horse. Once I start, he won't be able to get a shot off. He's helpless down there. Go!"

Victoria was on her horse and heading down to the valley as she heard Sam's first shot.

Montgomery was eating a breakfast bar and reloading his rifle when the shot ripped through the tree above his head. His horse immediately spooked and galloped off the way it had come. Montgomery scurried back behind the thicket of trees, crawled into a brush pile, and scooted up to where he could scan the area with his scope. He fired wildly in hopes of gaining a chance to escape.

Victoria rode across the little stream as Peter looked on in complete astonishment.

"Get on!" Victoria instructed as she approached. Peter quickly jumped up on the back of the horse behind Victoria, and she turned and galloped quickly into the woods back toward Sam.

Sam could no longer see Montgomery. He heard Victoria's approach but did not turn to look.

"Sam, are you ready?" Victoria shouted as she rode up.

"Yeah," Sam said as he scooted back from the edge of the rock. "Ride toward the cabin. I'll catch up."

"Hang on, Peter," Victoria said, as she quickly rode off. Sam slowly made his way down the slope and mounted his horse.

Montgomery was still crouched low in the thicket, working his way slowly backwards. The shots were coming from the distant ridge, he reasoned, so he fired a few quick rounds in that direction as he moved back beyond its reach. Finally, about 200 yards or so away, he saw his horse meandering through the grass. Confident the shooter could not reach him through the trees, he stood and made a dash for his ride.

Discovering the empty barn that morning, he thought, "No worries," saddled his horse, and headed out. "He can't get far on foot, and a little Peter-hunting sounds like fun."

Now, things had changed. Montgomery raced back to the lodge to call for assistance. As he rode, he wondered who would be helping this guy. He settled on two options. Either another reporter was in the woods, or a local rancher had stumbled upon his "hunt." He berated himself for not thinking of the possibility of another reporter. But a local rancher? That was a bigger problem. He might be facing a skilled opponent.

Montgomery reached the lodge after an hour's ride and quickly called his associates for help. A helicopter was dispatched, but it would take another hour to reach him. Montgomery was instructed to take his satellite phone and go back to track the target. He returned to the area where he had been pinned down by the unknown shooter and cautiously made his way toward where he had last seen Mercury. He found the horse tracks and followed their trail across the stream and toward a rocky cliff.

There, Montgomery dismounted and looked over the campsite Sam and Victoria had shared the night before. He determined there were two riders in addition to Mercury, and quickly headed off in the direction they had taken. Montgomery called his associates, reported the news and proceeded to follow the trail.

At the cabin, Victoria decided to stop long enough to water the horses. Peter, who was in bad shape from the whipping he had taken, not to mention the long night of running, was in need of food and water himself. Victoria got him off the horse and helped him walk up the steps into the cabin. He lay down on the bed as Victoria retrieved a towel and some bandages for his wounds.

As Peter lay face down, Victoria cleaned his wounds and started the painful process of dabbing them with hydrogen peroxide she'd found in the cabinet. Peter had already stuffed a corner of the blanket in his mouth. He bit down and groaned as she cleaned each cut. Then she applied an antibiotic cream and placed gauze over his entire back.

"Sit up, Peter. I'm going to have to wrap something all the way around you to secure these bandages," Victoria said. Peter pushed up from the bed.

She ripped a bed sheet into strips, then reached around him and tied them.

Peter watched her as he thought what to ask first.

"Everyone thinks you're dead," he finally said.

"They're supposed to," she replied as she reached around for another layer of the cloth. "Why are you out here?" she asked. "Were you looking for me?"

"You?" Peter pulled back. "No, I thought you were dead. I came out here because I thought Langley was at the Sims Lodge."

"Langley?" Victoria replied. "What lodge? What are you talking about?"

"I followed Langley a couple days after the VP was in that wreck. Langley said he was on the road that morning, and I was curious about why he was traveling in that direction. So I followed him. He went to a park outside DC, and I saw him, another man, and a woman talking. All of a sudden, the man pulled out a pistol and shot the woman. Langley took off running in one direction and the man in another. I was scared shitless. I made it back to my car and drove to a diner." Peter motioned for Victoria to pause a bit because he was hurting. The pain-controlling impact of adrenaline was wearing off, and Peter was starting to feel sick.

"I need a minute," he said as he let out a breath. "I've never felt pain like this." He gasped for air.

Peter drew long breaths as Victoria watched.

"You have to keep it together, Peter. We can get to Sam's ranch by evening if we ride hard. I'll give you something to bite down on while we ride. You have to do this, Peter. Think of Susan."

Victoria knew Peter would walk through hell for Susan, and it was the one thing she could say that would focus his mind if nothing else worked.

Peter motioned for Victoria to continue with the bandages as he gathered himself. His mind then returned to the recent events. "A few minutes later, Langley walked in the diner and sat across the horseshoe counter from me," he told Victoria. "He didn't say a word. He sat there and stared at me. Then all this crazy shit happened, including you getting blown up in your condo. But now I'm sitting here talking to you."

"Who was the man?" Victoria asked as she tied the last strand. "Did you recognize him?"

"I don't know him. I had never seen him before, but it was the same guy chasing me through the woods," Peter said as he lay back on the bed. "My editor told me his name is Hiatt Montgomery. He's former Special Forces."

"He kidnapped me from a DC parking garage the day before my condo was blown up."

Peter sat back up. "So, you know him?"

"No, I don't know him. I had never seen him before that day. But I recognized him when I saw him chasing you. Why was he chasing you anyway?" Victoria asked, as if Peter knew more than he was sharing.

"I went to the Sims Lodge thinking Langley might be there. His office said he was out west fishing, so I went there on a wild ass hunch."

Sam, who had been trailing slightly behind, rode up to the cabin. "We need to keep moving."

"He's right, Peter. You're going to have to ride." Victoria reached for Peter's hand and helped him to his feet.

"When we get to the ranch, you two need to tell me everything you know about this guy and what's going on. But right now, we need to move as fast as possible," Sam said. "I have a gut feeling that guy is right behind us."

With that, Sam turned his horse as Peter and Victoria joined him on the other horse, and the three were quickly on their way. Peter was weak and in bad shape, but he held on as Victoria rode ahead quickly.

After riding hard for hours, they reached the ranch as the sun was setting. Victoria helped get Peter into the house and then to the guest room she had used a few nights before.

"We aren't staying here," Sam instructed. "If this guy is the bad ass you two make him out to be, he'll find us here. We're going somewhere else where he wouldn't know to look. Someplace I know we'll be safe. We're not giving this guy any help finding us."

"Sam, Peter needs to see a doctor."

"I've got that covered. Don't worry," Sam said.

Sam pulled his Suburban up to the porch and started putting all the seats down in the back.

"We'll make a bed back here for Peter."

Victoria unrolled sleeping bags in the back. "You can get some rest now, Peter," she said as she helped him climb in through the rear hatch.

Sam walked into the ranch house and quickly returned with a bag. "Put some of that in your pockets and the rest in the glove box," he said, handing it to Victoria.

The bag was stuffed full of bills—hundreds, fifties, and twenties. "We need to use cash," Sam said as he pulled away.

"How do we get Peter to a doctor if we want to stay hidden?" Victoria whispered.

"I have an old friend who can cover that for us," Sam answered as he reached into his coat pocket. "Peter, are there any pain killers you can't take?"

"Nothing comes to mind," Peter groaned from the makeshift bed in the back.

Victoria handed two white tablets and a bottle of water back to Peter.

"He won't feel much of anything in about twenty minutes or so," Sam said. "I have an old friend less than an hour away who's a retired veterinarian. Henry Hancock and his wife, Katie. They can treat Peter's wounds and get him bandaged up without us creating a hospital record. If these guys are as connected as you say, we need to stay off the grid as much as possible."

Sam outlined the plan without any request for input from his passengers. "Once we get there, we'll figure out what's next."

It was dark out now, and Victoria was tired from the hectic pace and crazy events of the day. The beautiful morning view and soothing hot springs had given way to a frantic day, and now she was exhausted.

"I need you to drive, Pinky," Sam said after driving for about 30 minutes.

Victoria looked over as Sam started to slump forward. "What is it, Sam?" she asked.

"That asshole got in a lucky shot back there," he muttered as he slowed and pulled to the side of the road.

"What?" Victoria exclaimed. "Where?" she asked as she reached for the wheel.

"It's nothing serious. I think it grazed my side," he said as he stopped and opened the door.

Victoria quickly jumped out of the passenger side and ran to help Sam come around the truck. "Why didn't you say something?" she asked as she grabbed him and helped him back into the passenger seat.

"It's nothing compared to him," Sam answered as he motioned to Peter. "The address is in the GPS," he added as he leaned against the window.

"Sam," Victoria said in an anxious tone. "Sam," she repeated. Victoria looked over as Sam's body went limp as he slumped further against the door. As she turned to adjust the seat, she noticed a pool of blood on the driver's side floor mat.

"Oh, my God," she said softly, tears welling up in her eyes.

EARLIER THAT DAY back in Washington, the political heavyweights leaned in hard on the White House. It was after midnight on Capitol Hill, and only a few office lights were still on. Cochran and Reed sat together in Reed's House office, staring at a pile of papers on the table before them.

"Some of this crap is the usual bullshit," Cochran belted out as he stood to walk across the room. "But the changes that impact the House and our money—they're beyond the pale. Hell, we can't submit this crap."

He walked to a corner table and poured a drink from a newly opened bottle of Scotch. He motioned to Reed with an empty glass, and Reed nodded in approval.

"It'll set the Council on fire, Wilson," Cochran muttered as he returned to his chair and handed Reed his drink.

"I know," Reed said as he fiddled with his cane. "I'd hazard that they're already on fire."

Neither said what they both suspected. Such things were never discussed openly in the Capitol. Both knew that the changes Niles planned to introduce would forever change America's status quo. They both knew members of the Council, a powerful but secretive bipartisan organization based in Washington, would eventually show their teeth, and the President would be the target. The changes Niles was pushing meant a loss of control and money for the two parties.

"Do you think we can control this thing, Hamilton?" Reed asked.

"No," Cochran responded. "Not without a change in wording or a big shift in attitude from our people."

Both sat quietly for a while as they sipped their Scotch. "Better chance at a wording change than an attitude change," Reed finally said.

"No doubt," Cochran grumbled. "This is going to get real ugly before it's over, Wilson," he said in a low voice. "People, more people, are going to get hurt. I have a meeting with the Captain tomorrow. Nothing formal, a routine conversation, but we better get our arms around this or it's going to get bad. We both know there are elements that aren't going to risk this bullshit reaching the floor. They'll end it sooner rather than later."

Cochran set his empty glass down and walked to the door. "Wilson," he added. "Have you talked to Jack lately?"

"No."

"We need to," Cochran said as he walked out of the office.

THAT DAY AT THE White House, President Niles sat alone in the Oval Office. He knew he was in for the fight of his life. Miller Redding had been a marked man from the start. He and Miller had discussed it. But neither believed Niles was in danger. The brazen attack on his sister had come as a shock. It shouldn't have. He understood that now. Victoria's nomination had served as the flashpoint his opposition longed for. He had given them the justification to go ugly early. He should have seen it coming, but he was blinded by his devotion to put a superior mind on the bench. The fact that she was his sister was, to him, irrelevant. Her intellect was superior to all the other obvious choices. Still, he hated himself for not seeing something so obvious. In any event, it no longer mattered. As far as the world was concerned, Victoria was dead, and he was free to take his fight right to Congress.

THE GRAVEL ROAD Victoria turned on should have been enough to wake both Peter and Sam from their stupor.

"Sorry about the bumps," Victoria whispered, hoping someone might answer.

Neither did as she looked anxiously at Sam. He didn't acknowledge her. "I can't believe this is happening," she thought as she approached the small house at the end of the lane. The home was an old country bungalow with a porch that spanned the entire front. The tan clapboard siding was freshly painted, and the dark green shutters and porch swing completed a perfect picture. Plants hung along the front on either side of the wide central steps. As her lights flashed across the front porch, a man holding a shotgun appeared. He was dressed in denim overalls and a white t-shirt. His ruffled gray hair and old wire-rimmed glasses softened his appearance, but his large frame and lean body were intimidating.

"I think you're lost, missy," the man grumbled as Victoria opened her door.

"I have Sam McBride with me, and he's hurt badly," Victoria cried out as she fell to her knees. "He said you would help."

The man stood motionless for a second, then bolted down the stairs.

"Katie, it's Sam, and he's hurt," he called out as he reached the SUV.

His wife burst out the door, terror on her face. Katie Hancock bolted down the steps. The woman's long gray hair was pulled into a ponytail at the nape of her neck. She wore jeans and a long-sleeved pink shirt that added a whisper of softness to her strong and steady look. She was plain but with a natural elegance. She stopped momentarily as she made eye contact with Victoria, who had managed to stand.

"Can he walk?" the man yelled as he rounded the front of the Suburban.

"He's unconscious," Victoria answered as she wept. "He's been shot."

"Oh my," Katie exclaimed as she came around the suburban and joined her husband at the passenger door.

"Sam, Sam," Katie called out as she pulled the door open. "Oh, my God, Henry. Is he breathing?"

"Barely," Henry replied as he felt for a pulse along Sam's carotid. "Please, help me get him inside," he said as he removed Sam's seat belt. The three managed to carry Sam into the house and onto the dining room table. Henry quickly cut off Sam's shirt, revealing a bullet wound through his left side. Henry stepped back and bit his lip as he stared at the wound.

"I need my medical bag," he said. Katie scurried down the hall and returned in seconds with an old doctor's bag and a roll of gauze.

"I almost forgot," Victoria exclaimed. "There's another man in the car who's hurt worse."

"I'll work on Sam," Henry said. "See if you two can get the other guy inside."

Katie followed Victoria out the door to the back side of the SUV. As it opened, Peter tried to push himself up, but only managed to rise slightly.

"At least he's semi-conscious," Katie said as she took Peter's hand and helped him scoot toward them.

"Can you walk, Peter?" Victoria asked as she took his other arm.

"I think so," he mumbled.

Katie and Victoria led Peter up the steps and into the foyer. Henry looked over as they entered, relieved that this patient was able to walk.

"Put him in my study," Henry commanded.

The women helped Peter to a long day bed Henry often used for afternoon naps.

"Oh, my God," Katie said softly as she removed the sheet strips and saw the wounds on Peter's back. "We need to get these cleaned up right away."

"I need another pill or something," Peter groaned.

"Okay," Victoria said, and headed out to check on Henry and Sam.

"How's he doing?" she asked as she approached.

"I have him numbed up, and I think the wound is closed. I'm not much good at stitching people, but the bleeding has stopped," he said. "The bullet seems to have missed his lung, but I don't know how much blood he lost."

"There's a puddle in the car," Victoria said, her voice cracking. "It was running out the door when I opened it," she added as she broke down.

"His vitals are okay right now, honey. Try to stay calm. We'll do whatever we have to for our Sam. These things often look a lot worse than they are," he added, attempting a smile.

"How's your other friend?" Henry asked as he wiped Sam's blood from his hands.

"We need you," Katie answered as she hurried past with an armful of supplies.

"Who ... or what ... in the world did this?" Henry muttered when he saw Peter's back. "You can explain later, but right now I need to knock this man out."

Henry disappeared for a few seconds, quickly returning with a syringe. "Let me do this," he said as he stood over Peter looking at his wounds.

"Maybe you and I should go somewhere else," Katie said to Victoria as she gently took her arm.

"Will he be okay?" Victoria asked.

"Those are the deepest cuts I've ever seen on a human being, but I'll get them cleaned up," Henry said. "You should go with Katie," he added as he picked up a pair of magnifiers.

Katie and Victoria walked to the back of the house and exited into a large garden.

"Go sit in my gazebo, honey," Katie suggested as she turned back toward the house. "I'm going to get you something to eat and drink."

Victoria fell into a large, padded swing as she exhaled. Before she had time to think, Katie was back with a plastic tumbler, a pitcher of water, and a bag of pretzels.

"You'll have to forgive me. I wasn't prepared for company."

Victoria attempted to hold her glass still as Katie tipped the pitcher toward her.

"Let me do that," Katie said, taking the glass from her hands.

"I'm sorry. I can't believe this is happening," Victoria said softly as she took the glass back.

"Judge is the best. He'll take good care of them," Katie reassured her.

Victoria clutched the glass with both hands. "I'm sorry. I haven't even introduced myself," Victoria said. "My name is Victoria, and I want to thank you for helping us." For a moment, Katie did not say a word.

"Victoria, you said. How long have you known Sam?"

"Oh, we met in college," Victoria answered, tearing up at the memory.

"You're that Victoria?" Katie asked, nearly spitting out her water.

"Oh, I shouldn't have said that," Victoria said as she rubbed her face.

"Honey, this is the safest place in the world for you," Katie declared. "But the news says you're dead."

"My brother's idea of protecting me," Victoria confessed. A long moment of silence ensued.

"You used to be a strawberry blond back in college, didn't you?" Katie asked, with a slight smirk.

"Yes. I dyed my hair yesterday in hopes of being unrecognizable," Victoria answered with a flip of her new hair.

Another moment of silence followed.

"How would you know that?" Victoria finally asked as Katie's comment penetrated through the day's events.

"Oh, Sam has told me all about you, dear," Katie confessed with another smirk.

Victoria reached for a pretzel and nibbled along the salty edge. "Sam used to talk every week with someone he called 'K-mom.' Was that you?"

"Yes, I am his K-mom," Katie confessed with a big smile.

The two sat quietly for a long moment as each processed the unlikely meeting.

"I met Sam after his mom died," Katie finally shared. "He was the saddest little boy I'd ever seen," she added with a sigh of grief. "Judge and I both took an immediate liking to him when we met that summer."

Victoria remembered hearing about that part of Sam's life.

"He was in 4-H, and Henry was a judge—that's where the nickname comes from," Katie said. "He and Sam bonded immediately, and before long, he was out here riding with Henry almost every day."

Katie looked off as if she could see those days replaying before her. "I filled a need in his life back then, and we became like mother and son. He's been a part of our lives ever since."

Victoria pulled a blanket over her that Katie had draped on the chair. The summer night was cool, but the clean air was refreshing to Victoria. They sat in silence for a few more minutes. She had so much to process, but instead Victoria found herself listening to the sounds of summer in the countryside. Frogs croaked and crickets chirped as her mind resisted the memories pushing for attention.

"I know all about you, honey," Katie finally said softly.

Victoria squirmed. She had worked hard to distance herself from the memories of Sam, although she often found it impossible.

"That was a long time ago," Victoria said, sniffling.

"You still love him, though," Katie said.

"Oh, it's old news that just doesn't matter," Victoria answered with an attempt at disinterest.

Katie continued rocking in her chair. "I think there are some things you need to know," she said.

"No, there really aren't," Victoria quickly responded. "It was a long time ago, and it ended badly. The world thinks I'm dead, and I'm moving on. I want to be sure Sam and Peter are okay, and then I'm leaving," she stated forcefully.

Katie Hancock rocked back and forth and tried to control her smile. "I'm sorry, honey. I don't mean to make you uncomfortable. But you should know that my conversations with Sam about you didn't end when he left Yale."

"What are you talking about?"

"When he left that morning, he hurt you badly, didn't he?" Katie reached for Victoria's hand.

"Worst day of my life," Victoria confessed. "It still makes me cry," she added as she pulled her hand back and wiped her tears.

"Him to."

"What?!" Victoria asked in an almost angry tone.

"Let me explain, honey," Katie said in a reassuring voice as she again reached out and took Victoria's hand in hers. She contemplated how best to proceed.

"Did Sam ever tell you much about Sarah?" Katie asked softly.

"Nothing," Victoria answered.

"Sarah was a sweet girl, a lot like you, according to Sam. But she wasn't strong like you. She was a loving woman, but she was too dependent on Sam. He was about to tell her he wasn't coming back here. He had decided he was staying out east after graduating."

Katie paused as Victoria absorbed the words. "He wanted to stay with you, Victoria," Katie said, as if she needed to clarify and remove all doubt. Victoria looked over as Katie prepared to go on. Her discomfort was obvious.

"But Sarah felt it coming," Katie said softly as her expression changed to sadness. "She attempted suicide the night before Sam left you." The pain in Katie's face was obvious as she glanced over at Victoria.

"It wasn't a cry for help. Sarah was almost dead when they found her. I was the one who called Sam to tell him." Katie teared up as she recalled the events.

Victoria remained quiet. She noticed the lines in Katie's face tense up.

"That was an awful night," Katie said softly, as if no one else were listening. "Sam and Sarah met that same summer he found us. They were just little kids in 4-H. The two of them used to come out here and help Henry with the horses and then go for rides. We watched those two grow up together," she said as her voice dropped a little.

Victoria sat frozen as she listened. Silence took over as Katie closed her eyes, reliving that time in her mind. Victoria stayed quiet, not wanting to disrupt Katie's thoughts.

"I wasn't surprised he fell in love with you," Katie said finally. "He was captivated by you. But Sam couldn't turn his back on Sarah." Katie cleared her throat and sat up. "It wasn't that he was unhappy with her or with being out here—he loved it here. And they had a good life together—don't get me wrong."

Katie fidgeted with her glass. "I almost hate saying this to you after all these years, honey, but the truth is, he loved you more."

Victoria felt numb and expressionless. Her mind twisted and lurched as the words Katie shared ran through her soul.

"I'm sorry. Maybe I shouldn't be this candid," Katie added, putting a hand on Victoria's arm. "But his love for you never ended, honey. To this day."

Victoria fell back in her chair and let out a deep breath. "Why didn't he tell me?" she said with a touch of anger in her voice.

"He wanted you to move on," Katie quickly answered.

The two sat quietly as Victoria contemplated Katie's answer.

The silence was interrupted by the sound of a squeaky screen door opening.

"May I join you?" Henry asked as he approached.

"How are they doing?" Katie asked before Victoria could get the words out.

"Sam is still out, and your friend's out, too, but his wounds are awful," Judge said as he took a seat.

"Henry, are they going to be okay? Should we get them to a hospital?" Katie quickly followed up.

"The people after us are more dangerous than you can imagine," Victoria said before Henry could respond. "They may be looking in hospitals right now for Peter. I'm sorry you're involved in this, but Peter and Sam are in grave danger."

Henry looked at Katie as he rubbed his hand across his chin. "I can take care of them both right here, at least for now," he assured Victoria.

Katie and Henry exchanged an uncomfortable glance as each thought of Victoria's warning.

"I think you've been through enough for one day. Maybe it's time for some sleep," Judge said to Victoria as he stood.

"I would like to stay with Sam tonight," Victoria replied. She stood next to him, looking down at the ground and twisting a strand of her hair as she waited for a response.

"That's fine, honey," Katie said as she also stood. "We'll slide the sofa over by the table so you're right next to him."

"Yes, of course," Henry said.

The three walked back into the house and quickly moved the sofa.

"I'll get you a pillow and a couple of blankets," Katie said as she gently touched Victoria's arm.

"Thank you," Victoria replied softly, her focus on Sam.

"I'm sure Sam will be fine," Judge assured her as he walked toward Peter. "I need to keep an eye on this one, though," he added, pulling a chair next to the day bed.

Looking at Sam, Victoria had a million thoughts racing through her mind.

"Why didn't you tell me?" she thought as she brushed the hair back from his eyes. "You should have told me," she whispered as she kissed his forehead.

"I put on a pot of coffee for you, honey," Katie said as she handed Victoria a cup. "You need to have faith and be strong." She gently placed her hand on Victoria's shoulder. "He's going to be okay. Good night, dear."

Katie disappeared down the hall as she switched off the lights.

"I'm in here if you need me," Henry called out from the study. "I'm going to sleep a bit, but wake me if he stirs." He turned off the lights in the study.

Victoria sat next to the table watching Sam draw each breath. "God, I love you so much, Sam," she whispered as she took his hand. "I need you to be okay." She felt her long-suppressed love boiling inside.

"I always thought you were selfish," she blurted out through the tears. Victoria fell back onto the sofa and curled up, clutching the pillow.

In the middle of the night, the sound of Henry walking through the room woke Victoria.

"Your friend's in a bad way," he said in a low voice as Victoria sat up. She quickly joined Henry at Peter's side. "I'm worried about infection with him," Judge said. "I gave him another shot that will keep him sedated."

"Has anything changed with Sam?" she asked as she glanced back at the table.

"No, but that's a good thing," Henry replied with a comforting glance. "He's breathing fine, and his vitals are all stable. The bullet passed through, and the bleeding has stopped."

Victoria let out a deep sigh as she absorbed the news. "Thank God," she said softly.

"I'm going to heat up that coffee. Would you like some?" Victoria quietly asked Henry as she walked to the kitchen.

"No, I'm going to get some sleep," he said as he finished up at Peter's side.

Victoria returned from the kitchen as Henry turned down the lights and closed the doors leading to his study. Only the front porch light shining through the front window provided light. Victoria curled up with a blanket and her cup of coffee and watched as Sam slept.

"Would you have been happy as my husband?" Victoria whispered softly as she looked at Sam. She smiled in the darkness as the words left her mouth. "I wonder if we would have made it?" she added in an even quieter voice. With the exception of an old clock, ticking thunderously loud in the quiet, there was no sound.

"Sam, you should have explained things to me," she said softly as she sipped the coffee. "I would have understood. We could have parted ways and still been friends," she added as she began to cry. "You didn't need to try to make me hate you."

Victoria pulled the blanket up around her shoulders; the evening temperature had fallen. Her mind kept replaying that last day at Yale, but now she saw it through a new lens.

"I can't believe you chose to hurt me, thinking that was the right decision," she mumbled through her tears. She fell back on the sofa and gripped the blanket tighter. She quivered a little as the mix of emotions swirled inside her.

"I've hated myself for that day," came the whisper from the darkness.

"Sam, my God, you're awake," Victoria exclaimed as she rose to his side.

"I'm so sorry," he said softly. He had no strength to force the words out with any emotion. "I'm sorry," he repeated in a whispered and weak voice.

"Stay quiet, Sam. Don't try to talk." Victoria clutched his hand as she drew close to his face. "I love you, Sam," she whispered as she gently kissed his cheek.

"I love you. I've always loved you. I will always love you," she repeated.

Sam offered a slight smile as he looked up though glassy eyes. "I'm sorry," he repeated as a tear rolled from his eye.

"Shh. Stay quiet. Please," Victoria urged as her tears fell and merged with his. "Please rest."

Sam's eyes slowly fell shut as his breathing deepened and his hand fell from Victoria's grasp. She remained close as she wiped the tears from his face and stifled back her own.

In the quiet of the darkness, Victoria felt numb. Without knowing anything about Sam's motives, Victoria had been left to speculate. Over the years, she had contemplated every possibility for why Sam had left the way he did. But Katie's words presented a scenario she could never have imagined. The crickets and bullfrogs and other sounds of the Montana night now seeped into the house, mixing with the ticking of the old clock. Victoria thought of Sarah, and while she did not understand how a person could attempt suicide, she found herself feeling deep compassion for this woman she had never met. Victoria had many dark moments after Sam's departure, and she tried to remember if she had ever been close to crossing that line herself. "She must have suffered terribly," Victoria thought as the wind picked up outside and the house seemed to grow colder.

THE NEXT MORNING, Victoria woke to the aroma of bacon frying and fresh coffee brewing in Katie's kitchen. The house felt warmer now, and the smells comforted Victoria as she greeted the new day. "Where's Sam?" she asked as she sat up and looked over at the empty dining room table.

"We moved him to our bed this morning," Katie explained as she poked her head around the corner from the kitchen.

"What? How?" she asked as she stood.

"He was able to walk there," Henry explained, as his smiling face also appeared.

"He walked?" Victoria jumped from the sofa as the news set in.

"Sam's going to be fine, dear," added Katie, once again out of view.

"Have some fresh coffee." Katie emerged from the kitchen with a big mug and a bigger smile.

"You're going to be fine, too," she added softly as she gave Victoria a loving look and handed her the cup.

Victoria smiled shyly. "Can I go in there?" she quietly asked.

"Why don't you go into our bathroom and have a shower, too," Katie said. "I'll bring in some clean clothes for you. My daughter-in-law left a few things here."

Victoria set down the coffee and quietly entered the bedroom. Sam was sleeping deeply, but Victoria noticed that the color had returned to his face.

After a warm shower, Victoria emerged from the bathroom wrapped in a towel and found a pile of clean clothes on the edge of the bed. "That feels good," she thought as she slipped on a clean pair of pink shorts and a white t-shirt that had a matching pink stripe running diagonally across the front. She gently lay down on the bed next to Sam as he continued to sleep.

"I have a lot of questions for you, Victoria," Sam whispered as he woke up. "First, who is this Montgomery guy?"

"You need to rest," she said softly.

"I need to understand what's happening," he replied with as strong a voice as he could muster. "Who is the guy that's chasing us?"

"I don't know him. He threatened me in a DC parking garage the day before my condo blew up."

"You had never seen him before?" Sam asked

"No."

"Assuming he blew up the condo, why would he want you dead?"

"To keep me off the bench I suspect," she said.

"So, these people want you dead so you won't be on the bench when Jackson's reforms get challenged in the Court," Sam said.

"That's basically it, but I suspect there's more," she said as she sat up in the bed. "The reforms are going to scale back Washington's power. There are a lot of people angry about that."

"It has to be more than that," Sam said.

"That's the problem," Victoria said. "We know this Montgomery guy is out for blood, but we have no idea who's behind him. I hope Peter knows something. He started talking about Jack Langley when I was cleaning his wounds."

"Langley?" Sam said in astonishment. "Jack is career military. My God, he fought with Jackson in the Middle East. He would take a bullet for Jackson."

"He has been acting strange lately," Victoria said. "Jack has missed meetings and been late for appointments. Honestly, his behavior changed when Jackson started talking about nominating me."

"Still, Langley? There's no way he would be part of something like this," Sam said. "I agree he's an odd guy. I've never met anybody more hard-nosed and driven than that guy." Sam's voice grew stronger as they began to piece together the details.

"Wouldn't Jackson bring him in and quiz him up and down until he knew where Jack was mentally?" Sam asked.

"Jack has been distant lately, and Jackson has been going from crisis to crisis," Victoria said. "So, time has been a problem. Peter did tell me he went to some lodge because he thought Langley might be there."

"The Sims Lodge?" Sam asked.

"I don't know what that is."

"Clayton Sims has a big family lodge on the other side of the National Forest we were in. It's quite a place," Sam said.

"So that's what Peter was doing," she said. "He went there hoping to find Langley, but instead Montgomery found him. But that means Sims is in with Montgomery."

Her voice heightened as she realized the President's special advisor was connected to the man who had kidnapped her.

"I have to call Jackson," she said, jumping out of bed.

"No," Sam said, with all the force he could muster.

"What do you mean, no?"

"I promised Jackson you would disappear until this was over. If you start making phone calls, someone will find out you're alive," he said. "And if I call the White House, it will lead them to you. Victoria, I made a promise. But more than that, I'm not putting you at risk under any circumstances." Sam reached out for Victoria's hand. "Let's see what Peter knows when he wakes up, and then we will decide what to do. Okay?"

"Okay," Victoria replied reluctantly.

AT SAM MCBRIDE'S RANCH, Hiatt Montgomery walked silently along the back porch. As he reached the back door, he kicked it in and stepped inside, a small automatic gun pointed out in front of him. He searched through the house until he was sure it was empty.

He was still inside when he heard a helicopter landing. Out the window, he saw two men dressed in suits jump out of the chopper and approach the house.

"Anything?" one asked, walking past the busted door into the house.

"No," Montgomery said.

"Are you sure this is where the tracks led?" the second man asked.

"Yes, I'm sure. Hell, a blind man could have followed their horses here. They didn't even try to hide the trail." Montgomery stepped into the guest room and picked up a bloodstained towel from the floor. "They had Mercury in here before they left."

"Start checking hospitals," one of the men said. "They had to take him in for treatment. Find his ass and kill him and the assholes he's with. Got it?"

The two men walked out of the house back toward the chopper.

"There will be a car here for you shortly," the first man called back over his shoulder. "Sit tight and wait. You better get this mess cleaned up, or you ass is in deep—you understand?"

Montgomery nodded, but the man didn't wait for a response. Montgomery scowled with anger as the chopper and the two men lifted off.

"I GOT YOUR FRIEND'S wounds cleaned up as best I can," Henry said as Victoria emerged from the bedroom later in the day.

"He woke up a little bit ago and was in terrible pain, so I gave him two more of your painkillers. Once he was out, I took the opportunity to get the bandages off and get the wounds cleaned up more," he said. "If we don't stitch him up, he's going to have some awful scars."

The old doc picked up his coffee cup and walked to the family room.

"Get some coffee if you want," he said.

Victoria went into the kitchen and returned with a cup of coffee.

"If a bad infection sets in, there isn't much I can do out here," Henry said. "He's going to need an antibiotic drip if that happens, and that means a hospital. In fact, if that kind of infection sets in, you would be better off taking him down to Billings."

"Let's hope that doesn't happen," Victoria responded with a look of concern.

IN WASHINGTON, CLAYTON Sims sat at his desk in his large office in the Eisenhower Executive Office Building. He had considered an office in the West Wing, but after seeing the size of the only office available to him, he opted for the Eisenhower. His enormous eight-foot walnut desk looked right at home in this large office finished in natural woodwork. A set of matching bookcases ran along the wall to his left. To his right were windows with a view of the West Wing of the White House. He had chosen maroon paint for the walls, similar to his office at the lodge. The color was something of a trademark for Sims. He liked the strong, masculine look, but many colleagues and friends, women in particular, told him it looked like the color of blood. For décor, he had an authentic suit of armor his father had bought in England. It was a strange looking addition to a business office, but Sims insisted it be displayed. He often looked across at the thing when he was on a tough phone call as a reminder of how difficult conflict can get.

"My skin is as hard as that suit," he would often say when feeling challenged. This morning, he stared at his phone. The night before, he had been notified of a security breach at the lodge, but the caller had offered no details. Later he had been informed of the events involving Peter Mercury. Sims was incensed over the situation, but he was unable to do much except hope others could clean up the mess. He waited to see what was next.

"Surely they'll find that damned reporter and end this before it gets out of control," Sims thought. As he waited, he wondered if his worst fears would be realized or if the people he entrusted would come through as promised.

Finally, the phone rang.

"Tell me," he said.

"We lost him."

"Lost him? You damn fools," Sims shouted. "How?"

"Someone helped him."

"Who? You're in the middle of nowhere. Follow his trail and get him," Sims demanded.

"We did follow his trail. It led to a house, but they were gone when we got there."

"Check all the hospitals and find him," Sims insisted, losing confidence.

"We are doing that right now," the voice on the other end said.

"There aren't that many options out there. Find him this morning and get this cleaned up. Keep me posted." Sims hung up, stood, and paced the room. "I need better field people," he mumbled.

HIATT MONGOMERY DROVE to the nearest hospital and walked casually through the emergency room door. "I'm looking for info on a stranger I helped last night," he said to the woman at the desk. "I'm sure he's here."

"No, we have no one here who came in over the last day or so. It's been real quiet," she said.

"Can you tell me where else around here an injured person might be taken? I really want to make sure the guy's okay," Montgomery said.

"There's a small hospital about half an hour up Highway 36. He might be there."

Montgomery thanked her and left the hospital. He was mad at himself for letting this happen and intent on finding and killing Peter before he talked. He may have already talked to the locals, he thought, but he can't be allowed to get back to his paper and start real trouble in Washington. "Some little local bullshit cop won't matter," he reasoned.

Montgomery headed north on Highway 36, but he was already thinking things were going to get complicated. "If they aren't at the nearest hospital, then they could have gone anywhere," he thought. "This search will be a total waste of time."

BY LATE AFTERNOON, Katie and Victoria were in the garden together picking berries, carrots, lettuce, broccoli, and onions for dinner. In another area they dug potatoes and harvested mushrooms. The garden was a large, sprawling area with every sort of vegetable, fruit, nut tree, and herb one could imagine. The garden had taken years to develop, and several small, simple greenhouses were scattered about to offset the short summer season. The entire area was surrounded by a tall, mesh fence to keep out the critters. The large gazebo in the center provided shade during breaks, and an old hand-pump well next to the gazebo supplied the coldest and freshest water Victoria had ever tasted.

"This garden is incredible, Katie," Victoria said as the two finished picking raspberries. "Sam and I had a few tomato plants in college, but I've never seen anything like this. I think in my next life I'm going to have a big garden."

"It took years to get it to this point, but now it supplies us with most of what we want," she said as she set down her overflowing container. "I think I might make a pie with some of these. If Henry had any luck down at the stream, we'll be eating fresh trout. With these potatoes, vegetables, and berries, we'll have a feast tonight."

"Let's take a rest in the gazebo for a while," Katie suggested. She stopped at the water pump on her way and sat down the vegetables before pumping the handle. As the clean cool water began flowing, she cupped her hands and dabbed a little on her face. "Oh that feels good."

Victoria followed her into the gazebo. "You can have that big padded chair," Katie said as she sat down in her swing.

It was getting hot out as the noon sun heated up the garden. The mosquitoes circled around the women, growing more annoying as Katie and Victoria each swatted away at the pesky bugs.

"Use this spray," Katie suggested, grabbing a bottle from next to the swing and passing it to Victoria. "It's a natural blend we make from our citronella plants."

"Smells good, too," Victoria replied as she sprayed her arms. "Sam hasn't said a word about his kids to me." She put her feet up on a small wooden stool.

"He probably won't, and I wouldn't ask if I were you," Katie said as she sprayed herself with the sweet smelling spray. "They stay with his sister, Anna, a lot since Sarah's death."

Victoria looked over at Katie, hoping for more information.

"Sam's had a lot of issues since the accident," Katie said reluctantly. "He's feels terrible guilt."

The two sat quietly.

"Anna and her husband live just down the road from Sam's place. She and Jake—that's her husband—have two kids about the same age as Charlie and Molly. Sam's kids."

"I would love to meet them," Victoria said.

"I'm sure you will honey, but I wouldn't push it. Sam is a great dad, but he's struggled since Sarah passed and he feels terrible guilt over that, too. The kids are doing great. Anna and Jake have been a godsend. You just need to give him space on that subject."

"Thank you for being so candid, Katie," Victoria said.

"I know you two don't want to talk about whatever is going on ... " Katie said, pausing to see if Victoria would change the course of her thought before it was finished.

Victoria said nothing.

"Just know this: Henry and I will help you anyway you need. All right, Victoria?" she said as she stood. "Now, do you know how to make an old-fashioned berry pie?"

Victoria laughed. "Only if it comes in a wrapper and goes in the microwave."

They both laughed as they descended the steps from the garden and proceeded along the curving walkway to the house.

"Today you are going to learn."

"That sounds fun, Katie. I would love to spend the day cooking with you. Maybe one day you can teach me about gardening, too."

The two women smiled at each other as they walked along the garden path. There was something about Katie that Victoria found captivating. Part of it was that the older woman was well grounded and simple—a type of person she had seldom encountered in her previous life. Money, politics, power, and prestige: those things meant nothing to Katie and Henry. Victoria felt as if she was in the presence of an old soul who could see through the superficial into the actual person. It had intimidated her at first, but now Victoria felt a kinship with Katie she knew was mutual.

MID-AFTERNOON HENRY strolled into the back yard carrying a bucketful of fresh trout.

"What a day!" he exclaimed as he entered the house, finding the women in the kitchen. "The fish were practically jumping at me," he gushed, as he sat down at the small kitchen table. "I'm going to take a look at your friend, and then we'll get those trout cleaned up, deal?"

"Sounds like a plan to me," Sam answered as he entered the room.

"Should you be up walking?" Victoria asked.

"Judge told me to move around a little if I feel up to it. For a guy that got shot, I actually feel pretty good. Thank God that bullet only hit fat," he chuckled.

Katie and Victoria both smiled a little but were still worried over Sam's close call.

"So, I bet you two have been sitting around in the shade all day," Sam chided as he looked at the two women hovering over several pots on the large stove.

"I beg your pardon, Mr. McBride!" Katie exclaimed. "Show that ungrateful man what you made today, Victoria."

"I am now a graduate of the Katie Hancock pie baking school," Victoria said as she opened the oven door to reveal four pies, which were about ready to eat. "Raspberry, apple, peach, and pecan pies, Mr. McBride. All made from scratch, I must add." Victoria stood with the oven door open, genuinely proud of her day's work.

"I'm impressed, Pinky," Sam said, moving close to her. "Your extensive list of skills just got longer," he whispered in her ear. Sam and Victoria had moved beyond their past, and they both could feel it. A lightness hung between them now, something close to a childlike expectation. Katie could sense it, too, as she glanced over at Sam and Victoria standing close and looking into each other's eyes for a brief moment. The electricity between them made Katie feel younger.

"This is magic," Katie thought as she turned back to the stove. "Beautiful magic."

"We need to keep a close eye on your friend," Henry announced as he rejoined the others. "His temperature is up a bit. Might be nothing or might be the start of something bad. He did manage to eat a little last night when I had him awake. But if he doesn't show signs of coming around soon, I think you better plan on a trip to Billings. How dangerous is it for you to take him there?"

The old doc was afraid to ask too much, because he knew Sam wanted to reveal as little as possible.

"Look, Sam, if need be, I'll take him in and use my son's ID. They are about the same size."

"No way," Sam quickly answered. "Not a chance."

"The offer is out there if you change your mind."

Victoria spoke up. "We have to do whatever is necessary to get him well."

"I know, and I agree, Pinky," Sam answered. "We will do whatever has to be done."

CONTINUING HIS SEARCH, Hiatt Montgomery was leaving the fourth clinic when his phone rang.

"Anything?" the voice asked.

"Nothing," Montgomery answered.

"Okay. Go back to that house we were in and check there again. Maybe they've returned. If not, find out who it belongs to, and we'll start looking for them." The caller hung up as Montgomery pulled over to change course.

"Where the hell did that damned reporter go?" he yelled as he slammed his hands on the steering wheel.

CHAPTER FIVE

No Plan Survives Engagement

In Washington, Clayton Sims paced nervously in his office at the Eisenhower Building. "This is a stupid and unnecessary mess," he thought as he moved about the room.

He made several calls to his people on the ground in Montana, but so far, he had heard nothing back except, "We're working on it." This infuriated Sims, since he was helpless to do anything but trust that the people he had in place would perform. Sims had never contemplated real trouble from his involvement with The Council, but now he was worried.

Sims had been through many tight spots in his life, both professionally and personally. He often told his friends that he completely understood the principle behind the phrase, "Don't shoot 'till you see the whites of their eyes." He was known to take negotiations all the way to the edge because he could remain calm under fire. Now, he paced and reasoned and convinced himself that this problem would be handled.

ABOUT 4 O'CLOCK in the morning, Victoria woke to Henry's voice outside the bedroom door.

"Victoria, Sam," he called. "Peter's fever is getting worse. I believe you had better get him to a hospital. It's too dangerous to mess with this. I think he's developing a bad infection."

"We'll pack up," Victoria said, jumping up and dressing as Sam started putting items in the luggage. Within minutes Victoria had picked up the room, made the bed, and was heading for the front door with their bags.

Peter was awake but not coherent as he tossed around in his bed.

"Sam, I'm afraid this thing isn't going to clear up," Henry cautioned as he looked at Peter.

"I feel the same, Judge," Sam said as he walked out the front door and down the steps. The Suburban was in the same spot as when they arrived.

"Let's get the bed arranged back here, and Henry and I will get Peter out," Victoria said as she opened the rear door.

Sam made up the makeshift bed and soon Peter was settled in.

"I packed you up a little breakfast," Katie said as she came to their side. "I'm getting you a couple of large coffees so you don't fall asleep on the road. Oh and I put in a few of my favorite gardening magazines for you to start learning." Katie gave Victoria a little wink as she handed over the bag.

"Sam," Henry said as he approached him. "You two be real careful, okay?"

"We will, Judge," Sam answered, realizing his friend was scared for them.

Katie emerged with the two oversized coffee mugs. "This would keep an elephant awake," Victoria said, laughing as she took the cups.

Katie put her hand on Victoria's shoulder. "Promise me you'll take care of our Sam."

"I promise."

"And, Sam, you better take care of my new friend."

"I promise I will, Katie," Sam answered obediently.

"We look forward to your return," Katie added.

"Thank you both so much," Victoria said with complete devotion. "I promise you: we will be back."

Sam and Victoria pulled back onto the interstate and set a course for Billings. They were no longer thinking of Montgomery. Peter's well-being was their only concern.

FROM AFAR, MONTGOMERY watched the house he had been through earlier, anxiously watching for signs of life. After an hour of surveillance, he decided no one was home and drove up the long drive and walked back through the door he had kicked open. The house was dark, and it took him a few minutes to find all the light switches. Once the lights were on, he began searching for something that might help him locate Peter. He found little of interest, but did find some mail addressed to the occupant. He dialed his contact.

"This better be good."

"I'm back at the house, but no one has been here since we left."

"Damn it. Tear the place apart. There must be something," the contact demanded.

"I'm telling ya, this is some rancher who happened upon that damned reporter and helped him out," Montgomery said. "He doesn't know anything. He's some shit kicker." Montgomery was tired and agitated, and he had had enough of Montana.

"Give me the name, and we'll start a search for the rancher," the contact demanded.

"Samuel McBride is the name on the mail. There isn't much else here but a few bills and magazines," Montgomery said.

"Okay, get out of there and go find a hotel. I'll be in touch."

The phone went dead as Montgomery sat back on the family room sofa.

"What the fuck," he mumbled as he put his feet up on the coffee table.

SAM AND VICTORIA made great time as they sped down the interstate toward Billings.

"How are we going to do this?" Victoria asked.

"We are going to take him in as a John Doe. It's our only choice," Sam answered with a shrug. "We can't use your name.

We can't use his name. So I'm taking him in as a guy I picked up with no ID, and I will agree to pay if they need that."

Sam described his plan as if he had thought it through, but he was making it up as he went along. "It's our only choice."

IN WASHINGTON, THE phone rang and startled the usually alert Clayton Sims. "Tell me," he said.

"We don't have him, sir. We've been to every little clinic and hospital within sixty miles of the ranch where we tracked them. The guy has disappeared."

"This is unbelievable," an exasperated Sims responded. "Have we been back to the ranch yet? Do we know anything about that guy?"

"We got a name, but other than that, there's nothing in the house to offer any clues. It looks like they rode up to the house, got in a vehicle, and disappeared," the voice continued.

"At least we can track down the damned rancher," Sims countered.

"The mail inside the property is addressed to Samuel McBride, but we don't know if that is the owner or some tenant."

There was a long silence on Sims' end of the phone.

"The name is McBride? Is that what you said?" Sims asked.

"Yes, sir."

"Spell it," Sims demanded, knowing as he sat in his dimly lit office that things may have become even more complicated. "What are the fucking odds of this?" Sims thought as he sat in the quiet after hanging up. "If that is the same guy, I might have real problems," he thought.

Sims was known for his calmness under intense situations, but this was taxing his ability to think clearly. "There can't be two guys with that name in that area," he thought. "So the issue is whether or not he was out there for a reason, or by chance stumbled upon Mercury as he fled Montgomery."

Sims quickly realized it didn't matter. Either way, McBride needed to be located and eliminated.

"I never liked his ass anyway," Sims thought.

SAM AND VICTORIA pulled into St. Vincent Hospital after a hurried and stressful drive. Peter was unconscious and shivering badly. Sam parked near the emergency room doors and instructed Victoria to wait in the car.

"You stay invisible. Don't make me into a liar to your brother, okay?"

"Yes," Victoria said.

Sam went into the hospital and quickly emerged with a nursing assistant rolling a gurney.

"I found him a couple days ago up by the National Forest. We tried to get him cleaned up, but he now seems to have a bad infection," Sam said, opening the side door to the Suburban to reveal the gravely ill Peter.

Victoria was uncomfortable sitting in the truck, thinking it would seem weird to the woman.

"He doesn't have a wallet or any ID and so far has been unable to tell us anything," Victoria added, craning her neck toward the back of the Suburban where Sam was standing.

"Let's get him on the gurney," the hospital assistant instructed as she pulled it to the back of the Suburban and opened the double doors. "Sir, can you understand me?"

Peter tried to answer, but he was shaking so hard his speech came out more as a groan.

"Let's get him inside," the woman instructed with a bit of urgency.

Within minutes, Peter was in a room with a doctor, a nurse, and two other assistants who were busy removing bandages and getting IVs started.

"We can have the infection under control pretty soon," the doctor told Sam. "These cuts are going to take some work, but we will get him fixed up," she said.

"Can we get some information from you?" an administrative worker asked Sam.

"Sure," he answered, aware that not doing so would throw up red flags and likely complicate things for Peter.

"We will admit him as John Doe, but we need contact information from you for our records," she said as she scrolled through a computer screen. "Are you planning on staying in the area?"

"Yes, for a day or two," Sam said.

"Okay. I understand you found him by the park. Do you want a call about his status?"

"Yes, I would like to know the poor guy is going to be okay. Will you be treating him as a typical patient even though he has no ID?" Sam asked, wanting to make sure the John Doe status wouldn't hinder Peter's treatment.

"Of course. We are nonprofit, and we treat everyone, rich or poor, with the same level of care."

"Great," Sam responded. "I want to be sure he makes it."

"He will be fine," she said as she finished entering Sam's contact information. "There's a nice hotel a couple blocks down the street if you and your wife are needing a place to stay," she said, after thanking Sam for helping the man. "We'll give you a call later today or tomorrow."

Sam thanked the woman and thought about her reference to Victoria as his wife. "I should have corrected her on that one," he thought as he walked away.

"Mr. McBride," the woman called as Sam approached the door. "I almost forgot. We notify the police anytime a John Doe comes in. They will be here in a minute to meet with you and your wife."

"That's fine," Sam answered. "But she's not my wife. She's just a backpacker who helped me get the guy here. She already left."

Sam smiled at the woman, who looked at him with a puzzled expression.

"Okay. Whatever," she answered. "Can you stick around for a few minutes until they get here?"

"Yes, of course. I need to move my truck. I'll be right back in."

"Have a seat over there when you return," she said, motioning to a small table and chairs behind the admission desk.

"Okay."

As he got in the Suburban, he told Victoria to crouch down. "The police are coming to ask me about where I found Peter. That staff thought you were my wife, but I told them you were a backpacker and that you had already left. I'm going to pull around and park where we are out of view. There's a hotel about two blocks that way. Wait about a minute or so, and then take off down that street and find a coffee bar and wait for me. We cannot afford to have the police asking you questions."

As he parked, Sam said, "We need to get out of here by tomorrow morning. Okay, now wait a minute after I got back in and then get out and walk casually."

Sam walked back to the emergency room entrance. When he rounded the corner, he saw a police car waiting at the door.

"Are you Sam McBride?" the officer asked.

"Yes," Sam said, extending his hand to shake the man's.

"About where did you find our John Doe?" the officer asked as he took out a small notepad.

"I was riding up by Flathead, my ranch is up there, and I came across him out by a cabin I have. I couldn't believe my eyes when I saw him. He looks like he tangled with a bear."

"The nurse said his cuts look like whip marks," the officer countered.

"I've never seen whip marks on a man, so I wouldn't know about that," Sam answered as he looked around to see Victoria safely walking down the street.

"I doubt many people have," the officer smirked. "I'm going to need your address for the report."

Sam gave the officer all his contact information as requested.

"I sure hope the poor guy will be okay," Sam said as he took his keys back out of his pocket.

"The nurse said you had a woman with you?" the officer squinted at Sam. "I need to note it for the report," he said, turning the page on his notepad.

"I got the guy to my house and got him cleaned up. But he had a bad fever this morning, so I thought I better get him to a hospital that could treat the infection," Sam said. "When I got on the road, I saw a hitchhiker and stopped. I told her I would give her a ride if she would help me with the guy. She jumped in, and when we got here, she got out and started walking. I don't even remember her telling me her name."

Sam swung his keys around on his finger to let the officer know he was ready to be on his way.

"We get a lot of backpackers out here this time of year. All right, thanks for helping the guy out. I'll call you if anything else comes up." The officer put his notepad away.

"I'm going to stay in town tonight to do some shopping and be on my way in the morning," Sam said. "I'll probably swing by and check on the guy before I head out."

Sam headed for the Suburban, then the hotel. The hotel was new, and Sam was glad to see a morning breakfast bar so they could eat and get on the road in the morning. The man at the desk greeted Sam and asked how many would be staying.

"There are two of us," Sam answered. "My friend's out in the car." He was exhausted from the day's events and anxious to retrieve Victoria and get to the room. He also knew he had to figure out where to go next, to make sure Victoria was safely hidden.

"Okay, I need a card, and you are set," the clerk said, handing the sign-in form to Sam.

"I want to pay with cash," Sam said, as he handed the clerk two one-hundred-dollar bills, grateful he remembered not to use his real name.

"That's fine, too," the clerk said as he opened his drawer. "Okay, Mr. Smith, you are set." The clerk smiled and explained the location of the room upstairs just off the elevator, the next morning's breakfast times, when the pool and hot tub closed, and where best to get a meal.

"Okay, thanks," Sam replied as he stuffed the swipe cards in his pocket and turned to go get Victoria. He heard little of what the man said. He was thinking only of tomorrow's plans. Across the street, Sam saw a sign for the Java Roaster and guessed correctly that Victoria would be there. Inside, Victoria sat with a cup of coffee, a chocolate muffin, and a copy of *USA Today*.

"Have you missed much?" Sam asked as he looked at the paper.

"Nope," Victoria answered as Sam took a seat.

"I got you a muffin and some coffee," Victoria said as she slid the big chocolate muffin and a ceramic mug across to Sam.

"Thanks. I'm starving," he said as he unwrapped the muffin and took a drink of the coffee. "We'll get carry out or delivery tonight," he said, looking around at all the people sitting in the cafe.

"That's fine."

The waitress at the little café came by and offered to top off their cups.

"Is there a good Italian restaurant around here that has carry out?" Victoria asked.

"Right down the street," the waitress answered. "They have fantastic food and wonderful desserts, too."

"That sounds great," Sam said as he continued to devour the muffin.

"I would like to check on Peter tonight," Victoria said.

"You can't go back there," Sam said. "We cannot afford to have you confronted by the police. I think the guy bought that you were a simple hitchhiker, but if you go back, he's going to ask for identification. It's too risky. I'll go check, or we can call."

Sam was concerned about Peter, but he was more concerned about keeping Victoria safe.

"Then what?" Victoria asked.

"I'm not sure."

"I've been thinking about it, and I need to find a way to let Susan know he's okay," Victoria said. "We can't do anything to keep him safe now, so we need to let his editor know where he is and that he needs help."

"I'm okay with all that as long as you are not compromised."

"I know that, Sam. I don't want to put you in any more danger, either," Victoria said working through a plan in her head. "I think we have to call his editor and inform her of where Peter is and that he's in trouble. She'll notify the police and get him protection."

"An anonymous call?" Sam asked.

"That or a fake name," Victoria replied. "We don't have any other choice. If you give your real name, the police will circle back and be looking for you because you gave them a different story. Besides, my brother would be pissed off if you surface somewhere. So an anonymous call is the best we can do."

Sam nodded in agreement.

"His editor is Kyanne Fitzgerald," Victoria said. "She and Peter go back a long way. She'll do whatever's necessary to get him home safely."

Sam nodded again as he finished his second cup of coffee.

"I want to make the call," Victoria said as she stood up.

"I understand that," Sam answered. Sam knew Victoria and Susan Mercury were best friends, and he knew she would handle the call in a way that would ensure Peter's safety.

"I want to make that call now, Sam," Victoria said. "I need to know he's safe. That madman is probably searching for him right now, and unless he is protected by the police, Peter will be at risk."

She approached the coffee bar and asked if she could make a long distance call. The owner gave a puzzled look as Victoria offered him a $20 bill.

"Okay, fine," the cafe owner mumbled as he accepted the cash.

"Can I use your office?" Victoria asked as the man handed her the phone from behind the counter.

"That important?" the man asked.

"Yes, it is important," Victoria said, without reaching for the phone in front of her.

"Down the hall, last door on the left," the man motioned then went back to making coffee.

"This won't be a long conversation," Victoria told Sam as she passed by him, then turned and walked down the hallway.

She entered the little room and closed the door behind her. She first called information and retrieved the number for the *Washington Post*.

"May I speak with Kyanne Fitzgerald?" Victoria said as the newspaper receptionist answered the phone.

"May I tell her who's calling?" the receptionist asked.

"Tell her I am a friend of Peter Mercury, and he needs her help." There was a pause on the line for a second or two and then the receptionist said she would send the call through.

"This is Kyanne."

"Kyanne, you don't know me, but please listen carefully. Peter Mercury is in St. Vincent Hospital in Billings, Montana. He has been beaten badly and his back has been brutally whipped. He is being treated and will recover from his wounds. But, and this is the most important part, the man who did this is still looking for him. You must call the police and tell him who the John Doe is that they investigated earlier today. Ask the police to post a guard outside his room, and please make plans to get him back home ASAP."

Victoria paused, expecting a series of questions.

"What else?" Kyanne asked.

"Make sure you call Susan and let her know Peter is okay," Victoria's voice cracked a little as she spoke. She desperately wanted to let Susan know she was okay, too, but she believed Peter would tell her soon enough.

"You know Susan? Who is this?" Kyanne asked.

"Please act quickly, Kyanne. Peter's life is at risk. He is at St. Vincent in Billings. He is checked in as a John Doe. Please do it now." Victoria hung up and sat for a moment replaying the conversation. She knew Kyanne would do whatever she could for Peter.

"Okay, it's done," Victoria announced as she rejoined Sam at the table. "Let's get some dinner and figure out what we do now."

Sam and Victoria went down the street to the Italian restaurant. The place wasn't a typical Italian chain restaurant. The owner, who had been an exchange student at Billings High School, married the local football star the night of graduation. Her restaurant wasn't just Italian; it was *authentic* Italian.

Sam and Victoria walked in and were immediately captivated by the place. Everything about it was a recreation of the owner's hometown of Pescara. Sam and Victoria sat at a small table as they waited for their carry out. The environment was soothing and relaxing, and Victoria marveled at the odds of finding such a place in Montana.

"I told you it was great out here," Sam said after they ordered. Soon they walked out with a bag full of rigatoni, fresh bread, and two bottles of water.

"A long shower and a movie sound nice," Victoria said as they crossed the street.

"Yes it does. But we have to leave in the morning," Sam said as they entered the hotel.

"I know. But where to?"

"I don't know yet," Sam answered. "Let's relax tonight, and we'll figure it out in the morning."

In the room, Sam unpacked the food as Victoria searched for the TV remote.

"Not as good as Katie's chicken pot pie, but good enough," Sam said, as he tasted the rigatoni.

"I've been craving Italian, so this tastes perfect to me," Victoria said.

"Do you think we can check on Peter before we leave?" Victoria asked.

"Risky," Sam answered. "Assuming the police act, the hospital is going to be on edge about that whole event. If we go back, we may end up having to stay here and answer more questions."

Sam took a long drink of the bottled water. "We've done all we can do. Mercury knows you are alive. Do you believe he'll keep that secret for long?" Sam asked, knowing she already knew the answer.

"It's going to slip out," he said. "You know he will tell Susan. Who will she tell? How long will it take before everyone knows? Including the people trying to kill you." Sam's voice rose as he described the situation. He was mad that things had gotten so complicated, but he also knew they had done what they had to do.

"It'll be okay," Victoria assured him.

An hour later, Sam and Victoria were reclining on one of the beds watching a movie about a guy sailing around the world.

"We could do that," Victoria joked as she waved her hand in the air.

"You think so?" Sam replied.

"Yeah, no one would find us," Victoria said nonchalantly.

"That's true. We could take my plane down to Key West," Sam suggested, half joking.

"I do love it down there," Victoria said. "You aren't serious—are you?"

"I wasn't, but we have to go somewhere," Sam smiled as Victoria's face lit up.

AT THE HOSPITAL, in the middle of the night, Hiatt Montgomery approached the reception counter and smiled politely. "I believe a friend of mine might have been brought in here today."

"What is the name?"

"He probably came in as a John Doe.

"Okay, one moment," the woman answered. The receptionist scrolled through the computer screens and then paused for a moment.

"Okay, I'll be right back. I need to check on something." She got up and walked down the hall and disappeared around the corner.

Montgomery drummed his fingers on the counter as he waited, trying to appear casual. As he turned to look in the direction she had walked, he saw her coming back down the hallway with a policeman. Montgomery started backing up at the sight of the officer.

"Wait right there, mister," the policeman called out as he approached.

Montgomery reached into his jacket and pulled out a pistol.

"Get down," the policeman called out as he grabbed the receptionist and ducked behind a wide column. Immediately the policeman called for backup. Hearing the radio, Montgomery turned and ran for the ER door. Outside, another officer stood by his patrol car, watching the road. As the call came through on his radio, he spotted Montgomery running out of the hospital.

"Stop now," he shouted.

Montgomery turned and fired at the officer, hitting the car but missing his target. Montgomery ran around the corner of the hospital and disappeared from view. An officer in a police cruiser coming from the other direction saw Montgomery cross the street as he fled. He called out through the car's speaker for Montgomery to stop. Again, Montgomery turned and fired at the car, then ran down an alley and disappeared into the dark.

BY NOW, THE ENTIRE area was glowing with police lights as sirens blared from all directions.

Sam and Victoria stood by their hotel window listening to the sirens and watching as police cars raced up and down the streets. They knew Montgomery had found Peter at the hospital. Victoria sobbed at the thought of Peter lying defenseless in his hospital bed.

"Had the police arrived in time?" she wondered. "Or were they chasing him after he accomplished his goal?"

"We can't leave now," Sam said. "But we have to, as soon as things calm down."

"I know," Victoria said, sad and despondent as she curled up on the bed.

"If you want to shower, you should do it now," Sam said. "We'll leave as soon as the police cars clear out."

HIATT MONTGOMERY SPRINTED through downtown alleys until the sirens were far off in the distance.

"Fuck," he shouted as he dropped to his knees in an alley. He pulled a phone from his pocket and called his contact.

"Mercury has police protection. He's out of reach."

"What about McBride?" the voice on the other end asked.

"Nothing. The area is too hot now. Shots were fired when I entered the hospital. I need to be extracted," he said. Montgomery had yet to catch his breath.

"Sit tight. We'll send a car," the voice answered. "And try not to make things worse."

"Fuck you," Montgomery answered. He sat down behind a dumpster in the darkest corner of the alley he could find. It would take a few hours for a car to reach him, and he knew he could not move until then. He would sleep for a while. The microchip buried beneath his skin would guarantee he was located. There was nothing left for him to do but wait.

POLICE CARS STILL swarmed the streets when Victoria emerged from the shower. "What's the plan?" she asked as she approached Sam.

"I suspect we are as safe here as anywhere with all those police out there," Sam answered.

"So we stay the night?" Victoria asked.

"I think so."

"Let's get some sleep, Sam. We can get up really early and take off. Come on, close the curtains," she said as she pulled back the covers on the unused bed.

IN SIMS' OFFICE, a small desk lamp lit the otherwise dark room. Sims sat in a chair on the opposite side of the room with his feet up on a coffee table and a cigar dangling from his mouth.

"What a fucking mess," he mumbled as he contemplated his next move. He had been updated on Montgomery's failed efforts to get to Mercury. Now he was trying to determine the best course for damage control. It was 3:30 a.m., and the exhausted Sims was aware that more aggressive steps would need to be taken to keep the lid on his involvement. He could disavow both men, claiming Montgomery was a trespasser and Mercury was just in the wrong place at the wrong time. But that would leave a loose cannon running about telling stories that need not be told. Mercury had to be silenced and soon. Sims had dispatched new operatives to deal with the problem while Montgomery had been recalled to the base. Sims had not yet determined the best use for Montgomery, but his past special-forces experience made him a valuable asset—even though his drinking often made him sloppy in his execution. At about 2 o'clock, the phone rang.

Sims answered. The voice on the other end announced, "We got him."

"Excellent," Sims responded.

PETER MERCURY HAD been picked up at St. Vincent Hospital in Billings by an ambulance service that had all the right paperwork and credentials. He was to be taken to the local airport for a charter flight back to Washington, the forms indicated. Instead, the imposters took Mercury to a private airport where he was transferred into a van that was now on the road. At the last minute, Sims was successfully silencing the one person who realized something big was afoot.

"Do you want him terminated now, Mr. Sims?" the voice asked.

"No, we don't want any bodies turning up. Take him to the lodge, lock him up, and let's see what he knows."

As he hung up the phone, Sims stood to head for home. "That's done," he said to himself. "Now I just need to find McBride."

IT WAS STILL DARK out when Victoria woke up and walked to the window to see if things had calmed down. Outside, there was no movement, no police cars, nothing.

"Sam, wake up," she whispered.

Sam jolted up out of his sleep. "What is it?"

"It's completely quiet out there. Let's get going." Victoria walked to the bathroom and emerged a few minutes later in a clean pair of blue sweats and a gray t-shirt.

She packed the few bags they had, made fresh coffee in the mini-maker the hotel provided, and within a few minutes, they were out the door and in the Suburban. There were barely any cars on the road as they reached the interstate and drove north.

"Where are we going?" Victoria asked as Sam set the cruise control and took the lid off his coffee.

"We're going to get the plane and fly south," Sam announced.

"So you weren't kidding about Key West?" Victoria asked with a tired smile.

"Nope, that's where we are going."

"I'm worried about Peter."

"I know you are, but there's nothing we can do now," Sam answered. "We have to get back to our plan to make you disappear. I hope you like the ocean, because we're going to take my boat out to sea. Those assholes won't find you there." Sam grinned.

"How far out to sea?" Victoria asked with less enthusiasm.

"Far enough to get lost."

"I bet Henry and Katie would be glad to see us."

"I'm not bringing them deeper into this. What's wrong, don't you like the ocean?" Sam teased.

"I like walking next to it, but I've never been a big fan of not having dirt under my feet."

"Oh, the dirt's down there," Sam said with a little laugh.

"Can we check on Peter somehow today?" Victoria asked, changing the subject. "I can't stop thinking about him."

"We'll make a call soon, but you realize we've done all we can do, right?" Sam said as he put his empty coffee cup in the holder.

"I know," Victoria said, resigned to the situation. "I just want to be sure Kyanne acted, and the police did their job." Victoria looked at Sam in a way that told him she would make the call one way or the other.

"If these people followed us to the ranch, then they might be looking for me, too. We have to assume they are well-connected and organized and have access to any data they need," Sam said. "We have to disappear again and stay off the computer screens. So let's give it a few days and then call his paper again. Can we play it that way?" Sam wanted Victoria's buy-in to the plan.

"Okay, I get it," Victoria responded.

AT THE WHITE HOUSE, President Niles sat in the Oval Office with Cochran and Reed. There was no real agenda for this meeting, just a get-together to get the three up to speed.

"Jackson, I know this has been a terrible few days for you. Why don't we slow down and let everyone catch their breath," Speaker Reed said.

"It has been a terrible few days. There is no denying that," the President said as he let out a deep sigh.

"Jackson, you should at least nominate a VP before we try and move on the package. We don't even have a VP to chair the Senate," Cochran said. "You know that issue really needs to be dealt with first."

"I haven't thought much about the VP thing yet, but I'm inclined to look at a governor," the President stated as he rubbed his hands across his head. Cochran and Reed exchanged glances at this comment, neither excited about the word "governor."

"We think you need a friendly face in here with you. Hell, Jackson, we've had a VP killed, and, I'm sorry to bring it up, but your first Supreme Court nominee, too. You need someone in here who has your back."

"What about Sinclair?" Cochran asked.

"Sinclair?" The President reacted with a bit of amusement. "Hell, he hates politics," the President said, dismissing the idea.

"Come on, Jackson," Reed said in a strong voice, pointing his cane at the President. "He's a good friend, a smart guy. He will have your back, and he's been in two previous administrations. Hell, he's the perfect guy."

"You two have been discussing this a great deal," Niles said as he glared at them both. "It's my decision, but your thoughts are always welcome." He reached for a stack of papers. "Now, let's talk about the defense cuts."

Again, Reed and Cochran looked at each other, but this time they both seemed annoyed by the change of topic.

"You two are going to have to be willing to help sell these on the Hill. We've talked about this. If you two lead the way, you know those freshmen are going to come along. Hell, they're already scared to death of you two." The President stopped and smiled at his two old friends. "But you have to be on board first."

"Of course we are, Jackson," Reed answered.

"But we think you should wait until you get a VP in place," Cochran added.

"Not going to happen," the President countered. "Nothing is going to prevent me from introducing these reforms. Nothing. You guys may not like all this. Hell knows many don't. But the changes I campaigned on are coming to the Floor. Period. You will vote on these." Niles' voice rose as he jabbed his finger toward the two men.

"The Senate will sit on it till a VP is in place," Cochran announced nonchalantly. "That's a matter of protocol."

"Any idiot would know that," Cochran thought to himself.

"Bullshit. That's bullshit, and you know it," Niles responded. "That's a stall tactic. Hell, it could take months to get a VP in place. I'll bring these bills to the Floor myself if I have to. If you guys want a fucking war on the Capitol steps, I'll give you one. I was elected by 49 states, and I'll be God damned if I let a bunch of Washington insiders overrule the will of the people."

Jackson Niles gazed intently at his two old friends. Reed and Cochran stared back. For a few uncomfortable seconds, no one said a word.

"Mr. President," the voice of Susan Mercury came across the intercom.

"Yes, Susan."

"Mr. Sinclair is on his way."

"Send him in when he arrives."

As Anthony Sinclair entered, he immediately picked up on the mood in the room. "If it were a little later in the day, I think I would make you all a drink," the Chief of Staff said, smiling.

The other three men also cracked a smile and laughed at the tension that had built.

"Mr. President, I have been trying to reach Langley, but so far I've had no luck," Sinclair said as he took a seat on the vacant sofa across from the two wingbacks occupied by Reed and Cochran.

"He took a few days off," the President answered.

"Bad timing, if you ask me," Sinclair said.

"Perhaps," the President said. "But I'm sure he's working. Hell, he never stops."

The other three exchanged glances as they sat in uncomfortable silence.

"He'll be back in a day or so, and then he'll need to get focused and get busy," the President said. "There are plenty of questions that need to be answered, and Jack has been less than effective lately. But that's between him and me. If he can't handle the load, then I'll need to get someone else in there."

The President stood. "You will have to excuse me, gentlemen, but I have some personal matters to attend to," he said, opening the Oval Office door. The three men filed out without a word.

"We'll talk later," Sinclair told Reed and Cochran as he headed back to his office.

IN MONTANA, AFTER driving nearly straight through for eight hours, Sam and Victoria arrived at the small airport where Sam kept his plane.

"I need to file a flight plan and get the plane ready," he said as he parked the Suburban. "Sit tight out here for a few minutes, okay?"

Sam gathered his wallet and other needed items from the car.

"Won't that leave a trail they can follow?" Victoria asked.

"My plane is titled to a partnership. There are a bunch of owners," Sam explained. "My name won't show."

About a half hour later Sam emerged from the small building and opened the rear door.

"We're all set," he said as he started grabbing their few bags. "You might want to grab a couple of these blankets for the trip."

Sam handed Victoria the blankets they had used earlier to keep Peter warm. She folded them and started across the tarmac with Sam. The small jet was running, fully fueled, and ready to take off. The inside of the aircraft was more spacious than Victoria remembered from the flight out here from New York. Four large, tan, leather seats offered plenty of room for reclining, with space behind them for luggage.

Once in the air, Victoria reclined her seat and spread one of the blankets across her lap.

"Are you going to be okay—you'll stay awake?" she asked as she pulled the blanket up to her chin.

"Yes, I'll be fine," Sam said as he adjusted the flight instruments and got comfortable in his seat. Sam was an experienced pilot. He had received his pilot's license about the same time he started driving a car. "This little baby can really move. We'll be there in no time."

"In fact, we'll be out to sea and on the boat by tonight," he continued.

"Great," Victoria muttered with a smile.

As Victoria drifted off to sleep, Sam started thinking through the events of the past couple of days. He didn't know much, but he did know that Clayton Sims and his old family lodge were playing some role in whatever was going on. "It would be nice to know who's coming and going out there," Sam thought as he flew along.

Victoria was now in a deep sleep, and Sam thought it safe to make a call from his satellite phone.

"Charlie," Sam said softly when his call was answered.

"Is this Sam McBride?" the man asked.

"It sure is, you old rascal."

"Hell, I haven't talked to you in, what? Three or four years?" the man said with a friendly laugh. "What the heck are you up to these days?"

Charlie's ranch was a few hours away from Sam's place, and they had spent a lot of time together in earlier years.

"Charlie do you remember when we were in our twenties and we first joined the militia group?" Sam asked in a more serious voice.

"Yeah, Sam, I remember that," Charlie answered, matching Sam's change in tone.

"Do you still remember all the codes we used to have for describing threats?" Sam asked, waiting as Charlie thought.

"Yeah, Sam, I remember all that stuff. It wasn't that long ago," Charlie answered.

"You remember 'Red Alpha?'" Sam asked.

"That was a bad one, Sam, about as bad as it got, if I remember. Why are you asking me this?" Charlie asked as he walked across the den in his home and closed the door.

"Something might be afoot, Charlie," Sam stated.

"Something that bad?" Charlie asked. "Red Alpha?"

"Maybe."

"That's some bad stuff you're talking about Sam, real bad," Charlie said as his voice heightened. "I've been reading about the Vice President's death and the President's sister getting killed in that explosion. You know, a conspiracy freak like me might think that was all too coincidental."

"Charlie, do you remember that big old lodge on the other side of Flathead?" Sam finally asked.

"Sure, I remember that place. Big stupid place where some east coast rich guy vacations, right?" Charlie asked, puzzled but intrigued.

"That's the one," Sam answered.

"What about it?"

"Can you or some of the guys we used to hang with back in the day put some eyes on that place?" Sam asked.

"Sure, I've got time, and most of the boys are pretty free right now" Charlie said his enthusiasm growing. "But what are we looking for?"

"Just who comes and goes," Sam answered.

"Easy enough. I've got scopes we use to track the cattle. Hell, I can see a fly on a heifer's nose from a mile away," Charlie laughed.

"That's good, Charlie, because you need to stay at least that far away," Sam cautioned.

"What am I getting into here?"

"There are some bad people at that place, Charlie. You have to be invisible and at a safe distance," Sam warned.

"Okay then, so you aren't exaggerating when you say 'Red Alpha,' are you, Sam?" Charlie asked, more serious and cautious now that he had the details.

"No, I don't think I'm wrong about this," Sam said. "I need you to send me pictures from the field?"

"Sure. That's not a problem."

"Listen, Charlie," Sam warned. "You guys watch during the day, but retreat far away at night so your fires are out of sight, okay?"

"Sure, Sam, we can handle this. We all know that territory well. I can set up where those people will never see a thing. They won't have a clue we're out there," Charlie assured Sam. Then he added, "Sam, are you okay?"

"I'm fine. But worried about some old friends," Sam confessed.

"I get that," Charlie said. "I'll handle it. You can count on me."

"I know I can, Charlie. Be careful."

"You'll start seeing info from me in a few days," Charlie assured Sam as they both hung up.

AT THE SIMS LODGE, a confused and blindfolded Peter Mercury was carried in his wheelchair down a set of stairs, through a series of doors, and into a room with no windows.

His blindfold was removed, and a man he had never seen before set a pitcher of water and tray of food on a small table.

"That door over there is a bathroom," the man said. With that, he closed and locked the door behind him as he left the room.

Peter sat in his wheelchair, unsure of where he was, but confident that he wasn't back in Washington or with Sam and Victoria. "What the hell happened?" he thought.

Upstairs, Hiatt Montgomery walked back and forth in front of the three large fireplaces, talking on his cell phone.

"I understand," he said over and over again.

On the other end of the line, an angry and frustrated Clayton Sims barked out orders to his under-performing lieutenant.

"Leave Mercury alone for now. Are we clear?" Sims asked.

"Yes, sir, crystal," Montgomery said, resenting Sims' tone but also knowing who wrote the checks.

"I have an FAA report that shows a plane leaving from near Billings for Key West," Sims said. "We'll dig into the ownership from here, but we think it might be worth following. I want you to take the jet and get down there," Sims instructed.

"When?" Montgomery asked.

"Right now," Sims said, exasperated.

"What do you want done when I find the pilot?" Montgomery asked.

"First, find out if it's McBride. If it is, find out what he knows, who he told, and then kill him," Sims instructed, as if the answer were obvious. "Take his ass out to sea and feed him to the sharks. I've never liked that guy." Sims slammed the phone down.

Montgomery went to his room, packed a few things, and then made his way to the large building at the end of the airstrip. For Montgomery, it was just another day with another hit. "No big deal," he thought. "A couple of hours of racing a jet down to Key West sounds kinda fun."

A FEW HOURS LATER, Sam McBride landed his jet at the Key West airport. The weather was typical for South Florida—bright, clear, sunny, and very hot. He taxied the plane into a hangar, came to a stop, and turned off the engine. The taxi Sam had called while still in the air was waiting for them outside the building.

"We're going straight to the marina," Sam told the driver.

The marina was a sprawling complex with a restaurant, bar, supply store, and showers.

"I love it down here," Sam said as they got out of the car and started walking down the pier.

"Do you get down here much?" Victoria asked as they walked.

"Sarah and I used to fly down on a regular basis, but I haven't been down much since the accident."

Victoria didn't say anything more but squeezed Sam's hand as she walked beside him.

At the boat dock, an attendant was busy cleaning and checking over things to ensure all the equipment was in proper working order on Sam's 42-foot Grady White. He had purchased the boat years earlier with a group of friends, but over time he bought out the others' ownership shares. The boat was equipped for long stays out to sea. The large area at the rear was used mainly for fishing. Inside, the boat looked more like a well-finished condo. The cockpit included comfortable seating for four people and had retractable doors open to the back. Below deck, a large kitchen area finished in granite and stainless steel led to a master suite containing a king-size bed and full walk-in shower.

"She's about ready, Mr. McBride," the attendant announced as Sam approached.

"Great. How long do you need?" Sam asked.

"At least two hours."

"Okay, we're going up to eat and get some supplies. Leave it here running if you are finished before we return," Sam said.

He and Victoria put their bags on the pier and walked back up the dock.

"Let's get a decent meal, and then we'll go next door and get some groceries and maybe some clothes fit for a life at sea," Sam said, laughing.

"Clothes that float is what I want," Victoria replied.

The little marina restaurant looked out over the bay and was a welcome break from the hurried pace of the last few days. A myriad of mismatched umbrellas provided an abundance of shade. The chairs were similarly mismatched, with no two alike. Some kind of exotic parrot occupied a large cage near the entrance, apparently the namesake of the establishment, The Bird Cage. In the far corner a small stage surrounded by potted palm plants was being readied for the late night crowd, which had yet to appear. Sam and Victoria had the place pretty much to themselves with the exception of a few locals sitting at a long bar right inside the main building.

"I already feel less stressed," Victoria said as the waitress brought two glasses of wine and a plate of steaming calamari.

"Me, too," Sam agreed, lifting his glass.

"So, are we going out there?" Victoria asked as she motioned in the direction of the bay.

"No," Sam laughed. "I have friends up along the east coast. We're going to travel along visiting. Some nights we'll stay on the boat, some nights with friends, and some at small bayside inns. We'll have fun, but we're going to keep moving, too," Sam explained. "I promised Jackson I would keep you safe, and that means no more bizarre run-ins with those creeps."

Sam sat back as Victoria finished off the plate of calamari. "You were hungry," he said as he looked at the empty plate.

"Still am," Victoria mumbled with a mouthful of food.

About a half hour later the waitress returned with plates of oysters, shrimp, grouper, and hush puppies. Two salads and a few more glasses of water rounded out the meal.

"This should get you filled up," Sam said as the waitress spread the plates before them.

"Maybe, but where's the chocolate?" Victoria asked with a smile. It wasn't long before they both sat back in their chairs, plates nearly empty.

"Okay, now I'm full," Victoria said with a deep breath. "I think I ate too much."

"Let's go next door, get some clothes and a few basic items to have on board, and then let's hit the water," Sam said as he stood up from the table.

"Sounds like a plan," Victoria replied. They made their way back through the maze of umbrellas and left the little bayside restaurant.

Next door, a little shop sold shorts, hats, shirts, swim suits, and other items a northerner might forget to pack for a few days out on a boat. The store's entrance was only a few steps from the giant birdcage, and the creature made a series of high-pitched squawks as the entry door creaked and the tiny bell attached to the handle rang.

"That bird is crazy" Victoria said as she slipped into the store.

"I think it runs off more business than it brings in," the storeowner offered upon hearing her comment.

Inside, Victoria was struck by the shop's level of finish. How different it seemed from the restaurant. The store had been completely modernized and was as clean and polished as any boutique in New York.

"I need a swimsuit," Victoria said as they entered.

"Me, too," Sam said.

"I'm going to get you a Speedo," Victoria teased.

"Then I get to pick out yours. Deal?" Sam asked with a smile.

"I don't know. Show me the suit first," Victoria said, suddenly insecure.

"This one," Sam said as he pointed to a black string bikini.

"Okay, never mind," Victoria said as she walked away. "You pick out yours, and I'll get mine."

"Works for me," Sam said, still laughing.

A bit later, they met at the checkout, each carrying an assortment of shorts, shirts, hats, sunglasses, lotion, and bathing suits.

"Let's go next door and get a few food items," Sam suggested, "and then I think we're ready."

They arrived at the boat as the attendant was packing up his cleaning supplies.

"You are all set, Mr. McBride," the attendant said as the couple approached.

"Great. Thanks a bunch," Sam told the young kid, handing him a couple of $20 bills.

Sam and Victoria brought their purchases onto the boat and put everything away. The cabin was large and felt more like a family room than a fishing vessel.

"This is really nice," Victoria said.

"All the comforts of home," Sam said.

"I forgot to get a sweatshirt," Victoria said as she finished emptying her bags.

"Go back up and get one. We're fine on time," Sam said as he put food in the full-sized fridge.

"Be right back then," Victoria said as she stepped out of the cabin and climbed back onto the pier. She hustled through the door of the little clothing store where the clerk immediately recognized her.

"Hey, you're back," she smiled.

"I forgot a sweatshirt. I also wondered if you have something kinda like that little black bikini over there, but maybe one that covers a little more?" Victoria asked, feeling her cheeks redden.

The clerk, who was a few years younger than Victoria, smiled at her with a twinkle in her eye.

"We don't sell many of those around here," she chuckled.

"I'm going to be out on the boat for the next couple of months, and I need more than one suit," Victoria explained. Both women laughed as they walked down the aisle.

"What size?" the clerk asked as she looked at Victoria.

"A few weeks ago I was in a 12, but now I don't really know," Victoria said as she looked at what the clerk had picked.

"You aren't a 12 now, honey, I can tell you that," the woman said as she looked Victoria up and down. "What size shorts did you buy?"

"I bought 10's."

"You better try on an 8," the woman cautioned.

"No way," Victoria laughed. "There is no way I can wear an 8. I haven't been that size in ten years or so."

"Take these in there and try," the woman said, as she grabbed a pair of shorts off the shelf and handed them to Victoria.

A couple of minutes later Victoria emerged from the dressing room with a huge smile across her face. "I can't believe I can wear these," she said, standing in front of the mirror.

"Go grab your bag and let's get these switched for you," the woman instructed Victoria.

A few minutes later Victoria was swapping out the clothes she had just bought for the smaller size.

"Whatever you've been doing, keep it up," the woman said as she finished bagging up the items. "What about the suit?" the woman said with a wink.

"I think I'm going to try it," Victoria answered. "I can't believe I can wear that size again. I must be nuts."

"Hey, honey, if you still got it at this age, you should be showing it off!" she laughed.

"A few weeks ago I wouldn't have even considered wearing such a thing," Victoria confessed.

"How long will you be out there?" the woman asked.

"No idea," Victoria responded. "Long enough to get to know that guy again is my hope." They both smiled and laughed as Victoria picked up her bags.

"Good luck with that," the woman called out as Victoria headed out the door. "Another gold-digger bitch," the woman mumbled as the door closed.

Victoria boarded the boat as Sam removed the ropes holding it in place.

"All set?" he asked as Victoria descended into the main cabin.

"Yep," she called back up.

"Okay then, we're off," Sam said as he pushed down the throttle and the big boat started moving away from its slip. Thirty minutes or so later, Sam was in open water cruising at a comfortable pace. Victoria emerged wearing a pair of new red and white striped shorts and a white t-shirt.

"We're going to cruise along the coast for a while, and then we'll anchor for the night up here in a quiet, little cove I've been to before," Sam said. "It's about a three-hour ride from here, but it's worth the trip. It's a beautiful little spot."

Sam was as much at home on the ocean as he was on the ranch. He loved the wide-open space and freedom of the water.

AT THE MARINA, Hiatt Montgomery walked along the pier casually, wearing a large-brim, white hat and dark sunglasses and looking for signs of McBride.

On a hunch, he had asked the cab service where his "buddy" Sam kept his boat. At the marina, he walked into and quickly out of the restaurant. He went into the clothing store and asked the owner if a Sam McBride had been around.

"Not sure," she casually replied. "What's he look like?"

"Tall, rugged looking. He ranches up in Montana."

"Does he have some black-haired woman with him?" the clerk asked.

"I don't know," Montgomery answered with an attempt at a casual laugh.

"A guy left here about an hour or so ago. Sounds like your guy. He has some black-haired woman with him. A gold-digger, if you ask me. She said they were going out for a couple of months."

"Is there somebody around here who gets the boats ready for owners?" Montgomery asked.

"Yes. He's probably up in the boat storage building or over there on that lift," she said as she pointed to a boat lift moving around.

"Okay, thanks," Montgomery said. Then turned and asked again, "A gold-digger, you say?"

"Yeah. She was a real piece of work," the woman said as she moved about hanging up items others had left out of place.

"Hey, thanks a lot," Montgomery told the woman with a smile as he walked out the door.

The boat attendant confirmed for Montgomery that it was indeed Sam McBride who had left earlier.

"Two months out at sea with some bimbo," he thought. "That guy doesn't know jack shit. He's working on getting laid." Montgomery walked back up to the ship store to call for a taxi.

Once the taxi was scheduled, Montgomery went back over to the little restaurant, ordered a drink, and then went to an outside table where he could make a private call.

"We want you to stay down there for a few days and see if he comes in," his contact instructed him.

"What the hell for?" Montgomery protested. "I'm telling you, he's out there with some chick who's looking for a gold ticket. He's just trying to get some action. Hell, if he knew something important, he wouldn't be floating around out here with some damned woman he just met. What the fuck!"

"You better cool it, Hiatt. Get a room, go to the marina each day, and wait for instructions," the man said as he hung up.

Montgomery slouched back in his chair. Sims was putting him on ice for a few days.

"Oh well," he muttered, "at least I'm not in some shit town with nothing to do."

Montgomery walked back up to the ship store, cancelled the taxi, and went back to his table to get some dinner.

"A little action sounds kinda good," he mumbled as he drank his Scotch. "Good idea, Sam, you fuckin' prick."

Montgomery had married early in life, but his wife left him after a year or so. Since then, he had been alone, with the exception of a few prostitutes he regularly visited. Despite the money, even they hated to see him coming because he was rough and angry in bed and seemed to be more interested in degrading them than being pleased himself.

SAM'S BOAT CRUISED smoothly over the water as he and Victoria sat in the cabin together. The ocean air blew hard through the open windows, and an occasional spray of water made its way through the openings.

"I think I'm going to change into my suit and take up a spot in one of those lounge chairs on the rear deck," Victoria said as she stood and headed down to the galley.

"Works for me."

"You want anything?" Victoria asked as she passed him.

"No I'm fine," Sam answered.

Victoria emerged a few minutes later with a bottle of water, a tube of sunscreen, and a note pad and pen.

Sam kicked down the engine to idle and joined Victoria on the back of the boat.

"We are going to drift for a bit," he announced as he took a seat in the chair next to her. "Can I get some of that sunscreen?"

"Here you go. You think Peter is back in Washington yet?" she asked.

"I would think so," Sam answered as he finished putting sunscreen on his face.

"I wonder if he remembers that I was there with him in the woods," Victoria said.

"We have to assume he does," Sam said. "We simply can't afford to think otherwise."

"We know that Montgomery and Sims are connected," she said, moving the conversation in a new direction. "So we know that Sims wanted me dead—just like Redding. It has to be about more than the Court or any changes Jackson would be proposing. I mean, we're talking about the vice president here. This guy has committed murder, treason, the list goes on and on."

Victoria scribbled notes on a pad in the formation of a flow chart as she went through the recent events.

"For that matter, there has to be a lot of people involved in this," she continued. "This kind of thing doesn't happen without coordination. They even tracked us to the hospital last night."

"Your mind never stops," Sam said as he smiled at Victoria.

"Still," she said, ignoring his comment and turning to face him, "Sims is in Jackson's inner circle. What's to say some of the others aren't in on all this?"

"Who are you thinking of?" Sam asked, now taking the conversation much more seriously.

"Cochran and Reed," Victoria answered.

"To what end, though?" Sam asked. "That's the part I don't get. Kill the VP, kill a Supreme Court nominee, but to accomplish what? What would they possibly be going after if they were involved?"

"I don't know," Victoria answered. "I don't even have a guess. I know as soon as possible I need to get to Jackson and tell him about Sims and Montgomery."

"Your brother is a smart guy, Victoria," Sam said. "I can guarantee you he is already suspicious of Sims. He always has been."

"Are you sure of that?" Victoria asked.

"Yes. He has expressed to me over the last few years that he questions Sims' character and motives. Your brother is no fool, Victoria. You know the saying, 'Keep your friends close and your enemies closer,'" Sam said.

"Yes, of course," Victoria answered.

"I can tell you that's why Sims is where he's at—at least for now," Sam confessed.

"So you're saying we don't need to tell Jackson about Montgomery and Sims?" Victoria asked.

"Jackson hasn't trusted Sims for a long time. He's keeping him close so he can find out who else he should be worried about," Sam said.

"You know a lot more than you've let on," Victoria said. A lone seagull swooped in alongside the boat and dove into the water. They both turned to watch as the large bird surfaced with a fish clutched in its beak.

"Look, Jackson knew his victory would bring out opposition. He just wasn't sure how violent, harsh, or open it would be. He didn't know how deep the Washington political circles would be in the whole thing, either, for that matter," Sam said. "But he's not a fool. He knew his changes would bring out opposition, and he knew Sims would likely be on the other side. I'm sure your brother is having Sims monitored as we speak."

The boat rocked gently as a slight breeze picked up. Victoria quickly grabbed her hat as the wind threatened to send it overboard. The breeze felt good against the June temperatures that were becoming noticeable as they drifted.

"That's why he told me to get you hidden, Victoria. Jackson can handle what's happening in Washington. He's counting on me to keep *you* safe. That's my role. He has plenty of friends there, powerful friends. Never forget how tight he is with the military. They love him, and he feels the same about them. They'll have his back."

In the distance, they saw another large boat approaching. It slowed about 100 yards away. "That's a fishing charter,"

Sam announced sensing Victoria's concern. "An old ship was sunk right over there to create a reef. Fish use the wreck site as cover, and lots of charters come out here from Key West."

The boat slowed and circled as Sam and Victoria watched.

"What are they doing?" she asked.

"They have the location marked with GPS, and the system will put the boat right on top of the wreckage," Sam explained. As they watched, they could see the captain wave to the crew followed by an anchor dropping and fishing lines being prepared. Sam returned to his seat.

"If something really bad is brewing, and it may be, you can be confident that Jackson has a plan," Sam said. "Jackson always has a plan."

He offered Victoria an encouraging smile. "You can be confident in his abilities, like he is in yours," Sam said. "He didn't nominate you because you're his sister. It's because of your mind. But you need to appreciate your brother. He's a sharp cookie. He's on top of things."

Sam looked out toward the fishing charter as the sounds of excitement bounced over the water toward them. Sam looked just in time to see a large fish landing in the water after having jumped trying to free itself from the hook.

"My order was to keep you safe—at all costs—and to take no risk with your safety," Sam said as he looked back at Victoria. He could tell she still wasn't satisfied that Jackson knew all that was happening. "Jackson told me in no uncertain terms that I was to make you disappear for as long as necessary. Even for good, if that's what it takes. Period. Washington is his to handle. Your role is to be safe with me. That is what your brother, the President of the United States, ordered me to do. There was absolutely no ambiguity in his directive. Do you get it?"

"Okay," she whispered as she kissed Sam. "Okay."

IN WASHINGTON, Cochran and Reed sat in Reed's office.

"He's with the Joint Chiefs of Staff now before he meets with us," Cochran said as he poked at the wastebasket with one of Reed's canes. "It's a damned slap in the face that not a single member of Congress is in that meeting. Jackson won the election to be President—not the fucking emperor. He's going to have full military support before he even makes his plans public."

"It's going to be hard to argue against their unified position—assuming they get one," Reed said.

"True, so we are going to have to chip away at that unity!" he said, shaking his fist. "What the hell is that stink?" Cochran couldn't ignore the smell any longer. Reed had eaten lunch in his office earlier in the day and the smell of fish lingered. Though Cochran was often uncomfortable in Reed's office with all the flaunting he did through the pictures, at least he could ignore pictures.

"It was lunch. Just ignore it," Reed said, waving a hand as if to brush away the interruption. "All Jackson's supporters are in the service. They can't afford to argue with their Commander in Chief. That will be our angle with the press."

"There are plenty of retired generals and former National Security advisers who think his positions are crazy," Cochran said. "His policies will disrupt long-established positions and programs that simply do not need to be changed."

"We can't allow Congress to be overrun by the executive branch the way Jackson wants to," Reed said. "It's bad policy."

"Regardless of anything else, we need to slow him down, encourage him to take the proper time to look fully at any significant changes," Cochran said.

"I've known Jackson for a long time, but that's beside the point. Our two parties have served this country well. He wants to marginalize us, and that ain't going to happen," the Speaker said, his face growing red with anger. "It ain't going to happen!" Reed slapped the table as he finished talking.

Cochran flinched at the sound and then nodded in agreement. "You should have somebody spray something in here," he added as he struggled out of his chair.

OUT WEST, PETER MERCURY sat quietly in his little room in the basement of the Sims lodge. While the space wasn't cold or dark, it was still basically a jail cell. He could hear someone outside moving around, but he hadn't yet heard any voices. Food came in, without comment or question, through a slot in the bottom of the door. The slot would open and a tray would slide in. Peter was surprised that the food was actually good even though he had virtually no appetite. From this room he couldn't smell or hear food being prepared, but throughout the day it suddenly appeared.

By now, Peter's mind spun with thoughts of Langley in the park, Montgomery, and his own grand conspiracy theories. He thought about the rescue from the woods and wondered if he had imagined Victoria being there or if it really happened. "I must have been hallucinating," he thought as he lay back on his bed. Then there was the trip from the hospital to the airport. "How could these people pull that off?" he wondered. Peter had few answers for the questions swimming through his mind.

"Mercury," a voice said from outside the room.

"Yeah," Peter responded.

"Write down what you know on this tablet," the voice instructed as a notepad and pen were thrust through the food slot. "I suggest you be thorough if you intend to survive this." The door over the slot slid shut again.

Peter sat and stared at the paper. "I can tell the park story. But do I say anything about Victoria?" he wondered. "They're going to try and beat it out of me, that's for sure. Either way, I'm going to get beaten severely. I might as well try to hold something back."

"I might die out here," he thought. "At least I can protect her, if she was really there." His mind ran in circles as he tried to organize his memories of the last few days.

IN THE QUIET WATERS between the Keys and the Florida mainland, the sun was low in the sky as Sam and Victoria cruised along at a mild pace. They sat together in the Captain's chair, enjoying the beauty of the sea and the peace they felt being away from the real world. It had been hard for Victoria to switch off what was going on, but after Sam's speech, she now knew her brother was okay.

"I love the ocean," she said as she watched the dolphins jump in the surf beside the boat.

"They're chasing a school of fish," Sam pointed out as he slowed the boat. "Have you ever been fishing out in the ocean?" Sam moved the throttle to neutral and turned off the engines.

"Really?" she replied with a silly face.

"Today you learn," Sam announced as he went down into the galley to retrieve his equipment. Off the back of the boat, the dolphins rose to the surface and then dove in again.

"They are forcing the fish into a tighter and tighter group," he said as he finished tying a lure on the end of one of the poles.

"Watch this," he instructed as he cast the lure out into the middle of the group. Within seconds, Sam's rod bent hard. He jerked the pole up, setting the hook in the fish's mouth.

"Here," he said as he handed the pole to Victoria.

"What am I supposed to do?" she asked in a shrill voice as she grabbed the pole.

"Reel in the fish," Sam laughed. "Turn that handle." He pointed to the side of the reel.

Victoria struggled with the pole. The fish had no intention of being dinner.

"Let me show you," he said as he came up behind Victoria and put his hands over hers on the pole and reel. "Bring the pole up and then reel as you lower it back down," he said, helping her move the pole up and down as she reeled.

"Now, if the fish takes off, let it run. Otherwise, the line might break," he continued.

"You feel it pulling?" Sam asked as the pole jumped and twitched with the fish's efforts. "You want to work him up slowly. Don't try to force it, try to keep the line tight, and as the fish gets tired, you can work him to the boat." Sam watched as she worked the reel.

"I'm going to try and get another one hooked," he said as he cast the other pole out.

Soon, each of them where reeling as the dolphins and the school moved to the south. Victoria reeled as she brought the exhausted fish alongside the boat.

"Your first fish?" Sam asked.

"No, I've eaten fish before," Victoria said with a smile. Sam stuck his reel in a rod holder, quickly netted her fish, and dropped it on deck. He then finished bringing in his own.

"Whew, that was crazy," he said.

"What kind are they?" Victoria asked as she looked at the fish tangled in the net.

"Redfish," he answered.

"Redfish? Are they good to eat?"

"Oh yeah," Sam assured her as he hauled them to the back of the boat to clean. "They'll make a great dinner or two."

He restarted the engine and pressed the throttle forward. Victoria sat in the chair across from Sam and smiled as the wind cooled her off after fighting the fish.

"God, I love being with this guy," she thought.

Sam thought the same about Victoria. He remembered fishing with Sarah and how much fun they had had doing the same things, and he thought, "I never thought I would feel this way again." He smiled back at Victoria as the boat headed north.

CHAPTER SIX
Boxed In

By the time the sun was setting, a now semi-drunk Hiatt Montgomery still sat at the table outside the restaurant.

"You going to spend the night out here?" the woman from the clothing store asked as she locked up her shop and spotted him.

"I might," he replied with a rare smile.

"May I join you?" the woman asked.

"Of course," Montgomery said as he managed to stand and pull out a chair. The woman was attractive enough, but Montgomery wouldn't have cared either way. He was more accustomed to paying for company, so the thought of a freebie appealed to him.

"You think your friend is coming back tonight?" she asked as she sat down.

"Who knows?" Montgomery said, feeling liberated from the chase since he was being forced to stay in Key West while Sims decided his fate. "Fuck him," Montgomery thought. "I'll stay here and have some fun."

"Where you staying?" the woman asked.

"Don't know yet," Montgomery replied as he laughed at his situation. "Maybe I'll sleep out here."

"Where are my manners?" he said as he waved down the waitress. "What would you like?" he asked the woman as the waitress approached the table.

"A beer's fine. Miller Lite?" she said as she smiled at the waitress she knew well.

"By the way, my name is Jill," the woman offered as she realized Montgomery had not yet inquired.

"I'm so sorry," Montgomery answered with genuine embarrassment. "I'm a little preoccupied lately and haven't quite relaxed yet. My name is Hiatt, and I appreciate you joining me." Montgomery lowered his dark sunglasses and smiled at the woman sheepishly.

"So, the dock attendant couldn't help you out?" Jill asked.

"Not really."

"He's fairly new," she explained. "The guy that runs the marina said your buddy has been coming down here for years. Used to come with his wife, but he thinks she died."

Montgomery was now a bit uncomfortable—afraid of being found out since he had no knowledge of McBride's personal life.

"Yeah, that was a shock," he said, hoping Jill had no knowledge that would contradict his guess.

"So, how long have you owned the store?" he asked in an effort to change the subject.

"About a year."

"You like it?"

"It's fun. I meet a lot of nice people, and I love the ocean."

"You want to eat dinner?" Montgomery asked.

"Sure!" Jill answered enthusiastically. "The food here is really good. They actually have a real chef back there." She pointed to the kitchen door.

The waitress showed up with another drink for Montgomery along with Jill's beer.

"What do you recommend?" Montgomery asked as she set down his drink.

"It's all good," the waitress said with a smile. "How hungry are you?"

"Very, but I don't want heavy food," he said.

"Maybe you could get a bunch of appetizers?" the waitress suggested.

"That sounds good," Montgomery's dinner date chimed in.

"That cowboy that was in here earlier ordered about everything," the waitress laughed.

"That must have been your friend," Jill said. "He was trying to catch up with that guy but missed him," she explained to the waitress.

"I'll hook up with him when he comes in tomorrow," Montgomery said.

"Oh, I don't think he's coming back anytime soon," the waitress said. "They were talking about going up the east coast to see some friends. Besides, they were pretty chummy. I don't think he will be anxious to have anybody else around, if you know what I mean. And I don't think that Victoria woman is going to let him off that boat," she snickered.

"She was a piece of work," Jill said. "And how about that hairdo? Looks like she cut it herself and dyed it in the back seat of the car. God, it was like she spray painted it black."

The women continued chatting about different single women they had encountered at the marina.

Montgomery sat contemplating what he'd heard. Was it possible that he had failed in his attempt to kill Victoria Niles, that she was the second rider in the woods, and that a few minutes before he arrived at the dock, she was sitting where he was now? These thoughts all fought for space in his mind. "Fuck me," he thought.

"You sure her name was Victoria?" he finally asked.

"Yeah," the waitress replied. "Your friend called her that several times. Those two are pretty sweet on each other, you know. Okay, will it be the appetizers, then?"

"You decide," Montgomery said to his new friend, not caring anymore about food.

"I'll order a few items if that's okay?"

"Hmm," he said, distracted. "That's fine." He was re-engaged mentally with the reason he had been sent to Key West in the first place.

"What time does the marina open?" he asked Jill.

"6:00 a.m."

"I think I'm going to rent a boat and go find my buddy," he said, forcing a friendly smile.

"Sounds like your buddy wants to be alone. If you want, you could stay at my place for a few days and wait for him," Jill suggested with a look that meant more than offering a free room.

Montgomery realized he had been propositioned. He was genuinely surprised and even a little moved by her offer.

"Maybe just tonight," he said, looking over the rim of his glass. "I really need to catch up to Sam."

"Let's eat and then we can walk from here. My place is only a few blocks away."

Montgomery managed to carry on a meaningless conversation, but his mind was elsewhere.

He thought about the reaction Sims would have when he found out Victoria's assassination likely failed. He wondered about McBride and what he knew. He wanted to go back to the Sims Lodge and interrogate Mercury, but he couldn't stand the thought of leaving the trail of McBride and Victoria, if it really was her.

AT THE WHITE HOUSE, President Niles sat in a meeting in the Oval Office with a few staff members as documents were organized. He was about to meet with Cochran, Reed, and other party leaders. The fact that he was an Independent president had complicated things in Washington. He needed friends in Congress if he was to have his reforms passed, but so far he had met with only crises and delays. He had decided to bring in the powers-that-be to have a frank and candid conversation. The election was now a distant memory, but nothing he had campaigned on had even been introduced. So far, he had tried to get cooperation through good relations, but he had been met with smiles and no action. Now, five months after his inauguration, he felt it was time for a more direct approach.

"Mr. President," Susan Mercury's voice announced through the President's intercom.

"Yes, Susan."

"Your appointment has arrived."

"Okay, send them in."

Reed, Cochran, and the others entered the Oval Office. "Please, Ladies, Gentlemen, make yourselves comfortable," the President urged as he directed them to the sofa and chairs across from his desk. The President pulled up a chair for himself in the circle.

"I realize we could have a long conversation about where we are, but I would like to get straight to the point since it is late in the day," he began. The President paused and drew a deep breath.

"I need to get my reform package out of committee and introduced for a vote," the President said. "That's what this meeting is about. We've had the election. Now it is time for us to govern. That's what we are sent here to do, and it's time to get to work."

Those seated exchanged glances as each wondered who would speak first. The President's conciliatory tone was not what they had planned on, so their prepared answers now seemed inappropriate. Congresswoman Dienhart cleared her throat in an effort to let the others know she was going to step forward and speak.

"We are not comfortable with the language in the bills, Mr. President."

"They deserve to be introduced and voted on," the President countered. "I have a responsibility to push the reforms I ran on. There are members in Congress who will step forward and sponsor this package. These bills deserve a vote."

"Frankly, sir, that is *your* problem," Congressman Diaz added.

"We aren't going to ever get along, are we?" the President asked.

"We simply don't agree," Cochran answered.

"Elections have meaning," the President countered.

"Yes, they do, Jackson," Cochran said in a friendly tone. "You are the President, but everyone in this room represents the American people, too."

The sound of ice settling in a bucket on the snack and drink cart momentarily drew everyone's attention.

"Okay," The President said as he returned to his desk chair. "The fact that I am not a member of either of your parties should not be a factor here, but it is now clear to me that's where we are."

The group stared at him silently.

"Legislation is a process, Jackson. Parties have nothing to do with it," Reed suggested.

"Then introduce the bills, and let's get on with it."

"Not likely," Cochran answered.

Niles stared at them. "You do remember that I carried nearly every state?" he asked.

No one responded.

"I can tell you that many of your colleagues are expressing interest in joining me in a new party based on my reforms," the President said without showing any signs of posturing.

"Horse shit," Speaker Reed chuckled.

"It seems that we should prepare for an ugly public battle over this then," the President declared. "If you want a public fight over this, you've got it."

"You'll lose," Cochran declared.

President Niles picked up a single sheet of paper. "Here is a poll on term limits for the House. It represents 75-percent public support".

The President picked up another piece of paper. "This one is about campaign finance reform. It comes in at 83-percent support. I have polls on my desk about education reform, flat taxes, state's rights, prison reform, inner city programs, equal pay, you name it. Every damned thing I ran on is polling over 72 percent, and you people won't act." The President dropped the papers on his desk and let out an exasperated sigh.

"My plan to redirect oil industry subsidies to an inner city mentoring program polls at 92 percent, and you fools won't even discuss it," the President nearly shouted as his face grew red. "Every single governor in the country has expressed support, but because the oil lobbyists own your sorry asses you stand in the way."

Niles walked to a pitcher of water and poured himself a drink. "You should be ashamed of yourselves," he said softly as he kept his back to the group. "I've tried to work with you, but I'm done."

Niles returned the chair he had pulled out earlier to its proper place and turned to face the group.

"Well, we still think you'll lose a public fight over all this crap," Cochran stated with a huff.

"Do you really think so, Hamilton?" the President asked. "I beat your candidate, and yours," he said to the other members of the group. "If we have to have another debate about this, it will come with my effort to get members of *your* parties to jump ship and join me. Your parties have run this country for a long time, and I won because people are pissed off with the job you've done.

"You want another round of gridlock? That's fine with me, but I'm going to weaken your numbers until you don't matter. I'll build a new party that's about getting all these reforms into law. And your parties will be marginalized into obscurity at your own hand," the president declared. "You want hard ball? I can play hard ball."

"There will be no vote on these bills until we all agree on the wording. Period," Cochran announced as he stood up. "If you want to work with us, then let's rewrite these damned things into something that makes sense. Otherwise, we're sitting tight." He headed for the door.

"I've been over this with you people enough," the President declared as he looked directly at Cochran and Reed. "It's time for action."

The President stood up and motioned the group toward the door. "Meeting's over."

They silently filed out without the usual exchange of pleasantries.

"You think he's serious about a public battle?" Congresswoman Dienhart asked as they walked along.

Reed stopped once they were out of the Oval Office and had reached a point safely away from the others. "Yes, I do" he said.

"Then turn up the heat," she suggested.

THE NEXT DAY, Jackson Niles was scheduled to hold his monthly press conference. Many thought he would send someone else, but to their surprise, the President was at the podium at the scheduled time.

"Good morning, members of the press corps," the President said, stepping to the microphone. He wore a black suit and many noticed that his usual crisp white button down shirt had been replaced with a dark gray shirt and black tie. The room had been noisy when he first entered but quickly turned silent. There was not a single empty chair, and reporters from around the world stood along the sides and the back of the room. Members of the press held mixed opinions about the reform package; many thought it was ill advised. Once the reporters quieted down, the President stepped closer to the podium.

"I want to do something a little different today," he began. "A lot has happened the last few days, so I'm going to let you ask questions right from the start. Who wants to go first?"

A surprised group of reporters sat around in shock for a moment, then nearly in unison jumped to their feet, clamoring for recognition.

"Mr. President, we all express our condolences over the death of your sister," said Charity Webber from *The Washington Post*. "We expected you to be unavailable today because of funeral arrangements. We appreciate you being here. Can you tell us when another nomination for the Court will be made?"

"Thank you for the expression of sympathy. My sister's funeral has already taken place at a private ceremony. I intend to announce another nominee in the next day or so."

"Mr. President, will you be choosing a VP this week, too?" another reporter, Vanessa Singleton from *Huff Post*, shouted.

"That nomination will also come in the next few days," he answered.

"Can you tell us who is being considered?" Porter followed up.

"Not at this time. We're still vetting the list. We are fairly sure where we're going, but we aren't ready to subject them to all the attention just yet," he smiled sadly.

"What about the reforms you campaigned on? When are they going to be introduced?" asked Bill Craig, a veteran from the *New York Times*, from the front row.

"Now that is the question I was hoping for," the President said, motioning for everyone to sit down. "Since I arrived here, I have tried to get cooperation from the two parties that run Congress. So far, those efforts have been met with stall tactics and, frankly, nonsense. In fact, I met with the leadership of both parties yesterday, and the meeting did not go well. The truth is, they refuse to introduce any of the bills.

"I warned my supporters that this might happen, and it has. The only way we'll ever get Congress to pass term limits on themselves or end the grotesque campaign financing system is if the people complain loudly."

"Who's the problem?" another reporter shouted. "Who, specifically, is holding things up?"

"The two parties are the problem. They tell their members how to vote, and that's that. Our nation's people may vote for a person to represent them, but once that representative reaches Washington, he's locked into his party's collective thinking. The two parties control the members of Congress. It's that simple." The President stepped back from the microphone and scanned the room for reaction.

"Comments like that aren't likely to help the cause," one of the reporters said.

"It can't get worse than it is," the President responded.

"How do you get past this?" another asked.

"The people must make their will known in no uncertain terms," the President declared forcefully. "Party leaders will not act until they fear for their positions. I know there are some in Congress who support my changes, and they have even expressed an interest in joining me in a new party. I wasn't planning on going in that direction, but if that's what it takes, then so be it." The President threw his hands in the air as a sign of exasperation.

"It's amazing and scary that these two parties would unite against an Independent president, don't you think?" he asked as he looked around the room.

The gathered reporters glanced at each other, recognizing that the situation in Washington was changing before their eyes. Some in the room were opposed to term limits, but nearly everyone was in favor of getting super PACs shut down.

"All of you have an obligation to put a microphone in the face of every elected official in this town," Niles continued. "They have an obligation to think for themselves and represent their districts. This ends today's press conference, but I will hold these every day, if necessary, until we get this Congress to act."

The President thanked the reporters and exited.

"That will set the two camps ablaze," he said to his press secretary as he returned to the West Wing.

Chief of Staff Anthony Sinclair followed the President into the Oval Office.

"If you had asked me, I would have advised against those statements," Sinclair said.

"I'm sure you would have," the President answered.

"What do you hope to accomplish with a tone like that?"

"A reaction," the President answered. "The parties are more fractured than they know."

"It sounds as if there are things happening that I'm not privy to," Sinclair said with both frustration and a touch of anger. "I should be kept in the loop if I am to do this job."

"There are many in this Congress who support my changes," the President said. "They call me directly. They're tired of party leadership always leaning on them to vote a certain way. They recognize that it's time for a new direction."

The President sat down in his desk chair and motioned for Sinclair to take a seat across from him. "I'm not going to lose this fight," the President said.

"Jackson, I think it is more than a little unwise to force a public fight at this time," Sinclair cautioned.

"I disagree."

"You are an Independent. These people have been here a long, long time. We need them if we are going to get anything done. Anything at all," Sinclair said, his voice rising.

"They are perfectly happy with gridlock," Niles said.

"We have to be patient," Sinclair pleaded. "We can't come here and piss everybody off."

"I've been patient for a few months. That didn't work, so now it's time for action. If people get their feelings hurt, that's too damned bad. Your advice is needed and desired, but the final call is mine. This is my presidency."

Sinclair said nothing as he left. He was not prone to rash behavior and did not feel comfortable in such settings. He did not like this side of Nile's personality and was surprised to see it so early. "This will get ugly," he grumbled to himself as he walked down the hall. "What a stupid move!"

THAT MORNING, Hiatt Montgomery awoke to the sounds of sea birds.

The night before, he eventually quieted his mind about Victoria and Sam and instead enjoyed an evening of eating and drinking at the marina restaurant. He and Jill had made their way to her house and then to her bedroom. Now, he tried to quietly gather his clothes and make it to the door. Normally, he would be throwing a couple hundred bucks on the nightstand and making as much noise as he wanted, but this morning he didn't want the woman to wake up. He surprised himself as he turned and left a short note thanking her for a "lovely evening."

When he reached the marina, Montgomery decided it was time to make the call he was dreading. His contact, whom he had never met, listened but offered no emotional response to the news. He was quizzed over and over again regarding McBride and Victoria and then was told to wait for instructions. He took a cab to the airport to be close to his plane when the call came. An hour or so later a call came directly from Sims.

"What kind of a fuck-up are you?" Sims screamed. "You blew up her fucking condo, and she wasn't even there! God damn it! I've dispatched a helicopter. It'll probably be two hours before they reach you."

Sims calmed some, but his voice was still agitated. "When it gets there, you find that boat, and you end those two once and for all. Are we absolutely crystal clear?"

His voice rose again. Sims was about to blow a fuse. "I can't believe that woman is alive, and she hasn't shown up on CNN telling her bullshit story. You are damned lucky, pal. Damned lucky her brother is such a pussy that he has her hiding out with that cowboy. Find them and kill them."

Montgomery looked around the little airport for a place to sit out the wait.

AT SIMS' OFFICE, the infuriated conspirator paced back and forth contemplating his next moves.

"This is bullshit. Why don't we end this shit now. What the hell are we waiting on?" he said out loud as he sat down at his desk and rubbed his face. "We're playing with fire with this guy."

Sims stood and wiped a few flakes of dust off his suit of armor.

BY NOON, SAM HAD crisscrossed his boat around the area of Marathon and was now pulling into a small marina.

"We'll fuel up and get some lunch here," he told Victoria as she slipped on an orange and white t-shirt.

"Where will we go after that?" she asked as she spotted the small dockside bar.

"I don't know. I'm making this up as we go."

The little bar sat bayside and clearly had been added onto over the years. The outside eating deck spanned three different levels, and the inside looked like an old converted house.

"Let's sit outside," Victoria suggested when she spotted a table off by itself under a large, ocean blue umbrella with giant turtles printed on the underside. As they approached, Sam's cell phone rang. It was his old friend Charlie, finally getting back to him.

"I need to take this," Sam said. "Get me some kind of fruit drink." He walked away to talk privately.

"Hey, Charlie," Sam said.

"Sam, this lodge is like a little international airport. There are jets flying in and out of here all day long."

"Have you got any pictures yet?" Sam asked.

"Not yet. I'm waiting on some equipment. We did get close enough this morning to check the front of the place with a pair of binoculars. Shit, Sam, there are guys walking around with machine guns hanging off their shoulders. I get your point about the danger."

"If you want to leave, it's okay," Sam said.

"Not a chance. Me and the guys are loving this," Charlie admitted with a youthful laugh. "I'll start getting you pictures later today."

"Thank you, Charlie, and be careful."

"Everything okay?" Victoria asked as Sam returned to the table.

"Yes, a little ranch business is all," he said. Sam didn't have any real reason to keep Charlie's activities secret other than he didn't want Victoria thinking about all that stuff. She was relaxed and having fun, and he wanted to keep it that way.

"Did you order drinks?" Sam asked.

"Something called a mango tango or something like that," Victoria laughed.

A few moments later the waitress returned with two oversized goblets filled with a frozen yellow concoction and fruit hanging over the side of the glass.

"Next time, I'll order the drinks," Sam said, smiling as he inspected the overflowing glass of juice and fruit.

"Oh my gosh, this is fantastic," Victoria said as she drank though the curly straw.

"After we eat, let's take a long walk before we get back on the boat," Sam suggested as they scanned the menu.

"Did you see that giant chess board when we came in?" Victoria asked.

"Yeah, I saw it."

"Do you remember that chess set we had at Yale?"

"Of course I do," Sam replied, his smile revealing that he knew what was coming.

"I don't remember you ever winning a single game."

"Oh that's BS," Sam replied with a laugh knowing she was probably right.

The breeze picked up for a moment, and Sam quickly grabbed the napkins before they blew away.

"Good reflexes," Victoria quipped.

"After lunch you're in trouble, lady," Sam predicted with a wink as he looked at the giant chess set. "I probably should have asked you how often you play before saying that."

"I play ... *and taught* ... weekly," Victoria confessed, trying to hold back her confidence.

"Taught?"

"At the Boys and Girls Club in Harlem."

"When did you start doing that?" Sam asked, both surprised and impressed.

"One of my law partners started a program there, I don't know, probably 30 years ago, and I helped out a little at first. Then I just got completely absorbed by the program."

"Wow that's very cool, and I think I'm in trouble with my challenge."

Victoria smiled knowing full well that Sam was indeed in trouble unless he had also been playing regularly.

"I've seen lives changed by just a few hours a week of people giving of their time," she added.

Victoria looked out at the ocean and took in a deep breath.

"You've changed lives," Sam stated. He could tell Victoria was as proud of herself as he was of her.

"We have a partner at our firm now who was one of the kids I taught years ago."

"Tell me more," Sam urged.

"I met this girl who was only about eight at the time. She was so shy and backward she wouldn't even look me in the eye at first. Her dad was not in her life, and her mom worked three jobs just to barely get by. Her brothers came, too, but I only interacted with Tammy at first."

Victoria paused and bit her lip as she looked back out at the crashing waves. "She was so smart and nobody knew it," she added as her eyes filled with tears.

Sam had put down his fork and was now fully focused on the emotion he saw in Victoria.

"I started working with her, and I realized how deep her talent was. I couldn't stop with chess or with just her. It turned out her brothers were just as smart. Today, she's a partner in the firm. One of her brothers is an engineer, and the other owns a restaurant in Manhattan."

Victoria took a drink of her water and paused as the waiter inquired about the quality of the food.

"We're fine," Sam responded without taking his eyes off of Victoria.

"Has Jackson discussed his 'Inner City Mentors' program with you?"

"A little" Sam answered.

"I've pleaded with him for that one."

Sam was reminded of his earliest encounters with Victoria at Yale. He was in awe of this brilliant, loving woman. And while this story didn't surprise him, he was no less moved.

"You amaze me."

"Those kids would amaze you," Victoria said.

"Who would be the mentors?"

Victoria held her fork up, motioning to Sam that she needed to finish her bite of salad before she could respond.

"They would be paid. Former teachers, military vets, athletes, policeman, and retired professionals—you name it. But they would be paid, and we would fund the program by ending subsidies for industries that don't even need the money."

A large group being seated across the patio caused a commotion that interrupted Victoria's thought.

"I'm sorry I get emotional about this."

"It's fine—I want you to continue," Sam prompted.

"We have to break the cycle of poverty in our inner cities. But it won't happen without intervention. There are brilliant kids and average kids who all need a chance. If we intervene in the lives of an entire generation, then we can change what has become the norm."

They each took a few bites of their salads as Victoria cut the fresh bread and passed a piece to Sam.

"Eventually you get to a jobs problem," Sam said.

"Yes, you do, and that brings us to Jackson's plan for the 're-industrialization' of America."

"Which means what?"

"Robotics has evolved to the point where all those industries lost to cheap labor could be brought back. The end users are here, and transportation costs are high. We can produce electronics, textiles, and consumer goods here using robotics. The jobs created would be in programming, maintenance, etc. There would be hundreds of thousands of good jobs created if we brought those industries home."

"You two have talked about this?"

"It takes vision, leadership, and the right tax policies to get the entrepreneurs enthusiastic about this new form of manufacturing. But it's a huge job source and a good one. Jackson and I don't believe businesses should be taxed at all. Every company in the world would come here if we had such an environment. Jobs would be so abundant we would have to get our inner cities cleaned up so the demand would be met. Bring these two ideas together, and the mentors have a real, tangible direction to show these kids. We *can* change the world, you know."

Victoria laughed as she ended her sermon.

"You are still an amazing woman," Sam said.

"And I'm going to kick your ass in our chess match," Victoria said, pointing her fork at Sam.

"Yeah, I kinda figured that out a half hour ago."

They finished their salads and bread and then walked down the steps toward the chess tables.

Four moves into the game, Sam stood staring at his lost cause on the board. "Some things never change," he declared as he leaned over the table and pushed his king down. "Let's take a walk."

They browsed a few shops and bought some bottled water before strolling through a residential area across from the marina.

"I think I could live in a place like this after this is over," Victoria said spontaneously.

"Maybe in the winter," Sam agreed. "But I would have to be in Montana in the summers."

"That goes without saying, Mr. McBride."

"But you love Montana now, right?" Sam asked.

"I do. Is that important?" Victoria smiled.

"Let's get through this mess," Sam answered, squeezing her hand.

"I've noticed a few screened in gardens in some back yards."

"Are you a gardener?" Sam asked in surprise.

"Katie promised to teach me."

By mid-afternoon, they were back on the boat and heading out.

"Where are we off to?" Victoria asked as Sam started the engines.

"There are a cluster of tiny islands up the way," he said. "We can dock for the night in a little cove and hang out on a small private beach tomorrow. It will give you another day with earth under your feet," Sam said, remembering her earlier comment about her water fears.

"That sounds like a perfect day," Victoria replied. "What else is out there?"

"Nothing, it's a tiny little uninhabited island. We should have the place to ourselves."

IN WASHINGTON, Jackson Niles came down the West Wing hall after taking a quick 15-minute break in the family quarters. The day had been filled with a parade of Washington bureaucrats calling or visiting to express their dismay at his comments at the press conference. The President knew he was kicking at a hornet's nest when he made the comments, but playing nice got him nowhere. "Let's see who bitches the loudest," he thought.

"Mr. President," Susan Mercury called on the intercom. "Sir, may I speak with you about a personal matter?"

"Of course. By all means, come in."

As she entered, the President moved to greet her at the door. "What's on your mind?" he asked as they sat together on the sofa across from his desk.

"Mr. President, I've tried to never bring my personal life to the office, especially considering where I work," she said with a tearful chuckle.

"Susan, it's okay. It's only you and me here. I'm just Jackson now," he told her as he placed his hand on her shoulder. "What's going on?"

"It's Peter. I think something is wrong," she said, holding back tears. "He left a few days ago for a story he's working on, and I haven't heard from him. He isn't answering his phone, and that's not like him. Even when he goes somewhere out of cell range, he always finds a way to get word to me that he's okay. To hear nothing is—well—this has never happened before."

"Where did he go?"

"Out west is all I know," Susan replied.

"Have you tried his editor?"

"I've left a message, but I've heard nothing back," Susan said. "Usually the paper doesn't even know where he is. He does his own thing. That's the deal they made."

"Susan, I will instruct my Secret Service detail to find him," the President told her as he gave her shoulder a squeeze.

"Jackson, I can't ask you to do that."

"They are the best there is, Susan. They have access to everything they need. It might take a day or two, but they will find him," the President assured her. "We've been together a long time. This is about friendship, Susan. They will track him down."

"Hopefully they don't scare him when they come swooping in," he added with a laugh.

Susan smiled and managed a small laugh of her own at the thought of a secret service team showing up wherever Peter was. "I hope he doesn't get mad at me for this," she added as she stood up.

"It will be fine. These guys are discreet and smart. They won't blow things up for him," he assured her.

"Thank you, Jackson," Susan whispered as she gave the President a hug when she reached the door.

"It's not a problem," he assured her.

As soon as Susan left the room, Jackson immediately made a call regarding Peter.

"We'll get him," the man on the other end of the line said.

HIATT MONTGOMERY HAD fallen asleep in the corner of the airport.

"Are you Mr. Montgomery?" a young female airport attendant asked, waking him up.

"Yes," he said, rubbing sleep from his eyes.

"There is a helicopter outside that just landed. The pilot is looking for you," she said.

"Okay, thanks," Montgomery replied as he picked up his bags and headed for the exit.

On the tarmac, a black helicopter sat running. The pilot waved to Montgomery, then pointed at his wrist indicating that time was of the essence. Montgomery jogged to the craft and jumped up into the rear of the chopper.

"Your target just used a credit card at a shop in Marathon," the pilot explained in shouts as Hiatt boarded. "We need to move. It's a short trip. Get your weapon ready."

Montgomery opened his bag, took out a small case with a disassembled sniper rifle, and quickly assembled and loaded it.

"Who is this guy?" the pilot asked as he looked back at Montgomery.

"He's the fucking target," Montgomery shouted back as he gave the pilot an angry stare. "Fly the fucking bird."

The pilot raced across the sky and soon was over Marathon.

"Let's look south from here. I suspect he's heading for some open water," Montgomery advised the pilot. "His boat is a 52-foot sport fisher. I think it's a Grady White."

The pilot dropped down to get a closer look at two boats off the coast of Marathon.

"Those are too small," Montgomery shouted, looking out the open side door on the pilot's side. "There," he shouted, pointing to a large vessel cruising south about 15 miles off the coast. "Go down close for a look."

The pilot turned the chopper and pointed it straight toward the path of the boat. He dropped down low enough for Montgomery to make a visual identification. As they came close to Sam's boat, Victoria emerged from the galley in time to look up and see Montgomery's bleached blond hair blowing in the wind. Everything moved in slow motion as he stared at the woman with the black hair described by the waitress and she stared back at the man she had come to know as Hiatt Montgomery.

"It's him," Victoria shouted to Sam as she ran back to the cabin.

"What?" Sam asked, unsure what she was talking about.

"That helicopter out there. Montgomery is in that helicopter," she yelled as she pointed skyward.

Sam jumped off his chair and stuck his head out of the cabin in time to see Montgomery raise his rifle.

"Get below," he screamed as he rushed back in and headed for the lower galley. Sam opened a cabinet next to the bed and pulled out the biggest rifle Victoria had ever seen.

"Stay down," he commanded as he loaded the gun.

"Sam, for God's sake, please, stay down here. He can't land that thing out here," she pleaded.

"He'll try to shoot our tank if we sit still," Sam replied, pulling back the lever on the gun and loading the first bullet. "But he's hunting the wrong guy!" Sam stepped up into the cabin.

Montgomery's first shot blew out the window on the far side of the cabin, across from Sam.

"He's guessing where I am," Sam thought as he waited. He knelt down and used the now missing window as a shooting port for his rifle. Through his high-powered scope he could clearly see the pilot looking down toward the boat. Sam's first shot struck the tail of the craft, sending a trail of smoke into the air.

"What the fuck?" the pilot screamed at Montgomery as his ability to control the craft became much harder. "You're running out of time, pal!" Before he could reposition the chopper for a second shot, Sam fired again, striking the pilot in the chest. The craft spun as the dead pilot slumped over the controls. Sam reloaded and fired another shot, hoping to get lucky and hit Montgomery. The chopper moved further and further away and finally crashed into the water.

"Victoria, stay down below until we get a safe distance from here," Sam called down to the galley. "The helicopter is down. Unless another one shows, we're safe for now. I'm going to get moving as fast as possible. Stay down there and hang on." He pushed the throttle down and sped away from the area.

In the distance, an explosion occurred. He was not going to stick around to see if Montgomery survived. Either way, he knew they had to get moving.

"I used that card three hours ago. They found us that fast," Sam thought as he sped along.

Below deck, a despondent Victoria curled up on the bed in disbelief at the ongoing pursuit. "I can't take any more of this!" she cried hysterically. The roar of the engines drowned out her

constant cries. Any thoughts she may have harbored of
returning to her old life drained out with the tears. "I'm done
with this," she groaned as she cried. "I'm never going back.
Never." She screamed over and over as the boat sped along.

A few hours later when Sam finally slowed the boat,
Victoria looked out to see the Miami skyline.

"We're going to leave the boat at the marina here and
borrow a car from a friend and get away," Sam said. "They may
find my boat, but we're getting off the water. We're sitting
ducks out there."

"Let's go to the police," Victoria cried out from below. "This
is all ridiculous. I need to tell them who I am and explain what
happened. We can't keep running. It's crazy. I can't take any
more of this, Sam. I can't. I can't."

Victoria threw clothes and other items into bags. "I'm sick
of this. I can't take any more. Let's call the FBI or the police.
Please, Sam, I can't take any more of this. I can't. I'm going
nuts. I can't do this. Please, Sam!"

Hysterical, Victoria climbed the steps to the cockpit and
plopped down in the chair across from Sam.

"We can't do that," he answered.

"Why not?" Victoria said desperately.

Sam shut off the boat and turned his chair to face her. "This
is going to get a little more complicated," he said as he clasped
his hands together and brought them up to his mouth. He took
a deep breath as he looked at Victoria with the most serious
expression she had seen yet.

"What is it, Sam?" she asked through her tears. "What's
going on?"

"I had hoped things would not come to this," he said with
another deep breath.

Worried what she was about to hear, but having no idea
what Sam was thinking, Victoria waited for him to continue.

"Greystone," Sam said.

"Greystone? What are you talking about?" she asked, her
voice quivering.

"Jackson knows about your involvement with Greystone. He
knew if there were any serious troubles with your nomination,

it might come out. But he wanted to take the risk because of your skills and beliefs as a judge."

"What the hell are you talking about?" she screamed as she began to sob. "What else are you keeping from me? What else do you know? God damn it, Sam, I'm 'dead,' and they are still trying to kill me. I can't take any more of this."

Victoria tore apart her bags, separating her items from Sam's.

"I'm serious, I'm leaving. I'm going to a police station. I don't care anymore."

Sam stood in silence, unsure of what to say next.

"Jackson was approached some time ago to join the Greystone Board," he finally began. "It was before he announced his campaign for President. They thought he would jump at the chance, but they were wrong. He got angry over the thing and made some comments that he probably shouldn't have made. That's when they told him about your involvement. They showed him proof."

Victoria teared up.

"Then why would he nominate me?"

"Because he intends to change the laws that allow those kind of people to go free. Afterward he was going to circle back and get all those places closed up and keep the whole thing quiet. He didn't think your nomination would spark the reaction it did," Sam explained.

"Your brother believes you belong on the bench. But he was stunned to find out you were involved in the Greystone operation. He's not stupid. He understands the reasons. He thinks the laws should change, too. But hell, we can't have people operating secret prisons. For God's sake, Victoria, what the hell were you thinking?" Sam asked with a combination of disappointment and compassion.

"You don't understand what it's like seeing those creeps walk free. The system is broken," she said as she rubbed her hands across her face. "I couldn't stand against that system. It's been around for a long time."

Victoria felt the weight of Sam's disapproval. "I knew it was wrong," she confessed.

"It gets worse," Sam said softly.

Victoria looked at him with dread.

"Sims is on the Board. He's the one who approached Jackson. He has the file on you. Jackson didn't believe he would disclose your involvement because he had the same info on Sims. It never occurred to him that he would resort to killing you."

A passing sailboat glided by quietly as it came up behind Victoria. It startled her at first as she heard the sound of the sails flapping in the wind. The couple onboard waved with big smiles, catching Victoria off guard as she struggled to raise her hand and smile.

"If you go to the police, Sims will arrange for your involvement to be made public. Sims himself would likely disappear or claim he was a mole. The fact is, you are going to have to remain dead until Jackson gets Greystone cleaned up. Otherwise, you're going to go to prison. I'm sorry, Victoria."

Victoria didn't move or say a word. A large flock of seabirds flew low across the water. Their constant squawking was amplified by the dead silence she felt. A slight gust of wind along with the wake produced by a far off yacht shook Sam's boat enough that Victoria's eyes lifted from the passing flock and met Sam's.

"He knew the nomination was a big risk, but he thought he could navigate it. He thought you would be confirmed," Sam said. "Then he would change some laws and Greystone would go away quietly. The Board would be dealt with, and everyone would forget it ever happened. That was the plan. But when the condo exploded, he knew that whomever Sims answers to was not going to allow the nomination to go through."

Sam put his hands on Victoria's shoulders. "We can get through this," he whispered as he hugged her.

"So all this is about Greystone?"

"No, not at all. Greystone is an unfortunate coincidence. Jackson's agenda is the real issue," he said. "His changes will cost a lot of people power and money, and that's what's causing the real problems. Jackson thinks Sims was counting on the Court challenges to stop the reforms, but when he nominated you, that effectively cut them off before they could play that card. So with you on the bench, assuming Jackson can get the reforms passed, there will be nothing to stop them from being implemented."

The large flock of birds circled back as the water calmed and the slight rocking of the boat subsided. As the boat settled, Victoria noticed a dragonfly that had landed next to her earlier had now returned. "Even this bug can come and go as it pleases, but not me," she thought as she silently considered her predicament.

"Sims and his group didn't see your nomination coming. I suppose because of Greystone. But when Jackson nominated you, they knew you would support his programs if they reached the Court. So, they freaked out and thought they killed you," Sam explained. "They may have been shooting at me a few hours ago, but I suspect they now know you are still alive. They are afraid you'll go public, but Jackson can't save a family member from prosecution over Greystone without losing all credibility. So you have to stay quiet ... and dead."

Sam sat down again and opened a bottle of water.

Victoria tried to process all she had heard. "Let me have a drink of that," she said as her trembling hand reached out.

"Keep it," he said as he handed it over. "Jackson had already decided to run when Sims approached him about the board position. Then he found out about you. Jackson has strong, rich, and powerful supporters. But they are crystal clean. They would be horrified by what your group has done. Jackson had already agreed to run as an Independent. Money had already been raised, and Miller was already being pressured to join the campaign as the vice presidential candidate." Sam was now resigned to tell her everything.

A helicopter passing in the distance startled them both. "It's a news chopper," Sam said, trying to assure himself as much as Victoria as he squinted toward the helicopter.

"Jackson didn't want to jump ship, but he knew if he continued, Greystone was going to have to be dealt with immediately. He thought he could get it done and make it all go away."

Sam opened another water bottle for himself and walked to the back of the boat and sat down. It was now a beautiful evening, and the boat rocked gently in the bay. The evening air had calmed them both, and the soothing aroma of salt air had settled over Victoria.

"So is it all the reforms that are causing this?" Victoria asked, no longer sure what was true.

"It's a lot of things," Sam answered. "Many of the people who provided his initial financial support disapprove of most of what the two parties have done for the last eighty years or so. It's about power and money, same as always, you know?" Sam smiled at Victoria, who was still recovering from all she'd heard.

"Jackson thinks the two parties are too powerful at all levels. He wants them pissed off so they overreact. His supporters aren't a unanimous group, but most think the parties have run things into the ground and they need to go," Sam said. "Jackson intends to get under their skin and see if he can fracture them. If he can, he'll introduce a plan to pass term limits in the House and a restrictive campaign finance law. He wants to get the money out of the House. It's kind of a subtle thing, but he opposes the 'group think' they impose on their members."

"So what do we do now?" Victoria asked.

"I've got a good friend not far from here. He can get me a chunk of cash, which is all we'll use from here on. I'm going to cut up those damned cards so I don't accidentally use one again. Then we're going to take off and disappear."

"Is it dangerous for us to call Jackson?" she asked.

"Absolutely. We don't know who's listening. Let's go underground, so to speak, and let Jackson do his thing," Sam suggested. "We broke the trail when the chopper went down. If they're still looking, they'll find the boat, but the trail will end there. We only use cash, and we keep moving. We'll stay only in low-profile places. This will end eventually."

Sam laid back and looked at the sky. "We disappear," he repeated as Victoria wiped tears from her eyes.

"I'm tired, Sam," Victoria said. "I'm tired of being chased. There are a million boats in this bay. Can't we stay here for a while?" she asked.

"I think we're safe here for the night."

After several minutes of silence, Victoria took a deep breath and shifted in her seat.

"Katie told me about that day," Victoria finally said.

"I know."

"You should have talked to me that night. You should have given me a chance to understand." Victoria let out a sad sigh. "You hurt me so badly."

Sam fidgeted with his water bottle. Victoria wasn't making eye contact with him, which made the exchange easier for him. But it also made him feel small.

"You scared me," Sam finally muttered.

"I scared you?" Victoria asked.

"I was in love with a girl I had known since I was nine years old," Sam said softly as he tried to face her. "I didn't come to college looking for someone else."

Victoria sat up and faced him.

"I didn't know there were women in this world like you," he said, trying to choke back the emotion. "Sarah hadn't grown over the years. I didn't see it until I met you. She was a part of Sam-and-Sarah, but there was no Sarah. I never even contemplated meeting someone who would make me want to be somewhere else."

He drew a long breath.

"I was afraid," Sam confessed.

Victoria's face went blank. "If you had explained things and held me all night, I would have had some closure," Victoria finally said.

"If I had told you the night before, would you have wanted me to hold you?" Sam quietly asked.

"I deserved closure, Sam."

Sam felt her words cut through him.

The boat rocked gently as each sat in silence. The occasional splash hinted at marine predators feeding nearby, but the darkness covered their movements.

"Do you remember the night we both realized we had fallen in love?" he finally asked.

"At your fraternity dance," she said with a pained smile as she brushed her hair back.

"We were sitting at a round table off to the side of the dance floor. You had on a maroon dress with a diamond cut design across the back. I remember you complaining that the shoes you had on didn't match the color of your dress. You had on those silver loop earrings I bought you that you loved so much."

Sam chuckled sadly as he relived the moment.

"I still have them," Victoria admitted, tears streaming down her face.

"I was watching the others on the dance floor, but I could feel you looking at me. It felt good," Sam said.

Victoria shifted in her seat. Sam's detailed descriptions drew out her own memories of the night.

"All of a sudden I heard you say 'I love you.'" Sam's head dropped as he said the words. "Sarah didn't even cross my mind. God I loved you so much."

Victoria sat in shock.

"Every year since then, when the leaves start to change, I relive that moment. It still seems like yesterday to me," Sam added.

A long silence settled over them as they each remembered not only that night but also the years that had passed.

"You never had closure either," Victoria finally whispered, with compassion.

"I didn't want it. I didn't deserve it."

Victoria felt an end of the hurt she had carried for so long. The change was palpable and powerful. For a moment, she grew hot as the years of resentment left her completely.

"There were times I used to curl up in bed and cry, long after you left," she whispered, feeling embarrassed by her admission. "There were nights I would have sworn I could feel your spirit there with me. It was so real."

Sam knew he had missed her as much.

"I can't believe I'm hearing this from you, Sam," she said with love in her voice and tears rolling down her face.

"Sarah never had all of me," Sam finally said with deep sorrow. "I felt guilty at first, but after a while I realized I was paying the price for having walked away like I did. I thought saving her was right. She was my best friend growing up, but you are my other half." Sam stopped to wipe away his tears.

"I'm so sorry," his voice cracked as his emotions burst past his ability to control them.

"We have to try us again," Victoria finally said as Sam grew quiet.

"Can you forgive me?"

"I already have," Victoria said, standing and approaching him.

Sam drew a deep breath as her words helped him regain his composure.

"Can we start by just holding each other all night?" Sam asked hesitantly as he wrapped his arms around her.

"It's been a long time, Sam," Victoria replied as she contemplated his offer.

"Let's hold each other tonight," Sam whispered as he pulled her closer.

THAT SAME DAY at the Sims Lodge, the door to Peter Mercury's little basement room swung open, and a voice commanded him to come out.

"Where am I going?" Peter asked as a bald, muscular man grabbed his arm and led him toward the stairs.

"Fresh air time," the man responded, leading Peter out the front door. "Walk around if you want. But if you run, you get the whip again. Understand?"

Peter nodded. He had no interest in going through that again. He shuffled around the grassy area in front of the lodge for a while and then sat down on the ground. Eventually, he stretched out and lay back on the soft grass. The clean mountain air and the sunlight were refreshing, and Peter closed his eyes in an attempt to relax. His mind was tired of trying to figure things out, and he had determined asking questions was a bad idea.

"So I wait," he reasoned.

After thirty minutes or so, another man approached Peter. He was more fat than stocky, and his slicked back hair and black suit screamed "gangster." As he looked up, Peter noticed the man's pants weren't snapped at the top. The belt was holding them closed, but his belly had obviously grown beyond this pair's ability to close. Peter couldn't help but sneer. He had confronted many guys like him in New York over the years, and this character was as out of place in Montana as a cowboy in Manhattan.

"I read your report, or whatever the hell that bullshit is," the guy said. "I think you're holding back on us. Answer my questions honestly, and this all goes much easier for you. Hell, I don't want to beat you up. Shit, man, your back looks like Montgomery cut you up with a sword or something. Good thing that psycho got tired, or he might have killed you that night."

The man walked back to the porch. "Come up here, Peter," he said as he took a seat. "Sit down."

Peter took a seat in a rocking chair next to the man. The wind had picked up and the breeze felt refreshing on Peter's face. The air had a sweetness to it as the aroma of wild flowers wafted across the porch. Peter watched as a pair of western meadowlarks sat singing on a nearby fencepost.

"That wind probably means some rain is coming, but it sure is peaceful out here isn't it?" the man in the black suit said to Peter, as if they were just two men enjoying the afternoon.

The words brought Peter back to his predicament. "It would be."

"Look I'm not much into this "interrogating prisoner business," but I have a job to do. So here goes," the man said. "Who rescued you from the woods? Think hard before you open that mouth. I can't protect you if you lie."

"Some guy named Sam, I think."

"Some guy named Sam?"

"Yes. He's a local rancher. He picked me up in a stream. I was in bad shape, in and out of consciousness. He took me somewhere and bandaged me up. I was hallucinating a little bit, and when the infection set in, I lost consciousness and woke up in a hospital." Peter maintained eye contact the entire time and seemed believable enough to his interrogator.

"Who else was with him?"

"Nobody. At least I don't think so. He had another horse that was carrying supplies, but I don't remember seeing anybody, else," Peter said, staring straight at the man.

"You told Montgomery you were out here looking for Langley?" the man said, switching gears.

"Yes. Langley had been acting weird, and I thought it was odd he would take time off so early in the new President's term, so I came out here on a hunch to see what he was up to."

"Wait here," the man said.

Peter sat on the porch, looking around to see if he was being watched. It had started to rain, and Peter noticed guards who had been invisible to him pulling on ponchos. The number of men he saw surprised him. Clearly making a break for it was not an option.

"The boss thinks you're lying," the man said as he came back out. "We can't whip your ass. That's a given. You ever been water boarded?"

"What?" Peter yelled as he jumped up. "Are you insane? I'm a reporter. What the hell are you guys up to?"

"Shut up!" the man growled as he slapped Peter with the back of his hand. Peter tumbled backwards and then raised his hand to his lip to reveal blood.

"Come on," the man said, grabbing Peter by the hair and dragging him back into the lodge. When they got to the basement door, the man threw Peter down the stairs. He landed hard and lay there for a moment as he heard the man walk down the stairs.

"Get in there," he commanded as he pushed Peter into a room with a table in the middle and a sink off to one side.

"Get on the table. Get on the fucking table," he screamed as he grabbed Peter by the arm and swung him around and onto the table. Peter fought back, but the man punched him repeatedly in the face until he was so dazed he couldn't resist. The man strapped down Peter's arms and legs, then put a towel over his face.

"Show time, Mr. Reporter," the man laughed as he jerked Peter's head back.

Peter heard the door open, and a second man entered the room. He couldn't see him, but the man wore a dark suit with a starched white shirt and red tie. He was taller than most of the other men at the lodge and possessed a confident and intense demeanor.

"I'll take it from here," the man announced. Peter heard the other man say, "Yes, sir," as the door closed behind him. The new man's voice seemed familiar but he was unable to place him.

"I know it's not Montgomery's voice," Peter thought as he sought some comfort. The new man grabbed Peter's head and started pouring water down his nose. Within seconds, Peter was choking and screaming as he felt the sensation of drowning.

"You mother fuckers," he screamed in between coughs. Peter was pushed back down and the process repeated until he was nearly choking to death. The man then slipped a black cloth bag over Peter's head and violently dragged him out of the room and back up the stairs.

The man led Peter out the door, then out of the lodge and into a vehicle as Peter coughed and gasped for air.

"Lie down," the man said.

Peter heard the driver get in, and they took off. The driver said nothing as the car drove rapidly along the lodge's long drive. Peter felt the transition as the car turned onto a primary road and began traveling at a normal pace. After what seemed like an hour or so, Peter felt the car turn onto a rough road and drive along at a much slower pace. The road was bumpy, and Peter was hard pressed to keep himself on the seat.

"This asshole is going to take me out in the woods and kill me," Peter finally concluded. He thought about Susan and their children. Now resigned to his pending death, Peter managed to smile at the life they had had together and the fact that he had lived long enough to hold his grandbaby.

"We had such a good time," he thought as the car lumbered on. "But, damn, I didn't think I would die like this." He fought off the picture of Susan being alone.

"Fuck this. I have to try and fight off this guy," he suddenly decided. Peter swung his legs up and managed to kick the driver in the side of the head.

"What the hell are you doing, you dumb ass?" the driver yelled.

"Fuck you!" Peter screamed as he swung his feet wildly at the driver's side of the front seat. The car came to an abrupt stop as he heard the car door open.

"Come here, Mercury, you maniac," the driver said as he pulled Peter out and pulled the hood off Peter's head.

"Langley!" Peter shouted. "You fucking traitor mother fucker!"

"Oh, settle down," Langley said as he untied Peter's hands and stepped back. "You okay?"

"What? Fuck no, I'm not okay, you shit. You water boarded me. What the hell is this? What are we doing out here? Is this where the fucking FBI director takes people to shoot them, you fucking piece of shit!" Peter turned to run.

"Will you settle down, for God's sake? If I planned to kill you, you would already be dead. Calm down," Langley insisted. He lit a cigarette and walked over and sat down on a stump.

"You're fucking things up by being out here," Langley said.

"What?" Peter said, still not sure if he should run away or try to hit Langley.

"What the hell made you come out to the lodge, anyway?" Langley asked as he took a long drag off the cigarette.

"Are we having some kind of normal conversation?" Peter asked with disgust and astonishment. "Because an hour ago you almost drowned me, you. . . "

"Yeah, get over that, will you?" Langley interrupted. "I had to or they would have done it worse and then beat you to death afterwards. I saved your life, you dumb ass. But now I need to figure out how long to hide you."

"Hide me?!"

"Will you settle the fuck down before somebody hears you?" Langley said with growing impatience.

Peter walked in circles, thinking about the events of the last few days. The open, grassy area where they had stopped stood out from the surrounding woods, which was dense and rocky. Peter, now relaxing a little, looked up as an eagle flying overhead shrieked. The wind blew lightly, filling the area with the sweet, fresh aroma of the surrounding pines. Langley's exhale contrasted rudely with the fresh scent, reminding Peter how much he hated the smell of cigarettes.

"What the hell is going on?" Peter finally asked.

"Can't tell you much," Langley said as he smashed the cigarette under his foot. "Less you know the better for now, but I'm sure you will get the exclusive when this is over."

"When what is over? Damn it, tell me what's going on."

"Can't do that. But let's just say you've got friends in high places," Langley smirked.

"What was that shit in the park?" Peter asked, showing his anger.

"You mean when that psycho Montgomery shot that woman?" Langley asked, lighting another cigarette. Stress turned Langley into a chronic chain smoker. Ironically, he also was an exercise freak and worked out daily. He saw his doctor for annual exams, got regular lung scans, did their damned stress tests, and whatever else the doc recommended—except quit smoking. Langley loved cigarettes. They were like candy to him.

"Yeah, who was that? And what the hell was that about?" Peter asked as he sat back on a downed tree.

"She was from the State Department and was being recruited," Langley said.

"Recruited for what?"

"Not completely sure, to be honest. Not yet anyway," Langley said. "But she balked after showing some signs of joining in, and Montgomery freaked out. She was yelling about something Montgomery had done that involved Victoria Niles, but she didn't get a chance to say much else because that nut job shot her."

Peter jerked suddenly at the sound of movement in the woods.

"That was a rabbit," Langley said with a smirk. "I know you've been through hell. You get to be a little jumpy," Langley added with a bit of sympathy. "Most people wouldn't have survived your first encounter with that nut." Langley offered Peter a friendly look, knowing all too well what the encounter likely involved. Langley had met many lunatics in his years in the service and seen the result of their brutality.

"Look, Peter, you need to stay dead. I'm not kidding. I don't know exactly what all is going on, but I do know some powerful people are up to something bad, and I know it's about the President's reforms. I don't know yet who all the bad guys are."

Langley walked toward Peter as a helicopter approached from the distance.

"Shit," Peter said in a hushed, paranoid voice.

"Relax, Peter. This one is friendly," Langley said as he walked to his car and took a small pistol from his suit coat pocket. "Okay, this is what we have to do. You have to shoot me." Langley said, handing the pistol to Peter.

"What? No," Peter protested. "What the hell is going on?"

"Don't worry. It's a small caliber, and you're going to barely hit me. Have to do it, otherwise they'll suspect something." Langley shook the gun out toward Peter. "Come on, take it, God damn it. We don't have all day."

Peter took the gun and stared at Langley. Nearby, the helicopter was landing.

"Right here," Langley stated as he pointed to his side. "Make sure you don't hit the rib."

"You are out of your mind," Peter said, dropping the gun and walking toward the chopper.

"Hey, dumb ass. I saved your life. You were a dead man walking back there because you fucked up and walked right into the lion's den. Now take the gun and shoot me, or I'll be the dead one. Get it!" Langley said, clearly annoyed as he shoved the gun back into Peter's hand.

Peter looked at the gun, then at Langley. "You're serious?" he asked.

"Yes. I'm serious, and we're out of time. That chopper is taking you to meet a friend of mine. You'll have to stay there for a few days or maybe longer."

Langley stood up straight. "Come closer," he instructed. "Shoot me right there." He pointed to the spot on his side.

"Why there?" Peter asked, now playing along with Langley.

"Been shot there a few times. Not much left of the nerve endings," he explained with a sarcastic chuckle. "Go ahead."

Peter pointed the gun at the spot at nearly point blank range and squeezed the trigger. The bullet ripped through the outer edge of Langley's side.

"Damn, that still stings," Langley said as he grabbed his side. "Should do the trick though." He pulled his hand away, revealing a large blood spot growing on his white shirt.

"Good job. Now, you have to stay with my buddy, or they'll know I lied about killing you. Understand?"

Langley stuffed a handkerchief into his shirt.

"Not really, but okay," Peter answered. "Why did you do this for me?"

"Your wife will know you're okay," Langley said as he got back in his car. "You stay with my friend. Promise me. I won't be able to save you again, and if you turn up, I'm a dead man. Got it?"

"How is my wife going to know I'm okay?"

"I had you shoot me. Trust me. Oh, and by the way, the woman with McBride ..." Langley started to ask, looking square at Peter.

"Is it the President's sister?" Peter said, finishing Langley's question for him. He was now feeling more secure of his position.

"I need to know, Peter." Langley pulled up his hand wet with fresh blood and held it up for Peter to see.

"Yes, Victoria Niles is alive," Peter answered. "I don't know how or any details, but, yes, she is with McBride. And I would bet that psycho is still chasing them."

"Do you have any idea where they might be?" Langley asked.

"No, they got me to the hospital, and that was the last I saw of them."

"Fair enough," Langley said. "Stay with my friend until I say otherwise, okay?"

"I will."

CHAPTER SEVEN

Desperation and Reprieve

In Washington, President Niles sat in the family quarters watching CNN. He told the staff the place was completely off limits to them so he and the kids, when they finally arrived, would feel at home. He had removed all the original furniture from the family area and replaced it with a more casual and comfortable design. The furniture was mostly in earth tones and over-sized for comfort. He had the largest lazy boy recliner on the market situated in front of a 90-inch TV for those rare moments when he could watch a football game.

"In our next segment we will be speaking with the chairman of the Republican Party," the reporter, William Conner, said. "Chairman Cochran, you've been the head of the Republican Party for how long now?"

"Seven years," Cochran answered.

"And before that you served two terms in the Senate?"

"That is correct."

"Now, you and the President are actually old friends, isn't that true?"

"Yes, we went to school together and have been good friends ever since."

"So, I would suppose your opposition to these reforms has caused some stress in the friendship?" Conner asked. "I mean, it certainly appears you personally oppose the reforms

President Niles intends to introduce in Congress. Is that a fair statement?"

"Yeah, I would say our 'loyal' ties are frayed, you jackass," Niles said out loud while watching.

"Yes, in their present form I do not think the reforms have any chance of getting to the floor for a vote," Cochran answered.

"Much is being made of this right now, as you know. Many are saying the reforms should be put to a vote. Some think this is nothing more than typical party politics with a new player," Conner said.

"The President doesn't have a 'party,' so to speak, so he really is dependent on the two parties if he hopes to get anything done," Cochran said.

"I guess that goes to my point that you are viewing this as an 'establishment versus the new guy' issue. Is that correct?" Conner asked.

"No, it's about policy structure," Cochran said.

"With all due respect, Mr. Chairman, we had an election. Is it appropriate for your party to keep the President from bringing his proposals in for a vote? He did win. He won big."

Niles smiled as he watched the confrontation. "This is better than a ball game," he said out loud. He reached for a bowl of popcorn as he watched Cochran grow uncomfortable. The President knew Hamilton Cochran—and his body language—well. When they played poker in college, Jackson could tell when Cochran had a bad hand and had bid too high. Niles couldn't control his amusement watching Cochran's same "tell."

Cochran smiled politely at the interviewer. "Everyone in Congress won an election. They all have a responsibility to represent their constituents. Congress is not a rubber stamp," he said, taking a drink of water.

"Most of these proposals have been clearly discussed," the CNN reporter said. "The proposed bills are online right now, and many in the news business think you are stalling because these changes will reduce the two parties' powers."

"That is simply untrue," Cochran said. "Congress simply wants to be sure any new legislation is written as intended. It's that simple."

"Americans seem to believe otherwise. A poll released today shows that 65 percent of voters believe that Congress is stalling and that the President's package should be introduced and voted on now."

"We could beat this back and forth all night," Cochran said. "They will be introduced when they are in proper form."

"I have to tell you, Mr. Chairman, with all due respect, you have not made a strong case here tonight," he said, expecting Cochran to offer a more substantive argument for the obvious delay.

"I can come back in a few weeks and talk about why the President won't make an effort to address *our* concerns. Can we do that, William?" Cochran said, feigning a smile.

"Later tonight President Niles is going to be with us, along with several former members of Congress, who will argue that the bills are in proper form and that you and the Democrats are simply stalling."

"Fair enough," Cochran laughed.

"Well done, William," the President said as the interview ended.

Almost immediately there was a knock on the door.

"What is it?" the President said without getting up.

Anthony Sinclair entered the room looking annoyed and anxious.

"CNN?" the chief of staff asked.

"That's right."

"Is there a reason you aren't discussing these things with me?" Sinclair asked.

"Oh, I said yes to CNN on a whim," he smiled. "After we met with the party heads, I decided it was time to turn up the heat."

"But CNN? Why not another press conference?" he asked, a bit suspicious.

"Not everyone watches those things. I think we'll reach more people with a news interview," Niles said.

"Are we going to work on scripting some answers, or are you going to fly by the seat of your pants?" Sinclair asked. "And who are these former Congressmen he mentioned? What's that about?"

"It's just some of the people I've talked to along the way. It's not a big deal, really," Niles said nonchalantly. "None of them are running for anything. They like the changes and know these bills are ready, that's all."

"I think you are being incredibly confrontational here, Jackson. I don't understand why you would want to do this. We need to continue pushing behind the scenes in a methodical and professional manner. Going on CNN? For God's sake, Jackson."

"Behind the scenes has not worked, Anthony."

"You're kicking a hornet's nest," Sinclair said as he headed for the door.

"Good," the President said with determination.

"We should be getting a VP nominated before we start taking our legislative battles to CNN," Sinclair said as he left.

ON CAPITOL HILL, Reed welcomed Cochran to his office. As Speaker of the House, Reed occupied a large, well-appointed office. He had the room painted gold for a regal feel. But visitors often commented, after leaving, that they felt like they were inside a mustard jar. Reed had many photographs hanging on the walls, but even a casual observer would notice they were with people of higher stature or famous types. Former presidents, foreign heads of state, and Hollywood stars all shared the space. These were Reed's way of reinforcing his status and position of power. A cane collection hung on one wall. None had any documented historical significance, although Reed claimed Robert E. Lee had used one late in his life. On his desk sat an old gavel his father had used during his tenure in the Massachusetts House. Reed often told people it was proof that the "speaker's office was in his blood." But like the cane, there was no real proof of its origin.

"We better start thinking about a compromise," Reed said.

"Screw that. He wouldn't compromise anyway," Cochran retorted.

"He's not going to let up unless we give him something," Reed stated forcefully as he thrust his cane at Cochran.

"We aren't giving anything until *he* softens up," Cochran chuckled.

"If this stuff gets to the floor as written and we just vote it down, we'll be watching most of our friends—hell, even me—get replaced next November." Reed insisted.

"We need to keep our heads here, Wilson," Cochran cautioned. "Some of his policies are crazy, and we have a responsibility to be reasonable. And right now, reasonable is stalling him into compromise. It's that simple. And I don't give a shit about public opinion polls."

"You aren't running for office anymore," Reed countered. "My guys are running every two years, and I can tell you they are scared of this President. You've got yourself a nice cozy deal as party chairman, but my guys have to face voters."

"Wilson, this crap has to get through both chambers, and it's not even going to make it out of Committee. Period. Now, let's go get some dinner," Cochran said, slapping his old friend on the back. "You need a drink, anyway."

OUT WEST, EXHAUSTED and confused, Peter Mercury ended his helicopter ride on a small airstrip in the middle of nowhere.

"You must be Jack's friend," said a man dressed in plain clothes and holding a pipe.

"I guess so," Peter said, conveying some doubt.

"My name is Larry Cooper, and Jack asked me to pick you up here," the man said, smiling at Peter and shaking his hand.

The two walked to a car, and Cooper directed Peter to the passenger side.

"I'll bet you're hungry," Cooper said as he started the car and placed the pipe in a glass tumbler in one of the cup holders.

"Starved."

"You want anything special?"

"Anything."

Minutes later, they arrived at a small diner.

"Wait in the car. Jack told me to keep you out of site," Cooper said. "Give me ten minutes. Sit tight."

The diner didn't look like much, but the smell coming from inside was pure heaven to Peter. The place looked like an old drive up, with outside speakers next to each parking spot where visitors would order and have the food brought to their car windows. Peter noticed loose wires dangled from the stations where speakers had once been. An old neon sign now only partially worked. Peter squinted as he tried to make out the original name. "The Happy Buffalo" was now affectionately known as "Happpalo," as the remaining letters had long burnt out. Part of the big smiling buffalo head was still partially illuminated, adding to the quirkiness of the place. The restaurant was all by itself along the state highway, and Peter wondered what had prompted the original owner to locate his business in such an isolated spot.

A few minutes later, his new friend emerged with a bag overflowing with Styrofoam containers.

"Start eating," Cooper said as he handed the bag to Peter and slid back into the driver's seat.

"You can put twenty bucks in the pot and guess the date that buffalo head burns out," Cooper said, noticing Peter looking at the sign.

"How big is the pot?" Peter asked.

"It's probably up to a couple thousand now."

Peter opened the first container to find the largest beef Manhattan he'd ever seen.

"That's their special," the driver said with a sense of pride. "There's fried chicken and apple pie in there, too."

Peter shoveled the food into his mouth as he nodded in complete approval. Peter relaxed a little as they drove. He was happy to be eating and, at least for the moment, away from Montgomery. It was the first time in days he could actually take in the scenery of Montana. "I need to come out here with Susan when this is over," he thought.

A half hour later, Cooper turned off the main road onto a side road with small ranch homes. He pulled up in front of one. Peter was relieved to see other houses, since he was still a little freaked out by the day's events.

"We have a pool in the backyard behind that fence," Cooper pointed out as they got out of the car. At the front door, a smiling woman emerged and waved at Peter as he walked toward the house.

"Hello, Peter," she said. "I'm Barb, come in and make yourself at home." The woman was dressed in light blue running shorts with a matching shirt. Her short brown hair looked damp, as if she had just completed her daily run. Next to her a small chocolate lab lay panting.

"Looks like you both just got some exercise," Peter said.

"Yeah, he needs to come in for some water," Barb explained.

Peter entered, taking in the front room. It was warm and cozy, but even a casual observer would notice the abundance of military memorabilia. Pictures, medals in frames, and flags in cases all competed for space. Peter didn't make any comments about the items, but they did give him a sense of comfort. "At least these people don't look like gangsters," he thought as he smiled politely. The sound of country music coming from the kitchen mixed with the smell of some type of food being prepared.

"Something smells good," Peter remarked.

"It's for later," Barb explained.

"You want something to drink?" Larry asked.

"Water sounds nice," Peter said, beginning to believe he was no longer in danger.

A few minutes later, the three of them were sitting on the back porch enjoying the fresh air. Peter was also working his way through the apple pie from the diner.

"So, let me answer the question you want to ask," Cooper said.

Peter looked up from his pie, hoping his life wasn't about to take a crazy turn.

"Barb and I were in the service with Jack," Cooper said. "We go back twenty-some odd years together. Jack saved my life more than once. He's the best man I've ever known. He called me and said he had a friend that needed help, told me where to pick you up, and here I am. I don't know anything else except that your back needs some nursing."

He smiled at Barb.

"I'm a nurse, Peter," she said as she got up. "Another water?"

"Both of us," her husband answered.

"I need to check on something in the oven so give me a few."

"So, you don't have any answers for me?" Peter asked as he pushed aside the empty pie container.

"Nope, and I don't have any questions, either," Cooper said with a laugh. "Jack said to look after you until he called, and that's all I know." He downed the rest of his water.

AT THE SIMS LODGE, Jack Langley drove slowly along the driveway, contemplating how he was going to play his arrival. Several of the guards were gathered at the front porch, so the FBI director felt the time was right. He pulled his car right up to the porch and threw his door open.

"Who the fuck brought that asshole in here?" Langley shouted as he got out, opened his suit jacket, and revealed his blood-soaked shirt. The men all looked at each other and then back at Jack. "Fucking idiots!" he shouted as he took off his jacket and threw it at the nearest man.

"That fuck had a gun up his ass," he screamed as he pushed past the men and climbed the front steps. "You guys are a bunch of fucking amateurs."

"What did you do with him?" one of the men asked as Langley cleared the group.

"I shot the fucker right in the face and rolled his body in a ditch. Of course that was after he shot me first, you God damned idiot!" Langley screamed.

Inside, Langley went down the long hallway where the bedrooms were located and walked into his suite. Soon there was a knock on the door, and Clayton Sims entered.

"What happened?" Sims asked as he walked past Langley and sat down in a black leather wingback chair.

"You got a bunch of idiots out here," Langley said as he poured a drink and sat down.

"What did you find out?" Sims asked, ignoring Langley's critique.

"The woman with McBride is some ranch hand or ranch owner or some shit like that," Langley said. "It's a coincidence that her name is Victoria."

"So is Victoria Niles dead?" Sims asked.

"She's not with McBride," Langley said. "But whether she's dead or not, hell, I don't know, and that dead reporter didn't know shit."

Sims pulled a footstool over with the tip of his shoe. "The people upstairs are getting restless, Jack," he said as he crossed his legs on the stool.

"Who are these people you always make reference to?" Langley asked as he sat in the other wingback next to Sims.

"They will introduce themselves when the time comes," Sims said.

"And who is 'the Captain' you talk about?" Langley asked, rubbing his still bloody side.

"That is not something I can discuss, Jack. You've not been around long enough. But, listen, these people are excited to have you on board. You are the kind of guy they need on The Council. They all like you and respect you. Your time will come. Keep doing your job." Sims smiled as he stood and headed for the door. "So, the woman with McBride is some other broad named Victoria," Sims said as he stood in the doorway.

"I guess so," Langley said.

"What did you do with the body?"

"Kicked him into a ditch. He'll be eaten by wolves or coyotes in a couple of days," Langley said as he untied his shoes. "Someday, some hiker might find a bone or something, but by then nobody will care."

"I suppose that's true," Sims said as he pulled the door closed.

Langley walked into the bathroom, took off his bloodstained shirt, threw it in the tub, and turned on the shower. The damage was a flesh wound in his belly fat. He applied a bit of antibiotic cream and taped on a gauze bandage.

Down the hall, a nervous and angry Clayton Sims waited on hold as he paced back and forth. Finally, a voice came across the speaker.

"What is it, Clayton?" the voice demanded.

"We need action now," Sims declared, the phone still on speaker.

"You call me here to say that?" the man whispered in a harsh and angry tone. "What the hell are you thinking?"

"What the fuck are we waiting on?" Sims asked.

"You better get yourself calmed down right now, or I will get you calmed down. You understand?"

"This 'dance' we're doing with this guy is ridiculous. You need to take care of business, and now," Sims demanded.

"Goodbye, Mr. Sims," the voice said as the phone went dead.

"Damn it!" Sims screamed as he kicked over the small table the phone had been sitting on.

IN FLORIDA, SAM and Victoria were checking into a small, one-story motel near Everglade City. The place had been there for decades, but had been reasonably well maintained and updated over the years. Each unit opened directly outside. This style had been popular in the 1960s when crime wasn't much of a concern and travelers enjoyed the convenience of parking right outside the door of their rooms.

The owner who checked them in was happy to see Sam pay with cash, since that meant no taxes would need to be paid on the income. As far as the books were concerned, the room would remain empty for the night.

"Let's walk down the street and get something to eat," Victoria said as she threw her bags on the bed.

THAT EVENING THE White House was lit up like Christmas Eve as a CNN crew rushed about setting up for the interview with the President. Several former members of Congress were also milling about as they waited for the President's Press Secretary to sign off on the setup in the Oval Office.

Niles was alone in the family quarters, looking over notes he had jotted down over the last few days. Finally, a knock on the door indicated the room was ready.

"Come in," he said.

Anthony Sinclair entered, a look of exhaustion on his face. "Jackson, I do not think this is wise. I'm sorry, but I think you are making a mistake with this," he said to his old friend as he joined him on the sofa.

"Anthony, I am going to do what I promised the people. Come hell or high water, these reforms are going to be introduced into Congress and voted on. I have tried to be patient and reasonable, and I have made absolutely no progress," the President said.

"But this will simply inflame the situation," Sinclair said as he stood and raised his hands in the air. "You are making things worse with all these public challenges."

"I was elected to change things, and that's what I'm going to do. I intend to inflame the situation since 'reasonable' hasn't produced a thing."

"But why?" Sinclair asked in disbelief.

"This town is full of rotten people whose conduct has been damaging to the country," Niles said. "My reforms are going to flush them out and get them moving. I am going to run the bastards out of town. That's why I ran, and that's why I won, plain and simple." The President stood up and headed for the door. "Anthony, I need your help and your advice to make these changes work, but getting them to the floor for a vote is going to take public pressure. I'm lighting the fuse. Let's go."

IN THE OVAL OFFICE sat William Conner, who had interviewed Hamilton Cochran earlier in the evening. With him were four former members of Congress and the camera operator. No one else was allowed in the room during the interview. All of them stood as President Niles entered the room.

"Good evening, ladies and gentlemen," the President said as he came through the door.

"Good evening, Mr. President," they all responded in near unison.

"Please sit down and relax," the President instructed as he motioned to the chairs.

"Susan," the President said as he pressed his intercom.

"Yes, sir?"

"Please have coffee and sodas sent in for everyone."

Shortly, a staff member arrived with a cart of coffee, canned drinks, and an assortment of snacks.

"It's getting late enough that I thought a little caffeine and some refreshments might be appropriate," the President said as he poured a cup of coffee and grabbed a handful of nuts from a bowl on the table. "Please, folks, get a cup of coffee or a soda if you wish."

"We have about fifteen minutes before we go on air, Mr. President," CNN's Conner said. "Is there anything you want to go over before we start?"

"This interview will be unscripted and free-flowing," the President said. "I want you to point out to the American people that you came here with no script and no rules. There are no questions that have been declared out of bounds. I want the people to know that." The President took a drink of his coffee.

"And that goes for everyone in the room," the President added as he looked at the four former Congress members. Each nodded in agreement.

"What about a time limit?" Conner asked.

"No limit" the President said.

"Thirty seconds," the cameraman said.

"Okay, are you all ready to go?" Conner asked in the final minutes before going live.

The President walked to his desk, picked up a pile of papers and returned to his chair.

"I'm ready," he said as he looked at his watch.

"Okay, in 5-4-3-2-1, you're live," the cameraman announced.

"Good evening," Conner began. "We are coming to you live from the Oval Office tonight. In addition to Jackson Niles, President of the United States, we have four former members of Congress in attendance. Mr. President, thank you for this opportunity."

Conner shook hands with the President.

"It's my pleasure, William. I would like to introduce these former members of Congress: Representative Sheila Welsh from Michigan, Representative Alan McDermott from Georgia, Representative Nancy Phillips from Texas, and Representative Frank Evans from California."

Each nodded and smiled.

"Let's begin," Conner announced. "Earlier today I interviewed Hamilton Cochran, chairman of the Republican Party. It is no secret that both Cochran and Wilson Reed, the Democratic Speaker of the House, are publicly against your reforms being introduced into Congress. Their argument is that the bills are not in a format suitable for floor debate. I'm going to first ask these former members of Congress if that argument has any merit."

Conner turned to the four. "What do you each have to say about that? And before you answer, please confirm that you have actually read these bills."

"We have all read them," Congresswoman Welsh said. The others nodded.

"Their argument is complete nonsense," Congressman McDermott said.

"You all agree?" Conner asked. They nodded again, assuring him they did.

"So, the argument both parties are putting forth doesn't hold up?" Conner asked.

"That's right. It's absolute nonsense," Phillips said. "I was in Congress for three terms, and I can tell you the bills the President is proposing are absolutely no different in structure than any bill I voted on while I was in office. This is all a delay tactic, plain and simple."

"Okay, for the remainder of this interview, we are going to assume the bills are in proper form," Conner said, summing up the structure issue. "I don't want to talk about content since we spent the election debating the merit of the reforms. Let's instead talk about 'why' Congress is reluctant to introduce these bills."

Conner turned his attention to the President.

"I did not intend to leave you out of the opening conversation, Mr. President," Conner said, smiling.

"That's perfectly fine. That's why I invited them," Niles said.

"You have criticized the two parties in press conferences since you've been in office," Conner said.

"I have."

"How much of this is typical Washington maneuvering?"

"That's what so many want to think," the President said.

"But you say it's more than that?" Conner clarified.

"It is more than that. This is the two parties, or a faction within each party, trying to prevent the changes I ran on from being introduced. It's that basic. They want the status quo maintained."

"Can an Independent govern in this town?" Conner asked.

"Based on early results, I would say 'no,'" the President answered.

"How does this get settled, then? You won an election. You are the President. And you can't get the ideas you ran and won on introduced into a Congress held by the two parties. How does this get resolved?" Conner was animated as he asked the question.

"I'm going to do two things tonight that will likely anger at least some party members even more, but I also believe it is necessary," Niles said as he looked at the four former Congress members. "I am not going back on my word to the American people. There are many members of Congress who do support all or many of my proposals. They recognize that party leadership has grown too powerful and has too much authority over individual members of Congress. Tonight, I am inviting them to join me in a new party. It has no name, no structure, and no pre-approved positions. It is for patriotic members of Congress who want to break the grip the Republican and Democratic Parties have on this country. It will be a party of free-thinkers who are not bound to party politics and the nonsense that comes along with the Democratic or Republican parties."

"That was a lot," Conner said. "I suspect some screaming is going on right now on Capitol Hill. You invited and are urging a mass rebellion within both parties. Does that sum up what I heard?"

"Yes. That's right, and it's long overdue," the President said.

"How do you four feel about what the President said?" Conner asked as he looked at the former Congressional members.

"We have discussed this, and we are all in agreement with the President," Representative Welsh replied.

"You propose members of Congress leave their current party and join you in a new party?"

"Correct," the President said.

"Okay. You said you were going to do two things tonight. I can't wait to hear the second," Conner said, attempting to hold back a smirk. William Conner had interviewed more of the power elite in Washington than any other reporter. For him, Jackson Niles was something of a unicorn. He was without a party, yet he sat there as the President of the United States. Never did Conner, or anyone in Washington for that matter, think such a thing was possible.

"It's time for Americans to demonstrate their frustration with these parties in an undeniably visible way," Niles said.

"More so than your election?" Conner asked, now unable to hide the smirk.

"Apparently my presence in the White House is not enough to get these parties to accept the changes I ran on," the President said.

"What are you asking the people to do?" Conner inquired.

"We have all heard about this 'red state' and 'blue state' nonsense for the past 50 years or so. I think most people aren't 'blue' or 'red' but some combination of the two. This choosing of sides was the work of the two parties, and they have tried to get every voter in one camp or the other. I want to ask Americans to break out of this mold and think about a new paradigm. It's time for something different, something bigger, something that sets aside the old party crap, pardon the word," the President said, his arms raised.

"It's time for real change," he continued. "I ran on that promise, and I intend to see it through. But these two parties are trying to hold onto things as they are because professional politicians simply want to get re-elected." The President paused and took a drink of water. He then cleared his throat. "Excuse me I've been talking too much today."

"Take your time Mr. President," Conner commented.

"The Founders created a House of Representatives with the goal of everyday people coming to Washington for a two-year stint and then going back to their 'real' life." Niles paused again as he looked at the four former House members, who seemed to be enjoying the moment. "These two parties have hijacked the House and turned it into a 30-year career for professional politicians. That needs to change, and the people want that changed. I realize I'm asking members of Congress to join a movement that will result in them not being in Congress for much longer, but we live in a time of crisis, and we need statesmen and stateswomen to step up and lead our nation out of this mess. If we were at war, the President would ask the people to sacrifice, and they would do so. We are in debt up to our eye balls, our cities are in disrepair, our schools need improvements, our roads and bridges need to be fixed, the list goes on and on, and these two parties are trying to maintain the status quo."

The President paused, giving Conner a chance to speak, but the look of expectation on William Conner's face made it clear he was not going to interrupt the President's point.

"It's actually insane if you stop and really analyze their behavior," the President said, pausing again and raising his hands to emphasize the point. "I'm asking the American people to rise up and demand that these two parties get out of the way."

The President now sat back and waited for Conner to proceed.

"I imagine the screams on The Hill are even louder now," Conner said.

"I hope so."

"You hope so?"

"Yes, I want them mad. I want the people mad and marching. I want the reasonable people in this country who are sick and tired of the red-versus-blue nonsense to stand up and take over. They outnumber the fringe elements of each party, and let's face the plain fact: the fringe of each party is running the show."

"I suspect you are going to have a lot of visitors tomorrow," Conner said as he took a breath and smiled. "I don't think any President in our history has made such a strong appeal for civil disobedience as you just did."

"I won an election with overwhelming numbers, and my program can't even get introduced for a vote. I think some civil disobedience is in order," the President declared.

"I suspect you are going to see some after this interview," Conner said.

"It's time," the President stated.

"Thank you, Mr. President. You told me when we came in today that there was no time limit to this interview. I want to tell our viewers, although I think it is unnecessary, that there was no script or boundaries established before we started. I suspect this interview will be rebroadcast all or in part on every channel and likely in most countries for days to come. That being said, I am going to end this here so the public can focus on the two requests you made," Conner said.

"Thank you, William, and thank you four as well," Niles said as he shook hands with all five of them. "Your willingness to stand up and defend these bills will be a big help."

Then, turning to look directly into the camera, Conner said, "Thank you for joining us this evening. This is William Conner, CNN News."

The red light on the camera dimmed, and Conner, the camera operator, and even the four members of Congress left without any further comment. When the room was empty, the President sat down and put his feet up on his desk.

"Now comes the shit storm," he thought as he smiled. "Let's see who screams the loudest."

IN FLORIDA, A TIRED Victoria Niles sat with Sam in a crowded local bar. The place had multiple TV screens on every wall. Any college or pro sports team from Florida would have found at least one reference to their mascot or logo somewhere in the place. A series of autographed jerseys hung high off the ceiling.

The man seated next to Sam explained it was a custom for any Florida player of any fame to eventually visit and leave an autographed jersey for the owner's collection. The waiters and waitresses also were dressed in uniforms reflecting their favorite teams—as long as that team was from Florida.

Patrons were glued to the screens, but they weren't watching sports. Not tonight. They sat silently, listening to their new President. Victoria and Sam were as shocked as everyone else in the room. Sam was especially amazed that a sports bar would have tuned all the channels to a Presidential interview. As the interview ended, the owner shouted, "Give'm hell Jackson," as the room slowly returned to its typically lively atmosphere.

"You said he wanted to shake things up," Victoria said. "But, holy cow, that was unbelievable. I hope he didn't go too far."

"He wants the reaction," Sam said. "He wants them fractured and scared so they get out of the way. Tomorrow is going to be a crazy day in DC, that's for sure." Sam smiled as he took a drink of his beer.

"Let's stay here for a few days and keep an eye on the news. Can we do that?" Victoria asked.

"Sure. I don't see why not. If anyone is still looking for us, they probably haven't even found the boat yet," Sam said. "We can find a beach for part of the day, too."

"That would be great," Victoria said. "A few days of lying around sounds good."

AT THE LODGE, Clayton Sims and Jack Langley sat together in the main room along with a few of Sims' henchmen.

"That man is a fucking lunatic!" Sims shouted as the President's television interview concluded. "He's trying to subvert the government he's supposed to be in charge of. What the hell is he up to?" Sims stood and started pacing in front of the large fireplaces.

Langley sat quietly with a cigar in his mouth, knowing full well what his old friend was up to. He had heard all about Niles' disdain for the two parties over the years. He wanted to smile, but he didn't dare. He silently puffed on his cigar.

Sims was in a full-scale rant, anyway, and not looking for Langley to comment or speculate, so he had time to ponder the questions that would soon come. Langley was entertained by Sims' actions, but he also feared for Niles. He had not learned all he needed to know about who was involved in killing the vice president and the supposed killing of Victoria. Nor did he know for sure what their full intention was. But he knew things were about to start moving faster, and he needed to get past Sims and find out who was pulling the strings.

"Who's on this 'Council' and who's the 'Captain' he makes reference to?" he thought as Sims rambled on.

"I need to go back to Washington," Langley said as he stood. Sims followed him down the hall and into Langley's room.

"Why?" he asked, now completely exhausted from his rant.

"Because I am the director of the fucking FBI, and I can't sit out here smoking cigars."

"Settle down, Jack," Sims said, a bit shocked.

"Settle down? Fuck you, Clayton. I'm sitting out here listening to you rant and watching the President light the country on fire, and you want me to settle down? Shit, man, this place is about to come apart at the seams, and we're out here in the middle of nowhere screaming at the TV. I'm leaving right now. It's game-time, dumb ass. You better get your boys thinking about right now or we lose before the fight's even started."

Langley had begun packing his clothes as he made his little speech.

"I'll be in my office by morning," he said as he picked up his bags and walked for the door.

Sims followed him to his car, still parked in front.

"If you guys have a plan, you better get it implemented," Langley yelled as he closed his car door and drove off. He hoped his show of impatience might trigger some communication from a source other than Sims.

"I've got to get past that asshole," Langley thought, as he sped to a small, private airstrip.

IN KEY WEST, an exhausted and angry Hiatt Montgomery was recovering from his ordeal at sea. After the chopper went down, he drifted for several hours clinging to a small cooler. He had finally been picked up by a couple of fishermen who returned him to the marina. He had not seen the Presidential interview, but he knew something big had happened by the conversations he heard from people walking past him. He was still in damp clothes and attempting to get his bearings so he could find Jill's home from the night before.

ON CAPITOL HILL, Speaker Reed and Chairman Cochran sat in Reed's mustard-colored office with a few other senior members from both parties.

"This guy is a madman," one of the senators sighed.

"We need to stay calm," Cochran said. "I think this will blow up in his face in a week or so. Listen, if nobody jumps ship and only a few nuts show up out here with picket signs or some shit like that, then this guy is our prisoner. We need to control our ranks. That's all we can do for now. If you guys have any loose members, you need go get them by the neck and make sure they don't do something stupid. If we can prevent any defections, then this shit will blow over, and he's finished."

Cochran looked sternly across at Reed. "Can you control your side of the aisle?"

"I think so," he said.

"Niles is making a big gamble," Cochran said. "He's throwing all his chips on the table. We prevent defections, and his little challenge falls flat. Stay calm, talk to your buddies, assure your folks back home, and then we win. He'll have to back down, and this thing is over. Everyone agree?"

The group looked somber and worried, but all nodded their approval.

Speaker Reed said nothing. His confidence was low, likely because he was one of the House members who had made a long career out of a string of two-year terms.

"We're playing with fire, Hamilton," Reed finally said. "This President is popular, and he may succeed in getting people to join him. At the very least, we need to start thinking about our position if his appeal for civil disobedience works. Shit man, who knows how many nuts might show up out here?"

Reed rubbed his face as he slumped back in his chair. "My guys are scared, Hamilton," he said. The mood differed between the House, with its two-year terms, and the Senate, with the six-year-terms its members enjoyed.

"Start calling your guys tonight," Cochran said. "Start with the ones who seem the most vulnerable. Get your Majority

Whip to help out. Call the Minority Whip as well and get her started. You guys work through the membership and get a grip on all of them. Make sure they know the consequences of jumping ship."

Cochran stood and walked over by Reed's cane collection, lifting one with a carved ivory handle.

"We can have challengers lined up in a matter of days for anybody who leaves. Tell them that," Cochran said, thrusting the cane in air as if leading a charge. "Make sure they understand that this President is short-term, probably one term, but we will still be here when he's gone. If anybody defects, then we go after his seat with both barrels shooting. Make sure they know that."

Cochran waddled around the room, offering his speech as if he was trying to rally a football team losing at halftime.

"Get started now, and let's all meet here again tomorrow at the same time," he said. Cochran returned the cane to the case as he contemplated what else he might offer to motivate those gathered.

"We stay unified and he loses," he declared, as he turned around and looked at each person in the room. "It's that simple."

With that, the others in the room stood and filed out.

"Stay focused, Wilson," Cochran said to his friend as he approached the door. "We'll get through this."

AT THE LODGE, Clayton Sims sat in his suite listening to a conference call being conducted on speakerphone.

"Let's see what the morning brings," the Captain said. "We need to make sure we don't overreact to his little stunt. I think he's counting on the parties to do or say something stupid, and we need to make sure that doesn't happen. Stay calm and professional, and if anyone asks you about it, smile and express your 'support for the democratic process.' Everyone understand?"

The Captain waited for any dissent. None came.

"We will reconvene tomorrow, same time," the Captain said, ending the call.

"This guy is such a pussy," Sims screamed as he threw his unlit cigar at the fireplace. "It's time for action."

IN KEY WEST, Hiatt Montgomery finally approached the door of Jill's house just as the sun was setting. He knocked softly, fearing he may not be welcome after leaving without saying anything earlier.

"What happened to you?" Jill asked as she opened the door.

"My boat sank," Montgomery said. He shuffled through the door looking soggy and defeated.

"Oh, my God, you poor man," Jill exclaimed, helping him to a chair. "Let's get you out of these clothes. I'll get you something dry to put on."

She scurried away as he stripped off the damp and sand-filled clothing.

"Here, put on this robe," she said as she wrapped it over his shoulders. "I'll throw this stuff in the wash. Do you want something to eat or drink?"

Montgomery pulled the robe around and tied it in the middle. "Hot coffee would be great," he said.

"Did you lose everything?"

"Yeah. I hit something in the water, and it tore my boat open. The damned thing sank in minutes, and I was left clinging to my cooler. A couple of fishermen eventually pulled me in," he explained, filling in details where needed. Montgomery glanced around the little house he had slept in the night before. He was too drunk to notice much then, but now he was as sober as a person could be. The small bungalow was decorated in everything Key West. Even the lamps had shells in their base. Pictures of Jill's kids adorned the walls along with others of her and her many friends. For a moment, the nasty Montgomery found himself feeling a bit empty. Clearly this was the home of a happy person.

"Thank God they came along. Do you want to shower before your coffee?"

"I need to get warmed up, so maybe the coffee first?"

Jill got it brewing then brought him a blanket.

"Do you mind if I turn on the national news?" he asked as Jill delivered a large mug of coffee.

"Of course not," she said, handing him the remote.

"I was about to walk over to the market," Jill said. "I think I'll do that quickly since I don't have much here to eat. You don't mind, do you?"

"No I'm not going to move for a while," Montgomery said with a rare smile.

"I'll be right back."

Montgomery turned on CNN to see the usual talking heads discussing the President's earlier interview. Montgomery only needed to hear part of the details before he realized he better call Sims.

"Damn, this guy has balls," he thought as he watched clips from the interview.

"But, damn, dude, you are a dead man now," he sneered as his waited for Sims to pick up.

AT THE WHITE HOUSE, President Niles and Anthony Sinclair were watching TV in the family quarters. Niles sat in his big recliner with his shoes off and an iced tea on the table to his right. Sinclair was on the sofa to the President's left and sat with his legs crossed.

"You still think that was a bad idea?" the President asked his chief of staff.

"That doesn't matter much now," Sinclair said with a tired, almost-despondent smile.

"I suppose not," Niles said, clearly fatigued.

"What's done is done now, Jackson," Sinclair said, keeping his eyes on the screen. "Maybe you'll get the response you want. But if not, I think the parties will rally together and be even harder to deal with."

"We needed something to mix them up," Niles said. "They were already a fairly solid block. Without public pressure, I don't think we have a chance of getting our reforms passed."

"We'll find out soon, I'd think. If you don't need me anymore, Jackson, I'm going to head for home and get some sleep."

"You do agree with these reforms, don't you?" the President asked.

"Of course I do, Jackson. I simply thought a more subtle approach was better. But now we'll find out. 'The cat's out of the bag,' as they say."

THE NEXT MORNING, CNN was the first news service to start setting up in the National Mall. William Conner had told the network that he would be there whether anyone showed up or not. By morning news airtime, fewer than ten people said they were there because of the President's interview.

"Good morning," he announced as he began the 6 a.m. newscast. "As promised, we are broadcasting live from the National Mall here in Washington DC. As you look around the mall, you can see things have not changed much from a typical day."

The cameraman panned the Mall, showing only a small group milling around with signs that referenced passage of the President's reforms.

"We are going to broadcast from The Mall all day to see if President Niles' appeal to the people yields any public result. But I have to say, as it stands right now, this surprises me, and I would assume the President is both surprised and disappointed, too. I know it's early, but considering the appeal that was made, I expected to see some kind of response out here this morning. Certainly more than a few people."

Conner signed off, passing the airtime back to the studio, where the anchors were hard-pressed to contain their amusement by the situation.

"Did the President really expect some big crowd to show up?" one asked.

"This was a bad play on the President's part," repeated various talking heads on every channel as the morning wore on.

"If we had gridlock before, we're now looking at gridlock on steroids," another commentator stated.

By noon, it was obvious the number was not going to grow by much, since only a few more had joined the small group in the middle of the Mall.

IN FLORIDA, SAM AND Victoria were lying in bed, drinking coffee and watching the morning broadcasts.

"This isn't good for Jackson," Victoria said as she switched from channel to channel, hearing the same opinions.

"It's early," Sam said.

"Let's go find a beach," Victoria said, finishing her coffee. "I've already had enough TV for the day. Look at a map and find a beach for us." She headed for the bathroom.

"I'm on it," Sam said. He looked through the few tourist pamphlets he had picked up in the hotel office.

"There's a park not far from here that has a large beach area," he called out.

"That'll work," she said.

"I'm going next door to get a few things," Sam said as he pulled on a pair of green shorts and grabbed his wallet.

"Okay, I'll be ready when you get back."

AT THE WHITE HOUSE, President Niles was watching the same shows from the family quarters. Unlike the media, he remained optimistic that his call to the people would be answered. He had won the election, after all, so he reasoned it might just take a few days. His calendar was full of events and meetings with visitors from China, so it would be easy to avoid the media today. He was relieved to have a day away from party politics.

When he reached the Oval Office, Anthony Sinclair was the first person through the door.

"Jackson, we have an opening after 3 o'clock today," he said. "Let's get the two party heads over here and pencil out a deal. They don't want this fight to get any more public, or, for that matter, nasty. It's not good for the country." Sinclair poured a cup of coffee for the President and approached him at his desk.

"I think you made your point last night. You certainly got their attention. That's for sure," Sinclair smiled.

"I take it you've had some phone calls this morning?" the President asked as he sipped the coffee.

"Yes, Reed and Cochran both called, and each had the same attitude. They don't want any more public brawling over this.

They want to work out a deal and get something passed for you right away."

Sinclair poured a cup of coffee for himself and took a seat across from the President's desk.

"That's quite a change of tone," the President said.

"They were more than a little shocked by what you did last night," Sinclair chuckled. "The fact you were elected as an Independent has introduced a new environment to these people. I think now that you have their attention, we should take advantage and get a deal done."

"That will depend on what they're offering. Let's ask them for a simple, written outline, nothing formal, and then we can look that over. You know I have a full day with the Chinese, so see if you can get that, and we'll schedule something for tomorrow."

"Not today?"

"No. I want time to digest what they have in mind."

SAM CAME BACK to the hotel room to find Victoria sitting in front of the TV again.

"Anything new?"

"The same,"

"Are you ready?"

"Yep, let's go," she smiled as she jumped out of the chair.

In the car, Sam had a cooler full of drinks, along with a big beach blanket and a large umbrella.

"I got a few snacks, too," he said as he handed her a bag of assorted items.

"Did you get wine?" Victoria asked.

"No, I thought something different would be good today, so I got vodka, Sprite and cranberry juice. It's a nice hot-weather mix."

"Sounds good."

A few minutes later, Sam turned into the state park and followed the signs to the beach. It was a weekday, so the parking lot was empty, which made them both happy.

"Looks like we have the place to ourselves," Victoria said as they pulled in near the beach entrance.

"At least for a while," he said.

The beach was long and dotted with several pockets where the vegetation reached all the way to the water's edge during high tide.

"Let's find a real private spot," Victoria suggested with a wink.

"Works for me," Sam said as he scanned the beach. "Let's go down to that end." He motioned to the far left. After walking through a small area, which was completely overgrown, they emerged to find an isolated patch of beach.

"Perfect," Victoria said as she spread out the blanket.

"Will you put some lotion on my back?" she asked once they were settled.

Sam was busy mixing drinks in two large plastic tumblers with screw-on lids and flexible straws.

"Sure," he said, handing her one of the drinks.

"That's good! What are these called?" she asked as she took another long sip.

"Scannell," Sam said.

"Good stuff. Okay, get some lotion on me. I'm going to get some sun," Victoria said, pulling off her long t-shirt.

"I didn't think I would ever see you wearing a bikini like that," Sam said as he rubbed lotion on her shoulders.

"I left the other one on the boat," Victoria laughed. "That's why I wanted a private spot. There is no way I'm walking on a beach in this thing—at least not sober."

"I'm not sure I would want you to to be honest," Sam said. The bikini was the little black string one she bought in Key West. She had worn it once before on the boat but never took off her long t-shirt to reveal it. Victoria was not prone to skimpiness, but being with Sam brought out a side of her that seldom surfaced. The last few days she had thought a lot about what their time in Yale had been like. "We didn't wear much most days," she remembered with a smile one day.

"I hope Jackson is okay," Victoria said as she stretched out face down on the giant beach blanket Sam had bought that morning. It was mostly white other than a cluster of oranges that seemed to hang in the air in the middle.

"I'm worried, too, but I know he planned on getting those guys pissed off. Of course, he had expected them to push back against his reforms, so I think all this is unfolding as he had expected," Sam said.

"You don't think these nuts would go after him, do you?" Victoria asked as she rose up on her elbows and took a long drink.

Sam sat cross-legged next to Victoria with his own drink in his hand. "I'm worried about that, too," Sam confessed. "I think he was getting worried about that possibility. I think that's why he took the step he did yesterday. He either has to force the parties to move closer to his position, or he has to generate enough public pressure that the people force the parties to capitulate. He knew it was going to be an ugly process, but I know he never contemplated assassination attempts."

As the waves crashed a few feet away, Victoria noticed a coconut tumbling in the water. As she looked closer, she could see a small school of fish swimming through the waves. "Something must be chasing them," she thought as the fish darted off. A sudden gust of wind sprayed water on her face. She wiped away the water getting a small taste of salt. "I wish this craziness was over," she thought as she listened to Sam.

Sam added lotion to Victoria's legs and butt as he finished talking.

"We can't have you getting sunburned back here," he laughed, giving her a light, playful slap.

"Your brother has a plan. I'm worried, too, but we have to trust he has it covered," Sam said, stretching out next to Victoria. "Let's relax today. Let's pretend we're on vacation." He closed his eyes and took a long, deep breath.

"Fair enough."

PETER MERCURY SAT glued to the TV in the home of Jack Langley's friends. After watching the President's interview the night before, he had barely been able to sleep. His mind twisted in knots as he tried to unravel all the events of the past several days and figure out what was really going on. He couldn't help but consider the irony of sitting in a room decorated almost exclusively in military memorabilia. As a reporter he had often been suspicious of the military, but now he was comforted by the thought of their presence. "They're the good guys," he thought as he glanced about.

The aroma from the previous night's dinner lingered in the air. Barb called the concoction "western chowder." It was her own recipe and started with buffalo meat and potatoes. What she added after that depended on the season and what was on hand, she'd explained to Peter. He was alone now at the Cooper home, and he no longer worried about his own safety.

The President had gone after the two parties in a way that was shocking to Peter, but having been through hell the past couple of days, he suspected there was a lot more at play. He watched William Conner report from the National Mall and called out to the TV as if he were a cheerleader.

"Where are all the people?" Peter screamed each time Conner went live to show a rather empty field.

"This is incredible," he shouted each time Conner lamented the fact that no one seemed to be responding to their new President. Time after time, Peter threw his hands in the air.

"I guess we get what we get what we deserve then," Peter said, standing up and turning off the TV.

AT HIS LODGE, Clayton Sims sat laughing in his family suite. "You overplayed your hand, Jackson," he kept shouting. "You may have won the right to sit in the chair, but you're ours now, you dumb ass."

Sims was on the phone all morning celebrating the President's miscalculation and plotting the next move. The consensus was that the President was much weaker now. Some of his group saw this as a chance to reach a compromise deal that would carry through the entire four-year term while others saw a chance to make this Independent President a virtual prisoner of the two parties.

"He's our bitch now," Sims repeated to each caller, and that attitude was gaining momentum, even while calmer voices were appealing to reason as they saw a chance to secure the status quo indefinitely.

"Let's wait for a few days," the Captain decided after all the voices had been heard. "We let him sit in his pee for a while."

"YES, THIS IS CONNER," the reporter said as he pulled his cell phone from his bag.

"Bill, this is Jane from the studio. Are you seeing many people down there yet?" she asked.

Conner walked out from under the sunshade the crew had put up. "No, not really. Why are you asking?"

"My husband is a state trooper in Maryland, and we were just talking. He told me traffic into DC is ten times the normal volume. He said it's nuts out there."

"They aren't coming here, I can tell you that," Conner said. "But, hey, do me a favor and call the other states and see if they're seeing the same thing. Maybe it's a ball game or something. Let's check it out to be sure."

IN KEY WEST, Hiatt Montgomery was back at the airport waiting for a plane. His host had washed his clothes and provided him with a nice evening. He didn't understand such kindness, but he was more than willing to take advantage. "You can always count on a desperate woman," he always said.

Sims had ordered Montgomery back to Washington after he had reported in. The exchange had been colorful as Sims berated Montgomery for missing the target and losing the chopper.

"The next time you send me after some cowboy with a fucking elephant gun, you better have a better plan," Montgomery shouted back.

Jill had driven Montgomery to the airport and after a long and unexpected goodbye kiss made him promise he would visit the next time he made it to the Keys.

"I actually kinda like that girl," he thought as he walked to the plane.

"Here's your packet," the pilot announced as he handed Montgomery a large, sealed envelope.

Inside, Montgomery found a wallet with a driver's license, credit cards, and cash.

"That bag over there is for you, too," the pilot said as he pointed to a small suitcase. Inside, Montgomery found clothing and a sniper rifle similar to the one he lost in the helicopter crash.

IN FLORIDA, Sam and Victoria had fallen asleep on the beach as the warm breeze and lightly crashing waves eased all the stress from their minds. Of course the giant drinks Sam made helped, too.

"I'm going to walk up to the bathroom," Sam said, waking up.

Victoria rolled over for round two of her tanning session. "I'll be right here," she mumbled.

A few minutes later, Sam reemerged through the thicket. "There's not a single soul out here but us," he said as he sat down.

"Awesome. How about another drink?" Victoria said, smiling and holding her empty tumbler up in the air.

"Do you need more lotion, too?" Sam asked as he took her glass.

"Sure, smear it all over me," she laughed, her eyes closed.

"I like you on vodka," Sam said.

"BILL, IT'S JANE AGAIN."

"What did you find out?" Conner asked as he stood on a bench scanning the mall.

"Are you seeing anything yet?" she asked, sounding as excited as she was during the first call.

"A few more, I guess."

"We sent a chopper up, and it's the same story everywhere. The main arteries into DC are packed with traffic. It's incredible."

"I'm telling you, they're not coming here."

"Oh my God, look at that," Jane said.

"What is it? What are you looking at?" Conner shouted as he stood on his tiptoes trying to see.

"It's the Capitol, Bill. It's completely surrounded by a giant crowd. There has to be 10,000 people down there. Oh my God, look at that scene. Bill, get moving. They aren't coming to the White House. They've surrounded the Capitol. Oh my God, there are people everywhere. The streets are packed. Oh my God, it's crazy, Bill."

"We're already in the van," Conner shouted, his cell on speakerphone and rolling around the floorboard. "What streets are open?" The crew took off down Constitution.

"None. I'm serious. Park now. There's a flood of traffic coming from every direction. Park and get set up by the Capitol. We have to get this on air," Jane shouted.

Conner and his cameraman parked the van in the first spot they saw and jumped out.

"Forget the shade thing. Let's go."

As Conner approached, he heard the crowd chanting, "Pass the reforms. Pass the reforms."

"Hi, this is William Conner with CNN, and we are on site onside the U.S. Capitol Building," he began. "As you can see, it appears Americans are responding to the call the President made last night when he asked the people to show their displeasure with Congress. We estimate this crowd to number about 10,000, but our eyes in the sky are telling me that inbound traffic to DC is tenfold what is typical. Are they coming here? We don't know that yet. In the meantime we're going to talk to some of these folks to see what they have to say."

Conner and his cameraman started moving into the crowd as the people assembled continued chanting for Congress to take action. "Excuse me," he said as he approached a middle-aged, gray-haired woman. "I'm with CNN, and I would like. . . "

"I know who you are," the woman interrupted him.

"I assume you're here because of the President's request?" Conner asked as he put the microphone to her mouth.

"Yes, of course," the woman said almost sarcastically. An orange backpack hung from one shoulder, standing out against her white blouse. "I gathered up a few things, bought a tent and here I am."

"Tell us about the last 24 hours or so for you," Conner said as the people in the immediate area began to form around the news team.

"I saw the interview you did last night. Not live, I saw it rebroadcast later. And I decided I've had enough, and I'm going to Washington. I'm staying here until those assholes in that building pass the plan our President ran on."

The crowd around the woman started chanting again while many laughed at her description of Congress.

"I take it you all agree?" Conner asked as he looked around the immediate group.

"Yes, we've had enough. We want these guys out. The President is right. These two parties have crapped all over this country," said a big, burly man dressed in blue jeans and a tan t-shirt.

"Where are you from?" Conner asked the man.

"Chicago."

"What do you do for a living?" Conner asked.

"I've worked construction my entire life, and now I have my own cement contracting business," the man said proudly. "Those guys in there are nothing but professional campaigners. Most of them have never worked hard or had to worry about making ends meet. They're lawyers and children of a privileged class. I want to personally go in there and throw those bums to the curb. They wouldn't last a day in our world."

Again, the crowd cheered and some laughed.

"Let's go around the group here. Tell me where you are from and what you do for a living."

"Cleveland—teacher."

"Hartford—stay-at-home mom."

"Atlanta—bus driver."

"Baltimore—banker."

"Nashville—factory worker."

"I'm guessing some of you used to be a member of one of the two parties?" Conner asked.

They all nodded in agreement.

"So, what happened?" Conner asked as he scanned the group.

"There's no difference between the two really," one said.

"It doesn't matter which one's in power," another said.

"The debt goes up, the wars continue, special interests get their favors. It doesn't matter. They need to be gone. They have damaged our country," another one added.

"So, what's your plan?" Conner asked.

"We'll stay here until they pass our President's proposal," the teacher said. "I can tell you that employers have told their

people, 'Go and protest. Your job will be here when you get
back.' This is not a normal protest. The entire country is on its
way here. These guys have overplayed their hand. Their time
is over."

The woman talking pointed out toward a scene of tents
being erected in every direction. Kids were playing soccer in an
area that seemed to already be designated as 'the playground.'
In another section, folks were cooking on small grills and
encouraging people to pool their food.

"Is this protest coordinated at all? I mean has any group or
spokesperson emerged?" Conner asked as he looked at all of the
people gathered.

"No, we are that 'reasonable middle' the President always
talks about. I'm not 'red' or 'blue' all the time. We're tired of all
the crap. The parties have tried to reel everybody in to their
stupid red-versus-blue thing. It's a bunch of nonsense," one of
the onlookers said as others nodded.

"It's time for something different. This President isn't like
those two parties. He doesn't think like them," another said.
"That's what we wanted, and that's what we got. Now Congress
is standing in the way. They need to go. Every damned one of
them. We need everyday people in there who don't have a
desire to stay here their entire lives."

A bicyclist pulling a small wagon rode past Conner and
stopped near the grills. "I have hot dogs and hamburgers for
sale," the girl called out. She was immediately surrounded and
her inventory cleared out. "I'll be back soon," she announced as
she stuffed the money in her pocket and rode off.

"That's the heart of it right there," another woman said,
stepping up and shouting into the microphone. "Our founders
designed the House with two-year terms so any of us could
come here and serve and then go home. But these two parties
have stolen the House and turned it into a lifetime job with
retirement plans and all kinds of special privileges. If we fixed
the House, we would fix most of our problems."

A Frisbee landed in the middle of the group, and everyone
stopped and watched two boys racing to grab it. "Sorry mister,"
one of the kids called out as his buddy scooped it up and ran
back toward the play area.

"How would that fix things?" Conner asked as he regained his focus.

"Because lifetime politicians are vulnerable to these damned lobbyists," the woman answered. "If I came here, I would want to pass laws that were good for me and other normal people like me. I mean, I would be back living in my home two years later. If we had everyday people in the House, they wouldn't vote for all these special deals for whomever the party or the lobbyist told them to. It's over for these people. We aren't leaving until they pass our President's reforms. Everybody I know is coming here. We've had enough of these clowns."

The group around her started cheering and smiling.

Conner faced the camera. "We'll be broadcasting from the Mall as long as this protest against Congress continues. I've been out here all day, and I was growing convinced that the President's request had fallen on deaf ears, but . . ."

"Hey, buddy," the jean-clad Chicagoan interrupted. "You know we all have lives to live, bills to pay, kids and parents to look after. I dropped everything and made it here in less than a day. You're all out of touch with reality in this town. Even you media people have let our country down. You are here every day. You've had a front row seat to all this bullshit for years. For a typical American, dropping everything and coming here is tough. This town is full of people out of touch with reality, and you media people are right there with them." With that, he turned and headed back into the crowd.

"As you can see and hear, there is a lot of anger out here," Conner said. "I'm going to send this back to the studio for a few minutes and see if we can't get all of our equipment out and set up for an extended stay. This is William Conner reporting from outside the U.S. Capitol."

Conner walked to the van and climbed on the roof to get an idea of how large the crowd had grown.

"Hand me up the camera. You aren't going to believe this," Conner said of the sea of people assembling around him.

"This crowd has grown ten-fold in just the last 20 minutes," he said as he handed the camera back down. "Give me my phone. It's on the passenger floor board."

Conner called the CNN office to find out if the helicopter was still over the city.

"They're watching the traffic," someone from his office informed him.

"Get me an update. I need to know if this is it, or are they still coming," Conner requested.

"Stand by."

Quickly returning, the woman reported, "All inbound major roads inside the loop are at a virtual standstill."

"My God," Conner said in a stunned whisper. "That could be another hundred thousand people. Hell, that could be a million more."

CHAPTER EIGHT
Fracture

A t the White House, the President entered his family quarters after a long day with the Chinese delegation. He had downplayed the events of the previous day, but he was as curious as everyone else about how the people would react. The Chinese also were interested and tried several times to switch the conversation away from trade to American politics.

The President's open criticism of the two parties had struck a nerve with his Chinese counterpart who was fascinated by this renegade taking office against the will of the "establishment." In fact, the idea terrified the Chinese who wondered why the two parties would have allowed such a thing. Once upstairs and comfortable, Niles turned on the TV to see William Conner's interviews in the crowd. "I'll be damned," the President said as he turned the TV up.

Anthony Sinclair soon arrived, asking if he could join the President.

"I think this makes things much more complicated," Sinclair said as he took a seat.

"How so?" the President asked.

"They're going to feel like they're under siege."

"They are under siege," the President quickly responded.

"I haven't received anything from them yet, but when we do, I think we should take a hard look at it. This thing could swing back against us if we appear to be acting too dictatorial," Sinclair said with growing concern in his voice. "Jackson, let's get a deal done soon. Let's not take an all-or-nothing approach."

"It's their move," the President answered as he walked into the kitchen.

"I think it would make a big impact if you would reach out to the parties and indicate you are willing to negotiate a bit," Sinclair suggested.

"That's ironic, coming from you," the President said, smiling as he returned with a can of peanuts.

"Why's that?"

"A few days ago, you were lamenting the fact that good policy often gets ground up over there," Niles said as he motioned toward the Capitol. The President kicked his shoes off and put his feet up on the coffee table.

"I think you have a chance here to get nearly all that you want. That doesn't happen often," Sinclair said.

"There are a few hundred thousand people out there who left their real lives to come here and demand change. I owe them, Anthony. They aren't here so we can cut some watered-down, backroom deal. No, I'm not going to start making offers now," the President said. He pulled out his cell phone. "You'll have to excuse me, Anthony. I need to call the kids. They've been texting me all day."

IN FLORIDA, SAM and Victoria were now lying together under the big umbrella.

"Let's stay out here and watch the sun go down," Victoria whispered.

"Fine by me," Sam said as he squeezed her even tighter.

"Will you go with me up to the bathroom first?" Victoria asked as she sat up and pulled on the long pink t-shirt.

"Sure."

"I can't believe no one is out here," Victoria remarked as they walked up the beach.

"I guess it's because it's a weekday," Sam said.

When Victoria emerged from the bathroom, Sam was sitting by the water's edge. As she got close, she pulled off the t-shirt and threw it at Sam's head.

"What are you doing now?" Sam laughed.

"Guess what, you dummy? Didn't you see that sign back there? This is a nude beach. That's why nobody's here. Come on, let's take a naked walk, only for a minute, so I can say I've done it." Victoria walked backwards, taunting Sam, who was reluctantly untying his suit.

"This is wrong on several levels," he said as he caught up with her.

"I kind of like it," she said as she kicked sand toward an incoming wave.

"This is not something I thought I would be doing when I woke up this morning," Sam chuckled.

"Oh, relax. There's no one around, and there hasn't been all day. A little further and then back, okay?" she said as she waded into ankle-deep water.

A little further up, the beach curved back, and as they rounded the corner, they saw a wide section of beach dotted with big palm trees.

"Wow, it's so pretty," Victoria said.

"We could go get our stuff and move if you want," Sam offered.

"There is a better breeze out here," she said. "I love the beach."

Victoria grabbed his hand and came up close. "But I love you even more, Sam McBride," she whispered as she kissed him and wrapped her arms around him.

"I love you, too, Pinky, and I would love you more if we could go back to our little camp right now."

Victoria laughed. "Fair enough. I can cross off 'nude beach' from my bucket list now."

As they turned to head back to the other end of the little island, they spotted a group of college-aged kids rounding the corner. All, of course, were completely naked.

"Hey, you two want to join us in a game of volleyball?" one of the women shouted as she ran up.

"We need two more," another yelled.

Sam moved his swimsuit so it hung in front, giving him a little cover. Victoria, on the other hand, had left her t-shirt on the ground after throwing it at Sam. She did have on a big floppy hat and over-sized glasses, so being recognized was not a concern. What was a concern was that she was naked in front of a bunch of twenty-somethings who expected her to jump around with them.

"I think we'll pass, but thanks for the invite," Victoria said with an embarrassed smile so big it made her mouth hurt.

"Okay, no problem," one of the women said.

"It's really cool that two people your age are out here," another said as they walked away. Victoria waved over her shoulder as she burst out laughing and grabbed onto Sam's arm.

"Never again. Don't even ask next time," Sam said, walking faster and faster toward the far end of the beach. Victoria was laughing so hard she couldn't keep up.

"Oh, come on, you gotta laugh," she said as they returned to where they had started and she picked up her t-shirt and suit.

The two made it back to their hidden spot, and Sam quickly whipped up a couple of drinks. Victoria was still giggling when she sat down to join him.

"Come on that was crazy, right?" she asked as she tried to get a smile out of Sam.

"Crazy? Yeah, that was crazy," he said, handing her another Scannell.

"Wow, that tall guy in the back. Now he was something," she said as she jumped up and ran into the water.

"Oh, I'm kidding," she called out to Sam who was still sitting on his towel. "Let's take a quick swim." Then Victoria dove into the crashing waves.

INSIDE THE CAPITOL, nerves were fraying as members of Congress debated the best course of action. Reactions ranged from making statements to ignoring the "crazies." Some had left early, anticipating the strong reaction to the President's message.

Speaker Reed was in his office with other House leaders from both parties, watching the news broadcast.

"This is not good," Reed said. "Not at all." He had taken the cane purportedly owned by General Lee and clutched it with both hands. "How would a great general react in this situation?" he thought as he listened to the fear in the room.

The crowd outside had grown so dense that police were having trouble keeping the roads open. Tents had sprung up across the Mall, and it was evident the protesters were not planning on leaving soon.

"We're screwed," one of the House members said as he watched the interviews Conner was conducting outside their windows.

The others looked his way, but no one offered a reassuring comment. The room was dimmer than normal as a light bulb had burned out earlier in the day and the scene developing outside had prevented maintenance from making the trip to the Capitol. The lighting change actually softened the mustard color of the walls, and on a normal day someone likely would have noticed. Today no one seemed to care.

"It does look like the House will be the focus," Reed said. "We better come up with a plan to get this thing defused soon, or we won't have any wiggle room with this guy. Hell, we may not have any now."

"At the current rate, there might be a million people out there by morning," another said.

"At least" another mumbled.

"The Senate is going to dig in its heels," Reed said.

"They can afford to," another said.

"Every single one of us is up for reelection every two years. There's no way we can survive something like this. We need to make a move without the Senate," a leading Democrat urged.

"And do what?" Reed asked. "Capitulate? Sign our own mass termination? What would you have us do?"

"We make a deal that gives him everything he wants *except* term limits," another suggested.

"And you think those people out there would go for that?" Reed asked. "That would smack of self-preservation at any cost. No, we need a proposal that gives him almost everything but doesn't single out term limits. We need to hold back a few things, and that would be one of them. If we play this smart and get out in front of it, we can come out of this as friends of those people out there. If we don't, we're in trouble."

Reed scanned the room looking for input. Those gathered simply stared back at their leader.

"Let's all make some notes tonight and meet here first thing tomorrow. I'm going to go out there and tell the media we have a proposal coming tomorrow. Each of you write up a list of items we can hold back, carve-outs from what the President wants. Get as detailed as you can so this looks like we thought it out. We'll get that out tomorrow and see if we can't shift the focus off the House," Reed instructed.

He stood, put on his suit jacket, and walked to the door.

"Wish me luck," Reed mumbled.

IN FLORIDA, SAM and Victoria walked out of a little seafood restaurant with two bags of carryout. After a long and wonderful day on the beach, they were ready for a night in.

"I wonder if anyone has answered Jackson's call?" Victoria said as Sam started the car.

"I sure hope so."

"If not, I think he's going to be in a weak position," she said as she stuffed a hush puppy in her mouth. "Damn good, but hot, hot, hot." She scrambled for a drink of her bottled water.

"His reforms are going to hinge on public pressure. He always knew that. He did this knowing the risk," Sam said after putting the hush puppy he had grabbed back in the bag. "The parties have acted exactly as he expected. He knew the election was only one part of the fight."

Once they were in their room, Victoria went straight for the shower.

"That food is so hot I have time," she said as she disappeared into the bath.

After unpacking the food cartons, Sam searched the little kitchen for plates and forks. The room was sparsely furnished, but he came up with one plate and a large bowl. After a quick shower, Victoria emerged in a clean black and white t-shirt and matching shorts.

"Wow, does it feel good getting clean after a day on the beach," she said, taking a bottle of water from the cooler.

"How does DC look?" she asked Sam.

"I haven't turned it on yet. I'm going to shower real quick myself," Sam said.

"We can eat when you get out," Victoria said as she turned on the TV still tuned to CNN from the morning. Victoria sat down, stunned, as she watched the camera pan across the National Mall.

"Oh, my God. Sam, get out here," she screamed as she burst into the bathroom. Sam stuck his soap-covered head out of the shower.

"What is it?"

"Look at this," she yelled as she pointed at the TV.

Sam emerged seconds later with the soap rinsed off and a towel wrapped around his waist. "Holy cow," he said as he slid down on the little sofa next to Victoria. "It worked. His plan is actually working."

By now the Mall was completely inundated with Americans who had responded to their President's call. CNN was reporting that well over 1 million people were there, and inbound traffic had not slowed at all.

"It's a stampede to the Capitol," one reporter said describing the scene.

As the sun set, the Mall looked more like the scene at a giant tailgate party than a mass protest. Tents were everywhere, and people were cooking everything imaginable on hundreds of grills. William Conner walked through the crowd with his cameraman, doing interviews and showing pictures of the festive atmosphere. Many families had taken their children out of school so they could be part of what many were calling "The Second Revolution."

The scene intoxicated Sam and Victoria as they tried to imagine how happy and excited Jackson must be as he watched from the White House.

Interviews with the DC police confirmed that the crowd had been extremely well behaved, and one cop even pointed out, "This group doesn't even litter," as he smiled into Conner's camera.

By the time they finished their dinner, Sam and Victoria were more at ease than at any moment since all the craziness had started. Both felt secure knowing there was no longer anyone able to track them and that Jackson had executed his plan with perfect precision.

"This is incredible," Victoria said returning from the kitchen with a bottle of water. "I am so relieved." She fell back into the sofa.

"Come on, let's go get some ice cream," Sam suggested as he stood up and threw his towel at Victoria.

"Like that?"

"Uh, no," he said, looking for a pair of shorts.

They left the hotel and walked down the dimly lit street to a small grocery store by the main road into town. Sam had noticed earlier that the store had a big freezer of ice cream along with what looked like a larger-than-expected wine selection.

"Those are the biggest ice cream sandwiches I have ever seen," Victoria said as she pulled out two.

"I saw those this morning," Sam said, coming around the corner with a bottle of champagne in each hand. "If we are going to celebrate, then let's celebrate." He held them up for Victoria to see.

"That stuff makes me crazy," she said as she put her hands in the air and danced toward the cashier.

The boy at the front of the store was sitting on a bar stool and watching a small TV mounted in the corner behind the counter.

"Look at that! It's crazy," he said, pointing to the scene being broadcast from Washington as they sat their items down on the counter. "I loved studying history when I was in school, and this is like watching history being made. This is nuts. Man, I wish I was there. Have you guys ever been to DC?"

"No, but I would like to someday," Victoria said as the young man scanned their items.

"I voted for this guy, but I never thought he would actually be able to do anything. They all say the same crap," the clerk said and shrugged.

Sam and Victoria left the store, smiling as they recalled the young man's comments.

"I feel so happy for my brother," Victoria said as she and Sam crossed the street and headed for a small marina. It was old and dimly lit but offered a nice place to walk and enjoy the cool evening air. They walked along eating their ice cream and critiquing the boats.

"Wish we had some glasses for this champagne," Sam said as he placed his ice cream sandwich wrapper in a trashcan.

"Tastes the same out of the bottle," Victoria said, laughing while she twisted off the foil and pushed the cork out. The bottle bubbled out as she held it away from them both. "Here's to Jackson," she said taking a big drink and then handing the bottle to Sam.

"Here's to us," Sam said as he pulled Victoria close.

"I am so happy right now," she whispered as she put her arm around Sam and her head against his shoulder. "I have so much fun doing anything with you."

Sam leaned over and kissed her forehead.

"When this is all over, will you promise me that we will still get together?" Victoria asked. "I'm not asking for anything permanent. I want to see you from time to time. I'm going to be starting a new life somewhere, and I want us to stay close."

"We will, Pinky. I promise," Sam said. He set the bottle down and kissed her long and passionately. "I promise, Pinky, we will be close."

Victoria took a deep breath, and when she exhaled, it was as if she released the fear of losing Sam again from her life.

"I think I felt a rain drop," she said. Victoria rubbed her hand over her head.

"Walking in the rain and drinking champagne out of a bottle. Is that on your list, too?" Sam asked as they crossed the street and the rain became more consistent.

They walked along, passing the bottle back and forth until finally Sam tossed it into a trashcan.

"So, you did the nude beach thing today, how bout walking in the rain nude?" Sam smiled.

"I think once a day is my limit," Victoria said as they strolled along.

"Really?" Sam said as he paused and smiled at her.

"Yeah, really. Let's go. I'm getting soaked," Victoria said as she pulled on Sam's hand.

"So now you're chicken," he taunted as he pulled his hand away. "Bak, bak bak, come on chicky, chicky. Come on, Pinky, where are you now? There is no one out here, chicky, chicky."

Sam laughed as he circled Victoria, flapping his arms and bobbing his head like some overgrown, drunk chicken. The rain came down harder and harder.

"You don't think I'll do it, do you?" Victoria asked, hands on her hips.

"Bak, bak, chicky, chicky," Sam went on.

Victoria looked at the hotel, which was still probably 200 feet away. The area was dark, with the exception of the lights over each hotel room door. She stepped back from the drunk and dancing Sam and pulled off her t-shirt. Then in one smooth move she pulled down her shorts, kicked them up with her foot, caught them in the air, and took off for the hotel.

"Come on, chicken man, catch me if you can," she yelled running down the sandy shoulder of the road. Sam quickly followed. He continued taunting her while trying to get his own shorts off. Victoria reached the hotel first and expected to see Sam right behind her. Instead, she turned to see Sam standing behind a car at the edge of the parking lot. He waved and smiled.

"Come on, Sam!" Victoria pleaded in a hushed shout. "I'm naked out here, mister. Now, come on."

She reached the door under the light, as Sam stood laughing. Realizing he had the room keys and she had been scammed, Victoria quickly pulled on her shirt and then struggled to get her shorts turned right side out.

Just then, a man approached from the edge of the parking lot. Spotting the naked man standing by his car, he shouted, "Hey, you freak, get away from my car!"

Sam jumped back from the car and quickly ducked low and crawled around a couple cars further away.

"I'll tell you, this state is full of freaks and weirdoes," the man yelled as he jumped in his car and sped away.

Still naked, Sam scampered across the lot, keys in hand, and quickly opened the room. Victoria had been laughing so hard she was still on the sidewalk outside the door as an embarrassed Sam jumped over her and entered the room.

"Oh, my god the look on your face," she yelled, laughing hysterically. "That was awesome. Oh my god. If only I had a camera. Nobody will ever believe that happened."

Victoria was still lying outside trying to catch her breath as Sam emerged, now dressed, and sat down next to the still sprawled out Victoria.

"I need to catch my breath," she said as she lay there.

Eventually, Sam, too, started laughing at the scene he had inadvertently starred in.

"Now that was funny," he said.

"It was hilarious," Victoria belted out as she started laughing again. "Oh, I can't stop."

"Marry me," Sam said softly.

Victoria stopped laughing and looked up at him.

"What did you say?" she asked, suddenly serious.

"Marry me," Sam repeated.

"You're serious, aren't you?"

"Yes, Victoria Pinky Niles, I am completely serious. I want every day I have left of this life to be a day with you. Marry me. Please marry me." Sam's face was full of emotion and his voice cracked a little.

"Yes," Victoria whispered as she took Sam's hand. "Yes, yes, yes."

BY EARLY EVENING, Peter Mercury had gone stir crazy watching the events taking place in Washington. "This might be the biggest story of my life, and I'm stuck out here in Montana in the home of people I don't even know," he thought as he paced back and forth. By now, every news channel in the DC area was "live on the scene" as more and more people flooded into Washington. Several stations had helicopters filming the inbound traffic as cars continued to slowly move toward the Capitol. Countless reporters were in the crowd interviewing people who had come from virtually every corner of the nation. One group had flown in from California after watching the President's interview while they were at work.

"We dropped everything and went to the airport," one of the men said.

"Everybody here is basically in the same boat," another added.

"We've had enough of this system like it is. These people get elected and then spend their entire careers here. That's bullshit. Get a job and find out what it's really like in realityville," another chimed in. "They get elected a couple times, and then they get a lifetime retirement plan. It's wrong. We've been scammed by these guys and especially by these two frickin' parties."

A mother from Arizona spoke up, "I had a friend who wanted to run for office in Arizona," she said.

"What happened?" the reporter asked.

"She ran into the 'party' system," she answered. "They control the registration process; they set the criteria for debates; they have the big money from their lobbyist friends. It's simply a rigged system. If you aren't in their club, you aren't getting in. It's that simple."

"Why didn't she run as a candidate in one of the parties?" the reporter asked.

"Why do we have to? Why is that the system? Why do they control everything? Why don't you report on how much they control? Our problem is the two parties. The President nailed it from the beginning. We're sick of those clowns, and we want them out. They should lose all their perks. It's all ridiculous."

The woman turned and walked back into the crowd as those around clapped and patted her on the back.

"This protest is sure looking like the beginning of a new party," the reporter said as he faced the camera.

"The party of the reasonable," a man yelled from the back of the crowd.

"There you have it," the reporter said as he turned and acknowledged the man. "The self-described 'Reasonable Party.' You heard it here first."

Everyone in the group began to cheer and laugh.

Peter continued watching, but he was about to explode. "I'm going," he said as he jumped up. "But I can't put Jack in jeopardy," he thought as he sat back down. He sat a minute thinking, then jumped up and headed for the bathroom.

"I'm going to shave my head and be an anonymous face in the crowd," he finally concluded. "I don't have to be a reporter. I can be there as a citizen."

Peter pulled electric clippers from the cabinet and changed his appearance. He left a note thanking the couple and also asked them to assure Jack he would stay invisible until it was clear things were okay. He also promised the couple he would return their truck.

THE NEXT MORNING, Speaker Reed and the other House members arrived while it was still dark out, dodging the heckling that greeted later arrivals. Once inside, Reed assembled the leadership and quickly went to work on a simple, bullet-point outline of areas they were willing to concede. All were designed, of course, to protect the House members from term limits and their supporters from being restricted from giving to campaigns. Reed and the others went through the House, discussing the outline with senior members and hoping to reach a quick consensus so action could be taken immediately.

By mid-morning, Reed had enough buy-in that he felt comfortable getting the details to the White House. At this point, the discussion in the room was whether or not to involve the Senate, which had been completely silent about the protests going on outside.

"Those guys are going to keep their distance," a senior representative said, speaking for the majority of the House members present. The Senate wasn't the target of the President's term-limit issue, after all.

"But they're also hostile to many of the changes we are about to say we will accept," another member pointed out.

"We have a chance to get out in front here and offer some compromise on many key items," Reed said. "Hell, we have two million people out there screaming for our heads. We better come up with something. If we do nothing, the President ends up making us look like we won't even meet him half way. We're in a box here, people. We have to do something."

"Let's send it over," another member said. All nodded and looked around for confirmation from their colleagues.

"Okay, I'll call Sinclair and see if we can get a meeting set for later today. If this works, the Senate might be on the hot seat, but at least we'll be okay," Reed said as he left for his office.

BY NOW, HIATT MONTGOMERY had made his way to one of the downtown DC apartments the Council maintained for visiting VIPs. From his window he could see the crowd. It had spread out so much that protestors occupied all of central DC, including all the memorials. Reports were circulating that many streets had been abandoned by police because the volume of people was simply too great to contain.

Montgomery had been told to go and wait; instructions would follow. He was glad to be done with chasing McBride, but he also looked forward to circling back later and setting things straight.

AT THE WHITE HOUSE, a smiling Anthony Sinclair entered the Oval Office and handed the President the list from Reed. "I have to hand it to you," he proclaimed with a smile. "These guys have come around."

The President looked at the list and then got up and walked to his window.

"Look at all those people out there." he said as he pulled back the drapes. "Can you imagine the disruption those people have voluntarily caused to their own lives? It's incredible. I was hoping a hundred thousand would show up. The DC police told me this morning people are now parking sixty miles outside of town in backyards converted to parking lots and taking buses into DC. Can you imagine that?"

The President approached Sinclair and put his hands on his old friend's shoulders. "You tell my old friend Reed that he needs to come all the way over. He needs to embrace the term limits and the financing restrictions. He will go down in history as a great statesman. He has that chance. There will be no deal on those two issues. The money is coming out of these House seats."

"Jackson, for God's sake, what are you doing?" Sinclair asked in an uncharacteristically emotional tone. "You have them by the balls. Do you have to humiliate them, too? Why? Take the victory, and let's get on with it."

"Go walk through that crowd for an hour, and then come back here and tell me that," the President said. "Go out there and talk to those people. The average income out there is probably forty-five thousand a year or so, and that's the average. These guys in the House make five times that, and they get healthcare, retirement, and who knows how many free trips from lobbyists. No, sir, I am not quitting on them now. Send the message to Wilson. That's final."

The President got up and walked back to the window. *"They're* going to win this time," he said staring out at the crowd.

IN FLORIDA, THE SUN streaming through the small window across from their bed woke Sam and Victoria.

"I had a dream last night that you were a giant chicken running around naked," Victoria said as she started laughing hysterically.

Sam let her enjoy the laugh for a minute or so and then whispered, "I had a dream you were my wife."

Victoria snuggled up next to Sam. "I like your dream better," she whispered. "But, man, that was funny."

They spent the morning in bed, holding each other. The TV was off, and they didn't talk much either. They quietly enjoyed the moment, celebrating that this time what they had together was for good.

WHEN REED RECEIVED Sinclair's message, it sent a shock wave through the House. The sound of millions of average Americans outside chanting, "Pass the reforms," was becoming deafening to those inside the Capitol.

"Now what?" the leaders asked Reed as they huddled in his office.

"I don't know. I didn't expect this answer. Hell, I don't think any of us did."

Reed looked through the list they had sent over, then tossed the sheet in the air. "He's after us, plain and simple. He wants us out," Reed said as he slumped back in his chair. "He's demanding our unconditional surrender. That's what this boils down to. But, hell, look outside. There are millions of people out there on a witch-hunt, and we're the targets. Maybe the Senate is next. I don't know, but today it's us. There's no parallel in history for this. The President's demanding we vote ourselves out of a job."

AT THE LODGE, Cochran and Sims received a phone call from Reed informing them of the House offer and the President's response. Cochran nearly collapsed in anger as he learned of Reed's solo move.

"You shit on all of us, you dumb ass," he screamed at the phone. "What the fuck have you done?"

"We're surrounded here, and you're sitting out there in a goddamned fort plotting what? You guys better come up with something good, and fast. This city is going to burn down around us if these people don't get something," Reed responded.

For Sims, the news of Niles' reaction only bolstered his argument that this President, friend or not, needed to go. Neither Sims nor Cochran expected any serious response to the President's appeal to the people, so they had no contingency plan for what to do now.

"Has the Captain weighed in yet on all this?" Cochran asked.

"Not in any meaningful way," Sims answered. "He thought it would blow over, and the President would cut a deal."

"That ain't happening," Cochran said.

"No, it's not," Sims added.

IN FLORIDA, SAM AND Victoria packed and checked out after seeing a cockroach scurry up the wall. It was Sam's turn to laugh hysterically as Victoria jumped out of bed and had everything packed and outside before he could even find his shorts.

"Right now," she had yelled as she saw the giant creature. "We are leaving right now!"

As they turned onto Interstate 70, Sam's phone began to light up with messages from his old friend Charlie. Sam exited so he could look through them without sitting on the edge of the highway.

The messages were a series of pictures Charlie had taken over the last two days.

"This is bad," Sam announced as he went through the shots.

"What's bad? What is it, Sam?" Victoria asked.

"I've got a guy out in the woods watching the Sims Lodge," Sam confessed.

"What guy?"

"He's an old friend from my militia days."

"I always thought that was only a bunch of guys running around playing army," Victoria said.

Sam looked over at Victoria with a slight smile and a little disappointment.

"I'm sorry, I didn't mean anything by that. I guess I'm still a bit giddy from last night," she said. She kissed Sam on the cheek as he continued going through the pictures.

"No big deal," he said as he continued flipping through the photos. "We need to find out who all these people are. There might be a couple hundred faces in all these."

"I'm no help. My contacts think I'm dead," Victoria said as she slumped back in her seat. "But if all these people are coming in and out of the lodge, then this group is up to something more than opposing my nomination or Jackson's reforms." She sat sideways. Her voice rose as her mind considered the scale of the group. "Sam, what do you think this group is planning?"

"We have to find out who these people are, and to do that, we have to get these pictures to Jackson."

"How do we do that?"

"He has a cell phone in my name that he uses only to talk with me."

"Perfect," Victoria said.

"Not if the bad guys know about it," Sam said. "We used it during the campaign and never had any problems, but who knows now? They were all over that credit card as soon as I used it. This phone belongs to one of my ranch hands." Sam held up the phone with the pictures.

"If those guys know about the phone Jackson has, they will be on us in a matter of an hour or so." Sam said as he sat back and looked at Victoria. "We need to plan for that."

"We could get one of those prepaid phones. So we send the pictures, ditch your phone, and then get moving," she said. "By the time they send someone after us, we'll be an hour or two down the road. If we send the pictures, we don't need to go to DC. If we need a phone, we can use the prepaid one."

Victoria was clear-headed and determined in her speech. "We can only do so much under the circumstances. We'll help Jackson and keep ourselves safe. We're getting married, mister, and I'm going to make sure you stay safe." She gave Sam a long kiss.

"Okay, that's a plan," Sam said as he pulled the car back on the highway and headed toward a cluster of shops on a nearby road.

After sending the photos to Jackson, purchasing a prepaid phone, and driving for twenty minutes or so, Sam could feel Victoria start to relax a little. "You and Jackson have talked a lot about the reforms?"

"Certain areas," Victoria answered.

"Jackson and I have had long discussions about term limits and campaign finance reform, but I haven't heard much detail about the other things."

"Jackson listens to lots of people," Victoria said. "It's one of his strengths."

"You said something about business and taxes the other day that surprised me."

"If a person has a quality job, they have a chance for a quality life," Victoria said.

"But no taxes?" Sam said looking at her with a doubting smile.

"If our country had the best environment for business to go along with our huge and stable consumer market then every company in the world would want to be here."

"That's probably true."

"What follows then is a labor shortage which helps raise wages," Victoria explained. "If businesses have to compete for workers then it's natural to believe that wages will increase. The mentor program gets these inner city kids aware and prepared for this new reality."

"Half that idea pisses off the liberals and half pisses off the conservatives," Sam suggested.

"Yes, and that's a sad truth. Both sides are half right and half wrong all the time. Jobs are critical to a healthy society, but so are well-educated and trained workers. If business is punished and the uneducated ignored, a society starts to unravel. Combine two problems to form multiple solutions, and everyone wins. It's not about ideology; it's about results. Imagine what happens if everyone had the opportunity to earn a living wage."

Sam slowed down as the traffic backed up. He could see taillights lighting up on all the cars ahead of them.

"What is it?"

"I think just a work zone," Sam said.

As traffic started moving again, Victoria sat back. She felt safe, but she also was on edge.

"Jackson doesn't care about the old, tired political philosophies. There are issues he wants the states to handle completely. Education, for instance, just drives him nuts. Nobody cares more about a kids' education than a parent or teacher. We don't need a bunch of people in DC telling schools how to teach. But when a kid is failing because their home environment is terrible, that's when the government can and should help."

"That's the mentor program?" Sam asked.

"Right, but even that is administered at a local level. They become what Thomas Jefferson called the 'laboratories of democracy.' Let the states all experiment and create and share, and we end up with an always improving system. But once you try to standardize and regulate, you just kill off the dynamic spirit."

"I'm beginning to think you are far more involved than I thought," Sam said.

"I've only talked in detail with him about these two areas," Victoria insisted.

"Are you getting hungry?" Sam asked.

"A little."

"Well, it looks like the battery on the car is getting a little low, too. Let's pull off at the next exit. We can charge up the battery and grab a sandwich," Sam suggested.

IN WASHINGTON, the flood of citizens had reached a point far beyond what even the most optimistic person could have imagined. The DC police, who had been urged by the White House to be patient, were stressed to the maximum. The crowd was well behaved, and there had been no reports of violence or trouble. But now protestors, who had erected tents and set up for a long stay, occupied even most of the side streets. Local vendors had quickly adapted to the new environment, and bicycle-pulled carts moved through the crowd selling water and food.

AT THE WHITE HOUSE, the President sat alone in the Oval Office. By now he was sure that the mood in the Capitol had swung to complete desperation. He had hoped for a strong citizen response, but even he was shocked by what he saw as he flipped through the news channels.

"This truly is a revolution," he whispered.

With the exception of national security meetings, most of his schedule had been cleared due to the protests. His friends in the military were anxious to remain unseen during the events in Washington, so many attended meetings via teleconference. Although most were uncomfortable with the proposed changes, they also were loyal to the President. He had been to war and fought alongside many of the current high-ranking members, and as a result, his relationship with the military leaders remained rock solid.

Susan Mercury interrupted the President as she burst into the Oval Office. "Sir, there has been an explosion at a natural gas facility outside the city."

As she got the words out, CNN announced the same news from the location. A large ball of fire was burning out of control in the background behind the reporter.

"From what we've learned, the explosion resulted from an accident involving a service vehicle," the reporter announced as sirens blared in the background. "There are no reports of injuries, but officials have said it will take several days to determine the extent of the damages to this facility."

"We are told this facility connects to one of the main lines that supplies natural gas from Texas all the way to New York," the CNN reporter continued, as police moved onlookers away from the scene. "So it sounds as if gas service will be disrupted at least a few days for a large swath of the country. Officials do not seem concerned that the crowds in Washington will cause any complications regarding repairs, so that is good news."

"Has there been any mention of terrorism?" a studio anchor asked the onsite reporter.

"Not as of now. In fact, the feeling here is that an old valve that was in need of repair simply ruptured when the vehicle lost control and struck the line. There has been no suspicion of foul play."

"We'll keep you up to date on that story. Now, we return to Bill Conner on the ground outside the Capitol. Bill, are people there aware of the explosion at the gas facility?" the studio reporter asked.

"No, people here are focused on the issue at hand," Connor said. "And I have to tell you, the crowds are becoming impatient with their representatives inside the Capitol. I'm not suggesting they're becoming violent, but there is a growing sense here that the bureaucrats intend to wait this out. The feeling I get is that these people will stay here indefinitely if that's what it takes."

Conner looked around at the crowd, which was beginning to look like a unified movement. Purple shirts dotted the sea of people, and a few purple flags could be seen flapping in the wind.

"What is the meaning of the purple that I am seeing in the crowd?" Conner asked the first person he saw wearing one of the shirts.

"That's who we are," the man responded. "We aren't blue, and we aren't red. We are the reasonable people trapped in between these two idiot parties. We are Purple Reason."

The man pointed to several other people in the crowd who also had on the same shirts.

"So this crowd is forming into a united movement?" Conner asked as he panned the group.

"We have always been unified. Now, we realize those bums in there are not going to act unless we show them it's over. The age of the professional politician is over," a woman said, moving in closer to the microphone. "We'll stay here until they pass the President's reforms or until the next election. We're going to replace the entire House if that's what it takes."

The crowd cheered as she stepped back into the throng.

"Wait a minute," Conner said as the woman disappeared. "Is there a leader, has anyone emerged as a spokesperson for this Purple Reason?" Conner looked around waiting for someone to respond.

"The President," the crowd said in almost perfect unison.

"There you have it," Conner said as he looked into the camera. "The President seems to be getting his wish. He now has a party, and it looks as though it will be called Purple Reason."

AFTER FULLY CHARGING their electric car, Sam and Victoria were back on the road in about 30 minutes. After eating a sub and taking their water bottles to go, they were set for another few hours of driving. Traffic had thinned out, too.

"Did you know Miller Redding at all?" Sam asked.

"I actually met Miller years ago at an environmental conference in Mexico," Victoria said.

"So were you involved in getting him on the ticket?"

"No not really. He called me before he committed, but he had already made his decision. Miller was a great guy. He had a few pet projects he wanted in the platform and asked me if I thought Jackson would go along."

"So you were the go between?"

"No nothing like that. He just needed to hear that he could count on my brother. He wanted the national debt resolved, and it made him crazy mad that Congress just went on year after year doing nothing."

"That makes a lot of people crazy mad."

"He wanted the national debt taken out of the budget and set up on a long-term bond tied to a national sales tax. But that would require a balanced budget amendment and removing the lid on social security tax. It would also mean the states would be given more control over some assistance programs," Victoria explained. "He had tied them all together to eliminate fraud and get better services and assistance to those who need it. 'Local people know who the con artists are.' That's what Miller always said."

"You talk to someone in Montana about welfare or assistance, and you'll get an earful."

"Well, about half the country feels the same way.'

"And that's your gridlock," Sam said with a laugh.

"True, but again you take this subject and twist it together with another problem, and you produce solutions. The people who are on assistance would be required to work. If you can't find a job, then the government provides one for you in a recycling center. Then, we stop burying our trash and aim for a 100 percent recycled society," Victoria said. "I've worked with young people with all kinds of disabilities, and the thing they want most is to be productive. No one thinks it's cruel to give a young adult in a wheel chair a job working as a dispatcher or at a computer screen or something where the physical handicap isn't a limitation. Yet we let con artists walk out with a check for doing nothing while young moms struggle to work and raise a family on a small income."

"You won't get either party on board with that one," Sam countered.

"Which is why Jackson won. The two parties only care about the status quo and getting re-elected. They won't take any risks. Try something like this in one state, and let others do different variations. That's what should be happening. Try a solution in Oregon. Then Maine tweaks it, and tries something else. Before you know it, we have a working model that solves real problems. This liberal versus conservative nonsense is pointless. People are interested in solutions, and the states are full of smart people who are ready, willing, and able. The feds should be making sure the constitution isn't violated—that's the rule book—but otherwise, set the states free to create solutions at the level where everyday people live."

Victoria paused and took a drink of her water.

"I'm sorry I keep getting worked up about this, but I've had this discussion many times over the holiday table with Jackson. I guess it's been well rehearsed."

"Actually, I'm enjoying it. I've had my own discussions with Jackson."

AT THE WHITE HOUSE, the President watched the news reports with Susan Mercury.

"Can you get me a purple flag?" he asked, smiling at Susan.

"I suppose I can. Jackson, what are you going to do?" she asked, one old friend to another.

"I'm going to hang it off the White House balcony so all those people know I'm with them. They deserve to know I appreciate what they've done. Send someone out in that crowd, and get three or four of those flags. And purple shirts, too, if you can find them."

The President sat back with a big smile across his face. "We're going to win."

SAM AND VICTORIA crossed the Georgia border and were making good time in their effort to distance themselves from the cell phone they used to send Jackson the photos of Sims' ranch. Now, they were heading north, having decided a cabin in the Smokies would be a nice place to hide out for a few days.

"Let's keep moving until we get lost in some small mountain town," Sam said.

"That's fine, but since we won't have a beach, can we at least get a place with a hot tub?" she said, laughing.

"And someplace clean!" she added, remembering the cockroach from the morning.

"How soon do you want to get married?"

"How about today?" Victoria answered with a girlish smile.

"I want my kids there," Sam said.

"I know. I was just kidding, but I love you enough to marry you right now."

"We're going to have to figure out the identity issue, too, since your brother has you officially listed as 'dead.'"

"My guess is he's already started the process to put me in the witness protection program. Now that I know what an issue Greystone has been, I suspect my new identity is already in the works. The bad news is I may have to testify someday."

Both sat quietly at the prospect of such a thing. A passing semi shook their little car.

"Let's hope that can be avoided," Sam said.

OUT WEST, A FURIOUS Clayton Sims putted a golf ball back and forth in the lodge's large gathering room. He had wanted to take action right after the election and had attempted to get the Council to agree that waiting was simply too dangerous. Now he watched as purple-clad protesters occupied Washington, chanting for an unacceptable level of change.

"We fucked up," he mumbled as he hit the ball back and forth, puffing hard on his cigar.

"Damn it!" he yelled, with no one to hear him. "We waited too long. We did this to ourselves. Some Captain!" He looked again at the scene in Washington.

"Waiting around here for somebody to do something is going to kill me," he thought as he plopped down in one of the large wingback chairs.

ALONG INTERSTATE 65 in Indiana, a tired and dirty Peter Mercury pulled into a hotel parking lot. He had been on the road for hours and knew if he didn't stop, he'd soon fall asleep at the wheel.

"After what I have been through, I can't die in a traffic accident," he'd told himself as he made the decision to stop.

Once checked in, he picked up carryout Chinese from the restaurant next door and settled in for the night. Before he even finished eating, he decided he had waited long enough and picked up the phone to call Susan.

"My God, Peter, I've been worried sick," she said as she heard his voice. She had sworn to the President she wouldn't disclose that she already knew he was okay. She didn't understand the reasons for secrecy, but went along, thankful the President had somehow made sure Peter was safe.

"Where are you?" Susan asked.

"Somewhere in Indiana," Peter answered. "Look, I can't explain right now, but you can't tell anyone you've heard from me."

Susan agreed. "I'm just happy to know you're safe and on your way home."

"Some people helped me out of a jam, and they must stay anonymous," he said.

"You *are* coming home, right?" Susan asked, wondering what his plan was.

"Yes, but are things still crazy in DC?"

"It's incredible here. Some reports estimate the crowds at well over 5 million," Susan reported.

"Sounds crazy."

"It's really amazing. Jackson ordered all federal buildings be opened to the crowds. Even the Congressional gym is being used so people can shower."

"I'll bet that really pissed off Speaker Reed and his gang," Peter said, laughing.

"Well they can't get to the gym anyway, so I don't think they're too worried. There are food vendors set up in the oddest places. I think there's a McDonalds in the lobby of the Smithsonian now, and I just heard the Frederick Douglas Museum has a pizza parlor operating on their first floor. It's crazy."

"I'll call when I get near town," Peter said. "I love you, Susan. These last few days have made me think a lot about life after DC. I'm going to be ready for that quiet life on our little place, but right now I have to sleep."

"Please be careful, Peter. I love you, too," Susan said with a sense of relief.

Peter ate his dinner and was soon in a deep sleep. Not even the biggest story of his life could keep him awake any longer.

AFTER A LONG DAY OF driving, Sam and Victoria pulled up in front of a cream-colored house on Lake Junaluska in North

Carolina. The place was small but clean and quaint with old rockers on the front porch that looked out across the scenic lake. Inside, the little house surprised them both. The kitchen and family room had been merged together into one large, open space. The trim was all freshly painted off white, and built-in bookcases painted the same color flanked an old wood mantle and stone fireplace. The old house had hardwood floors throughout that were interrupted by a series of rugs all sharing a common dark green design.

"This is darling," Victoria declared upon entering. "I love these quaint old houses."

"Well this one has certainly been updated," Sam commented as he walked into the kitchen. He had kept his promise; out back in the small, private yard was a large hot tub. The leasing agent had been reluctant to lease the unit at first, because Sam refused to use a credit card. The fact that Victoria had no identification didn't help matters, either. But after explaining that they had gotten engaged the night before and left on a whim, the woman was swayed. Of course, a few extra $100 bills didn't hurt their effort either.

Victoria unpacked the car and put away the few groceries they'd picked up before heading for the hot tub.

"Wine and tub," she announced as she walked past Sam and opened the porch door.

"I'll be right out," he answered as he looked up to see his naked fiancé pass through the door.

"Damn, I love that woman," he thought as she turned and smiled.

IN WASHINGTON, SUSAN Mercury returned to the Oval Office with her arms full of purple items.

"People started throwing them over the fence when they heard you wanted one," Susan said. "I sent an intern out there, and she was overwhelmed by the crowd. Those people are not going anywhere until they get what they want."

Susan smiled as she held up a t-shirt in the President's size. Across the front was "Purple Reason" in big white letters. She then stretched out several large flags and banners with the same writing.

"Looks like they've formed their own party, doesn't it?" Susan asked as she folded the remaining shirts and placed them on an end table.

"It's their party," the President declared as he looked at the shirt. "This one belongs to the everyday people."

He picked up the flags and banners and instructed Susan to have them hung from all the White House balconies.

"I want it done immediately so they can see them before it gets too dark," Niles said.

Susan headed out with her arms full of purple to get the task accomplished.

Niles turned on CNN, hoping the flags would be quickly seen. He felt the people could use a boost from his office. It wasn't long before he could hear the crowd respond when the first of the flags went up. Before long the President could hear "Purple Reason" being chanted by the sea of people now occupying the nation's capital.

"That ought to finish off those bastards," he said softly as he thought of the House members huddled inside the Capitol.

"Susan, I'm going to the family quarters for the rest of the day," he said as he passed her desk and headed down the hall.

As he entered the family quarters, the lights in the room flickered a few times. He could hear the crowd outside getting quiet.

"Mr. President," Susan called via the intercom. "There has been another explosion, sir. This time it's a main electrical facility feeding the Washington area. We're on the backup system, but it won't last long because the earlier explosion took out the gas service. The Secret Service wants to evacuate you immediately."

Susan waited for an answer.

"Collect all the candles you can find. I'm not going anywhere," the President replied. "But you can tell the staff they are free to go. Instruct the Secret Service that I'm staying, and I am requesting a second team be dispatched to get people out of here and safely to their homes."

Niles rummaged around in his dresser draw and retrieved the phone given to him by Sam McBride.

"Mr. President." It was Susan again. "I would like to stay, sir. Would that be okay?" she asked, in a tone reflecting more of a desire than simply a willingness to stay.

Niles paused for a moment. "Thank you, Susan, but I want you to go home, at least for the night."

He thought of Vivian and the kids, thankful they were safe in New York. "I'm glad they're safe, but I miss my kids," he said softly as he looked at a large family portrait hanging in the foyer. He left the family quarters and headed back to the Oval Office.

Anthony Sinclair met the President in the hallway as he emerged from the stairs from the family quarters.

"Jackson, we need to leave. This is crazy. We can be at Camp David in a few minutes."

"Out of the question," the President responded. "I'm not leaving when all those people are out there at my request."

"But you aren't safe here. You are taking an unnecessary risk." Sinclair was adamant that the President immediately board the Marine One chopper he had summoned and evacuate before all power to the White House went out.

"No, and that's final," the President stated defiantly as he began lighting candles in the Oval Office.

"This is ridiculous," Sinclair yelled, slamming his hand down on the President's desk. "What are you going to do here without electricity, Jackson? Sit here in the dark doing what? This is ridiculous. This city is a mess. Those people out there are making things worse. Get on the damn helicopter and end this madness!"

Sinclair fell back into a chair.

"You had a chance to make a deal, Jackson. It was a good deal, one that would have made those people happy and accomplished what you wanted. But you had to take this thing to the wall. Now we sit here in a building about to go dark in a city that is occupied by God-only-knows-how-many nuts, and things are going to spiral out of control. You chose this."

"I'm leaving, Jackson," Sinclair said. He walked out of the office and immediately boarded a Marine chopper already near capacity with other high-ranking cabinet members. "I think he's lost his mind," Sinclair announced as he sat down.

As the helicopter lifted off, a series of small explosions occurred in the distance, close enough to the White House to be heard by all inside. A few screams came from the throngs of people gathered in the city, but within a few seconds most stared in silence at the blasts. The crowd was so enormous that running was impossible, so most gathered their loved ones and stood or sat quietly.

The chopper pilot announced emergency measures and shot up and out of the area at an uncomfortably fast pace.

In the White House, Niles sat at his desk looking through the pictures Sam had sent earlier in the day. The vast majority of the faces were unknown, but a few were career bureaucrats who had held high-ranking positions in Washington for decades. Sam's brief note, "Taken by friend watching the Lodge," was all Jackson needed to know. Whatever Sims and his cronies were up to, it was headquartered at the lodge, and a lot of people were involved.

SAM AND VICTORIA sat across from each other in the hot tub with a bottle of wine perched precariously on the edge. Tonight's conversation became more about wedding plans than politics. Victoria was completely immersed in the idea of being Mrs. McBride, and her mind raced through the details. Colors, flowers, a dress, a church, and the pesky matter of her "death" all streamed out as Sam sat listening. He loved seeing her this happy and knew that he felt the same.

For Victoria, planning a wedding with Sam McBride was a chapter out of an unlikely romance novel. How many times as a young woman had she dreamed of spending her life with Sam? And now, in spite of all the odds life could possibly stack against them, it was going to happen. At times, Victoria wondered if she was dreaming.

For Sam, who only a few days earlier felt constrained by the direction his own life had taken, the entire situation was like an answer to his prayers. He had been in anguish since Sarah's death, and Victoria's abrupt arrival in his life was a gift from God. He sat there listening and agreeing and loving every minute of this time with his bride-to-be. By the time the sun set, they had emptied the wine bottle, and Victoria was lying against Sam.

"I think I'm getting pickled," Victoria said.

"Maybe some dinner would be good," Sam said, setting his glass down and turning off the jets.

"Let's go take a shower, and then we'll eat," Victoria said as she climbed over the edge and wrapped a towel around her.

Inside the cabin, Sam turned on the oven and placed a pan of frozen lasagna on the middle rack before joining Victoria in the shower. Fresh bread and salads from the little market down the road would complete dinner for tonight.

"This shower is nice," Victoria announced as Sam joined her.

When the timer went off, Sam made a dash out of the bathroom to turn off the oven and remove the lasagna.

"Time for dinner," he called out.

Victoria emerged from the bath in a new navy blue robe she had picked up earlier in the day. Sam turned on the TV and searched for CNN.

"Tonight, things in Washington have taken a turn in an unexpected direction," the announcer said as Sam and Victoria both stopped what they were doing. "Power, including emergency power, is out throughout the city, and even cell towers have been hit."

They set their plates down and took a seat in front of the TV.

"We don't know if this is a foreign terrorist act or the work of some domestic group, but we do know it has been deliberate."

Victoria and Sam sat speechless watching the scene as a shot from a helicopter showed a blacked out Washington DC.

"At this time the police have appealed to the crowd to remain calm and stay put or follow an orderly path out of the city," the newscaster said. "As you can see, no one seems to be leaving. We're going back to Bill Conner, who is still able to broadcast from location. Bill, how is it out there?"

The picture changed to Conner, who was surrounded by purple-clad citizens gathered around a small grill that had been converted to a campfire.

"Actually the mood here is quite positive. These people are serious and not planning to leave," he said. "This movement, which is calling itself Purple Reason, is committed to standing with this President."

Conner looked around as everyone nodded in agreement.

"What about the rumors that the President left in the chopper we saw take off from the South Lawn right after the power trouble started? Has that given anyone doubts about what you are doing?" Conner asked the crowd.

"The President put the Purple Reason banner up on the White House," one of the women said.

"He was telling us he is with us, and we are with him. I think he's still in there, but even if he did leave, we know he's standing together with us," another added.

"Bill, we have to break away. There is a report coming from another station about more explosions."

The TV screen went dark for a moment, and Sam and Victoria sat in stunned silence.

"Do you think this is a coup attempt?" Victoria asked. "Are these people so drunk on their positions of power that they would pull crap like this? Is this really happening?"

Sam grabbed the remote and began flipping through the channels, trying to find some network that was still broadcasting.

"Explosions have ripped through this area, and we can confirm there are casualties," a reporter said as Sam stopped on Fox News. In the background, screams and chaos erupted as people struggled to vacate the area. Police were struggling to clear the streets so ambulances could get through to the wounded.

Again, another blast went off, and the resulting fireball was visible on the screen.

"That was a car that exploded," a man yelled as he ran past the reporter.

"The first three were trash cans," another yelled in the distance.

"It is absolute chaos out here now," the reporter said as he fought to keep his place in front of the camera. Sirens screamed from all directions as police forced people to clear the roads and make space for treating the wounded. Soon police cars utilizing their speakers pleaded with people to stay calm and move away from all vehicles and trash containers. As had been the case since the protests had started, most quickly complied, making room in areas deemed safe by the police for makeshift triage centers. Soon, officers led bomb-sniffing dogs along the roads and through the crowds. Emergency security forces spread out to conduct a methodical search of all trashcans and parked vehicles.

"My God Sam, they're going to try to assassinate Jackson," Victoria said.

Sam knew she might be right. Jackson had ordered Sam to keep Victoria safe, but as he watched in disbelief, he knew Jackson was the one in danger now. Sam silently considered what would be the smart move for Jackson, as well as for him and Victoria. The scene on the TV was surreal as sirens screamed and police walked arm in arm through the streets.

"Who's behind this?" Victoria asked. "Is this all Sims?"

She paused and looked at Sam for a moment. "Or the military? I know some of them are pissed off by Jackson's plans, but would *they* do something like this?"

"It has to be Sims and his group," Sam said. "We don't know how deep they go. We know they wanted you dead so the Court wouldn't be upset. We know they are flying lots of people in and out of that lodge. Whoever they all are and whatever they are doing or trying to do, it's them. It's Sims. It's got to be. Jackson's reforms are so dangerous to that group that they'll do anything to stop him. I don't know why, but that's the bottom line."

Sam got up and walked into the kitchen and retrieved his plate of food.

"You can eat at a time like this?" Victoria asked.

"I'm hungry, and I can't think straight on an empty stomach," Sam said as he gobbled down the lasagna. "We know if they are willing to do this, they will never stop chasing us."

"Do you think they are still looking for us?" Victoria asked as she retrieved her own plate.

"Yes, we should count on that. I'm afraid this is a fight to the death."

"We have to find a way to win," Victoria said. "These assholes need to be taken out. Do you think Jackson has seen those pictures yet?"

"Considering you are with me, I would think he has that phone nearby all the time," Sam answered.

"Then he's getting those pictures analyzed right now then. I know how he is. He does everything 'right now.' He never waits. He'll have an ID on everyone in those pictures by morning. We should count on that," Victoria insisted.

"So then what happens? What will he do once he knows who all or most of the players are?" Sam asked.

"He has to find out who's at the top," Victoria said calmly. "It's like an undercover operation. You would get a mole into the mix and let them work until they reach the top. Then you would take down the entire group. Jackson needs to know who is at the top. We know it's not Sims. That would be too easy. And besides, he's a dumb shit when you get right down to it. There is no way he's the mastermind of anything. He answers to someone. The question is whether that person is at the top, or is there someone else higher up?"

Victoria had reverted to her prosecutor days and was now unraveling the situation in her mind.

"But what's the intent? What are they trying to accomplish?" Sam asked as he looked at his beautiful fiancé, now fully in her element. "Is it as simple as stopping the reforms? Is it the term limit issue? Campaign money? Military reforms? Why would any of those motivate a guy like Sims to commit treason? Because that's what we're talking about here."

"I don't know, but we have to help Jackson, Sam. We can't hide out in the hot tub while this is going on."

AT HIS HOME, FBI Director Jack Langley sat in his small office as a computer program analyzed the pictures sent over by the President. Out of his own paranoia, Jack had built redundancy into his security software, which allowed him to access the system under any conditions. Years earlier he had installed a whole-house generator that ran on propane to keep his house fully functional for days. His systems were common in areas of the country prone to power outages. For Langley, such measures were simple common sense.

As the program analyzed the faces, it printed out names, addresses, titles, and bios. As the pages began to accumulate, a pattern emerged. These were career bureaucrats from every government department in Washington. Langley sat back in his chair and looked through the photos. Like McBride, who had asked his friend to shoot the photos, Langley recognized the scale of the group. But he was equally baffled as to their intent.

"I have to get this information to Jackson," he thought. But that was no easy task. Langley had been brought into Sims' group after its members suspected that he also was opposed to the President's reforms and that his relationship with Niles was strained. Langley couldn't simply show up at the White House now without ruining his credibility with Sims.

Langley gathered up the dozens of bios, stuffed them in a large envelope, and headed for his car.

"The only person I can trust to get these to Jackson is that reporter's wife," he decided as he pulled out of his garage. He would have to take a long detour to get to the Mercury home, but it was the only option he could think of. Events were moving fast now, and he knew he had to get back to the lodge or Sims and the others would begin to question his absence.

After an hour of dodging roadblocks and jammed streets, Langley arrived at the Mercury home. When Susan opened the door, she was still in her work clothes and stunned to see the FBI director at her door.

"Please let me in before anyone sees me," Langley insisted as he pushed the door open and then quickly closed it behind him.

"Mr. Langley, this is a bit uncomfortable. Are you here on official business?" Susan asked as she backed away from him.

"May I sit down, Susan?" Langley asked as he removed his suit coat and hat. "And please call me Jack."

"Okay, Jack, yes, that's fine. Please sit down. Would you care for some coffee?" she asked as Langley took a seat on one end of the sofa.

"No, but a beer would taste awfully good right now," he answered.

"Okay. Let me see what I've got," Susan said, disappearing into the kitchen. Within a few seconds, she returned with two bottles of Miller Light and a couple of plastic tumblers.

"I have a feeling I'm going to need a drink, too," she announced as she opened her beer and poured it into a tall glass. "What's this about?"

Susan sat down on the opposite end of the sofa.

"I need you to get this envelope to Jackson as soon as possible," Langley instructed as he placed the large package on the coffee table.

"Why don't you take it over there yourself?" Susan asked, her eyes narrowing as she glanced from the envelope then back to Langley.

"I can't. It's a long story," Langley said. He took a drink of his beer. "Have you spoken with Peter yet?"

Susan stared at Langley for a few seconds. "What does he know?" she thought.

"Earlier today, in fact," Susan said.

"A few days ago, you asked the President to help find him, right?" Langley asked.

"Yes, that's right," Susan answered.

"I'm the one he called. I saved Peter's life that day. He was in a bad place, and the people behind all this had him in custody. I don't have time to tell you everything, but I know I can trust you. And Jackson has to have these documents as soon as you can get them there. This is the most important pile of papers you've ever laid your hands on. We need this to happen tonight."

Langley finished his beer and stood up to leave.

"Only the President can know I was here tonight, okay?" Langley waited until Susan nodded. "Use your White House credentials to get a police escort to the White House. They'll know who you are."

Back in his car, Langley headed directly for a small airport where The Council kept a jet for special personnel. He would return to the Sims Lodge after making a couple of stops.

SUSAN MERCURY IMMEDIATELY got in her car and left for
the White House. She wasn't accustomed to Jack Langley's
cloak-and-dagger style, but the urgency of his words was
palpable. Susan had assumed that whatever was happening
had to involve the President and his proposals because no one
in the White House thought for a second this was a foreign
attack. She drove until she came to a roadblock stopping any
traffic from crossing into central DC.

"Miss, you're going to have to turn around," the officer
announced as he approached Susan's car.

"Officer, my name is Susan Mercury. I am the President's
personal secretary, and I have papers here that he must have
immediately," she said.

The officer thought for a moment then asked her to wait
while he made a call. When he returned a few moments later,
he inspected her credentials and instructed her to pull over
and wait for an escort. Within a few minutes, a black sedan
arrived. The driver told her to leave her car behind.

"I'm sorry, Mrs. Mercury, but orders are orders, and we
cannot allow any vehicle inside the security zone. I have to
drive you in," the man said. He opened the door for Susan, who
quickly complied and got in the back seat of the sedan. They
drove along the outskirts of DC through streets lined with
emergency vehicles and security personnel. Once beyond the
roadblock, the car turned down a small alley.

"This is a strange route," Susan remarked as she looked out
of the back seat windows.

"It'll save time. A lot of the roads are full of people," the
man explained.

As they reached the midpoint of the alley, the car abruptly
stopped, and the back door was pulled open. Two men dressed
in black pulled Susan from the car and quickly hustled her into
a van parked behind a garage. Inside the van, she was gagged
and blindfolded.

"Let's see what you have here," one of the men said as he
ripped the package out of Susan's hands.

"Call Hiatt and tell him we have something that looks
important," he instructed as he leafed through the papers.

"What about her?" the other man asked as he wrapped tape around her ankles.

"They want her taken to base," the man answered.

BY NOW, SAM AND Victoria were on a mad dash to Washington. After arguing for thirty minutes or so, Sam had given in and agreed that reaching Jackson was critical. After watching Victoria stand over him demanding they go, he knew he had no choice. They had been apart for a long time, and he knew if he resisted he would wake up to find her gone again. She had ironclad resolve, and nothing would stop her from going to her brother now that she feared for his safety.

Victoria had no idea how to get to Jackson, but she knew she had to make sure he had received the pictures from Sam. It was an eight-hour drive under normal circumstances, but at the pace Sam was driving, Victoria hoped to be there in six.

CHAPTER NINE
All In

Around midnight, an exhausted Peter Mercury pulled the beat-up old truck he had been driving to the front of his home. He had decided to surprise his wife and simply show up. Inside he nearly collapsed from relief that he was actually home and would soon be holding Susan in his arms.

He turned on lights as he looked around and soon came upon a note taped to the mirror in their bathroom. "Langley came to see me. I'm on way to WH with important papers. If I don't get there something went wrong. Copies in printer. I'm scared."

Peter staggered back and dropped to his knees. He wanted to scream, but quickly realized Langley was reaching out to a person he knew he could trust. Peter grabbed the papers from the printer and dashed out the door and jumped back in the truck. He paused for a moment and then got out and threw his bike in the bed of the truck and quickly drove off. He followed what he thought would be a logical route for Susan, given the circumstances in DC. He pulled the truck over a safe distance back from the first roadblock and removed the bike. He peddled along, slowing as he approached the officers manning the barricades.

"It's a crazy time to be a reporter," Peter stated as he pulled his press credentials from around his neck.

"Good thing you got a bike, Mr. ...," the guard stopped as he read Peter's badge, "Mercury. We aren't letting any cars in. Be safe out there."

"Yeah, you, too," Peter said. He continued past the barricade and to his right saw Susan's parked car. "If she's not at the White House, those bastards got her," he thought as he peddled on.

Peter got as close as possible on the bike, but eventually he gave up and proceeded on foot. The crowd had settled down, and small flames flickered from grills that had been converted to fire pits to burn whatever scraps of wood or paper could be found. He worked his way through the sea of people until he reached the outer gates surrounding the White House. Inside the fence, uniformed guards stood a few feet back.

"Excuse me," he said as he pressed his face up against the iron bars. "Please listen to me. My wife is the President's secretary. I have papers here that I must get to the President. My wife should be in there. Can you call someone inside?"

The guard stood motionless as he continued scanning the crowd.

"I'm a reporter. I have credentials. I'm not some nut. My wife has worked for President Niles for years."

The soldier again ignored him and looked only at the people around Peter, who were beginning to notice his pleas.

"Hey, mister," said a woman who'd heard Peter. "Go over to that section. I think those guys are Secret Service. They might be more willing to listen."

Peter thanked her and made his way toward the area she had pointed to.

"No offense, kid," the woman said to the young Marine as Peter walked away.

"None taken," the Marine said, with a slight smile. "I have my orders."

"You keep our President safe, soldier. That's fine with us," another added, as the crowd cheered with support.

Peter worked his way around the fence until he found what appeared to be Secret Service personnel. The two men were nearly fifty feet from him and showed little interest in his repeated attempts to get their attention. Finally, he saw a member of the President's press team he had known for years approach the two men.

"Mary, Mary," Peter yelled as loud as he could. The woman turned and looked at Peter for a moment, waved, and then turned back to discuss something with the two agents.

"I have something important for the President. Please, Mary."

The woman said something to the two agents, and one of them joined her as she approached the fence.

"Mary, is Susan in there?" Peter pleaded through the fence.

"So that's all you want?" the woman said in disgust.

"No, please, Mary. Come over here." Peter held up the envelope he had been clutching and thrust it through the fence. "The President must be handed this envelope. You do it personally."

The woman took the envelope and looked inside for a few seconds. "What is this?" she asked.

"I honestly don't know," Peter answered. "But look, I've been through hell." He paused, turned around and pulled up his shirt.

"Oh, my God," the woman said as she stepped back with a look of horror on her face. "What happened to you, Peter?" She moved toward the fence closer to him.

"It's a long story, Mary. Is Susan in the White House? Please, I have to know."

She stepped back to the Secret Service agent and said something. He raised his radio and made a call, then looked at Mary and shook his head no.

Peter slid down the bars of the fence until he was on the ground. He knew Susan had gotten caught up in the mess, and he wondered if she was even still alive.

"Peter, is there anything I can do?" Mary asked as she knelt down to meet Peter's eyes.

"Personally hand that to the President. Tell him it came from Langley. Tell him Susan tried to deliver the same info but disappeared on her way here."

Peter stood up and turned to walk away as the woman reached through the fence and grabbed his sleeve.

"Where are you going now?" she asked in a voice of sincere concern.

"Back to hell I suppose," he replied as he disappeared into the crowd.

IT WAS THE MIDDLE of the night when Sam and Victoria entered the National Mall. After a night of intense driving, it felt good to get out and walk, even if the circumstances were disheartening. Many in the crowd were sleeping, but there remained many groups who continued to keep small fires burning and conversation going. Purple flags dotted the landscape. The Purple Reason movement had now taken hold over the entire gathering.

In the distance, Sam and Victoria could clearly see the light emanating from the CNN van as its small generator continued keeping Conner's area fully lit. They started walking in that direction, hoping to encounter someone from the White House that would get them inside to see Jackson. As they approached Conner, they were surprised to see him standing under his media tent and conducting yet another interview with a purple-clad protestor. As they approached, the crowd around Conner began to grow as more people made their way there.

"I can't believe he's out here," a woman said as she pushed past Victoria and hurried toward Conner. As they got close, she recognized the sound of her brother's voice. President Jackson Niles had slipped out of the White House, dressed in one of the Purple Reason shirts Susan had delivered, and inconspicuously made his way to Conner's van.

As the crowd gathered, the President turned to face them.

"I want to thank all of you for the sacrifice you are making. You are all heroes, and this nation will be reborn because of what you have done here."

The crowd started to cheer but was quickly asked to remain calm so the interview could continue.

"I'm one of you," the President said. "We're going to win this battle, and we will fix this government."

He shook Conner's hand and turned to make his way back to the White House. As he turned, a shot fired, and a man standing behind the President was struck in the chest. The crowd screamed, and many turned to run. The Secret Service men with the President pushed him into a nearby tent, next to where Sam and Victoria stood. They quickly jumped into the tent with them. One of the agents pulled out his pistol and demanded Sam drop face down. The President, recognizing his friend, reached for the agent's gun and assured him there was no danger.

"What the hell are you doing here?" Jackson shouted at Sam. Then, realizing what Sam's presence meant, he turned and looked at the black-haired lady sitting in the corner of the tent.

"Why are you in DC?" he asked. The President's anger and disappointment were obvious.

"We had to be sure you got the pictures," Sam said.

"I sent them to Langley to be analyzed. We can trust him. Damn it, you were supposed to stay far away from this mess," Jackson said as he glanced back and forth between the two of them.

"Mr. President, we have to get you back to the White House right now," the agent with the drawn pistol demanded. Another pair of agents entered the tent and didn't wait for approval.

"Right now," the man demanded from the entrance to the tent.

"Get her to safety, Sam. I have the pictures," Jackson said. The four Secret Service men surrounded the President and immediately made a run for the White House.

By now, the crowd had parted to form an open corridor that closed in behind them as they passed. The President was shielded from view and quickly passed back through the gate and inside the White House to safety.

OUTSIDE, AMBULANCES continued to crawl through the streets, sirens blaring, as security personnel spread out through the crowd. Word spread that a shooting had caused the commotion, and within minutes, the news circulating through the rumor mill was that the President had been shot. This time, the people did not respond patiently. Angry mobs began vandalizing any building rumored to contain a lobbyist's office, and several were soon on fire. Rocks, bottles, and other solid objects were hurled at the Capitol as the mob pushed against security forces ill prepared for this change of attitude.

Sam and Victoria moved as quickly as they could through the Mall area and made their way back out of the city. Once in their car, they were content to sit for a moment to catch their breath.

"They're going to keep trying to kill him," Victoria finally said, her voice shaky but strong.

"He won't give them another chance," Sam said.

"This group is trying to pull off a coup," Victoria continued. "It's that simple. We elect a President who goes against what these two parties have been doing, and the result is this. They, whoever 'they' are, are willing to kill the President to hang on to whatever it is they fear losing from the reforms."

"I wish we could have found out what Jackson knows," Sam said. "I would sure like to know who those people are in those pictures. The Secret Service will keep Jackson on lockdown now. He probably won't be seen in public again until this is resolved."

"But how does it get resolved?" Victoria asked, desperate for her brother's safety. "How does he end it without rooting out these people? He could find a reason to arrest Sims tomorrow, but there are obviously hundreds of people involved. I don't see how this ends until everyone involved is arrested or dead. We don't know how deep this goes."

Victoria let out an exasperated sigh.

Through her car window, Victoria watched as families moved as quickly as possible to get back to their vehicles. It saddened her to see the anxiety on the faces of the children as their parents hustled them along. Some groups, primarily made up of young people, were angry, and Victoria saw them kick trashcans and throw bottles at anything representing "official Washington."

"We do know that the pictures taken at the lodge are of people coming to see Sims," Sam said as he brought Victoria back from the scene developing on the streets. "We know they are involved in some way. Whoever is at the top of this will eventually show up. I say we meet up with Charlie and the guys and watch the place. We know Jackson is using the phone or will be once the towers are repaired around DC. So we watch and wait to see who else goes there. I say we head back to Montana and hide out in the woods. We have to do something, and I don't know what else we can do."

"Okay, let's go," Victoria said.

INSIDE THE WHITE HOUSE, President Jackson Niles sat at his desk looking through the packet left for him by Peter Mercury.

"This has to be a coup," he whispered as he leafed through the pictures. "But where's the muscle to pull off such a thing?" He tried to imagine how such a group could actually take power.

"These people are insane," he concluded as he threw the packet across his desk.

Just then Anthony Sinclair entered with a group of security officers.

"It's time to leave, Jackson," Sinclair stated as he stood across from the President's desk.

"We've been through this already," Niles responded.

"It's not safe, and you are leaving now," Sinclair said, staring at the President, who looked around the room at the men gathered.

"We must go now, sir," one of the Secret Service agents said as he approached the President.

"Fine, but I'm coming back as soon as the power is restored," he said. The President placed a few files along with the packet of pictures and Sam's phone in his brief case.

"The remaining members of your staff have already packed your personal items," Sinclair said as they walked for the door.

Outside, the President quickly boarded the waiting Marine One helicopter and was soon airborne.

"Camp David?" the President asked as he looked through a stack of papers he was holding.

"No sir, Camp David has been compromised. We're going to board Air Force One and head to a base in Missouri. The rest of the Cabinet will be arriving there as well."

"Very well."

ON A SMALL PLANE flying west out of the Washington DC area, Hiatt Montgomery sat staring at a handcuffed Susan Mercury lying on the cabin floor. As was Montgomery's MO with women, she had on only her underwear. Her face was already bruised from the backhand slaps he had administered shortly after takeoff.

"You will eventually tell me why you have these pictures with you. Who gave them to you?" he asked as he pressed his boot down on the side of Susan's face.

"If you have any plans to see that grandkid of yours again, you will tell me. You know I could make this much worse for you right now," he sneered as he looked her up and down. "For a secretary, you ain't half bad." He ran his leather boot down her side.

"It's a four-hour flight, lady. If you don't answer me before we get there, you will once we land. I guarantee you haven't been through anything like what you're going to experience there. Who gave you those pictures?" he screamed as he thrust his heel down on the side of Susan's head.

"Fucking answer me!" Montgomery screamed again and kicked her.

By now Susan was sure that her fate was sealed, and to frustrate this maniac was the only purpose she could think of to make her last hours meaningful.

"Fuck you," she muttered as she tried to tighten up into a ball.

"That might happen next, you bitch," Montgomery laughed. He always carried a flask of whiskey in his bag and decided a drink now might be a good idea.

"Want a drink, tits?" he said as he poured a little over the side of her face.

Susan pushed herself up and spit the little that made it to her mouth onto Montgomery's pants.

"Oh, this is going to get fun now," he said as he grabbed a handful of her hair and started swinging her from side to side.

"If you want it rough, I can give you some real fun," he yelled as he dragged her across the aisle to a bench seat and threw her down. "You lay there and think real hard, baby. You know what's coming next."

Montgomery sat back down in his seat across from Susan and continued drinking his whiskey and leering at her.

Susan had turned sideways on the seats and curled into a fetal position.

"You've got about ten minutes to tell me where those pictures came from. After that, things get real ugly," he said as he reached across and ran his hand across the back of Susan's thigh.

Without hesitation Susan turned and kicked Montgomery square in the nose. He stumbled back as blood poured out.

"You fucking bitch," he screamed as he came back toward her. Her second kick was a solid shot into the groin that doubled him over in the aisle. The third kick, another to the nose, was delivered with such force that Montgomery collapsed in the aisle. Susan quickly sat up and retrieved the handcuff keys from Montgomery's pocket. She then pulled his hands around the base of a chair and cuffed him in place.

"Land this thing now!" she screamed at the pilot as she stood shaking, Montgomery's Colt 45 clutched in her hands.

"Okay, settle down, lady," the pilot answered in shock.

"Turn this thing around and land it now," she screamed again.

"Hey, I only fly the planes," the man said as the plane banked for a turn.

The youngest of five kids and the only girl, Susan had been known to take out a boy with a swift kick.

"You land this plane, and I get off. Any bullshit, and I shoot you. You touch that radio, and I shoot you. You got it?"

"I told you, I'm just the pilot. Look, we're flying east," he said as he motioned at the compass.

Susan slowly sat down in the chair behind the door to the small cockpit.

"Relax," the pilot said. "I'm going to land at the first airstrip I can find. Don't start shooting in here, or you'll kill us both."

She pulled a blanket over her nearly naked body and sat with the gun clutched in her lap.

"There's a small airstrip up here, but there's nothing around it. I don't even think there's a phone down there," the pilot announced as he glanced back at Susan.

"Give me your phone," she demanded.

"Fine, take it," he said as he tossed it over his shoulder and into her lap.

Susan felt the plane descend as she picked up the phone. "After I get out, you take off and go back to wherever we were heading in the first place. If you don't, I'll start shooting at the plane from outside. You got it?" she commanded as she rummaged around for something more than a blanket to put on.

"Fine by me," he said as he pushed the plane lower for a landing.

The small jet taxied across the remote runway. At the far end, Susan saw a small hangar with two trucks parked outside. "Stop up there," she motioned.

The pilot taxied up close to the hangar and brought the plane to a stop.

"You're going to need to get that guy to a hospital," she said as she opened the plane's door.

"Oh, I think he'll recover," the pilot said without looking back.

Susan walked back toward Montgomery and fired a shot into the back of his left foot. Montgomery jolted forward, screaming.

"You bitch, I will kill you. I promise you are going to die slowly," he screamed.

"I told you he needed a hospital," she said as she went down the stairs with Montgomery's suit coat wrapped around her. "Take off or I start shooting at your gas tank," she said.

The pilot pulled the door shut as the sound of Montgomery screaming for the key to the handcuffs slowly faded.

Inside the small hangar, Susan found two young mechanics working on an old plane.

"I will pay either of you a thousand dollars if you fly me as close to Washington DC as you can get," she announced as she came up behind them. The two men turned and looked at the beat-up woman standing before them.

"You need a doctor, lady?" the shorter of the two asked.

"I need to get to Washington right now," she answered.

"How 'bout two thousand?" she asked without waiting for them to respond to her first offer.

The two men looked at each other for a moment.

"How about three?" the taller man said.

"Where are we?" Susan asked.

"Western Kentucky," the tall man answered, hardly believing what was happening.

"You don't know where you're at?" the shorter man asked.

"Fine, three thousand, but we leave right now," Susan answered, ignoring the question. The two quickly closed up their toolboxes and prepared the plane for takeoff.

"We need to hurry," Susan shouted as the two pushed the plane out of the hangar.

"Are you being chased by the police, lady? We don't want no trouble," the shorter man said.

"Chased yes, by the law, no," she answered as she walked behind them. "How close to DC can we get?"

"There's an airport outside of Harrisonburg, Virginia, we can probably land at," the tall man said. "That's about four hours outside DC. We can't get any closer than that."

AFTER CRAWLING DOWN the interstate for a few hours, Sam and Victoria finally cleared the traffic congestion around Washington. About three hours west into Virginia, there was a small airport owned by a friend of Sam's.

"He'll loan me a plane we can land at my ranch," Sam assured Victoria.

"Then what?"

"We take the horses out and meet up with Charlie. We need to see who is coming and going as it happens. We know now that Jackson is getting the pictures. This is going to come to a head in the next few days. If we find out who's at the top, we can take these guys down before they make their big move."

"So, more camping is what you're saying," Victoria added in her usual disarming style.

"We can find a nice little spot for the two of us," Sam winked.

"Make me one promise, Mr. McBride."

"What's that?"

"When I become Mrs. McBride and we take off for a honeymoon, there will be a nice, comfortable room with a big, soft bed." Victoria unsnapped her seat belt and slid over close to Sam. "Maybe a place where we have our own private little beach?" She smiled.

"That does sound nice," Sam said as he put his arm around her.

"I want to get this stuff all over with so we can get on with our lives," Victoria said as she put her head on his shoulder. "Even with all this craziness, this is the happiest I have ever been. I love being with you. I can't wait to be your wife."

THE PRESIDENT'S HELICOPTER landed at a small airport after the pilot announced a slight mechanical problem.

"We can take a private jet from here," Sinclair said without fanfare.

Once the President boarded, the jet quickly took off and was on its way west. Sinclair stayed behind, claiming he had a few issues in Washington to deal with immediately.

"I will be along shortly, sir," Sinclair had said as the President boarded the plain

"Has the cabinet all reached Missouri?" the President asked as the plane took off.

"Mr. President, I have been told the cabinet is meeting at Mr. Sims' lodge," the pilot responded.

BACK AT HIS HOUSE, Peter Mercury was trying to determine his next move. "I have to tell Langley," he thought, dialing the main number at the FBI and trying to explain to the person on the other end that this was a matter of extreme importance.

"Call him on his cell and tell him to call me. Trust me, he needs to know what I know," Peter said as he pleaded with the young woman.

"Sir, I will send a message to the director. That is all I can do."

A few minutes later, Peter's home phone rang.

"You realize the chance you are taking with both our lives," Langley said as Peter picked up the phone.

"They got Susan. She didn't get the papers there," Peter blurted out. Langley remained silent on the other end of the line. "She left copies here, and I took them to the White House myself."

"Who did you give them to?" Langley asked.

"An old friend of mine. She's in the press detail."

"You think you can count on her?"

Peter hesitated. "I think so. Where do you think they took Susan?"

"To the same room you were in, I would guess," Langley said. "Is she strong, Peter? Can she hold out?" Both men knew that things were likely going to be very bad for her.

"I don't know, Jack. I'm scared for her," Peter answered as he sank down in the couch.

"Listen to me, Peter," Langley said. "You stay low and out of sight. I'm on my way back out there. I will help her if I can, but if you turn up, then we're both dead. You understand?"

Langley hung up the phone and continued driving to Hyde Field in Prince George County, Maryland, where The Council kept its jets. He knew things had developed to a point that his own safety was now compromised.

"But I have to get to the top of this thing," he thought as he parked his car.

PETER SAT ON THE couch thinking of the best course of action. He picked up the phone and called his editor.

"Kyanne, this is Peter," he announced as she answered her office line.

"Peter, for God's sake, where are you? Where have you been? I had a phone call from some woman that you were in a hospital in Billings, and then you disappeared."

"It's a long story, and we don't have time now. I need you to run a story that I have been found dead."

The line was silent for a moment. "What did you say?"

"I need you to report that I'm dead," Peter repeated. "This thing in Washington is more than a protest. There's a group trying to do something bad. I don't know if it's a coup or what, but they are up to something really bad. I don't have time to explain, but they need to think I'm dead. It's important."

"Okay, Peter, I trust you. Give me some details, and I'll get it out there. Where are you anyway?" she asked as she grabbed a pen and notepad to take a few notes.

"Doesn't matter. Say campers found me in the woods near Flathead National Forest in Montana. It's important that that detail is in the story."

"That should help, Jack," he thought as he hung up with Kyanne and looked across the room at the pictures of him and Susan.

The phone rang, startling him.

"Hello," he nearly shouted as he answered.

"Peter!" Susan gasped, surprised he answered.

"My God, Susan, where are you?"

"I'm at a small airport in western Kentucky. I got away, Peter! I got away from that sick bastard," she screamed as she broke down crying.

"Stay where you are. I'll come to you," Peter said as he started for the door.

"No, I can get closer. Listen, get three thousand dollars out of our safe and start driving west. We will be landing in some small obscure airport somewhere. I'll call your cell once I know where we are. Just bring the cash and head west. Bring me some clothes, too. I have to go, but I'm okay," she assured him as she hung up.

Peter scurried around the house gathering the money and clothes and ran out to the old truck.

"I need to tell Jack," he thought as he stopped at the truck. He ran back inside and quickly dialed the number for Langley's office.

"May I tell the director who's calling?" the woman asked.

"Peter Mercury," he said without thinking.

"One moment please."

Peter sat there for a few minutes waiting for the call to be transferred to Langley. After a few minutes the line clicked a couple of times and went dead.

"I can't wait any longer," he said as he ran for the truck.

ANTHONY SINCLAIR WAS NOW at Camp David along with
Cochran and a few Cabinet members.

"It's time," Cochran said as he joined the others around a
table.

"I know," Sinclair answered in a voice of sad resignation.
"But let's be clear about what happens next. Jackson gets a
chance to come around. Reed will stay in Washington. The rest
of us will go to the lodge and explain things. I still believe
Jackson will come around when he sees the big picture. But
this is all going to come as a shock to him."

Sinclair looked around the table at the others. "I thought he
would have figured this out a long time ago," he continued.

"What if he flat out refuses?" Cochran asked.

"If that's his final position, then we do what has to be
done," Sinclair answered. "But I think we can avoid that.
Members of the press are on their way here, and I will make
the appropriate announcements. Once that happens, we make
plans to get Wilson sworn in. But we're doing this with the
expectation that Jackson comes back to office. Agreed?"

"Agreed," the others said.

THE PRESS ROOM AT Camp David was packed with reporters
from every major news channel and newspaper, along with
several cabinet members and White House press personnel.
The room had been prepared quickly and consequently lacked
adequate seating. Reporters fumbled around with laptops,
phones, recorders, and cameras as they adapted to the cramped
environment. A few reporters had moved a long table in the
back, which usually contained a coffee service, near the center
of the room. It was now an impromptu workspace for anyone
lucky enough to have elbowed in for a spot.

"Good evening," Sinclair said softly as he stepped to the
podium. "I realize that rumors are running rampant regarding
the condition of the President. He was wounded in the shooting
that occurred earlier tonight in the National Mall. Doctors do
not consider the wound to be life threatening, but it is serious
enough that the President requires surgery.

A reporter's ringing phone interrupted Sinclair who glared
at the man as he fumbled with the device.

"I'm sorry," the man said softly, raising his hands in a mea culpa.

"Of course that means he has to undergo anesthesia and may spend a lengthy time incapacitated," Sinclair continued. "He has made the decision that Speaker Reed be temporarily sworn in as president, pending his return to office. Speaker Reed is meeting with Cabinet officials right now and will be sworn in later this evening in a private ceremony."

Sinclair cleared his throat as he exchanged a glance with a Cabinet official.

"We are awaiting the arrival of the Chief Justice for that event. The last few days have been dramatic, and I know I speak for the President when I ask that everyone remain calm and return to their homes. I am not going to be taking any questions right now except as they pertain to the health of the President."

Sinclair stepped back for a moment and took a drink from a bottle of water.

"Where was the President shot?" several voices called out in virtual unison.

"The bullet hit the President in the chest and pierced his right lung. Unfortunately, the impact did considerable damage, the extent of which is not yet clear. But I can tell you he was awake and alert after the shooting and was able to participate in the discussion regarding the actions I have outlined," Sinclair said.

"That man is one tough cookie," Sinclair added with a slight smile.

"Where is he now?" another shouted.

"The President has been taken to a private, secure facility and will be treated by the best surgeons available. For security reasons we will not be providing any details concerning his location."

Sinclair looked at his watch and whispered something to his Press Secretary.

"We have to cut this short for now, but updates will be forthcoming as soon as possible," Sinclair said, turning to leave as the gathered reporters shouted a multitude of questions.

"Was this an act of terror?" one shouted above the other voices.

Sinclair stepped back to the microphone.

"Yes, it was a domestic group who took advantage of the situation in Washington to get near the President. The shooter is still at large, but we have a good idea who we are looking for," Sinclair said, then stepped away.

"What do we know about this group?"

"Nothing more for now," Sinclair said as he exited and returned to the room where Cochran and the others were waiting.

"We need to get to the lodge and settle things with Jackson," Sinclair announced as he approached the men. "Reed has meetings in DC set with the top tier of the Council. By morning, he will be up to speed on everything he needs to know. Everyone stays the course."

"What about all those nuts in DC?" Cochran asked.

"They need to be sent home. We can't pull this off until we get the public's focus off these damned reforms," a cabinet member added.

"There are some events planned for tonight that should take care of that," Sinclair assured them in a somber tone.

"It shouldn't have come to this. I now realize Clayton was right. We should have done this earlier. Get an update from our security detail. I want to know that all loose ends are tied up," Sinclair concluded.

The group exited down a side hall.

PETER MERCURY WAS NOW about 100 miles west of DC and searching for a small airport used mostly by hobby pilots. He had called Susan and coordinated the location with the pilot. As he pulled in, he saw an old, two-seat propeller plane making its way along the tarmac to the fueling area. Once stopped, the plane's door flew open. His heart jumped as he saw Susan emerge nearly naked and clearly banged up. He raced the old truck toward a small hangar, threw it into park, and quickly jumped out.

"I thought I had lost you," he said, tears streaming down his face.

"Me, too," said a sobbing Susan as she clung to Peter. "That maniac was going to kill me," she cried, finally feeling safe from Montgomery's reach.

"Let's get out of here," Peter said. He took the cash to the pilot and thanked him profusely for saving his wife.

The pilot quickly stuffed the money in his backpack, refueled, and was back in the air before the Susan and Peter had time to leave.

"Do you have your cell phone?" Peter asked as he returned to the truck.

"The one I took from the pilot," she said.

"Throw that thing out," Peter instructed as he neared the exit of the small airport.

"Are we going home?" Susan asked as she pulled on the sweats Peter had brought.

"No way. We aren't going home until this is over. There is no way we are going any place those creeps might look."

Susan finished dressing and threw Montgomery's coat out the truck's window.

"I almost forgot to tell you," Peter said as he smiled at Susan. "Victoria is alive and well."

Susan stared in astonishment.

"She is out west with Sam McBride. They saved my life ... the first time," he said with a slight chuckle.

"She's with Sam!?" Susan said, excited but confused.

"Yes. I was in bad shape, but they got me fixed up. I don't remember much, but I know she's okay. I'll tell you the details later. How did you get away?" he asked.

"My God, she's alive!" Susan said again as she put her hands over her face and sunk down in the seat. "I can't believe it. That makes me so happy. And she's with Sam! My God, she must be walking on air! She has loved that man since college. I'm so happy for her. This is unreal."

"So, how did you get away?" Peter asked again.

"The asshole who had me on the plane got drunk, and I kicked him in the balls and then in the nose and knocked the asshole out," Susan said, her voice getting higher and louder as she talked. "I can't believe I pulled it off, but I pointed his gun at the pilot and made him land. It's crazy. I can't believe I'm sitting here with you."

Susan moved over next to Peter and was as close to her husband as she could possibly be.

"Got drunk, you said?" Peter asked as he drove on.

"Yeah, why?"

"Did the guy have bleached blond hair?" Peter asked.

"Yes," she said as she pulled back to look at Peter. "Do you know what's going on?"

"Not entirely," he said. "But I know there's a group so opposed to the President that they will do anything to stop him. I don't know who or why, really. But I do know you and I are safe, and we are going to hide somewhere until this whole thing is over."

Peter and Susan drove along on a small Virginia highway enjoying the unlikely reality that they were together and safe.

"Peter," Susan said softly. He looked over at her, curled up on the truck's bench seat and sitting as close to him as possible. "This is the biggest story of your career, isn't it?"

"Yes. I suppose it probably is."

"Did you bring plenty of cash for us?" she asked as she sat up.

"I've got another three thousand or so. Why?"

"Let's buy a tent and a couple of sleeping bags and join the crowd in the Mall," Susan said with a smile. "I know you want to, and we can be two more faces in the crowd for a few days. I'll let Jackson know what happened, but all things considered, I'm due for some time off. You can talk to people and take notes, and when this is over, maybe write a book. You deserve a front row seat to whatever this is, and I want to be there with you."

She curled up close to him as he drove on, thinking.

"By the way, when this is over, you need to grow your hair back out," Susan said with a giggle. "The shaved head thing isn't working."

Peter laughed, but his mind was now in the middle of the protests. "Okay, if you're serious, we're going," he said as he picked up speed.

"I love you," he whispered as he wrapped his arm around her.

IT WAS NOW LATE, and Sam and Victoria were still waiting at the small airstrip. Sam's buddy, Paul, who owned the facility, had agreed to loan them a small plane, but it was at another location and needed to be flown over.

"Let's get a room somewhere and fly out in the morning," Sam suggested as he walked around inside the small hangar. "I'm too tired to fly anyway."

Sam helped an exhausted Victoria up off the ground where they had been sitting.

"Fine by me," she mumbled as they walked back to their car.

"We passed some motels a few miles back. We can try one of them."

"Fine by me," she repeated as she fell into the front seat.

A few minutes later, they had pulled into the first motel they could find, and Sam emerged with a key card and a bag full of snacks. "It's the best we can do right now," he said, handing the bag to Victoria.

"All I need is sleep," she said.

Sam pulled around to the side door of the hotel and grabbed their luggage as Victoria followed carrying the snack bag.

"A hot shower and some Oreos and you'll be good as new," Sam said, smiling at Victoria as she shuffled to the elevator.

Once inside their room, Victoria turned on the shower and dug through her suitcase for something clean to put on.

"Hey, it looks like I can still get a pizza delivered," Sam announced as he looked through the hotel's welcome packet.

"Whatever you want," Victoria called out.

WHEN THE PRESIDENT'S PLANE landed in Montana, Clayton Sims and a few additional Secret Service guards greeted him.

"Jackson, these are crazy times," Sims said as he slapped his old friend on the back.

Niles was sure he was about to learn what Sims was up to.

"Who has arrived from the Cabinet?" the President asked as the two climbed in a golf cart and headed for the lodge.

"A few are here," Sims answered.

Inside, some Cabinet members and the lodge staff greeted the President.

"I have the main suite ready for you," Sims said, feigning a smile. "I know coming here wasn't the original plan, but we all thought this would be a lot more comfortable for you. It's hard telling how long it will be before we get DC straightened out."

The two men walked down the hall until they arrived at the main suite. Sims opened the door and gestured for the President to enter.

"It's been a long day, Jackson. Let's get a good night's sleep, and we will get back to business in the morning," Sims said. "I am having the staff make dinner for you. It'll be brought to your room shortly. Unfortunately, we're having trouble with our satellite, so the TV is out right now."

Sims pulled the door shut, and Niles sat down in an old tan leather chair next to the fireplace. "These guys have me where they want me," he thought as he sat back and put his feet up on a small wooden stool. "At least the truth will finally be out."

IN WASHINGTON, HIATT Montgomery sat in the small apartment kept by The Council. His foot was in a heavy bandage and a bottle of Jack Daniels sat on the desk next to his brief case.

"Okay, it's go time," he said as he held his phone to his ear. He picked up the bottle and turned to face the TV across the room. When someone finally answered, he spoke just two words into his cell phone: "Execute all." From this makeshift headquarters, he directed the next phase of the Council's plan. Tonight would be a night few would ever forget, and it would certainly lead authorities to empty DC of the nuts. Still, as he sat in the little apartment, he could think only of circling back and finishing off the bitch who shot him. Then, he would find McBride and Victoria and do the same to them.

AT THE MALL, Peter and Susan walked along wearing backpacks crammed full of newly purchased supplies. To any onlooker they would have appeared as any other anonymous couple camping in DC. Things had settled down for the most part, and many people had decided to leave. Most of the kids were gone now, too. But many more people were making their way into the area. All who remained, or recently arrived, were planning to be there until the end. A much different feeling hung in the air. The light-hearted, spontaneous joy of a people's movement had been replaced with angry resolve. Most now suspected that "the system" was responsible for pushing back against the President. Few in the crowd accepted the idea that a foreign group was responsible for shooting the President or bombing the city.

"Let's stay away from that guy over there," Peter said as he looked across the Mall and saw William Conner's van. He and Susan walked along until they came across a group of kids in their twenties.

"You guys mind if we set up over there?" Peter asked as he pointed to a small clearing in their midst.

"No. Go ahead," one of the guys said. "Some of our friends just left, so that was good timing."

Peter and Susan set up their tent and dragged their backpacks and supplies inside.

"Let's get some sleep," Peter said as he unrolled his sleeping bag.

"Sounds good," Susan replied as she stretched out. "We've never had a day like this."

"You haven't seen my back yet," Peter said as he sat up and pulled his shirt off.

"Oh, my God," Susan whispered, as she ran her hand across the healing wounds on her husband's back.

"Who did that to you?" she asked as she moved closer.

"The same sick bastard that had you," Peter answered as he pulled his shirt down. "I escaped into the woods out by the lodge, and then that guy started hunting me and shooting at me. I was in the middle of nowhere hiding, and all of a sudden this black-haired woman came riding up and told me to get on her horse with her. That woman was Victoria. She was out there with Sam McBride."

Peter pulled out a bottle of rum and poured a little into a metal camp cup.

"They saved my life that day," he said, choking up. He handed Susan the cup. "But somehow I ended up back at that lodge. Some lunatic was about to water board me."

He hesitated a moment as he relived the terror.

"I was blindfolded. The door opened, and another guy came in and took over. He put me through two rounds of water boarding and then dragged me out and threw me in a car."

Peter looked down and took a deep breath.

"It was Langley. He drove me out in the country and pretended to kill me. He even had me shoot him in the side so he could convince them I fought back. That guy is the most intense person I have ever known."

Peter took the cup back from Susan who sat listening in disbelief. She had worried about her husband but never anticipated the story she was hearing.

"Langley had a helicopter pick me up and take me to his friend's house. But I couldn't stay there any longer knowing all that was going on here. I hope Jack makes it through this. He's really putting himself out there."

Susan clutched her husband's hand. "Let's hold each other," she whispered as she pulled Peter down next to her.

For the first time through the last few crazy days, Peter felt tears well up in his eyes. They surprised him at first. He felt safe now.

Susan felt her own tears forming, shaken by her husband's story and grateful they both had escaped a certain death.

SAM MCBRIDE AND Victoria Niles sat next to each other on one of the small beds in their hotel room near York, Pennsylvania. The nightly news was numbing to each of them.

"We were there, Sam," Victoria whispered as she watched footage of the Mall.

The footage of Anthony Sinclair conducting the press conference based on a total lie was the most chilling site either had ever seen.

"It's all of them," Sam said.

"The entire city is at war with my brother," Victoria said. She moaned as tears rolled down her cheeks. "And he's gone. They've got him, Sam. He saved me, but they have him. Oh, my God. He's probably already dead!"

Sam reached for his cell phone and called Charlie.

"Have you seen much lately?" Sam asked.

"Hell, yes, man. They're coming in and out of here like a damned convention is going on," Charlie said enthusiastically. He was far enough way he could not possibly be heard.

"Are you still getting pictures?" Sam asked.

"Oh, yeah, buddy. I've got guys all over that place. Hell, I've got snipers set up, picture-takers from every direction. Sam, I've even got a few former Special Forces guys in camo within 500 feet of the front door. We outnumber those Uzi-carrying bastards by five-to-one."

Charlie laughed for a minute, truly relishing his newfound purpose.

"Charlie," Sam said in a more serious tone.

"What is it?" Charlie asked, sensing his old friend's stress.

"The news is reporting that the President has been shot. Have you seen anything come in that looks like it might be carrying a stretcher?" Sam's voice dropped a little as he ended the sentence.

"No, Sam, we haven't seen anything like that," Charlie answered, nervously glancing around at the men standing near him. "The President? Shit. What's going on here?" Charlie thought.

"A small jet came in here a little while ago that had one passenger and four guys that sure acted like Secret Service," Charlie described to Sam. "The four guys got out first and were met by four other guys who also acted like Secret Service. Some fat guy in a suit came out and greeted the passenger. That flight stood out because normally we don't see any guards or security types."

"Did you get pictures?"

"Yes. We are photographing everybody that gets near this place."

"Send me that one as soon as you can. I mean right now if possible." Sam turned to Victoria with a look of expectation and excitement as he considered what Sims and the group might be doing.

"Okay, Sam, you'll have those shots in a few minutes," Charlie promised as he hung up.

"What did he say?" Victoria asked.

"A plane came in a little while ago that was handled differently. It may be nothing, but he thought Secret Service or some type of security guys met the plane. Only one passenger got off," Sam explained. "He's sending pictures as soon as he can." Sam poured himself a glass of wine.

"You and Anthony Sinclair are Jackson's best friends. My God, Sam," Victoria said as she rubbed her hands across her face. "Jackson didn't stand a chance. These guys are all rats that have played along. They've had this planned."

"But we still don't really know why. A few reforms wouldn't provoke a response like this," Sam said.

Sam's buzzing cell phone jolted both of them. "It's the picture," he announced as he picked it up.

Both stared at the screen as they waited for the picture to download.

"That's Jackson!" Victoria screamed as she saw her brother's profile.

"Yes, and that's Sims coming to greet him," Sam said in disgust.

"He's alive, Sam. At least we know he's alive," Victoria said, falling back on the bed and letting out a deep sigh of relief.

Sam redialed Charlie's number.

"Charlie, that picture is the President. Listen to me. Keep taking pictures, but pull back any guys that are close enough to be seen. If they find out they're being watched, all hell will break loose. Leave your snipers in place if they have a clean shot near the airstrip. How many guys are out there, Charlie?"

"Right now I count about thirty, but there have been more."

"How many men can you get there that are properly armed?" Sam asked in a tone that gave Charlie a chill.

"I'm not sure what you mean by 'properly armed,' but we have a couple dozen guys out here with combat experience."

Charlie paused as those around him glanced at each other with stunned looks.

"That's what I mean," Sam said. "Divide your guys up into three groups based on experience. We are going to need to ring that place. The inner ring needs to be ready for the worst. I'm going to get out there as soon as I can. Send me the rest of the pictures you have, and if anybody else shows up, get a picture and send it right away. It's critical your guys stay undetected, Charlie. You understand? That's the President in there. Those guys are holding him there against his will. I don't know why. Maybe it's a coup. We don't know. But the media's reporting he's been shot and taken to a hospital. Lay low until I get there."

Victoria had already finished throwing their clothes back into suitcases before Sam hung up the phone.

"I will get him out of this or die trying," Sam announced as he grabbed the bags, opened the door, and turned for the stairs.

It took them less than thirty minutes to return to the small airstrip owned by Sam's friend.

"You waited too long, Sam," Paul said as they entered the hangar.

"What do you mean?" Sam asked as he dropped the bags.

"We're being told to ground everything. There's been more terrorism somewhere, and the FAA has issued restrictions. I haven't turned on the news yet, but they're making a lot of noise," Paul explained.

Sam stared at his friend for a moment and then looked at Victoria.

"Listen to me," Sam said. "We have to get out west right now. I don't care what kind of bullshit story we have to tell. I know this is all going to sound nuts, but the President's life is at risk, and we have to go. We're *going* to go. If I have to steal that plane, I will."

The men stared at each other in silence as Victoria glanced back and forth between them.

"The President of what?" Paul finally said.

"Our President," Sam said with growing urgency. "The President of the United States."

Paul stared back again as he rubbed his chin.

"You're messing with me, aren't you, Sam?" Paul said, forcing a smile. The two men had known each other a long time.

"No, Paul. I don't have time to explain everything. You remember that story a few days ago about the President's sister being killed?" Sam asked in a hurried tone.

"Yes. The judge, right?"

"That's the one. Paul, I'd like you to meet the President's sister, Victoria Niles."

Victoria stepped up and shook Paul's hand. "My brother is in trouble. We need to get to Montana. How can we get a plane up?" she pleaded.

Paul studied Victoria. "You dyed your hair. But I do recognize the face."

Victoria leaned forward and revealed her blond roots.

"I noticed that when you came in. My wife does hair," he laughed. "Okay, here's what we do. But, boy, are we going to get in trouble if they decide to check us out."

Paul retrieved a badge and some papers from his desk.

"I fly emergency organ donations," he said, handing Sam a laminated card with ID numbers. "When you get contacted, and you *will* get contacted, you give them the info on that card. It's all I've got, but it should get you through. If the FAA upgrades this thing one more level, they'll force you down no questions asked."

Paul walked across the tarmac to the jet. "She's filled up and ready, Sam. You won't have much company up there, so you should be able to go full throttle."

"I voted for your brother," he said to Victoria. "I sure hope he's okay."

JACKSON NILES SAT alone is his private suite at the Sims Lodge. The room felt more like a prison cell than luxury accommodations. Everyone had gone to bed early, and without the TV or a cell phone connection, the lodge was uncomfortably quiet. Jackson knew he was in the middle of the hornet's nest. All he could do was wait and find out what his "old friends" were really up to. He did have to laugh at himself a little as he walked around the large room looking at old pictures of the

Sims family. These guys had managed to get him here without much trouble. He had known Sims was up to something, but Cochran's presence was a shock. His gut now told him his whole inner circle was rotten, but he didn't know the extent of their plans. He had gently tried the doorknob earlier and was not surprised to find the door locked. This would be explained away tomorrow as an accident, he was sure.

Eventually, he decided to try to get some sleep. Tomorrow, he was sure, would be an eventful day.

HIATT MONTGOMERY SAT back and watched as all the 24-hour news networks covered the latest rash of "terrorist attacks." This time, the targets were more obscure and scattered. A bus station in Baltimore, a shopping mall in Ohio, two different car bombs in California, and a major overpass in Florida. Newly sworn-in President Wilson Reed would address the American people the next morning.

Montgomery laughed as scenes of the spectacle he had created with just a few random acts flashed across the television screen. "Sources close to the White House" were speculating that President Reed would declare martial law and order Washington evacuated. Certainly the plan to change the focus of the public away from DC and the reforms was working.

AT THE NATIONAL MALL, Susan and Peter awoke to the commotion of people reacting to the news.

"This isn't foreign," Peter said.

"These creeps are trying to kill this movement," Susan said.

They left their tent and moved around the crowd so Peter could gauge reaction. As they walked, they began to realize how much they had missed since their reunion at the airport.

"I can't believe someone would shoot the guy," Susan heard someone say.

"What guy?" she asked as she stepped into the group.

They all looked at her for a minute without saying anything.

"The President," one of them finally said in a tone of almost sarcastic disbelief at her ignorance.

"He got shot right over there by that CNN van," another said.

"Was Conner there?" Peter asked.

"Yes, he had just interviewed the President when the shooting happened," another explained.

"Come on," Peter instructed Susan as he grabbed her hand and moving rapidly through the crowd toward the CNN van. When he got close, he realized the area had been fenced off and was now being treated as a crime scene. He scanned the crowd and finally located Conner, who was sitting with his cameraman watching, like everyone else.

Peter quietly approached Conner and found enough room to sit next to him in the crowd.

"Bill, I need to know something," he said as he removed his sunglasses.

"Peter, what the hell, man? Your paper is reporting that you are dead." Conner's voice was too loud for Peters' comfort. He quickly hushed his colleague.

"You were there when the President got shot?" Peter whispered.

"Hey, I'm on a gag order, buddy. You shouldn't be here right now. But, yes, I was right next to him," Conner said.

"Did you see him get hit?" Peter asked as others on the scene started to take notice of the conversation.

"He didn't get hit, Peter," Conner said. "Now get the hell out of here."

Peter was nearly frozen to the ground as the same fear he had felt at the lodge found him again.

"Susan, start for the tent," Peter said under his breath as those inside the fence stood looking at them.

Susan scooted back nonchalantly and pretended to be talking with another group as she left the area.

Peter was the center of the attention of those inside the fence.

"Go, Peter," Conner said, rubbing his face and looking in the opposite direction.

Peter stood up, turned, and quickly disappeared into the crowd. A few feet back, frightened and confused, Susan met up

with her husband, desperation on her face. They quickly
returned to their tent and gathered their things.

"Come on, we need to go," Peter said as he grabbed Susan's
hand and led her through the crowd.

"Where?"

"Not here," he said as he moved quickly.

THE NEXT MORNING at the lodge, President Niles had
showered and was on his way to the dining area. As he turned
the corner, the first face he saw was also the least expected.

"Good morning, Jackson," Anthony Sinclair said in a big
voice with a smile and open arms. "Did you sleep well?" He
handed the President a cup of coffee.

"Is this safe to drink?" the President asked, staring at his
old friend. An uncomfortable few seconds of silence followed.

Finally, Sinclair smiled. "Come on, Jackson. We have lots to
discuss today." Sinclair put his hand on his old friend's
shoulder and led him into the main dining area. Sims and
Cochran were already seated, joined by several cabinet
members, Secret Service agents, and support staff. For a
moment, President Niles just looked around at the gathering
then eventually took his seat near Sinclair.

"We have a fantastic breakfast coming out, Jackson,"
Sinclair said. "Everything's okay. What we have to tell you is
going to come as a shock, that's all. But once your hear it all,
you'll understand."

Sinclair took a drink of his coffee. He was almost giddy that
they had finally gotten to this point. He was tired of the cloak
and dagger and confident his old friend would be on board once
the truth was known.

"Ah, here we go," Sinclair said cheerfully as the staff
emerged from the kitchen with rolling carts full of every
imaginable breakfast delicacy.

"Jackson, the crepes are the best I've ever had," he said as
the waiter offered a plate to the President. Breakfast continued
with only slight small talk popping up here and there. Sinclair
was the most talkative, moving fluidly from sports to history to
his favorite recipe.

Niles sat silently through it all as he ate and listened, wondering what was to come.

Near the end of breakfast, Jack Langley walked into the room. He was greeted by Cochran, Sims, and Sinclair as the old friend he was. He intentionally avoided eye contact with Jackson as he filled a plate and took a seat at a table on the other side of the room.

"Jack, we'll let you catch up, and then a few of us will have a meeting," Sinclair said.

Little by little, the room cleared as people filed out. Finally, Sinclair invited the President, Sims, Cochran, and Langley to join him in Sims' private boardroom.

SAM AND VICTORIA were now close to the cabin after a slow, nighttime horse ride through the Montana wilderness. The flight had gone off without incident, and both were relieved to be moving closer toward Jackson's location.

"There have been too many riders through here," Sam said as he looked at the worn trail leading past his cabin. They dismounted so the horses could drink some water and take a brief rest.

Victoria rubbed her lower back and walked slowly up the stairs. Inside, she pulled off the quilt bloodstained by Peter's wounds and stretched out on the bed.

A few minutes later, Sam entered and joined her on the bed.

"What are we going to do?" Victoria asked.

"I'm not sure yet. I suppose it goes back to what you said about getting to the top. If they have Jackson out here, then it's safe to guess that whoever is at the top is here, too."

Sam took a deep breath and stretched his arms out over his head. "The real question is, what do we do then?" he said as he rolled on his side facing Victoria. "We need to get going, Pinky."

"I'm worried, Sam. This is heavy stuff. These are bold and powerful people," she said. "They will kill all of us at the drop of a hat. Hell, they've kidnapped a President. We better have a good plan or we're all going to die out here."

"We're going to find a way. I promise. We are going to get through this."

AFTER SPENDING THE NIGHT in the truck, Peter and Susan walked through the crowd to his office. Inside, Peter rounded a corner and quickly entered the stairwell.

"Where are we going?" Susan asked as she tried to keep up.

"I need to get to my editor," Peter said as he reached the third floor. He peeked out the stairway door and down the hall leading to Kyanne's office. There was still no power in the city, but the windows of her corner office made it bright enough.

"Come on," he said as he entered the hall and dashed for her door.

Kyanne Fitzgerald sat at her desk looking through newspapers with a flashlight. Peter and Susan entered and quickly closed the door behind them.

"Peter!" Kyanne exclaimed as she jumped up and hugged her reporter. "My God, what the hell are you doing here?"

"Listen to me," Peter said as he sat down. "By the way, this is my wife, Susan," he said.

"I'm sorry, Susan. I'm afraid my manners have been a little lax lately," Kyanne said. She walked across the room and gave her a hug. "I can't imagine what you've been through, honey."

"It's been a week, hasn't it?"

"Kyanne, the President wasn't shot," Peter said. "We were in the park. Conner interviewed the President right before the supposed shooting. He was standing right next to him. Conner has been told he can't talk about it. The Secret Service, or whoever they are, took his camera and gear. This thing is big, Kyanne. As big as it gets. These people have taken the President, pretended he has been shot, and have sworn in their stooge. We're watching a coup take place right here, right now!"

He paced the room as he spoke. "What the hell are we supposed to do?"

"We need to get what we know down on paper so we can take it apart and find a trail to follow," Kyanne said as she grabbed a note pad.

"Peter, it's the pictures!" Susan said. "That's the trail we need to follow. Those people are the key to this thing."

"What pictures are we talking about?" Kyanne asked.

"Jack Langley came to my house yesterday and gave me a packet to get to the White House. I was abducted on the way, but I escaped," Susan explained.

"Langley came to your house?" Kyanne asked.

"Yes, he's in this thing up to his neck," Peter answered.

"So the White House never got the pictures?" Kyanne asked.

"I think the President did get them because I found her note, and she had left a copy for me. I took them there myself and gave them to Mary what's-her-name. Remember, from the White House Press Corps?" Peter said.

"Mary Mitchell," Kyanne said.

"Yes, that's it," Peter answered.

"She would get them to him," Kyanne said. "But wait, Langley brought them to your house?"

"He also saved my life," Peter said. "We don't have to worry about Langley. He's with the President on this thing."

"I just remembered something, Peter!" Susan said. "Our printer has a memory. Those photos are still in our system. We have to go home and print them again."

"No way!" Kyanne declared, as she walked in front of her office door. "You guys aren't going back there. I've got friends in the police force. I can get a couple of guys to go over there and bring the printer to us. I need to get out of here anyway. We'll get the printer, take it some place safe, and set up shop. We have to dig into this thing and find out what role all these people are playing. That's all we can do."

Kyanne glanced back forth at Peter and Susan. "My God, look at you two. You look like shit. You smell like shit. You've been beaten, kidnapped, chased, and God-knows-what-else," she said. "I can have a team on this, and we can help smoke out these rats. We need a place to go that's safe."

"We have an old farm house in southern Indiana. It's in a trust. No one knows we own it," Peter said.

"It's so isolated it's hard to find when you *are* looking for it," Susan added with an exhausted laugh.

"Let's go there," Kyanne said.

"Hey, that's fine with us," Peter blurted out, relieved.

"Thank God," Susan said. "No one will be able to track us or find us."

She wrote down the address and handed it to Kyanne.

"You guys take off and meet me there tonight," the editor said. "I'll bring the printer with me."

Peter and Susan nodded in agreement.

"You need to get out of here and out of town without being seen," Kyanne added as she looked out her door and down the hall.

SAM AND VICTORIA RODE into Charlie's camp after being met by four different lookouts.

"You need to change the path of entry," Sam said to Charlie as he dismounted.

"Already done," Charlie answered as he tipped his hat to Victoria.

"Any more arrivals?" Sam asked as the three of them sat down around a makeshift table.

"One. This guy." Charlie held up his phone with a picture of Langley walking to the lodge.

"Good. He's on our side," Sam said as he looked at the photo. "Okay, this is where things change. Victoria, you're staying back here."

She immediately started to argue, but Sam grabbed her by the arm and led her away. "I can't be worried about you if I'm going in there after Jackson," he said. "This is not about you. Not right now. This is now about Jackson, and I need to know you are back here safe. Okay?" Victoria looked at Sam for a long moment and then wrapped her arms around him.

"Promise me you won't get hurt, Sam. I waited a lifetime for where we are. Promise me, damn it. You come back to me in one piece. You let the younger guys take the risk," she pleaded. "Please, Sam, please play this smart. Come back to me, Sam McBride." Tears rolled down Victoria's face.

CHAPTER TEN

Truth and Consequences

Sims' boardroom was stunning and majestic, patterned after a castle his grandfather had visited in England as a young man. The walls were stone and walnut and rose to meet an ornate, coffered ceiling. Large, medieval sconces hung from the walls on all sides, and a huge stone fireplace dominated the far end of the room. In between the stone columns running from floor to ceiling were large paintings of the Sims family.

"Quite a room, Clayton," the President remarked as he entered and looked around at the paintings and other furnishings.

"It's a special place for my family," Sims said as he closed the old, giant wood doors behind him.

"Please, Jackson, make yourself comfortable," he suggested, motioning to the oversized leather chairs situated around a large, oval wood table in the middle of the room.

"Jackson, we've all been friends for a long time, and I know I speak for all of us when I tell you we value that friendship," Sinclair said, offering his old friend a comforting expression. Sinclair knew how difficult it was going to be navigating through this situation.

"Jackson, we have a real problem right now, and we want to work through it so everyone wins in the end. That's what we want," Sims said.

"Who's 'we'?" the President asked.

Sinclair shifted in his chair and looked down the table at Sims and Cochran, who sat motionless.

"Jackson, things in Washington aren't what you think they are," Sinclair said. "The fact is some of the changes you're proposing simply cannot happen. They can't. It's not a question of whether they should or not. They simply cannot happen."

Niles looked around the room then focused on his old friend.

"Put it on the table in black or white, or I'm walking out of here right now," the President said.

Sinclair took a few steps to the corner of the room where a bottle of brandy and several glasses sat on a small table. "I know it's a little early, but I think given the circumstances, I am going to have a drink," he said. "Anyone care to join me?"

Sinclair stood there for a moment with his hands out to his side. He smiled at the other men in sad resignation then turned to pour a drink, keeping his back to the other men.

"You can't leave, Jackson," Sinclair said, still facing the wall. "You can't leave, and as of yesterday at 9:00 p.m., you are no longer the President. As far as the public is concerned, you were shot and left incapacitated. Clayton, show Jackson the tape."

Sims sat a laptop down in front of Niles and played the video of Wilson Reed being sworn in by the Chief Justice. Sinclair slowly turned around and approached Niles with the saddest look Jackson had ever seen on his old friend's face.

"But, you can go back. We can undo this," Sinclair said. "I want you to know that right now. That is our intention. We want you to go back."

Niles said nothing and just stared at this man who now seemed like a stranger.

"Jackson, there aren't two parties in Washington," Sinclair said. "There haven't been for eighty years or so. Yes, we have elections to keep the people happy and involved. They get to cheer for their red team or blue team." Sinclair waved his hands in a mocking gesture as he referred to the public's enthusiasm and involvement in one party or the other.

"Our fathers decided a long time ago that it was simply too dangerous to turn over the government to some farmer or playboy," Sinclair said. "Come on, does anyone really think the most powerful nation in the history of the world is going to risk moving in a completely different direction every four years? If you stop and think about it, it's preposterous."

Sinclair walked around the table as he spoke. He avoided eye contact and looked more like an eccentric professor lecturing a class than a civil servant addressing the President.

"You guys think you can pull off a coup to save these stupid parties?" Niles said, laughing.

"A coup?" Sinclair laughed, too. "I never thought about it that way, but it would seem like that to you. That's funny," he said as he looked at Cochran and Sims, who also looked amused.

"You are the coup, Jackson," Sinclair finally said as he walked to refill his glass. "The system we represent has been in place since the end of World War II. Every president since Roosevelt has been involved. Sure, some chafed a bit, and some even rebelled. The Kennedys were the most defiant, but the rest understood and played their role. You get to sit in the chair for four or maybe even eight years. But you simply can't take the system apart and change everything."

Sinclair stood looking at Niles.

"Okay, this is some kind of joke you assholes are pulling off," Jackson finally said, laughing for real this time.

"It's no joke, Jackson," Sinclair said, taking a deep breath and looking at the others. "The United States government is controlled by a ruling Council. The Council is made up of 200 or so handpicked members of society. Some Senators and Representatives are involved. In fact, all the past presidents have gone on to serve on the Council. Some have even been appointed to the Captain's chair. The notion that we can risk turning over this government to a group of uneducated reactionaries is simply naïve. The parties do what they are told. They serve their purpose."

Sinclair walked back to his chair and sat down.

"Jackson, this system works. The people are free to live as they choose but also are kept safe by having a consistent and stable government. Change can happen in this system. We expanded rights for minorities and gays when the people demanded it. We have better healthcare now. We made education improvements, adopted environmental restrictions, tightened banking laws—the list goes on," Sinclair said.

"But we cannot allow a group of people who know nothing about the 'real world' to take over. We cannot turn our national security over to a bunch of amateurs."

Sinclair stood again and walked around the table. "Jackson, the two party heads take their direction from the Council. The overwhelming majority of both parties have no idea they are unwitting actors in a grand play. If you think about it, this is the greatest political theater ever staged," he said, laughing and throwing his arms in the air. "So many of those elected commoners make their way onto television and rant and rave and argue, and all along they believe—and the public believes—they're going to change things. It's a beautiful system. Everyone gets what they want." Sinclair circled the table.

"What if the people want your 'stable' system to be different?" Jackson asked, interrupting Sinclair's lecture. "What if they are tired of the debt, the poverty, the wars, and professional politicians? What then, boys? What happens to your perfect little world when your policy no longer works for the poor bastards being sent to God-knows-where to kill or subdue whoever you think needs it? I got elected fellas. That should be a wake-up call that the party—in this case the one 'big party,' as it turns out—is over."

Niles had stood, and now he was the one circling the table. "You guys can kill me and bury me out here in these woods, but that won't be the end of it. Those 'commoners,' as you call them, they know they can win. You guys fucked up when you let this thing go through an election. If you didn't want me to win, you should have taken me out a long time ago."

Niles walked over to the corner, took off his sport coat, and poured a drink for himself. "You guys are done. You don't think so, but you're all done," he said, "and those people in the Mall will burn that city down if you don't get out of the way. You're nothing but a bunch of traitors to your country. You will be despised for eternity." Niles glared down at all the men seated at the table.

Jack Langley had been taking all this in as he sat at the other end. Now, he spoke up: "Jackson, you'll agree once you've seen the whole picture. It was hard for me at first, too, but once I had the entire picture, it was clear this is best."

Sinclair and the others looked at Langley as he spoke. "Thank you for adding that, Jack," Sinclair said as he turned back toward the President.

"You will have to excuse me for a moment, guys," Langley said as he stood. "Something in that breakfast is going right through me. I'll be back in a few."

"I think all of this will seem much more real for you if we go into the Council room," Sinclair said as he stood.

Clayton Sims walked toward the wall with the fireplace. He pushed open one of the large walnut panels, revealing a wide, winding staircase that descended to a meeting room. The large room looked the part of a "ruling body." Rows of oversized chairs formed an arch, all facing a podium flanked by thirteen black leather seats. The walls were lined with portraits of the Captains through the years on one side and with paintings of the nation's founding fathers on the other. Niles walked along, looking at the pictures and various framed memorabilia.

"What if I refuse?" Niles asked as he turned and faced the men.

"Let's not go there," Sinclair said, smiling as he approached the President. "Spend some time with us and try to keep an open mind. Many in your cabinet are also on the Council. Listen to them, Jackson," he said as he walked to the front of the room and sat down in one of the black leather chairs.

"Is that the Captain's chair?" Jackson asked, disgusted.

"As a matter of fact, it is," Sinclair said, leaning back and patting the arms of the chair. "Jackson, you're a smart and capable man. We want you to join us. Your presence would be a tremendous asset. And ... we can pass most of the reforms you want."

Sinclair stood up and walked back toward the other men. "But we can't turn the House over to those nuts running around in the Mall in their silly, purple shirts. It can't happen. And we cannot eliminate campaign money from our corporate sponsors. Do you understand? The rest of it I'm sure we can reach an agreement on, but not those two items."

Niles walked away from the men and sat down in the chair Sinclair vacated.

"It looks good on you, Jackson," Sinclair said.

"So, it's the House that has you guys all worried?" the President asked.

"That ... and the Court," Sinclair responded.

"Are you responsible for Victoria's murder?" Jackson asked with some hostility.

"First of all, she's not dead. You know that. And we all know that now, too. And second, to answer your question, no, I did not order a hit on her, if that's what you mean. That was an act of an over-zealous man who needs to be brought under control," Sinclair said.

"It was never the Council's intention to harm Victoria. We know she's running around out there somewhere with Sam McBride. When you join us, that chase ends. In fact, I think we could all agree that her nomination will be reinstated and she takes a seat on the Court. We all know she's qualified," Sinclair said with his arms raised and another big smile. "But if you won't join us, then I'm afraid I can't guarantee she'll be safe."

Sinclair walked toward Jackson and sat down in the chair next to him. "That's the way it works, Jackson. If you're in, then the whole family benefits, including kids, grandkids, aunts, uncles, etc. We take care of our own, Jackson."

"To the detriment of the people," Jackson countered.

"The people have what they want, Jackson. Come on, face the music here. The average American doesn't care about the reality of the world. For God's sake, just look at the polls asking commoners who we fought against in the Revolutionary War. Hell, most of them don't even know. You want them coming to Washington to lead our country? What a joke!" Sinclair said as he waved his hand dismissively. "The average American is stupid, but happy."

"Sounds like your education policy could use some work," Jackson said as he stood and walked toward the stairs.

"You can't leave, Jackson," Sinclair called out.

The President ignored him and walked up the stairs, back into the boardroom, then passed through the large, old wooden doors and into the great room. A few people were standing around talking, and all turned and stared at their President suddenly standing in their midst.

"Treason," the President said in a calm voice as he walked to his room.

BY NOW SAM AND Charlie had placed a handful of their best-equipped men in close proximity to the airstrip. Another group had moved in as close as they could to the lodge. Sam also sent two men with explosives experience to the electrical poles along the highway that eventually fed power to the lodge.

"Let's see how they like darkness," Sam said, planning to give them a taste of their own medicine.

"WHERE'S JACK?" Sinclair asked as Sims and Cochran approached from the Council room.

"Based on how he looked earlier, I'd guess he's sitting on the pot," Cochran said as they all chuckled.

"Go check on him and don't worry about Jackson's reaction. Every President has reacted that way when they first learned the truth," Sinclair said as he walked to join a group of cabinet members.

Cochran and Sims passed through the great room and knocked on the door to Langley's suite.

"Jack, you okay in there?" Sims asked as the two waited.

"He must have it bad," Cochran added.

"Let's leave the poor guy alone," Sims suggested as the two laughed and walked back down the long hallway to the great room.

"I think Jack is going to be out for a while," Cochran suggested as they approached Sinclair and the others.

"Something he ate didn't agree," Sinclair explained to the men who hadn't been in the earlier meeting.

"Jack Langley? He went outside," one of the men said. "He told us he needed some fresh air."

Sinclair, Cochran, and Sims all exchanged uncomfortable glances.

"Go check on him, Clayton. Make sure things are as they should be," Sinclair said.

Sims walked toward the door and Sinclair followed.

"Take a guard with you," Sinclair whispered, squeezing Sims' forearm.

Outside, Sims and the guard looked around to see if Jack was actually getting some fresh air. They jumped in a golf cart and made a dash for the airstrip. Upon arrival, they spotted Langley, gun drawn, waiting for a pilot to fuel a small jet. Immediately, the guard with Sims radioed for backup. Within seconds, Langley was surrounded by several men wielding machine guns.

"Give me your radio," Sims barked as he approached Langley. "You are a damned fool."

Through the radio, Sims said, "Looks like Jack is a turncoat."

"Put him in the barn," Sinclair answered. "I'll be there shortly."

A few minutes later, Sinclair entered the barn and approached the men. "Why, Jack? Why couldn't you join us? Why do you want to cause trouble? What did you think you were going to do?" Sinclair said, rubbing his chin as he stared at Langley. "You've put me in a bad spot here."

"You'll all hang someday," Langley answered.

"We can't let Jackson know what has happened here," Sinclair said, ignoring Langley's remark. "Damn it, Jack."

Sinclair paced back and forth under the beam that Peter Mercury had been tied to a few days earlier.

"You've left me no choice, Jack. You did this. Take him out in the woods a ways. You know what has to be done," he instructed then stepped close to Langley. "I'm sorry, Jack. I truly am. But Jackson can't know, and you can't live. Not now. You did this."

Sinclair and Sims exited the barn and drove the golf cart back to the lodge. The two guards tied Langley's hands behind his back and led him to the far edge of the runway.

"We have to go a lot farther than this," one of the men said as he gauged the distance back to the lodge.

"I hate walking through this crap," the other said lifting his boots high enough to clear the thick undergrowth surrounding the runway.

"Head back up, then. I can take care of this guy," the other said as he pushed Langley forward.

On a bluff a few hundred feet away, Sam McBride and his friend Charlie watched as Jack Langley walked, hands tied, to his pending execution. Sam raised his radio. "Must save that guy," he said.

The man leading Langley walked along a deer trail until he felt they were a sufficient distance from the lodge.

"Coyotes and wolves will have you gone in a day or two," the man declared with a sadistic laugh as he raised his pistol.

A shot startled Langley as his would-be executioner collapsed next to him.

"What the fuck?" Langley muttered as he looked down on the dead body.

"Mr. Langley, we were told to secure your safety," a man said as he approached and saluted.

"Who the fuck are you guys?" Langley asked motioning for them to untie his hands.

"Montana Militia, sir," one of them announced.

"Formerly U.S. Special Forces," the other added.

"Whatever you are, take me to whoever's in charge out here. And get the uniform off that asshole," Langley commanded, pointing to the dead guard beside him.

Sam and Charlie, meanwhile, had descended the bluff and were on their way to meet Langley.

"I'll be God damned," Langley said as he saw them approach. "I'll eat crow, my hat, and whatever else you want later. What kind of forces do you have out here?" Langley asked, looking around at the men gathered.

"We have about thirty or so now," Charlie answered.

"Thirty!" Langley said in disbelief. "Are you well armed?"

"You could say that," Charlie answered with a smile, as several of the men politely laughed. "We have two snipers set up around the main house. We have two hiding inside the hangar. There are two inside the barn, four former Special Forces personnel within a hundred feet of the house, and the balance in a ring of perimeter control. Oh, and we have two guys up by the highway waiting for the order to cut power."

Langley looked around at the group and smiled in amazement. "And I see you have Victoria safe and sound as well," he added as he spotted her standing off to the side.

"What's it like in there?" Sam asked as the men all closed in to hear the answer.

"The entire story is too unbelievable to try to tell quickly. Suffice it to say, the President is a hostage."

"Jack, is his life in danger?" Victoria asked desperately as she approached.

"Not yet, but it will be when they figure out he can't be swayed to join their treason," Langley said disgusted. "Listen, those people inside don't have any suspicion at all that you're out here. Hell, I can't believe it myself." He lit a cigarette and sat down. "Anybody got a drink?"

One of the men standing nearby handed Langley a bottle of whiskey.

"Thanks," he said as he took a drink. "I thought I was a goner this time. I'll tell ya, I've been in some tough spots before. Never thought I'd be rescued by a state militia, that's for damned sure."

"Our President saved my life on three different occasions when we were fighting together years ago. If I have to, I'll shoot every one of those fucking traitors to get him out of there," Langley said as he took another drink and handed the bottle back. "But the only way we get him out without blowing that place to hell is to go quietly through his bedroom window." Langley looked around at those gathered. "We need to get him out and then keep those people pinned down inside long enough for us to put some distance between us and them."

"What if he's not in his room?" Charlie asked.

"We wait till it's late. We watch for the lights to come on in the bedroom on the end of the main wing. Once his lights go on, we assume it's him, open the window, and make our play," Langley said. He looked around for input but none came.

"Can your special force guys get to that far end where the bedrooms are without making a commotion?" Langley asked Charlie.

"Not without taking out at least one guard," Charlie answered.

"They're all going to die tonight or by firing squad anyway, so that's not a problem. The question is, can you do it quietly?" Langley asked as he scanned the faces for reactions.

"We have Navy Seals down there, sir," Charlie answered with a sense of pride.

"Okay, that answers my question. Now understand, these people have a lot of resources. They could blow the woods to hell if they felt the need. They have satellite phones in there, so there's no way to cut communication. Once they discover the President is gone, the cavalry will be on the way. We'll have to blow the hell out of that place for a while, and then we have to scatter and I mean damned fast," Langley said. "Anybody have anything they want to add?"

Langley looked around at the group. "You people are patriots. This President and this nation owe you all. You should be damned proud."

The men gathered waited for final instructions. Most were former military and had been deployed overseas. The idea of treason made their blood boil, and getting on with the fight was fine with them.

"Okay, here's what we do. We put one of your best guys in the uniform we took off that guard. Put that guy by the hangar and have him make sure the plane is fueled up. He'll need to take out that pilot they have standing by that plane. How many pilots do we have out here?" Langley asked.

"I can fly," Charlie said.

"Whoever takes that plane is going to be a decoy," Langley said. "So you better be good and able to land someplace where they can't shoot you up."

"Hell, I can fly that thing at full throttle and drop it down on Main Street, if need be," Charlie said with a confident chuckle. "I'll give those boys a hell of a chase."

Langley looked around the group for input.

"I have a small jet at my ranch," Sam added.

"How far is that from here?" Langley asked.

"If we ride hard, it takes about four hours," he said.

"Okay, when we get Jackson out, you move as quickly as you can out of here and toward your place," Langley instructed Sam. "Charlie, you take off as soon as you see us move past. I don't care where you go, but fly in the opposite direction of Sam's place. Once we have the President and Charlie takes off, they'll be crawling out of there like cockroaches. Your guys are going to have to open fire on them. That's when you give the order to cut the power, too. We need them pinned down as long as possible."

Langley stopped and looked around the group for more feedback. "I'm warning all of you that hell fire is going to rain down on this place once they discover Jackson's gone."

Langley looked at Victoria, then at Sam. "You two and Jackson take off for Sam's ranch. The rest of your men are going to need to help me keep this place pinned down for an hour or so. After that, we all get as far from this place as fast as possible. There'll be helicopters swooping in here like locusts."

He looked at Victoria, seeking a response.

"What about you, Jack?" she asked with sincere concern.

"I'll follow you toward Sam's place. I want two or three guys with me to give you guys some back side protection. We'll ride an hour or so behind you. If any of those people try to follow the President, we'll take them out. Don't worry about me. When you get to Sam's ranch, get in his jet and get the hell out of Montana. You understand?"

Langley looked at Victoria with an expression that surprised her, then added, "You and I are going to need to have a talk when this over."

IN WASHINGTON, A BLACK police car slowly approached the Mercury home.

"She warned me we may have company when we get here," the officer said to his partner, referring to Kyanne Fitzgerald. "We grab the printer, and we go. If anyone tries to stop us, we shoot to kill."

The car pulled up silently. Both men exited and approached the front door. Once inside, they followed Kyanne's directions and located the printer.

"Grab it. I've got your back," the other man said. They had the printer loaded and were on their way in less than two minutes.

"That was easy," the driver said.

"Maybe too easy," his partner said.

The officers drove outside Washington and pulled into a grocery store parking lot where Kyanne waited.

"Any trouble?" she asked as she got out and opened her trunk.

"Nope. We were in and out," the man shrugged.

"You need anything else?" the other asked, smiling at Kyanne.

"I got it from here," she said and winked.

Across the lot, a black van watched the police car exit the parking lot.

"Let's see where she goes now," Montgomery said from the back seat. Kyanne quickly made a few turns and was on her way.

"We follow until she stops, and then we stick a GPS chip on her car. I'll follow by chopper after that," Montgomery instructed as they rode along.

OUT WEST, IT WAS getting dark, and the men outside moved into their assigned positions. Unfortunately, the room occupied by the President had been lit up all evening, so trying to guess if he was in there was just that—a guess.

About 8 o'clock, Jack Langley and Sam McBride made their way down to the hangar where Charlie was waiting near the small plane.

"Considering the environment in there, I'm guessing he's been in his room all night," Langley said to Sam and Charlie.

"I say we go now," he added with a deep exhale. The three exchanged handshakes.

"Charlie, you fly to a safe place. You understand me?" Langley commanded. "There's no need for a suicide mission here. You understand me?" Langley had the man's hand grasped tightly in his as he gave him a sincere and stern stare.

"I want to get drunk with you when this over," Langley finally said as he smiled and let go of Charlie's hand.

"I will hold you to that Mr. Langley," Charlie said as he saluted his new friend.

"These are your people. You give the order," Langley said as he returned Charlie's salute.

Charlie licked his lips as the weight of the moment set in. "Maybe a drink right now might be in order," Charlie said as concern flashed across his face. The three passed Charlie's flask around one last time.

"It's go time," Charlie said in a whispered voice as he pressed the button on his two-way radio. A few feet outside the President's window, a former Navy Seal dressed in camo waited for the guard to pass by. The guard was sloppy and loud and absolutely clueless he had walked by the Seal on several previous occasions. As the guard approached, the Seal pulled his knife. Within seconds, the guard was dead and his body hidden behind a shrub.

Almost immediately, two others joined the Seal outside the President's bedroom window. The first looked through the window and was relieved to see the President sitting in a chair reading. The Seal scanned the room for any others, and then knelt down next to his two cohorts.

"He's alone," the man reported. He stood back up and tapped lightly on the glass. At the sound, the President glanced over, but he continued reading. The second tap was in a Morse code pattern that was unmistakable to anyone with military experience. Niles walked to the door to his room and turned the lock from the inside. Then he returned to the window and cranked it open.

"We are here to get you to safety, sir," the Seal whispered. The President looked down at the men with a sense of relief as he stood at the window.

"We really need to hurry, sir," the Seal suggested as he cut the screen out with his knife.

The President struggled to get through the narrow window and was soon standing with the three men outside the lodge.

"Follow us quickly," the Seal instructed as they moved toward the tree line. Once there, the lead Seal raised his radio.

"We have him," was all he said as he turned toward the President. "We need to stay quiet and together, sir. Please stay one step behind me and on my right side."

The four men looped around the woods, heading for the hangar. As they made their way, they passed several other militia members who had also killed guards. All saluted as the President passed. When they reached the hangar, they heard gunfire coming from the lodge.

"The President is safe. Fire on any guards you see," Charlie instructed as he, Jack, and Sam caught site of Jackson emerging from the woods.

"Thank God," Sam said as he gave his old friend a big hug. "We don't have time to explain, Jackson."

"Follow Sam and get moving right now," Langley instructed as he put his hand on the President's shoulder. Niles looked at the three men who led him to safety and quickly shook their hands.

"Dinner at the White House, fellas," he smiled as he and Sam ran into the thicket and followed the trail Langley had been led down earlier.

By now, several guards had been shot and killed and were lying face down on the front porch.

"Cut the power," Charlie instructed as he started up the plane and prepared for takeoff.

"Play it safe, you crazy bastard," Langley said through his radio as he waved at Charlie.

The small plane shot down the runway and was quickly airborne.

"What the hell is going on out there?" Anthony Sinclair screamed as he looked out and saw the guards on the porch. He moved quickly down the hall toward the President's room. By the time he reached it, Cochran and Sims were already there looking at the opened window.

"Who's flying that plane? And who the hell is shooting at us?" Sinclair yelled as he ran back down the hallway. Just then, the power went out as all the men outside opened fire on the lodge. Shots smashed through all the windows, and those trapped inside quickly dove to the floor for cover.

"God damn it, Clayton, get some help brought in," Sinclair screamed with an uncharacteristic show of emotion. "Who the hell is out there?" he yelled as he crawled to his room. Inside, he reached up to retrieve his phone. Immediately, shots smashed through the window.

"Damn it, we're surrounded!" he screamed. "Who the hell is doing this?"

Sims scurried in to join him. "You get everybody. You understand me? You get everybody after Jackson and after whoever is out in that damned woods. You blow these sons of bitches to hell. You understand me? Damn it, Clayton, this should never have happened."

Outside the lodge, militia members reveled in their success in rescuing a kidnapped American president. Unbeknown to Langley, the true number of militiamen at his service was in excess of sixty. Charlie, much like Langley, didn't trust many people and kept his cards close to his vest. Now the sixty-some odd men were blistering the lodge with gunfire from every direction. One of the men had even landed a few flaming arrows through the busted out windows.

Inside, absolute chaos unfolded as a crowd of smug and calloused "rulers" now found themselves crawling around in the dark. A constant hail of gunfire crisscrossed above their heads as they clumsily tried to find a safe spot. Many made their way across the floor and into the basement, but they quickly abandoned their underground cover when small fires began breaking out, raising fears that their hiding spot might become a death trap.

"THANK GOD, YOU'RE SAFE," Victoria whispered into her brother's ear after she ran to greet him.

"Take these cell phones and get moving," Langley instructed as he came up on the three. "Right now. Get moving."

McBride led three horses up. "Let's go, Jackson. We can answer questions later," he said as he mounted his horse. The three rode off into the darkness as the gunfire continued.

"Whoever has the flaming arrows, keep shooting," Langley said into the radio as he watched from the tree line. Almost immediately, flames appeared in the woods from three directions. All three landed inside the lodge. Screams rang out from inside as the cascade of bullets continued and the fires burned out of control.

Suddenly, the lights inside the lodge came back on as the emergency backup power finally kicked on. Within seconds, the interior fire sprinklers were activated, and the fires slowly brought under control.

"Fire arrows at the roof," Langley said. Again, flaming arrows rained down on the lodge.

"I want that place burned to the ground," Langley yelled into the radio. "If we cook those rats to their death, we will be doing a great service to our country. Keep shooting, everybody, keep shooting."

Langley moved around the perimeter until he could see the back of the building.

"The large green box on the back is the emergency power unit. If anyone has a way to blow that sucker, let it rip," he encouraged as he anxiously looked around. Almost instantly two men ran out from the woods and placed a bag containing an explosive device between the green box and the lodge. The two then scurried back and disappeared into the woods. A few seconds later, an explosion blew the unit off the ground. Again, the interior of the lodge was plunged into darkness.

"Fire arrows inside again," Langley again commanded. As before, arrows shot out and lit up the interior of the building.

"More, every window, burn that fucker down!" Langley yelled through the radio. He looked skyward as he heard the sound of a helicopter.

"We have airborne company in less than two minutes," Langley said through the radio. "Everybody reload and prepare to engage. There is no time to retreat right now. I'm proud of all of you. I hope I get to meet you all someday."

The helicopter appeared above the tree line and started a slow dissent over the lodge. Large-caliber machine guns were visible on the front, and two men on each side also manned guns. In a sudden bust of fire, the men on the ground redirected their weapons at the chopper. Caught by surprise, the crew was almost immediately incapacitated by the hail of bullets. The helicopter spun sideways and then exploded above the lodge. The resulting crash sent the lodge roof into an inferno.

"There will be many more coming, boys. It's time to go," Langley instructed. "That's an order this time. Get the hell out of here now!"

Langley barked his last command, then slowly made his way around the lodge and back toward the main campsite. As he moved through the woods, he watched as the lodge was nearly engulfed in flames. A couple of people attempted to exit the front door and were promptly shot by those still watching the exits.

When he reached the campsite, the men assigned to go with him waited on horseback.

"Great job, guys," Langley radioed. "Now, get going. It's going to get real ugly here. If you stay, you'll die."

He walked up to the horse and pulled himself up in the saddle. "I hate horses," Langley said as he shifted in the saddle.

"Let's go, sir," one of the men said as he turned his horse and trotted away. As they cleared the immediate area, they heard helicopters coming from multiple directions.

BY NOW, CHARLIE was flying along at maximum speed in a southwest direction. The two helicopters that followed were struggling to keep him within site.

"If you can't force him down, shoot the dumb ass out of the sky," Sinclair screamed into the phone to one of the pilots as he, Cochran, and Sims huddled in a safe room off the kitchen. They could hear screams of their fellow conspirators outside the room, but they were helpless to do anything.

Charlie laughed as he flew the plane low to the ground, then climbed as high as he could fly. "Come on, you bastards, try and catch me," he yelled.

MCBRIDE, MEANWHILE, dismounted his horse and led it down to the little stream they were about to cross.

"Let's let them rest for a few minutes," he said to Jackson and Victoria. Both got off their horses and walked over to a small clearing and sat down on the cool grass.

"Do you think Jack is close behind?" Victoria asked her brother.

"I've seen Jack lead an assault before," the President answered. "I can guarantee you that place is destroyed and almost everyone inside's already dead. Jack's a warrior, and he hates people who do what those people have done. He wouldn't have stopped until he had to. He's smart and tough. He'll catch up."

"Sam, you need a hand?" Jackson asked as he stood up and stretched.

"Where do we go now?" Sam asked as he walked over to them. "We can't simply fly into DC and announce that a coup has been uncovered. Hell, our enemies would take advantage, and chaos would break out. We need a plan, Jackson."

Sam helped Victoria to her feet and gave her a hug. "You and I need a shower," he laughed and gave her a squeeze.

"This all has to end behind the scenes," Victoria said as she stepped back from Sam.

Jackson walked down to the creek and washed his face in the cool water. "Those pictures you sent were likely most of the Council, as they call it," the President called out as he switched to washing his arms. "I left them in my briefcase at the lodge. Jack ran them through his system and sent the results over. Many are career bureaucrats in DC. But there were some Wall Street guys, old-family-money types, former judges, and former Congress members—a mix. He identified the entire list. We need those pictures so we can round those rats up. Assuming he killed off those in the lodge, it's a mop-up operation after that. I'm willing to bet Jack cut the head off this thing back there, though." The President wiped his arms on the side of his shirt and walked back to his horse.

"Jack is as hard core as they get when it comes to situations like this. He would line those guys up and shoot them point blank," the President said bluntly as he climbed back in his saddle. "I don't know yet where we go. But you're right with that behind-the-scenes thought. The world can't find out that its leading democracy has been run by a bunch of thugs for decade. Let's get to your ranch, and then we'll figure out where to go next."

CHARLIE'S PLANE DESCENDED over Las Vegas like a dive-bomber coming in for an attack. His control panel was lighting up with FAA warnings as he buzzed over the main drag. Four helicopters hovered above, unsure how to proceed.

"This lunatic is buzzing Vegas," one of the helicopter pilots communicated to Sinclair, Cochran, and Sims. The three had managed to flee the burning Lodge once the gunfire stopped. Now they waited for a helicopter to get them to a private airstrip and then back to Camp David.

"The streets are lined with people watching him. You want us to shoot him down in front of all these people?" the pilot asked in a tone of self-doubt.

"Hell, no, I don't want you shooting the damned President down in the middle of Vegas. Land two of the choppers and get boots on the ground," Sims yelled then hung up the phone. "What the hell is he up to?"

Cochran and Sinclair looked across at Sims.

"Get a sniper on the ground," Sinclair instructed without a hint of emotion. "Take him out at the first opportunity. We'll have to deal with the fallout."

Sinclair looked up to see a helicopter approaching the airstrip at the lodge. "You were right, Clayton. You were right all along. We should have done this during the campaign."

Sinclair kicked a bullet casing with his foot. "Look, we get rid of Jackson, we set off a few more bombs, and Wilson declares martial law. Then, we arrest some nut and shoot him like they did with Kennedy's assassin, and it's all over. We can have some big committee investigation to placate the press, but it's over," he said. Sinclair spit on the ground and wiped his mouth.

He looked at Sims and Cochran. "Hey, you two need to stiffen up. Stop rubbing your damned heads and get in the game," Sinclair huffed.

"He's landing on a main thoroughfare," the pilot reported.

"Give me that radio," Sinclair demanded as he grabbed it from Sims' hand. "Are the snipers in place?"

"We have four in place on the roofs of the tallest buildings in Vegas."

"As soon as you see Niles in your scope, take him out," Sinclair instructed. Sims and Cochran nodded in approval.

Police cars, fire trucks, and ambulances lined the Las Vegas streets in preparation for the expected disaster. As Charlie came in at an alarming speed, most watching expected to see a crash. Being Vegas, many in the crowd were drinking. They cheered as Charlie came to an abrupt stop. Police cars raced toward the plane as he climbed out and waived at the crowd.

"The pilot's out and waving like he's some damned celebrity," the chopper pilot reported across the radio to Sinclair.

"Let us know when Niles gets out," Sinclair instructed.

"The police have handcuffed the pilot and are putting him in a car. They're now entering the plane," the chopper pilot said.

"Get ready," Sinclair responded.

"There's no one else in the plane. The police are pushing the thing off the road and into a nearby plaza," the pilot reported.

"Who are these people?!" Sinclair screamed as he threw down the radio.

SAM, VICTORIA, AND Jackson reached Sam's ranch and began cooking a couple of frozen pizzas while Victoria took a quick shower. There had been no sign of helicopters or any other trouble, so a brief stop for food and hygiene seemed okay. Sam and Jackson sat in the dimly lit kitchen debating what move should be next.

"We need to know who to arrest," Jackson said as he took a drink of water.

"We need those pictures," Sam answered.

"I know Jack had them printed from his home. That was the email I sent them to," the President said.

"Can we get anybody in there?" Sam asked.

"Possibly. But I don't know who could do that when I'm sitting out here. Hell, I don't know for sure who I can trust."

"To do what?" Victoria asked as she entered the room.

Sam looked up to see Victoria wearing a pair of red sweats he hadn't seen in years.

"I found these in your room," she said, taking a drink of his water. "Hope it's okay." She opened the oven and checked on the pizzas.

Sam hadn't seen that pair of sweats walking across his kitchen since Sarah died. The site of them brought up memories that had been buried for years.

"I'm going to take a quick shower," Sam said.

Victoria and Jackson sat quietly together in the kitchen neither knowing where to begin. When the timer went off, Victoria got up and pulled the pizzas out of the oven.

"Are you hungry?" Victoria asked as she slid a pizza onto the table in front of her brother.

"I am, but I have a feeling we need to get moving," Jackson said. He quickly gobbled down a slice.

"Go tell Sam to hurry up. We need to go," Jackson instructed and then began rummaging through the cabinets.

Victoria entered the bath and stuck her head into the shower. "Jackson's worried we need to get moving now," she said.

"Okay."

Victoria looked around for a towel as Sam finished rinsing his hair. When he exited the shower, he didn't expect her to be in the bathroom.

"Sam, your eyes," she said as he reached for the towel. "You look like you have been crying. What is it?" She stepped closer.

"Those damned sweats. I know it's crazy, but I haven't seen those since Sarah died. She used to wear those around the house when the four of us would be hanging out together watching movies or doing homework or whatever. I forgot they were in there. I'm sorry. I know it's stupid. It hit me wrong."

Victoria hugged Sam. "I'll find something else. I'm sorry."

"No," Sam said as he pulled her back. "Leave them on. I want to go forward—with you. Leave them on."

Jackson packed the pizza into a plastic container along with a cooler full of drinks and other snacks.

"Come on, let's go," he insisted as Sam and Victoria emerged from the bath.

"Where?" Sam countered.

"We make a plan to get someone into Jack's house to retrieve those pictures. If that fails, we'll go to a military base or some other safe place and go public. If that causes trouble, then so be it, but we can't let those people control this government any longer. We have a duty to fulfill."

Sam gassed up the small jet as Jackson and Victoria loaded the cooler and other supplies. Once airborne, Victoria distributed the pizza slices, which quickly disappeared.

"We have about a day, maybe two, to bring these people under control, or I think we are looking at going public," Jackson said as Sam leveled off the jet.

"You go public with this story, and the status of America changes forever in the eyes of the world," Victoria offered in a desperate tone.

"The American people come first," the President countered.

A few minutes later, as they flew along in silence, a strange sound erupted in the cockpit.

"What the hell is that?" Jackson asked looking around at the gauges and dials on the flight panel. Victoria pulled open a bag and dumped out the contents. The three cell phones Jack Langley had pushed into their hands at the lodge were all vibrating.

"Hello!" Victoria nearly yelled into one of the phones as she pulled it to her ear.

"Hell, it's about time," Langley said. "Where are you three?"

"In the jet," Victoria said.

"You could have left some pizza," Langley chuckled.

"You're at the ranch?" Victoria asked.

"Yep, haven't had any problems. The decoy worked perfectly except Charlie was arrested in downtown Vegas," Langley said, laughing as he exhaled a deep drag off a cigarette. "Where are you going now?"

"Give me the phone," Jackson said as he reached back for it. "Jack, I need another set of those pictures you identified and sent over."

There was a long pause on the phone. "My home cc or Mercury," Langley responded.

"Where is Mercury?" the President asked.

"No idea."

"Can you get to your system?" Jackson asked.

"Yes, but it will take a few hours. And of course, that assumes those bastards haven't been to my home."

"Get there and call back. I don't know where we're going yet," Jackson responded as he hung up.

"Where would Mercury go if he were hiding?" Jackson asked Victoria.

"I don't know, Jackson. Why does it matter?"

"Jack gave him a copy of the pictures."

"Why him?" she asked.

"I'm not sure. I know he's been in trouble lately, and I know Jack saved his ass," Jackson said. "Now think, Victoria. Where would he go to stay safe?"

Victoria stared out at the sky, trying to remember all she knew about Susan and her family, as Sam flew along. "Their farm," she finally realized. "He would go to their farm in the Midwest."

"It's all we got," Jackson suggested to Sam with a shrug.

"Where is it?" Sam asked.

"Southern Indiana by some big lake," Victoria said. "I've been there, but I don't remember exactly where it is." She sat back and rubbed her head as she contemplated the location of Susan's little oasis.

Jackson picked up the phone and called Langley. "Can you do an online search and know for sure it's secure?" the President asked him.

"Of course. My staff is solid, Jackson. I guarantee it," Langley said.

"Run a search on property owned by the Mercury family in Southern Indiana. Keep the search broad enough to pick up relatives, estates, all that kind of stuff," the President directed.

"Yes, sir," Langley said.

"We'll go there to find Mercury. If he's not there, we'll wait to see if Jack can retrieve the pictures from his home," Jackson said. "If both of those options fail, then we'll go to a secure base and go public. We have no choice. We simply can't do anything else until we find out who all the bad guys are."

They flew in silence until the phone the President held finally buzzed.

"We have an address," Jackson said as he looked at the screen. "Find a place to land near this spot," he said, handing the phone back to Victoria.

RESCUED BY HELICOPTER, then transferred to a private jet, Sinclair, Cochran, and Sims were on their way to Camp David to regroup after the debacle at the lodge.

"We will find him, and we will end this," Sinclair said as he made notes on his tablet. "Do you have the completed list of who was lost?" he asked Sims.

"Yes, this is everyone," Sims said handing Sinclair and Cochran a list of names.

"Could have been worse," Sinclair remarked as he laid the list on the empty seat beside him.

"We can replace those members in short order," he added nonchalantly. "Call the White House and notify Reed about what's happened. We need to button up some issues while our teams locate Jackson. We deal with him within a day or two."

"THERE'S A PRIVATE airstrip a couple miles from their farm," Victoria announced.

"Is it big enough to land this thing?" Sam asked.

"That I don't know. The planes sitting around it look like this one."

"We'll need ground transportation once we get there," Jackson said.

"I doubt there's a taxi service out there," Victoria laughed. "Not that it's funny."

"I say we put it down and hope for a ride," Sam offered. "Hell, it looks like it's close enough to walk if we had to."

"The President of the United States walking along a country road in Southern Indiana. Now, that's funny," Jackson said with a self-deprecating chuckle.

"No room for ego now, brother," Victoria replied, squeezing his shoulder.

"Hell, I'm just glad to be alive at this point," Jackson said.

"I could use a nice walk," Sam added with a laugh of his own.

BY NOW JACK LANGLEY was on his way to Washington after having been picked up by a military jet at Sam's ranch. His ties to the top military brass were personal and beyond question. He knew he could count on them if things got worse.

"I need a quick ride to my house after we land," he told the pilot as he climbed in the jet.

"How fast?" the pilot asked.

"Fast as possible."

Langley had called the chairman of the Joint Chiefs, who quickly offered to help but also issued a frank warning. "We have a sitting President, Jack. Don't expect the military to get involved."

Langley understood clearly what his old friend was telling him. They would help Jack as much as possible, but they answered to the President, no matter how he got there.

SAM LANDED THE plane at the small airstrip, stopping short of the fence at the far end of the runway.

"That was scary," Victoria said as she let out a deep exhale.

"Let's pull it up to that old building over there and see if anyone's around," Sam said as he taxied back down the runway and parked next to several other planes.

"Let's get going," Jackson suggested as soon as they stopped. He opened the door and stepped down. "Based on the map, we should be there in thirty minutes or so." He took off walking toward the main gate.

The little airport was really nothing more than a runway and an old green pole barn. At one side sat a cluster of old crop dusters with tarps draped over them. On the other, a group of newer propeller planes in a nice tight row. Sam's jet stood out.

The three walked out of the gate and headed in the direction of the Mercury farm.

"Hey, what the hell are you three up to?" a voice called out from inside the fence. "You can't park here and take off. Where the hell you going?"

The man approached from inside the gate. The old man's short gray hair was wet with sweat as was the old white t-shirt he wore. But he was fit and lean and had deep penetrating green eyes.

"We're meeting a friend at his place down the road and doing some fishing," Victoria said as she walked back toward the man.

"Fishin', huh?" the man asked as he wiped sweat from his forehead with a cloth. "You don't look like fishermen to me." The air already felt hot and sticky, even though it was early morning. A pair of morning doves was filling the woods with song while the stifling humidity and lack of breeze already had the three perspiring.

"Actually, we could use a ride, mister," Jackson said as he walked up to the man. The old man looked at Niles and rubbed his hand across his chin. He stared at the President for a solid minute without saying a word. Finally, he stepped closer.

"That's my van over there. It's all I got out here." The man continued to stare at Jackson without saying another word. The back of the old red van was covered with bumper stickers from national parks. Jackson also noticed a Marine Corp sticker among them.

"That would be great," Jackson answered as he smiled at the old man.

The four climbed into the van and rumbled down the road toward the Mercury farm.

"This is it," Victoria announced as he turned up the drive. When they approached, the house looked deserted and only a small security light on the front of the garage indicated a human presence.

"Our friends will be here soon," she added, hoping to make their driver comfortable with leaving them. The four got out of the old van and gathered their belongings. As Jackson reached down to pick up his bag, the man grabbed it and lifted it for the President.

"You need anything else, my number is on this card," he said as he offered Jackson a casual salute. The President reached out to shake the man's hand as he took the bag from him.

"I didn't get your name," Jackson asked quietly as the two maintained a firm handshake.

"Evans, Sergeant Eric Evans, sir," the man said with a wry smile.

"Thank you, Sergeant Evans," Jackson said with a wink.

The old man smiled as he released the President's hand. "It's my honor, sir," Evans said as he took a deep breath and returned to the front of the van. "I'm at that field every day. Retired last year and just work on my planes now. You call me, and I'm here," he said as he started the van and backed down the drive.

The three walked up to the house as the van disappeared down the road.

"There used to be a key hidden up here somewhere," Victoria said as they climbed the front stairs. The old white farmhouse with black shutters was nestled in a small valley. The Mercurys visited often and had the place looking like a postcard. A large, old red barn sat off to the right surrounded by a white fence with two cows inside. Just left of the house, an old chicken coup was still in use. Peter had partnered with a local man who needed a place for his livestock. Peter liked knowing the place was looked after and having the animals around gave the house that extra "country feel" both he and Susan craved.

Suddenly, the front door flew open, and Susan Mercury burst out and threw her arms around Victoria.

"My God, how did you three find your way here?" she yelled as she released Victoria. "I thought you were dead," she whispered as she hugged Jackson.

"Peter!" Jackson called out as he walked into the old house. "Where's Peter?"

"I'm here," Peter answered as he came around the corner looking stunned. "Holy shit," he said softly as he realized he was answering the President.

"Do you have the pictures Langley gave you?" Jackson quickly asked.

"No, I don't have them. I gave them to you already. I gave them to Mary Mitchell."

Jackson looked around at the group and let out a disappointed sigh.

"But we have copies in our printer. Peter's editor is on her way here with it," Susan interjected.

"She'll be here any minute," Peter added.

"Come on, come in here, and sit down. My God, you all look exhausted," Susan said as she led them into the large family room. "Peter, get them some drinks and the leftover chicken." Susan moved about the room clearing off chairs of the bags they had brought with them.

The three sat down as Peter emerged from the kitchen with a platter of fried chicken.

"We have bottled water, soda, and a few beers from our last visit. What's it going to be?"

"I think we all need some water," Jackson said answering for everyone.

"Jackson, what the hell is going on?" Susan asked as she distributed glasses of water. "Pardon the informality, but we have been whipped, beaten, kicked, kidnapped, shot at, and God-only-knows-what-else. What the hell is going on?" she repeated as she sat down on the couch.

"The short version amounts to a small secret group that's been controlling the two political parties for the last eighty years or so," Jackson said as he gulped water. "They've controlled the White House, Congress, and, I believe, the Court. It's all been subtle. They've done it through the party leadership. The parties control the senior members, the members control Congress, and Congress controls the White House. The Court's different, but I know they've had their hands in there somehow. On top of that, they have controlled campaign finance to the point where all the big money flows to the two parties, which their ruling Council controls."

Peter and Susan stared at the President as he reached for a piece of chicken.

"What? Oh my God," Peter said nearly spilling his water as he jumped up. "What are you saying?"

"Sit down, Peter," Susan instructed as she caught a look from her boss. Peter stopped and looked around the room. Everyone was staring at the emotional reporter.

"I'm sorry," he muttered as he sat back down.

"How do we stop them?" Susan asked.

"We need the pictures. Then we start arresting people. They think Jack Langley's dead and the FBI's compromised, but he is not and it is not," the President explained. "If we know who all the players are, we take them down in one swoop. I'll meet with the House leadership and make sure they know the game is over. Then they pass the reforms and their hold on Congress ends. There are other changes that will need to be made, but once we pass term limits for the House, the gig is up, and they all know it."

Jackson took a drink and looked around the room for any responses.

"Once we have the pictures, Peter will do an interview with me at some local station. I will assure the people all is well. At the same time, Jack is going to be taking down these creeps. After that, I'll give Reed an ultimatum about stepping aside or facing prosecution. This all needs to happen behind the scenes, or America's reputation and standing will be destroyed. And the world doesn't need that."

The President walked across the room to where Peter was sitting. "You need to play your role here. You can't be just a reporter anymore. You're on our team now. This nation needs you to be a team player."

Jackson walked back to his seat and looked at the rest of the group. "We all know what we're up against and what we're after. We need to be willing to do whatever it takes." Silence filled the room.

Finally, Victoria raised her water glass, "Whatever it takes," she said.

"Whatever it takes," the others repeated as they raised their glasses.

A knock on the door startled them for a moment, then Peter said, "That must be Kyanne," and he jumped up.

"Isolated is an understatement," Kyanne said as she marched into the room. "The printer is in my trunk." She took off her suit coat and tossed it onto a chair.

"Oh, my God," she said as she caught sight of the President. As she made her way across the room, she spotted Victoria. "Oh, my."

"I'll explain later," Peter assured her as he took the keys from her hand and led her to a chair. "I'll go get the printer."

Susan gave her a glass of water, put a hand on her shoulder, and smiled to help Kyanne accept the moment.

Peter quickly reappeared with the printer in his arms. "Go get my laptop and some paper from the office," he said to Susan as he entered the house and set the printer on the dining room table.

"Here we go," Peter announced as he finished hooking things up. Immediately, the printer started spewing out the same photos and bios Langley had delivered to Susan.

"That's it," Jackson declared. "Where's the bag with the cell phones?" he asked Victoria.

She threw items out of a duffle bag until she found the small bag with the phones.

"Jack," the President said over the phone, "we have them. We have all the pictures. Stay at the base so I know where you are. Let me think for a minute, and I'll call you back in a few."

As the printer continued to work, everyone began passing around the pages to see who might be in the photos.

"Put these in piles according to where they're located," Susan instructed.

"How many are there?" Jackson asked from the sofa. Susan counted the stack: 165.

"Most are in DC, but a couple dozen are scattered around the country," she explained.

"Okay, it's time for a plan," Jackson said. "If we're going to get this done without the world unraveling around us, we have to be quiet about it. The FBI can get these people arrested. That part is easy enough. But we should assume the leadership is still out there, and we know we have a traitor sitting in the Oval Office."

"Do you have a scanner?" he asked Susan.

"Yes but it's really old."

"Scan those so we can send them to Jack."

Jackson picked up the cell phone. "Jack, how many teams can you send out to round up 165 people?"

"I have my best 100 men and women ready to go."

"Okay, send me a secure email address, and the pictures will be on the way. Get a plan together to take down these people in one swift move. Call back when you are ready."

Jackson hung up and turned to the group.

"Peter and I will make a TV appearance on some local station. Their network will get it out nationally. I'll assure the people I'm fine and am coming back to office right away. Langley will start rounding up the rats as I do the interview. Once we have their Council in custody, I'll go to the White House and give Reed an ultimatum," Jackson explained.

"What if Sinclair and the conspirators are still out there?" Sam asked.

Kyanne jerked forward at the mention of the President's Chief of Staff in such a context.

"We'll fill you in on everything," the President said as he recognized Kyanne's shock. "Does the TV work? I need to find out what kind of bullshit these guys are putting out right now." The President walked to the screen on the far wall.

"There's a box out on the dish that needs to be switched on," Peter said as he jumped up.

"I'll get it," Sam said. "You scan those pictures."

"He'll need a screw driver," Peter said to Victoria as he pointed to a toolbox sitting by the door. Victoria retrieved one and left to catch up with Sam.

Inside, Peter grabbed the prints and went upstairs to his office to scan them.

"I'll call Jack and get the email address, and we can get this done in one motion," the President said as he followed Peter.

Sam approached the base of the dish and looked around for the control box. A few feet away, behind an old oak tree, Hiatt Montgomery watched in disbelief as he realized several of his targets were now in one location.

"Who else is here?" Montgomery asked as he stepped out. Sam slowly stood up and turned around.

"Look, buddy, I don't know who you are, but this thing is unraveling for you guys. Your friends are being arrested. You should leave now and just disappear." Sam stood with his hands out to his side as Victoria rounded the corner and froze at the site of Montgomery.

"Oh, this is too much," Montgomery said with a sadistic laugh. "Who else is in there? Shit, I'm going to clean this mess up in one stop," he said with a big smile.

"Sam," Victoria whispered in desperation.

The first shot hit Sam in the chest as he staggered back and collapsed into the shrubs.

"No!" Victoria screamed as she rushed to him. Montgomery's second shot hit Victoria in the shoulder as she collapsed next to Sam.

Inside, Susan scrambled across the house, stuffing shells into a shotgun. She reached the door as Montgomery approached the steps. Her first shot hit Montgomery in the left leg. He fell back but quickly gathered himself and pointed his gun at Susan. Her second shot hit his side, but he was able to fire again, hitting Susan in the thigh. She fell through the screen door and landed on the front porch. Montgomery stood and approached her. "If you're going to use a shotgun, you dumb bitch, you better carry extra shells."

He pointed the pistol at Susan's head. "Don't worry, that piss ant husband of yours will be joining you," he said as he smiled at Susan.

Montgomery's expression suddenly changed as Victoria's left arm came around Montgomery's throat. "That's a screw driver in your back. Do you fear me now, you piece of shit?" Victoria said as she stumbled while still gripping Montgomery. Victoria slid her bloody hand up and grabbed a handful of his blond hair. Montgomery spit up blood as he tried to respond. In a single motion, she pulled out the screwdriver and shoved Montgomery to the ground.

As he fell, he pulled the pistol around and shot at Victoria. The blast blew her back, and she rolled over as she writhed in pain. Montgomery laughed as he gathered himself and tried to stand.

Victoria, now crawling toward Montgomery, thrust the screwdriver down again, and this time pierced his right eye.

Montgomery twitched and shook for a moment and then stopped moving.

Hiatt Montgomery was finally dead.

Victoria turned and began crawling toward Sam McBride. Peter and Kyanne were the first two out and nearly tripped over Susan. Peter fell to his knees at the site of his wife bleeding on the front porch of their dream home.

Kyanne, frozen in place, stared at Montgomery with the screwdriver protruding from his face.

"Sam, Sam, Sam," Victoria mumbled as she crawled across the grass to the love of her life. "Sam, please Sam, say something. Please move, please, God." Victoria, now covered in her own blood, reached Sam's body as the President emerged from the house.

"My God," he said as he jumped down the steps and ran to his sister.

"Please Sam, please be alive," she cried out as she crawled up next to him.

"Let us die here together, Jackson," Victoria said softly, looking up at her brother. "There's nothing anyone can do out here." She wrapped her arm across Sam's chest.

Jackson stepped back from the scene and quickly dug into his pocket. He dialed the number he found on the card and waited for an answer.

"Sergeant ..., God, I forget your name," Jackson said into the phone.

"Sergeant Evans, sir," the man replied.

"You know who I am?" Jackson quickly asked.

"Yes, Mr. President, I do."

"I need a doctor our here right now. I can't explain. There's been a shooting. Three are down. Two are critical. No media. Can you help?"

The phone was silent for a few seconds.

"Ten minutes, maybe fifteen. Apply pressure to the worst wounds," the man said as the phone went dead.

"Tear a sheet into bandages," Jackson yelled to Kyanne, who was tying a shoestring around Susan's leg to try to slow the bleeding.

"I'm on it," Peter yelled as he burst through the door. In a few seconds, he was back with an armful of clean linens and began tearing them into long strips.

"You aren't dying out here," Jackson said in a calm, reassuring voice as he tied a bandage around Victoria's shoulder.

"Press down on that," Jackson directed Peter as he placed a large bandage on Sam's chest.

"Jack, it's time. Get going," Jackson said into his cell phone while still on his knees next to his sister.

"Jackson," Langley said, "Sinclair, Cochran, and Sims survived the attack at the lodge. They're at Camp David. I've got a guy in their security team."

The President considered his next move. "Get a team there. Take out the guards and seal the place off. Try to do it so those inside don't know they are now prisoners," he commanded.

"Jack," he said as walked a short distance from the scene, "Sam, Victoria, and Susan have been shot by that psycho the Council had running around. Sam and Victoria are critical. Sam's in real bad shape. He won't make it unless we see a miracle out here." His voice cracked.

"Take these people down. No mercy. Then you get to Camp David. Make them give you a list of everyone past and present who has served on that damned Council. Make them talk. Understand?" The President took a breath and looked back at Victoria.

"I'm going to some local TV station to assure the people I'm okay and coming back to work. That'll turn up the heat and get the rats squirming. We're going to win this thing, Jack," the President said as he hung up.

The lights coming up the driveway sent a jolt of fear through everyone.

"We got here as quickly as possible," Evans said as the four doors of his van opened.

"Introductions will have to wait," he said as he knelt down next to Sam. "Is he the worst?"

"Yes, and then her," Jackson said as he motioned to Victoria.

"Clear a table inside. We don't have much time," Evans said.

Jackson walked to the steps where Susan sat against the side of the house. Her leg had been tied with a tourniquet, and adrenaline had now made the pain tolerable.

"I have to leave, Susan. I have to end this," Jackson said as he knelt down by her side. "I need you to take charge here. I'm taking Kyanne with me. She's the closest thing I have to a press secretary, and I need to go talk to the people. Can you do that for me?"

"Yes, sir, I'll make sure they're all taken care of," she answered as tears rolled down her cheeks.

"Kyanne, you're coming with me," Jackson announced as he stood.

"Okay, I guess. Where?" Kyanne asked, looking around confused. Jackson walked into the house where he saw Sam and Victoria side by side on the dining room table. The Sergeant, his wife, and grown daughters worked side-by-side trying desperately to save their lives. The old man looked up at the President and offered an unwelcome expression of fear. The President walked over to the coffee table and gathered up the printouts of the Council members.

"You better wash off that blood," Kyanne said as Jackson turned for the door. He looked at his hands, which were covered in blood.

"Do you have different clothes?" she asked as she followed him into the kitchen.

"Go through Sam's bag and see what he has," Jackson said as he scrubbed his hands. He broke down as the blood of his best friend and sister swirled together and disappeared down the sink drain.

"Let me wipe off your pants," Kyanne suggested as she came back into the room. She knelt down and wiped dirt and grass from his knees.

"I found this shirt," she said, holding up a light green, short-sleeved shirt she had found in Sam's bag. "Take that thing off." Jackson pulled off the bloodstained shirt and quickly put on the clean one.

"This is his favorite fishing shirt," Jackson said with a sad smile.

"You want a press secretary? You got one. Let's go." Kyanne said, grabbing the papers the President had gathered and heading for the door.

Jackson stopped at the door and looked back at the scene in the dining room. The hurried and frantic activity did not give him a good feeling as he turned and walked out the door.

OUTSIDE CAMP DAVID, a group of eight men moved slowly through the woods.

"The main gate is over there," the lead man said, pointing. "We go on my mark. We shoot to kill. These are traitors."

The group crept slowly through the forest. A few seconds later, four dead guards were dragged into the woods and covered in leaves.

"Gate secure, sir," the man radioed to Langley.

"Send a team in either direction. Establish a perimeter. No one enters and no one leaves," Langley said, then turning to his driver, he barked, "Head for Camp David."

As they rode, Langley reviewed a list he had of the conspirators.

"All teams," he said through his radio. "All teams go. All detainees are to be brought to Camp David."

Across Washington, a swarm of FBI teams started knocking on the doors of people who were completely unprepared for what was about to happen. One by one they were removed from their homes and led to small buses. Once inside, they were handcuffed, and if necessary, gagged. Those who protested aggressively were informed, in front of family if necessary, that they were suspected of treason. At that point, all left quietly with their FBI escort.

Two hours later, Langley arrived at Camp David along with a dozen more FBI agents. The men and Langley pulled into the compound and parked their SUVs directly in front of the building occupied by Sinclair.

"We took out all their men on the outside and replaced them with our people," Langley was told as he pulled in.

"Secure all entry points. We enter on my command," Langley instructed as the men quickly fanned out around the building. As he looked back, the first of the small black buses began arriving.

"Hold them right inside the gate," Langley commanded.

"All in position, sir."

"All go now," Langley announced as the men with him breached the main door.

Inside, a stunned guard looked confused. He was immediately shot as the men made their way down the long hallway. Within a few minutes, all the teams converged on a large, central room where Sinclair, Cochran, and Sims sat relaxing before a television.

Langley entered the room with the other men following him. Sinclair was the first to realize those entering were not his people.

"I thought you were dead," Sinclair said, smiling as Langley approached them.

Cochran and Sims quickly jumped up and turned to see Langley point a pistol in their direction.

"Jack, sit down, for God's sake. Spare us the big lawman routine," Sinclair said.

"It's over," Langley said. "You have a chance to save your life, but that's all you have."

The other FBI men dispersed to the edge of the room.

"Your Council has been arrested, and you are going to write down the names of every person who has ever been involved with this treason," Langley informed the three.

"You do have a flair for the dramatic, Jack. I'll give you that," Sinclair said in a mocking tone.

"Get out a piece of paper and start writing," Langley said again.

"Jack, this thing is way beyond you, and you are really starting to annoy me." Sinclair sat back down and returned to his glass of Scotch.

"Bring me the tablet," Langley said as he turned to one of the men. "Look at this." He tossed it onto Sinclair's lap.

"What's this?" Sinclair said without even looking at it. "Those are pictures of your Council sitting on buses after being arrested tonight."

Sinclair picked up the tablet and then dropped it on the floor. "I'm not buying your bullshit, Jack," Sinclair said.

Langley walked toward Cochran and Sims, who stood watching the encounter.

"Either of you want to save your life tonight?" Langley asked.

"Fuck off, Jack," Sims snickered.

Langley raised his pistol and shot Sims point blank in the middle of his forehead. Sims collapsed to the floor as Sinclair jumped out of his chair and turned to see Sims dead on the floor.

Sinclair approached Langley and stood close, looking Jack in the eyes. A slight smirk spread out across Sinclair's face. "He probably had it coming," Sinclair said as he looked indifferently at Sims' dead body.

"Look out the window, Anthony," Langley said. Sinclair walked to the window and looked toward the long lane. A dozen or so buses were now lined up in a long row.

"Now look at the tablet," Langley instructed.

Sinclair scanned through the pictures without showing a hint of reaction.

"Was your great grandfather a rich man?" Langley asked as Sinclair looked up.

"What difference does it make?"

"You despise the commoner, as you like to call them, but somewhere in your past one of those commoners worked hard enough to get a better education or a better opportunity for the next generation. Never did he think that someone like you would come along, standing on his efforts, hating the place he came from. You disgust me, Anthony. And if you are lucky enough to meet that person in the next life, the one who made your opportunities possible, he or she will tell you the same. Now write down the list, right fucking now!" Langley screamed.

Sinclair took a deep breath and walked to a desk at the edge of the room. He removed a pen and paper from the desk and sat quietly staring at the wall.

"You fools have ruined everything," Sinclair said softly. "Those purple-clad idiots will take over, and chaos will be your prize. I may be far too cynical, but you and Jackson are far too naive. Given the direction this world is headed, I'd take cynical any day. Good luck, Jack."

Sinclair looked at the other men with a sad and despondent expression as his eyes drifted toward the floor. Sinclair then opened the drawer again, removed a pistol, and without saying another word, pressed the pistol to his temple and pulled the trigger.

"Your turn, Hamilton," Langley said to Cochran as Sinclair's dead body rolled out of the chair and hit the floor. "Start writing."

IN JASPER, INDIANA, a stunned news team looked on as a part-time makeup girl worked on the President's face.

"Relax," the President said to the 19-year-old girl as her hand shook. "I'm just a guy, probably the same age as your dad, right?"

"That's probably about right," she answered, still shaking.

"Mr. President, we're ready whenever you are," the newscaster announced as she came in and stood next to Kyanne.

"It's up to ..." the President began, looking at the girl doing his makeup. "You never told me your name."

"Darbi. My name is Darbi," the young girl answered with a shy smile as she brushed a hair from her eyes. She was dressed in a pair of red shorts, leather sandals, and black and red t-shirt. She had been at home relaxing when her boss called and demanded she make the short trip to the studio.

"This better be important," she'd muttered as she ended the call.

"Darbi, you decide when I'm ready, okay?" the President smiled.

"Cool," she giggled. Darbi stepped back and looked at the President's makeup. "I think that'll do it."

"Thank you, Darbi. I know it's late, and this face is a challenge," he told her with a wink.

"We're coming to you tonight with a special guest," the anchor announced with a nervous smile. "President Niles, welcome."

"I appreciate you taking the time tonight," the President responded.

"The American people have been worried about you, and I know I speak for all Americans watching when I say we are thrilled to see you looking so healthy."

"Thank you. It turned out that the wound I suffered was not nearly as severe as first thought. After being treated, I spent the last few days at a friend's house here in Southern Indiana. I expect to be back to work in the next day or so." The President smiled politely.

"Please forgive me for asking, but we were told you suffered a nearly fatal gunshot wound. So this is more than a little shocking. Were we given the wrong information?"

"The doctors were scared," the President replied. "They are paid to be overly protective. Honestly, they scared me, too." Jackson chuckled. "But I'm fine. The bullet did not hit anything vital, and the doctors were able to quickly remove it and get me patched up. Honestly, I feel great."

"Okay, then let's talk about the scene in Washington," she said. "Millions of Americans are still camped out in Washington, even as we speak, demanding Congress to pass your reforms. What do you have to say to them?"

"They are American heroes, plain and simple," the President said taking on a more serious tone. "I promise them and all Americans that the reforms I ran on and was elected on will be passed. They will become law."

"You are that confident?"

"I am. If I had a Purple Reason shirt with me, I'd be wearing it. I admire those people. They get it. They *will* win," the President said in a strong tone.

"What about the outbreak of terrorist acts? Do you think they are related to the recent events in Washington?" she asked.

"I think it's likely the act of some domestic chaos group. They will be rounded up and prosecuted," the President explained. "Any time you have an event like what's going on in DC right now, you have the risk that something like this could happen. It's likely the act of a few people who have some level of hatred of our system. I'm told that power has been restored and the situation is well in hand."

Niles looked at Kyanne, who in turn motioned the producer that the interview was over. The anchor signed off, and the cameras stopped rolling. Within a minute or two, Jackson and Kyanne were leaving the station.

"Now what?" Kyanne asked, as the two of them reached her car.

"I need to call Jack. Then I'll know," he said.

"Where are we, Jack?" the President asked when Langley answered.

"Everyone in DC is in custody. Clayton is dead, and Anthony took his own life." The line was silent for a moment. "Cochran is making the list right now. I'm standing here watching him do it," Langley reported.

"Okay, leave someone in charge, keep them all there, and meet me at the White House," Jackson instructed. "Oh, and I need a ride to pick me up in ..." the President turned to Kyanne, "Where are we?"

"Jasper, Indiana," Kyanne replied, smiling.

"Nice town," Jackson said as he looked around. "Jack, send a jet to Jasper, Indiana. We'll be waiting at the longest airstrip in the area, wherever that is."

"It's already there. I sent it after you called earlier," Langley said.

"I'll call you when we're airborne," Jackson said as he hung up.

The President rubbed his hands across his face. "I'm afraid to ask about Sam and Victoria," he said as they rode to the small airport.

Kyanne looked over at the President, unsure how to respond to this man she barely knew. "If they die, sir, it will have been in a heroic effort to save their country. They are true patriots, heroes. You should be proud of them."

Jackson wiped tears from his eyes. "You're right about that," he said.

AT THE OVAL OFFICE, Wilson Reed nervously watched the interview with Jackson Niles. The crowd outside was now louder than ever as a greater sense of energy and purpose took hold. All the idealism that had been drained out by the violence and strange events of the last few days was now magnified by their President's reappearance. Reed had been a reluctant participant in the Council, at least at first. Now, he shook nervously as he realized he was the target of Jackson Niles. His calls to Sinclair and his best friend Cochran went unanswered as the crowd outside chanted louder and louder for the reforms to be passed.

"Mr. President," his secretary said as she buzzed the Oval Office.

"Stop calling me that," Reed responded in a voice of self-disgust.

"The FBI is here. They are waiting outside for the arrival of Jackson Niles," his secretary reported.

"Shit," Reed responded as he began removing his papers from the President's desk. The roar that went up from outside was deafening to those inside the White House.

"Tell the staff to pack their things right now," Reed instructed his secretary.

OUTSIDE, PRESIDENT NILES walked through the crowd, shaking hands and thanking as many people as he could reach. When he came upon William Conner and his CNN crew, he smiled. "William, my friend, you're still out here," he said, and shook the reporter's hand.

Conner leaned in close to the President as he squeezed his hand tightly. "I would like to know the entire story," he said softly.

"I just needed a short break to recover from a bad day," the President said as he looked at Conner with a wry smile.

"We'll leave it there," Conner said as he winked. "Will you go live on air right now?"

"Absolutely," the President said as the crowd cheered.

The red light of the news camera flashed on as Conner lifted his microphone.

"We're here outside the White House where an invigorated and healthy-looking President Niles has just arrived," Conner began. "Sir, I have to say you look great for a man who is recovering from a gunshot wound."

"Paranoid staff and paranoid doctors," Niles responded. "I'm fine."

"Are you prepared to resume your duties as Chief Executive?" Conner asked.

"As soon as we get the Chief Justice over here, I intend to be sworn back in," the President said to the enthusiastic cheers of those around.

"Tonight?" Conner asked, surprised.

"Yes, right here, right now if we can get him out here," Niles answered.

"You mean literally out here on the North Lawn?" Conner asked, realizing he was about to witness something unprecedented.

"Yes, that is my intention," Niles answered. Cheers spread through the crowd like a wave as word spread of the possible event.

INSIDE THE WHITE HOUSE, a terrified Wilson Reed worked as quickly as possible to repack his belongings after a couple of days of "sitting in the chair."

"Mr. Speaker," his secretary now correctly addressed him, "the Chief Justice is on his way over."

"Good," Reed responded as he placed a box in the corner of the room. "Tell the staff to bring their belongings to one location. I don't care where; we just need to get out of his way."

Reed finished gathering his items as Jack Langley and three FBI agents entered the Oval Office.

"Jack, I'll do whatever you guys want," Reed said quickly as he backed away. "I never wanted this. I came to this town as much an idealist as Jackson." He dropped his head and looked down. "But I didn't have his courage. I wasn't willing to fight them. I went along."

Reed walked toward Langley. "Is anyone left alive?"

"Hamilton," Langley answered.

"That's fitting," Reed responded as he pulled off his glasses. "He was a chicken shit like me. We both knew it was wrong. But we both caved to the pressure."

Langley took Reed by the arm and led him over to a sofa.

"Sit down," Langley said as he nearly pushed Reed into the sofa.

"Jack, I told you I'll do whatever you want. There's no reason for you to get violent."

Langley looked around at the men gathered, who all held back smirks at the sight of Reed's weakness.

"You have a chance to redeem yourself, Wilson. You don't have to die a miserable piece of shit," Langley said as he lit a cigarette. "You go back to the House, and you lead the charge for term limits and finance reform. You do that, and Jackson might put up a statue of you out there somewhere."

Langley motioned toward the Mall with a wave of his hand. The cigarette left a trail of smoke floating in the air.

Reed looked up. "I don't want a damn statue, Jack, but I will introduce the bill. Hell, that's the least I can do to salvage some dignity," Reed said. He turned to say something else to Langley as President Niles entered the Oval Office. Reed froze when he saw his old friend.

"Give me your pistol," Niles said to the guard closest to the door.

"Hey, come on, what the hell are you going to do?" Reed said as he hovered down into the sofa quivering.

"I will shoot you myself if you give me any more trouble. You understand me?" the President said in a hushed but aggressive tone. "Because of you fucking assholes, my sister and Sam are dying. I ought to strap you down and peel you like an orange, you miserable piece of shit. You aren't worthy of that building." He motioned toward the Capitol. "You will do what I say, and then you'll resign and go home. You get to live only because the country needs your sorry ass for this one last act. Then you get your ass out of here, you understand me?"

Niles walked across the room and handed the pistol back to the agent. "You make me sick, Wilson. You're a fucking worm, a gutless, fucking worm. I wish I could take you out back and beat your fucking brains out right now."

Niles stood staring at Reed with his fists clinched and his body tight and hardened. He then turned and walked toward Langley. "He deserves a firing squad," Jackson said as he looked back at Reed.

"It would feel good," Langley said with a look of disgust.

"The Chief Justice will be here in a few minutes. We're going to go out in that crowd, and I'm going to be reinstated as President. Tomorrow morning, you'll introduce the reform package. Once it's passed, you'll resign so we can have the Speaker's office fumigated to get the stench of you out of that building. Are we crystal clear?" the President asked as he stared at Reed.

"Yes, sir," Reed said.

THE CROWD CHEERED wildly as President Niles and Speaker Reed emerged from the White House with big smiles. Now clad in a Purple Reason shirt, Niles walked ahead of Reed, who tried desperately to play his role. The CNN tent had been converted to a makeshift stage as the Chief Justice waited for their arrival. Once face-to-face, Niles gave the Justice a cold stare. The man quickly looked down in shame, unable to hide his guilt. The ceremony was over in minutes.

Niles turned to Reed. "Now, you tell these people that what they've been out here for will become law," Jackson whispered to him.

Speaker Reed approached William Conner as the President stepped over and stood next to the Chief Justice. "I want your resignation by morning," Jackson whispered in the Chief Justice's ear.

"You'll have it tonight," he answered.

"If it were up to me, you'd face a firing squad," the President whispered.

The Chief Justice turned and swallowed hard as he looked at the President. "I need to be on my way," he said to his aid as he stepped out of the tent. The crowd cheered as he walked through waving politely.

Niles stood listening as Reed completed his interview with Conner.

"Tomorrow we'll celebrate the liberation of the people's House," Jackson declared as he stepped over and addressed the crowd around the tent. "I want all of you to know that you are my heroes. You answered the call and came here to put pressure on a party system that locked you out of your own government. Tomorrow, that will change forever when the professional politicians get their termination papers."

Those who heard the President cheered wildly at his declaration of victory.

"The next challenge for all of us is continued involvement and diligence. Well-intentioned people must now be willing to run and serve in the House. Two years, as the founders designed it. For two years, once in your life, you will come here and serve your nation. Afterwards you will return to your normal life. That's the way Thomas Jefferson envisioned it, and that's the way it will be from now on. Tomorrow we celebrate! I thank you and your fellow citizens thank you."

Jackson Niles made his way back through the crowd, shaking hands with as many people as possible. Behind him, Kyanne Fitzgerald walked with Speaker Reed.

Jack Langley and the other agents oversaw the removal of Reed's staff and their boxes.

"Wilson, you better deliver," the President declared as he turned to Reed and walked closer to him. "If you screw this up or play any games, I will personally put a bullet in your head." He turned and left the Speaker standing in the White House foyer.

"Kyanne, try to reach someone at Mercury's farm," the President said as they entered the Oval Office.

"I have tried calling there, sir. There's no answer." Niles rubbed his hand across his face as he contemplated his next move.

"Jack, we need to send a team to Mercury's farm right now," Jackson said.

"Yes sir. They will leave immediately."

"Kyanne, I need to review a list of active Congress members who are on Cochran's list," Niles said.

She stood motionless.

"What's the matter?" the President asked.

"We're in the White House. You're the President again. Shouldn't someone else be in here doing this?" she said with a bashful look.

"How long have you been at The Post?"

She stepped forward and sat down in one of the chairs across from the President's desk. "About twenty years."

"My Chief of Staff committed suicide. Half my cabinet is about to be tried for treason, and a whole bunch of the usual staff is gone. I'm betting they're running for their lives right now. You are a capable, smart, and strong woman, and I know I can trust you. Are you ready for a new challenge?"

"Okay, what do you have in mind?" she asked slowly, staring across the desk at the President.

"I need a Chief of Staff who can start immediately. You want the job?" Niles smiled at Kyanne as she struggled to find her words. "You'll have to relax so you can answer questions faster than that," he said, laughing.

"Oh, what the hell. After what I've seen and heard these last few days, I don't want to leave," she concluded with an even bigger smile.

"That's the spirit."

"I'll be back in a few," she said, standing and leaving the Oval Office.

Outside the office, she found about a dozen people milling around. "We'll make introductions later," she announced in a loud and clear voice. "My name is Kyanne Fitzgerald, and I am the new Chief of Staff. I need a simple list containing each member of the House and his or her position on the President's reform package spelled out. Nothing fancy. We need to know where each member stands. I need it in fifteen minutes. And could someone please show me where my office is?"

A young intern stepped forward. "It's right there," she said, pointing to an office across the hall.

"Great, now get me that list. The President's waiting." She walked into her new office and looked around at the various items belonging to Sinclair. The desk, bookcase, and walls were covered with memorabilia from his long service in Washington.

Pictures and plaques from previous administrations mixed
with functional items.

"Can someone also get me a box?" she said over her
shoulder as she perused the office of the dead man. The intern
quickly arrived with a couple of packing boxes.

"What do you do here?" Kyanne asked the young woman.

"I'm an intern," she happily answered.

"Perfect. Box up anything personal in this office and get it
out of here," she instructed.

JACK LANGLEY ENTERED the Oval Office unannounced.

"Jackson, there's no one at the Mercury place. My men say
there's blood everywhere. No bodies, no cars, no nothing, but
lots of blood."

Niles got out of his desk chair and walked over to the sofa
where Langley was standing. "Sit down for a minute," he said
to Jack. "We have to assume some of their security teams are
still out there. That guy who came to the farmhouse is likely
one of many. I have to accept that they're likely all dead,"
Jackson said.

"They wouldn't have taken the bodies, Jackson," Langley
said. "They would have killed them and left them there. They
either left on their own or they were taken alive somewhere
else. I'll do a search of hospitals within a hundred miles or so.
We will find them." Langley shook hands with the President as
he stood and left.

ON CAPITOL HILL, Speaker Reed walked to his old office
followed by his staff. The senior members of the House were
gathered outside his office waiting.

"What's the plan?" the Minority Leader asked as he
followed Reed into his office.

"The plan is to pass the President's reforms," Reed said in a
dejected tone.

"What!?" the man said with exasperation. "You've lost your
nerve, Reed."

"I lost my nerve a long time ago," he said in a low voice, as
he stood motionless. "I'm personally introducing the bill in the
morning, and you're all voting for it. You will all vote yes."

"This is madness!" the Minority Leader shouted at Reed.

"Madness? You think what I am saying is madness?" Reed screamed as those gathered bristled in shock. "Are you blind? Are you deaf?"

Reed stood breathing hard, terror on his face. "Have you missed everything that's happened? Are you completely ignorant of what has been going on here? How many of our members are gone? How many are not coming back here tomorrow or ever, for that matter? For God's sake, you call *my* actions madness? Ten million people are camped outside this building, wearing purple shirts and screaming for change, and you think listening to them is madness? I swear to you this building will be in flames tomorrow night if we defy this any longer. That would be madness, and we'll be hated and despised. That's madness," Reed said as he fell into his chair.

"How many members of the House are already running around here wearing purple shirts?" Reed asked as he looked up.

"At least a hundred, at last count," a woman in the back answered.

"We vote yes tomorrow, and we go home heroes. Or we vote no, and we're replaced in two years anyway, and we go home hated," Reed said as he took a deep breath.

"Let's open a bottle of Scotch and have a drink to change," Reed suggested as he threw his hands up and laughed in sad resignation.

The next morning, as promised, Speaker Reed was at the podium on the House floor requesting a vote on the President's package.

JACKSON NILES SAT in the Oval Office with Kyanne and a few loyal Cabinet members. The chant, "Pass the reforms," was now so loud outside that many in the White House had given up trying to work.

"Are you confident?" Kyanne asked the President as she sat across from his desk.

"I worked that list you gave me pretty hard last night," the President smiled. "Considering that crowd outside and the conversations I had last night, I know we're there."

"Do you anticipate any issues with the Senate?"

"No, all the Senators I spoke with will go along. These changes impact the House for the most part. Those guys want to do whatever it takes to get these people to go home."

"Any word from Jack?" the President quickly asked, fear quivering in his voice.

"I'm afraid not."

SHORTLY AFTER 2 O'CLOCK in the afternoon, word came that the reform bill had passed both the House and Senate. Once the President signed it, his reform package would be the law of the land.

Outside Niles' window, the crowd celebrated with unbridled enthusiasm. American flags waved wildly alongside flags emblazoned with "Purple Reason." America was now becoming what the President had promised. This time, the change would come from the people. The commoners had their House back.

ABOUT A MONTH LATER, in a remote corner of Arlington Cemetery, two hearses sat quietly waiting. The day was wet and overcast and unusually cool for late July.

A small group of people gathered as a misty rain soaked their shoes. Two tents were visible, each open on one side. The tents shielded the gravesites from the constant rain. The President stood with Kyanne and Langley, along with a few Cabinet members. Also in attendance were a number of high-ranking military officers who were old friends of the President's.

The families of Clayton Sims and Anthony Sinclair stood together as a military chaplain conducted the service. The President had argued, against stiff opposition, that Sims and Sinclair be awarded a burial at Arlington. He had arranged for their bodies to be moved to the Lodge and then, to hide the truth, "discovered" in the burned-out structure. The event was blamed on an act of domestic terrorism. President Niles saw no gain in exposing their acts of treason.

Sinclair's widow, who was an old friend of the President's, stood with her two sons.

"I'm sorry, Brian," the President said to Sinclair's oldest son. The young Sinclair offered no response.

As the service came to a close, Langley approached the President.

"I know this is hard for you, Jackson," he said as he put his hand on the President's shoulder.

"It shouldn't have ended this way," Jackson said. "This never should have happened."

Niles turned and slowly walked to his waiting limousine. "The helicopter is waiting outside the cemetery," Kyanne said as she entered the car.

"Good, I want to get out of this place," the President remarked as he brushed water off his coat.

He, Kyanne, and Langley boarded the helicopter and made a quick trip to Air Force One.

"How long is this flight?" Niles asked as he boarded the plane and removed his wet coat.

"About two hours," Kyanne answered. "I have a few things to go over with you on the way." She opened a case and removed files.

"If it's nothing urgent, I'd like to wait," the President said as he kicked off his wet shoes.

"I understand, sir," she said as she put the files away. "There wasn't anything you could have done differently," she said as she placed her hand on the back of the President's. "You did everything you could."

Niles reclined his chair as Kyanne retrieved a blanket and spread it out over him.

"Why don't you rest now?" she said as she turned off the overhead lights. "I think it's safe to say you've earned it."

TWO HOURS LATER, as the plane prepared to land, Langley walked over to the President's seat, carrying a framed photo.

"I had this picture on the wall in my home office," Langley said as he handed it to the President. In the photo, a young Jackson Niles was pictured with a group of other teenage boys. Langley, Cochran, Reed, McBride, Sims, and Sinclair all stood together. They stood arm in arm, big smiles on their faces, and their entire life in front of them.

"I remember that day as if it just happened," Langley said, smiling.

"That was the first time we all met," Niles said as he managed a smile. "God, we had fun that year."

"Jackson, they chose their path. You don't need to feel badly about their fate," Langley said as he set the photo on the President's lap.

"I know, Jack," the President replied. "It's been hard to accept that people with such ability and opportunity would go in the direction they chose. We were all so sure we were going to change the world for the better." The President laughed at the youthful idealism they had each possessed at that young age.

"You did that, Jackson," Langley said with a soft laugh. "You certainly did that."

"It was a team effort, Jack, and would not have happened without your sacrifice. You put your life on the line, and the world will never know."

"All right, enough of this," Langley said as he reached for a bottle of Scotch. "Let's drink a toast to that picture, that time, and the great fun we had when we were young and dumb. And then let's agree that we leave this all behind forever."

Langley poured two bigger-than-usual glasses of Scotch and raised his in a toast. "To old friends."

"To old friends," the President echoed.

The two swallowed the Scotch in a big gulp and then looked at each other as big smiles spread across their faces. "And that's the end of it," Niles said as Langley nodded in agreement.

THE PLANE CAME to a stop on a private airstrip on a small island in the Caribbean.

"Look at that view," Kyanne said with excitement as the doors opened. At the bottom of the stairs, Peter and Susan Mercury were waiting.

"Peter, I've never seen you with a suntan," Kyanne said as she reached the bottom of the steps.

"Jack, we owe you so much, how can we ever thank you?" Susan said to Langley as she gave him a big hug.

"There's no need for any of that kinda crap," Langley said as he returned to his usual gruff style.

"Is everybody already here?" the President asked Peter and Susan as they walked toward the waiting van.

"Yes," Peter answered.

"Jackson, I have missed you," Susan said as she hugged her old friend.

"Let me tell ya, honey," Kyanne interjected, "we miss you at that crazy house we work in." They all laughed as luggage was loaded into a van and the group piled in.

As they drove, Peter took the opportunity to quiz the three on events in Washington.

"Sounds like the old reporter wants to get back in the game," Kyanne teased.

"Not a chance," Peter said as he looked to assure Susan. The van turned up a long drive and headed for a large but quaint private resort. The small, stone building was fairly new but the Spanish Mediterranean design made it look old. It had been built by members of the Barceló family of Mexico.

"We have it all to ourselves this week," Susan said as they approached the front door.

A group of people came out to meet the van.

"Hello, Jackson," Victoria whispered as she wrapped her arms around her brother.

"You don't know how happy I am to see you," he said as his eyes filled with tears. "Where's the man?" he asked as they entered the main building of the resort. While designed to look old, with marble floor tiles and carved fireplace mantles reclaimed from old structures in South America, the inside was equipped with every modern convenience.

"He's right in here," Victoria said as they stepped in. With the help of a cane, Sam McBride stood waiting for his two old friends.

"That was close," Sam said as he smiled at Niles and Langley.

"Too damned close," the President smiled.

"I got you a shirt, Jack," Sam said, holding up a t-shirt with "Montana Militia" on one side and "Honorary Member" on the other.

"I'll wear it with pride," Langley said as he held it for all to see.

"Hey, where's crazy Charlie?" Langley asked, looking around.

"Right here, you crazy bastard," Charlie said as he stepped through the crowd. Everyone laughed at the greeting as the two embraced.

"Sorry it took a few days to get you out of that Vegas jail," Langley laughed, putting his arm around Charlie.

"Hey, I needed the rest," Charlie answered with a laugh of his own.

"Where's my Sergeant?" the President asked as he scanned the crowd. Out stepped Sergeant Evans, along with his wife and two daughters.

"The odds that you were a retired military doctor are too high to calculate," the President said as he embraced him.

"Dumb luck or divine intervention," Evans said.

"You saved their lives, and I am forever in your debt," the President said as he hugged him.

Evans stepped back and saluted the President. "It was my honor, sir."

"Okay, what's the plan?" Jackson asked.

"I want everyone to get changed and get comfortable," Victoria announced. "We'll have dinner on the terrace in an hour."

Resort staff started leading people to their rooms.

"Can I speak with you for a moment?" Langley said to Victoria as the room began to clear.

"Of course, Jack."

The two walked outside and took a seat on a bench facing the ocean. The wind had picked up and the waves were crashing hard on the sand.

"I'm taking down the Greystone crowd next month. You know I'm a law-and-order guy. The law has to be enforced. It's all that separates us from chaos." Langley reached over and took Victoria's hand. "You are now in the witness protection program. I'll keep you out of this thing as long as we have plenty of people willing to testify, and right now it appears we have dozens trying to cut a deal. I have a new identity for you."

Langley held up a large envelope. "I went with Victoria Smith since you're going to change it to McBride tomorrow anyway."

Langley smiled as big as Victoria had ever seen him smile. "Jack Langley, you're my hero," she said softly as she hugged him.

"I'm your friend, Victoria, not your hero. I owe your future husband my life—along with those crazies he runs around with," Langley chuckled. "It was incredible those fools thought I would betray Jackson. We've always been like brothers. It's hard to believe they bought the entire act."

Langley looked out at the ocean and drew a deep breath as he sat back against the bench. "Everything you need is in there—birth certificate, social security number, driver's license, credit cards, school transcripts, everything," he explained as he handed her the packet. "Now you can get married legally tomorrow."

"You're the best," Victoria said as she stood and gave Langley a big hug. "Not a bad actor either, I might add."

THE NEXT MORNING as the sun rose, a barefoot Victoria Smith walked across the cool sand. She wore no veil, and her white knee-length dress was elegant but simple, accented by one small purple carnation. Her hair, now returned to its natural strawberry blond, moved gently in the ocean breeze. Her brother walked alongside her, smiling widely as he approached his old friend.

"I know you will take care of her," Jackson said as he passed her hand to Sam.

Next to Victoria, Susan Mercury held back tears as she watched her best friend marry the only man she had ever loved.

Next to Sam were his two children. Sam had surprised Victoria when they had suddenly appeared at the Sergeant's house to help with his recovery. The two stood glowing in the morning air as they watched their father finally move on with his life.

SAM AND VICTORIA EXCHANGED vows as those gathered watched. For Victoria, the insanity that had gripped her life had been replaced with a joy she never expected. Sam, who had been torn in half by the death of Sarah, was again whole. After the ceremony on the beach, the group moved to the large terrace. With the ocean as a backdrop, the group took pictures, ate a simple white wedding cake Victoria and Katie had made from scratch, and drank champagne. Finally, with music provided by a string quartet, Sam and Victoria took to the floor for their first dance as husband and wife. As they danced, the President stood to the side watching in amazement as his little sister married the best friend he had ever had.

"What an ending to such a crazy time," he thought.

THAT EVENING, THE couple sat on the beach with Jackson and Susan, watching the sun set over the Caribbean Sea.

"So where are you two going to live?" Jackson asked with a wry smile, knowing the history of Montana.

"That will depend on the season," Sam answered as he squeezed Victoria's hand.

"It will also depend on whether I win or not," Victoria added as she winked at Susan.

Sam and Jackson looked at each other, expecting the other to explain.

"Win what?" they asked simultaneously.

"My House seat, of course," Victoria said, smiling with confidence. "Jack set me up with a background so tight I can live as Victoria McBride without fear. I'm joining Jackson's purple revolution. I might do a little cosmetic work first and keep the black hair, but then I'm running." She raised her glass.

"I suppose I could handle some city life," Sam replied as he raised his glass, too, leaned over, and kissed his bride.

"About time," Victoria shouted as she raised her arms in victory. "It's about time!" she repeated with a laugh.